Born in Paris in 1947, Christian Jacq first visited Egypt when he was seventeen, went on to study Egyptology and archaeology at the Sorbonne, and is now one of the world's leading Egyptologists. He is the author of the internationally bestselling RAMSES series, THE JUDGE OF EGYPT and THE QUEEN OF FREEDOM trilogies, and several other novels on Ancient Egypt. Christian Jacq lives in Switzerland.

Also by Christian Jacq:

The Ramses Series
Volume 1: The Son of the Light
Volume 2: The Temple of a Million Years
Volume 3: The Battle of Kadesh
Volume 4: The Lady of Abu Simbel
Volume 5: Under the Western Acacia

The Stone of Light Series
Volume 1: Nefer the Silent
Volume 2: The Wise Woman
Volume 3: Paneb the Ardent
Volume 4: The Place of Truth

The Queen of Freedom Trilogy
Volume 1: The Empire of Darkness
Volume 2: The War of the Crowns
Volume 3: The Flaming Sword

The Judge of Egypt Trilogy
Volume 1: Beneath the Pyramid
Volume 2: Secrets of the Desert
Volume 3: Shadow of the Sphinx

The Mysteries of Osiris Series
Volume 1: The Tree of Life
Volume 2: The Conspiracy of Evil
Volume 3: The Path of Fire
Volume 4: The Great Road

The Black Pharaoh
The Tutankhamun Affair
For the Love of Philae
Champollion the Egyptian
Master Hiram & King Solomon
The Living Wisdom of Ancient Egypt

About the translator

Sue Dyson is a prolific author of both fiction and non-fiction,
including over thirty novels, both contemporary and historical. She
has also translated a wide variety of French fiction.

The Mysteries of Osiris

The Conspiracy of Evil

Christian Jacq

Translated by Sue Dyson

POCKET
BOOKS

LONDON • SYDNEY • NEW YORK • TORONTO

First published in France by XO Editions under the title
La Conspiration du Mal, 2003
First published in Great Britain by Simon & Schuster UK Ltd, 2005
This edition first published by Pocket Books, 2006
An imprint of Simon & Schuster UK Ltd
A CBS COMPANY

1 3 5 7 9 10 8 6 4 2

Simon & Schuster UK Ltd
Africa House
64–78 Kingsway
London WC2B 6AH

www.simonsays.co.uk

Simon & Schuster Australia
Sydney

A CIP catalogue record for this book is available from the British Library

ISBN-13: 978-0-7434-9224-9
ISBN-10: 0-7434-9224-2

Typeset by SX Composing DTP, Rayleigh, Essex
Printed and bound in Great Britain by
Cox & Wyman Ltd, Reading, Berks

Iniquity may take hold of people in great numbers, but evil will never bring its enterprise to a successful conclusion.

Ptah-Hotep, *Maxim 5.*

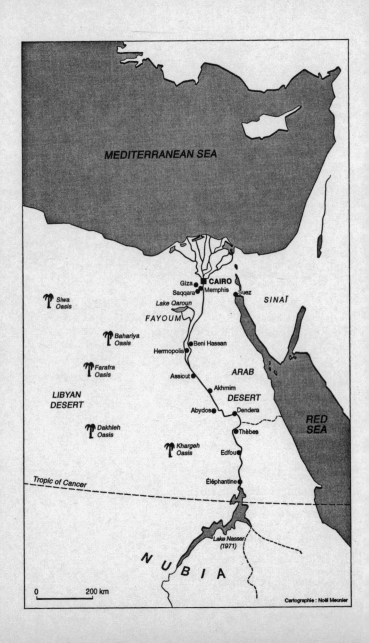

MEDITERRANEAN SEA

Siwa
Oasis

Bahariya
Oasis

Farafra
Oasis

LIBYAN
DESERT

Dakhleh
Oasis

Khargeh
Oasis

Tropic of Cancer

Giza
Saqqara
Lake Qaroun
FAYOUM

Beni Hassan
Hermopolis

Assiout

Abydos

CAIRO
Memphis

Suez

SINAÏ

ARAB

DESERT

Akhmim

Dendera
Thèbes

Edfou

Éléphantine

RED
SEA

Lake Nasser
(1971)

N U B I A

0   200 km

Cartographie : Noël Meunier

ABYDOS

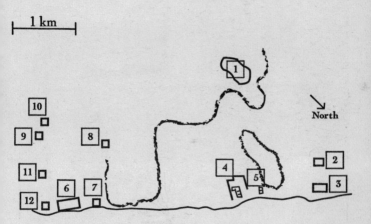

1   Royal Tombs of the first dynasty

2   Ancient Tombs

3   Temple of Osiris

4   Temple of Sethi Ist and Osireion

5   Temple of Ramses II

6   Cities of the Middle Kingdom

7   Temple of Sesostris III

8   Cenotaph of Sesostris III

9   Cenotaph of Ahmose

10 Temple of Ahmose

11 Pyramid of Ahmose

12 Chapel of Teti-Sheri

1

The Acacia of Osiris at Abydos had been attacked by evil magic, and might not survive. If it died, the Mysteries of resurrection could no longer be celebrated, and Egypt would pass away. Unable to make the essential secret shine forth, the Two Lands would become no more than a country like any other, delivered up to the ambition of a few men, to corruption, injustice, falsehood and violence.

Pharaoh Senusret would fight to the last to prevent that happening, to preserve his ancestors' priceless inheritance and pass it on to his successor. But the battle would be ferocious and, despite his innate authority, his courage and his determination, he might not emerge the victor.

At fifty, the third pharaoh to bear the name of Senusret was still a giant of a man. He had an inscrutable face, with deep-set, piercing eyes, heavy eyelids, prominent cheekbones, a straight, thin nose and a curving mouth. It was said that his large ears enabled him to detect the quietest word spoken in the furthermost depths of a cave.

Pharaoh poured water at the base of the Tree of Life, and the Great Royal Wife poured milk. The king and queen had taken off their gold and silver bracelets and collars, for the Rule of Abydos decreed that no metal was permitted within the domain of Osiris.*

*Abydos is 485 km south of Cairo and 160 km north of Luxor.

Abydos was the centre of the Egyptian spiritual universe, the land of silence, the domain of righteousness, the island of the just, over which the soul-birds flew, and it was protected by the deathless stars. Here reigned Osiris, creator of the heavens and the earth, he who was perpetually regenerated, who had been born before birth existed. Triumphing over death, he was reborn in the form of the great acacia tree, whose roots plunged into the *Nun*, the ocean of energy from which all forms of life emerged. A small protrusion, lost amid all this immensity, the world of humans was in danger of being submerged at any moment.

The situation was so grave that, in an attempt to produce enough spiritual energy to save the Tree of Life, Senusret had built a temple and a house of eternity at Abydos. The acacia's decline had been halted, but only one branch had grown green again.

The search for the cause and instigator of the disaster was bound to produce results soon, because the pharaoh was about to launch an all-out attack on Khnum-Hotep, governor of the province of the Oryx, who was suspected of being the perpetrator of this crime.

Bearing the Golden Palette, symbol of his office as High Priest of Abydos, the pharaoh read out clearly the words of knowledge it bore. Behind him stood the few permanent priests permitted to live inside the sacred enclosure, where temporary priests came to work each day, screened and overseen by vigilant guards.

The king's official representative at the temple was the Shaven-headed One, a gruff, blunt-spoken priest who was in charge of the archives of the House of Life. He took no decisions without Senusret's formal agreement. He had spent all his life at Abydos and had no wish to explore any other horizons. His only concern was to see that the duties entrusted to the permanent priests were carried out meticulously, and he permitted no laxity. Anyone fortunate enough to belong to this select body must be a stranger to weakness.

'Are the ancestors being venerated?' asked the king.

'The Servant of the *Ka* is fulfilling his office, Majesty,' said the Shaven-headed One. 'The spiritual energy of the beings of light is still reaching us, and the links with the invisible world remain strong.'

'And the offering-tables are being replenished?'

'The priest who pours the daily libation of fresh water has carried out his duties.'

'Is the tomb of Osiris unharmed?'

'He who watches over the wholeness of the great body has checked the seals placed on the door of the god's house of eternity.'

'Is knowledge ritually passed on?'

'He whose actions are secret and who sees the secrets has not betrayed his office, Majesty.'

However, one of those four permanent priests was in reality no longer thinking sincerely about the performance of his sacred duties. Bitter and resentful at not being appointed High Priest after service which he himself considered exemplary, he had decided to make himself rich by using the knowledge acquired during his years of training. Since Senusret refused to recognize his merits, he had determined to take his revenge both on the king and on Abydos itself.

'The gate of the heavens is closing again,' lamented the Shaven-headed One. 'The *neshemet*, the ship of Osiris, no longer sails the starry spaces. Little by little, it, too, is deteriorating.'

Those were words the pharaoh had dreaded hearing. The weakening of the Tree of Life would provoke first a series of disasters, then the collapse of the entire country. But it would have been unworthy and cowardly to stop up his ears and cover his face.

'Summon the seven priestesses of Hathor,' he ordered, 'and have them assist the queen.'

These priestesses came from varying backgrounds, and they resided permanently at Abydos. Like their male colleagues, they were sworn to absolute secrecy. The Shaven-headed One showed them no more favour than he did the priests, and would tolerate no mistakes on their part. Within the temple no post was held for life, and any priest or priestess found to be inadequate was instantly dismissed – the Shaven-headed One showed no lenience.

The youngest of the seven priestesses had only recently been raised by the queen to the rank of Awakened One. She possessed an almost unreal beauty. Her face was radiant, her features flawless, her skin matchlessly smooth, her eyes an entrancing shade of green, her hips slender; and she moved with a nobility and grace which charmed even the most jaded eye. Drawn to initiation since childhood, she had distanced herself from the outside world, learnt hieroglyphs and passed through the gates of the temple, one by one. Whenever she was called upon to leave the temple and celebrate rituals in outlying provinces, she always returned to Abydos with great joy.

The young priestess's life had been mapped out for her, and would have unfolded peacefully if three dramatic things had not happened. The first was the sickness of the Tree of Life, which spread anguish in a place where only serenity should have reigned. Next, it had been predicted that she would not be a Servant of God like the others, for she was to be charged with an all-important mission, perilous beyond imagining. Lastly, she had met a young scribe named Iker, whom she could not drive out of her mind – she found herself thinking of him more and more often.

But now all her attention was on the sacred rites, in which she wore a robe patterned like a panther's skin dotted with stars, signifying that she represented the goddess Seshat, queen of the House of Life and of sacred writing. The latter was made up of words of power, the only things that could combat invisible enemies.

'Let the seven Hathors form a circle round the Tree of Life,' ordered the queen.

Once they were in position, the Great Royal Wife tied a red band round the trunk of the tree, to imprison the forces of evil within it. But Senusret knew this protection would not be enough. Saving the acacia required a gathering of the Golden Circle of Abydos.

The ritualists withdrew, with the exception of the Shaven-headed One.

The royal couple and the priest waited in contemplative silence for the members of the Golden Circle to arrive. They had travelled to Abydos by the canal created by Senusret; along its banks stood three hundred and sixty-five offering-tables, evoking the celestial banquet celebrated throughout the year.

General Sepi, General Nesmontu, High Treasurer Senankh and Sehotep, Bearer of the Royal Seal, disembarked from a light boat. Only one initiate was missing; he was away on a special mission.

The four men bore a relic-holder. It was in the shape of four lions back to back, and in the centre of the hollow cylinder thus formed was a pole topped by a cover. The pole embodied the venerable pillar created at the beginning of time, the spine-like column around which the entire country was organized. The relic-holder was set down beside the Tree of Life. The lions, tireless guardians whose eyes never closed, would prevent attackers from approaching the tree.

In the relic-holder's cover, the king and the queen each fixed an ostrich feather symbolizing Ma'at, the justice, righteousness and harmony on which Egypt was built from day to day. An emanation of the Divine Light, Ma'at was the highest form of offering, which nourished the land of the pharaohs.

A sudden gust of cold wind swept through the site.

'Look! Over there!' exclaimed General Nesmontu.

5

A jackal had appeared at the top of a sandy mound on the fringe of the desert. It stared fixedly at the ritualists with its black, orange-rimmed eyes.

'The spirit of Abydos approves of what we are doing,' declared the queen. 'Khentimentiu, He Who Leads the Western Ones, the dead who have been recognized as Just, gratifies us with his presence and encourages us to pursue our quest.'

This sign from the world beyond reassured Senusret about his decision to alter the area around the sacred site.

'Plant an acacia tree at each cardinal point,' he decreed.

The members of the Golden Circle did so. By this means the Tree of Life would be protected by the four sons of Horus, who from now on would watch over the dwelling-place of Osiris. Witnesses to the resurrection, they would form an effective talisman against destruction.

After the pharaoh had dedicated the young trees, he visited the new settlement of Wah-sut, which he had had built to house the creators of his temple and his tomb. A heavy atmosphere hung over the whole site, but no one balked at the work. Senusret would allow no slackening of effort in the domain of Osiris, where the fate of Egypt was being played out.

At the end of his inspection, he withdrew into a shrine and summoned the young priestess.

'In accordance with the information you garnered from the ancient texts,' he said, 'I have taken as many precautions as possible to prolong the acacia's life. But that will not lift the curse and heal it.'

The priestess bowed. 'I shall continue to search the archives, Majesty.'

'You must not let up, on any account. The misfortune afflicting Abydos cannot be due to chance, and it probably has several causes. One of them may even be concealed here.'

'I do not understand, Majesty. Can you mean . . . ?'

'The priests and priestesses of Abydos must show that they are absolutely beyond reproach. If they are not, a crack will open in the magical wall erected to preserve Osiris from harm. I therefore ask you to be vigilant and to pay close attention to even the smallest incident.'

'It shall be done according to your will, and I shall not fail to inform the Shaven-headed One.'

'You are to inform me, and no one else. You may come and go as you wish, and you will no doubt have to leave Abydos more than once.'

The priestess bowed again, but this obligation would cost her dear. It was only here that life acquired meaning. She loved this land outside time, the contemplation engraved in each stone of the great temple, the daily celebration of the rites. She shared the ever-present thoughts of the initiates who, since the origins of the city of Osiris, had taken part in its Mysteries. Abydos was her land, her world, her universe.

However, an order from Pharaoh, guarantor of the very existence of this place, brooked no argument.

2

Sekari maintained a steady, sensible pace as he worked in the gardens. He had a square face, thick eyebrows and a round belly. To avoid getting back pain and an abscess on his neck from carrying the yoke with its two heavy water-pots, he paced himself and was careful not to work too hard. Hurrying would not make the leeks grow any more quickly.

Sekari dug up the largest ones and thrust them into one of the sacks carried by North Wind, the big donkey with the huge brown eyes who belonged to his friend, Iker the scribe. The tireless animal obeyed only his master, who had saved him first from the hands of a torturer, then from being killed as a sacrifice. As Iker had given North Wind permission to accompany Sekari, he helped the gardener in his work, which was as lowly as it was difficult.

According to custom, during hot periods Sekari did not water the plots until sunset. The water evaporated much less quickly during the night, and the plants could store more of the precious life-giver and thus withstand the sun's ferocity better.

Sekari wanted to extend his plot of onions, so he knelt down to pull up the weeds. But what he discovered took away all wish to continue.

To kill Pharaoh Senusret by whatever means possible: that was Iker's obsession. The young man had suffered so much from the king's cruelty that no other solution now existed.

Since he had become a member of the scribes' elite in the town of Kahun,* in Faiyum province, Iker ought to have been content with his success. But he could not forget the past and his several brushes with death. Those scenes constantly came back to haunt him in his sleep, ever since someone had stolen his magic ivory amulet, which drove away the demons.

He saw himself again, tied to the mast of a ship, the *Swift One*, and promised as an offering to the dangerous sea, then as the sole survivor of an unforeseeable shipwreck. The ship's destination was the legendary land of Punt, so she could only have belonged to the king. And Senusret had also ordered a fake desert guard to kill Iker, in order to prevent him from bringing the truth to light and provoking a scandal liable to shake the king's throne. This criminal tyrant was enslaving Egypt, the beloved land of the gods, by trampling on the law of Ma'at. The young scribe's way was therefore clear: he must stop the murderer doing any more harm.

But many questions remained unanswered. Why had the pirates who crewed the *Swift One* kidnapped him? Why, on the Island of the *Ka*, in a dream, had an enormous snake asked him if he would save his world? Why had the captain called his kidnapping a 'state secret'? Why had his old master, a scribe in the village of Madu, predicted: 'Whatever your ordeals may be, I shall always be by your side to help you accomplish a destiny of which you are as yet unaware'? Iker had been through many ordeals, but had found no answers to these questions. Still, at least he would be doing something extremely worthwhile by killing Senusret.

In his official house, the young scribe had everything he needed for a comfortable life. A small room devoted to the cult of the ancestors, a modest reception room, a bedroom, privies, a washroom, a kitchen, a cellar, a terrace, furniture

---

*About 100 km south-west of Memphis.

which was simple but sturdy and elegant: what more could he want? But Iker did not even notice this material comfort, so fixed was his mind on his sole aim, even though he knew it might be impossible to achieve.

He often thought of the young priestess with whom he had fallen in love and whom he would probably never see again. It was for her that he was progressing in his profession, for her that he wanted to become an elite scribe, so that he would not disappoint her if they met again and he had a chance tell her of his feelings. For a long time he had believed that that miracle might happen. Now he accepted that it was nothing but a marvellous and inaccessible dream.

North Wind's braying roused Iker from this gloomy meditation.

'I'm back,' announced Sekari. 'Feed your donkey, and I'll make the soup.'

'Are the crops doing well?'

'I've got green fingers.'

Sekari's speciality consisted not only of vegetables but also of pieces of meat and fish, bread, cumin and salt. It was a good, filling meal, and enabled one to sleep peacefully until morning.

Sekari had met Iker when they were prisoners doing forced labour at the turquoise mines of Sinai. They had escaped together, and their paths had later crossed again at Kahun, where the authorities had appointed him Iker's servant. Sekari did gardening work to boost his modest wages, and he sold what he produced to the scribes.

Iker took North Wind to his stable and fed him, then returned home with dragging feet.

'You don't look happy,' observed Sekari. 'Why don't you look on the bright side of life? Dress in fine linen, go to beautiful gardens and banqueting chambers, breathe in the scent of the flowers, get drunk, celebrate. Life's so short that it passes like a dream. If you like, I'll introduce you to a very nice girl. She makes a noose with her hair, to trap boys in. With her ring, she brands them with red-hot iron. Her fingers are as slender as lotus-stems, her mouth is a lotus bud, and her breasts are mandragoras. But before you let yourself be seduced, eat.'

Iker took a very small mouthful.

'Starving to death won't cheer you up,' said Sekari. 'Would you rather have something else?'

'No, thank you. The soup's delicious, but I've lost my appetite.'

'What's the matter?'

'Even if I can't understand why the pharaoh decided to kill me, an unimportant petty scribe, I must act.'

'"Act"? what does that mean?'

'When you know the root of evil, it is absolutely vital to destroy it.'

'You scribes, you can always find reasons for doing what you want to do. Well, I'm just a simple man and I advise you to keep clear of trouble. You have a house, a profession, an assured future. Why go looking for problems?'

'The important thing is to obey the dictates of my conscience.'

'If you start using big words you'll lose me. All the same, I must tell you . . .' Sekari paused, frowning. 'I've made a sad discovery. But perhaps you don't want to hear about it?'

'Of course I do.'

'It's to do with your ivory amulet.'

'Have you found it?' asked Iker eagerly.

'Well . . . yes and no. The thief crushed it into tiny pieces and scattered them among the weeds on the edge of my vegetable plot – the amulet couldn't possibly be put back together again. The thief may have been that fellow who attacked you and who was later found dead in the canal, so we'll learn nothing from him, will we? To me, these aren't good signs. Whatever your plans may be, you'd better give them up.'

'I still have the little amulets you gave me,' Iker reminded him, 'the ones with the falcons, incarnations of the sky-god Horus, and the baboons of Thoth, master of scribes, so I'm still well protected.'

'But those amulets are very, very small. In your place, I wouldn't place too much trust in them.'

While Iker gazed abstractedly into space, Sekari finished the soup. 'Next time, I'll add some more spices,' he said. 'Shall we go to bed now? We've got to start work early tomorrow.'

Iker agreed.

Sekari unrolled a high-quality mat on the threshold of the little house. Since the attempt on Iker's life, which had almost succeeded, his servant had been taking precautions.

Once he was sure Sekari was deeply asleep, Iker slipped out by way of the terrace. Making sure that no one was following him, he went silently through the empty streets until he came to a narrow alleyway. He ducked into it, and waited there for what seemed like a long time.

Kahun was a remarkable place. Built according to the laws of divine proportion, it was divided into two main districts. The western one consisted of about two hundred small and medium-sized houses, while the eastern one contained several huge ones, some of which had as many as seventy rooms. To the north-west lay the mayor's immense residence, built on a sort of man-made hill.

Iker no longer knew what to think of the mayor. On one hand, he had employed Iker and then fostered his career; on the other, he must inevitably be the faithful servant of the pharaoh. The young scribe sometimes wondered whether he himself was a mere pawn, being moved around in a game whose rules he didn't even know.

Everything was quiet, so Iker headed for the meeting-place. Neither the mayor nor Iker's superior, Heremsaf, knew about his meetings with a young Asian woman called Bina, a servant who could neither read nor write but who, like him, was fighting against Senusret's tyranny. Bina was very pretty, with big brown eyes, and was full of vivacity and charm.

She was waiting for him in a disused house. As soon as he entered, she closed the door and led him into a storeroom where only old, broken jars were kept; no indiscreet ears would overhear their conversation there.

'Did you take all the necessary precautions?' she asked.

'Do you think I'm irresponsible?'

'No, of course not. But I'm afraid, so afraid . . . Won't you reassure me?'

Bina pressed herself against Iker, but he did not react. Each time she tried to seduce him, the young priestess's face came back to him and quenched all desire to respond to Bina's advances.

He said, 'We haven't much time, Bina.'

'One day this town will belong to us, and we won't have to hide any more. But the road is still a long one – you're the only one who can lead us to its end.'

'I'm not sure about that.'

'Why not?'

'I'm not a murderer.'

'Killing Senusret will be an act of true justice.'

'Still, I ought to find absolute proof of his guilt.'

'Haven't you already got all the proof you need?'

Iker shook his head. 'I want to consult the archives.'

'Will it take long?'

'I don't know. In my present post I'm not authorized to do it, and I'd have to rise by several ranks before I could gain access to the archives without the mayor and Heremsaf being told about it.'

'What are you hoping to find, anyway? You already know that the pharaoh is solely responsible for all your misfortunes and for Egypt's. You are well aware of the gravity of the situation. You have no right to give up.'

'Can you imagine me plunging a dagger into a man's heart?'

'You'll have the courage to do it, I'm certain of that.'

Iker turned and paced up and down the storeroom. He trod on fragments of an old pottery jar, and one of them broke underfoot. He wished killing the monster was that easy.

'Senusret is still trying to wipe out my people,' said Bina with deep emotion. 'Before long he'll start persecute yours, at the end of the civil war that's coming. Not far from here, Governor Khnum-Hotep is raising an army to fight the tyrant, but how long will he be able to hold out?'

'Where do you get your information from?'

'From our allies. They'll be arriving here soon, I hope, and when they do our strength will be increased tenfold.'

'How will they get into the town?'

'I don't know, but they'll manage it. You'll see: they'll give us invaluable help.'

Iker sighed. 'This is mad, Bina.'

'I assure you it isn't. There's no other way to free ourselves from Senusret's oppression, and you will be the weapon that gives us freedom. What higher destiny could a man have? By attacking you, Senusret has unleashed the very power that can destroy him.'

Bina's last words convinced Iker that he was following the right course of action. However, the goal was still very far off, and his chances of attaining it seemed very small.

Bina read his mind. 'I have doubts and anxieties, too, Iker. But soon we won't be alone any more.'

Stretched out on his terrace, Iker lay awake all the rest of the night. His plan was taking shape, and this time he felt capable of carrying it through. There was nothing more unbearable than injustice, whether it was committed by a king or a pauper. And even if no one besides him would rebel, he would not back away.

A cry of pain from below made him jump.

'You're off your heads!' protested Sekari vehemently. 'You don't wake people up by kicking them on the backside!'

Iker went down to see what was happening.

Two guards were standing in front of his house. They were carrying clubs, and did not look very friendly. Sekari, still half asleep, was on his feet, rubbing his behind.

'Who is this man?' demanded the elder of the guards.

'Sekari, my servant.'

'Does he always sleep on the doorstep?'

'Yes. It's a security precaution.'

'With a lookout who has so much trouble waking up, I'd feel more in danger than secure. Anyway, we haven't come for him. Scribe Heremsaf wants to see you urgently.' With that, the two guards marched away.

At least, thought Iker as he watched them go, they aren't putting shackles on me and dragging me through the streets of the town like a common criminal.

Unfortunately it was only delaying the evil hour. If Heremsaf had sent a summons like this, it must be because he'd found out about the plot to kill Pharaoh. If Iker stayed in Kahun he'd be arrested and convicted. His only chance was to run away, but would the guards at the main gate allow him to leave?

3

Pharaoh Senusret had named his new settlement at Abydos Wah-sut, 'Enduring Places', in order to embody the first of the two founding values of the pharaohs: perseverance. The second, vigilance – or, more precisely, the awakening of Osiris at the resurrection – conferred on the pharaonic tradition the supernatural dimension that enabled it to build lasting monuments.

The pharaoh was examining the service roster for the temporary priests; they were divided into five teams which performed the rites in succession, one after another. Face to face with the king, the scribe responsible for drawing up the roster, a small, timid man, could not help trembling.

Senusret eyed him closely. 'If you have obeyed my instructions and done your work correctly, why are you so nervous?'

'The . . . the privilege of meeting you, Majesty, the—'

'Neither you nor I have privileges. We are the servants of Osiris.'

'Indeed, Majesty, that is what I meant, and—'

'How do your teams operate?'

'In the traditional way. Every crew is divided into several sections, each of which is allocated specific tasks. None must interfere with the work of another, and all tasks are carried out at the correct times.'

The scribe launched into a detailed account of cleaning the statues, washing the vases of purification, preparing the oil so that the lamps would burn without giving off smoke, choosing the food to be laid on the offering-tables and then shared out under supervision. He gave the king the names and service records of the guards, the workshop overseers, the sculptors, the painters, the gardeners, the bakers, the brewers, the butchers, the fishermen, the perfume-makers, not omitting the most modest bearer of offerings. 'Each priest,' he ended, 'is identified by the forces of order, which keep a register showing the days and times of arrival and departure, as well as reasons for absence and lateness.'

'Up to now, how many temporary priests have been excluded for serious misconduct?'

'None, Majesty,' replied the scribe proudly.

'That proves that you are incompetent.'

'Majesty, I—'

'How can you assume for one moment that perfection has been reached? Either you are trying to deceive me – an unforgivable mistake – or you trust the glib reports of your subordinates, and that is scarcely less unforgivable. As soon as I have appointed your replacement, you will leave Abydos.'

Senusret visited the workshops, storehouses, slaughter-houses and breweries, and noted several failures to follow orders regarding security. Sobek-Khu, 'Sobek the Protector', commander of the soldiers who guarded the king's person, took the necessary measures there and then.

Then Senusret received his master-builder. He saw that the man's face was drawn with fatigue, and asked 'Have there been more problems?'

'Nothing serious, Majesty, now that we have the protection of the priestesses of Hathor: the tools have stopped breaking and the stone-cutters no longer get ill. In fact, I am happy to inform you that your temple and your house of eternity are

both finished – the painters have this very morning completed
the last divine figure, that of Isis – and are ready to supply the
greatest possible amount of *ka*. When do you wish to bring
the treasure to life?'

'At sunrise tomorrow.'

At Thebes ceremonies were accompanied by much celebration by the general population. But at Abydos even the
brewers had a religious role in the service of Osiris. In any
case, in the current circumstances a display of joy would have
been out of place.

Watched by the priestesses and the permanent priests,
Senusret placed the following items in the storehouse in the
foundations of his temple: twenty-four ingots of metal,
among them gold and silver bars, and precious stones
including lapis-lazuli, turquoise, jasper and cornelian. These
materials, which had come from the belly of the mountains,
entered into the composition of the eye of Horus, the most
powerful of talismans.

Then men and women brought offerings to the shrine, so as
to furnish it with the things needed for it to function properly:
basins for purification, cups, vases, chests, altars, censers,
fabrics and boats entered the temple treasury, with its ceiling
of gold and lapis-lazuli, its silver floor and its doors of
copper.

'Today I shall celebrate the three rituals of morning, noon
and evening,' announced the pharaoh, 'so that the supernatural powers maintain the spirit of this place, a dwelling-
place for gods, not humans. Its role is to diffuse energy.'

The young priestess saw enacted the texts she had
deciphered in the House of Life; they dealt with the vital role
of the King of Egypt, master of the creation of rites. It was up
to him to replace disorder with order, falsehood with truth,
wrongdoing with justice. There was only one chance to
experience celestial harmony in an earthly society: perform

these rites at the correct time and possess a pharaoh capable of truly fulfilling his office fully.

'Let the light illuminate the altars,' ordered Senusret.

The perfume-burners filled the air with sweetness. Flowers, meat, vegetables, aromatic spices, jars of water, beer and wine, loaves of various shapes and sizes were laid on the diorite, granite and alabaster offering-tables. All these riches were presented to the gods so that they could taste their subtle aspect and transform them into substances they could assimilate. The offering strengthened the link between the visible and the Invisible. Thanks to it, creation was renewed.

Senusret entered the covered temple, entry to which was permitted to only those few priests charged with representing him. Here, in this place barred to outsiders, they must preserve the divine wholeness and ceaselessly push back the forces of chaos that strove to destroy this space belonging to Ma'at.

At the far end of the shrine stood the primordial mound, towards which the ceiling sloped downwards and the floor upwards. It had emerged from the original waters on the first morning, and was the plinth on which the Creator unceasingly built his work.

In the twilight of the Most Sacred Place, there was revealed the realm of Light,* whose doors the pharaoh opened. At the heart of the heaven of the powers, the king was causing the first times to be reborn.

'For as long as the cosmos remains set upon its four pillars,' said the monarch to the Presence, 'for as long as the annual flood comes at the right moment, for as long as the sun and moon reign by day and night, for as long as the stars remain in their places and the constellations carry out their task, for as long as Orion makes Osiris visible, this temple shall be as stable as the heavens.'

*The *akhet*, a word constructed on the root *akh*, 'to be radiant, useful'.

*

Bringing life to the temple would slow down the decline of the Acacia of Osiris. Surrounding it with beneficial waves would build a magical wall, which would protect the Tree of Life from new attacks, though it would not remove the cause of the tree's sickness.

The time to take action of a different order was approaching. So the king summoned the Golden Circle of Abydos to a meeting with himself and his Great Royal Wife, in order to tell them his decision.

'Only one provincial governor still refuses to submit,' reported General Nesmontu. 'Let us launch a great offensive against Khnum-Hotep in order to stamp out all traces of rebellion. When Egypt is truly unified, the acacia will grow green again.'

As full of energy as ever, the rugged old officer was not in the habit of mincing his words. Indifferent to honours, he lived only for the greatness of the Two Lands. And what embodied it, if not Pharaoh Senusret, to whom he was ready to offer his life?

'I agree with Nesmontu,' said General Sepi. 'The fighting will cause many casualties on both sides, but I can see no way of avoiding it.'

Sepi was a tall, thin, authoritarian man, who never let emotion get the better of him: he was contemplative and thoughtful, and detested warmongers. He was in charge of one of the most brilliant scribes' schools in the land, and had formerly been the right-hand man of Djehuty, governor of the Hare province. The Golden Circle had entrusted him with the vital mission of preventing war with Djehuty, and little by little he had brought Djehuty to see that war would have disastrous consequences: the governor was now a loyal subject of the king.

'I abhor violence,' said Sehotep, Bearer of the Royal Seal, an elegant, well-born thirty-year-old whose eyes sparkled with intelligence. 'But I agree with Nesmontu and Sepi that Khnum-Hotep will never surrender, and that negotiations with him are doomed to fail. Although he is the last provincial governor to hold out, he will never recognize that he is in the wrong and will prefer to spill blood in order to attempt to retain his privileges.'

The Shaven-headed One, guardian of the archives in the House of Life at Abydos, merely nodded in agreement. He paid little heed to the upheavals of the outside world, but he was struck by the convergence of views between individuals as different as Nesmontu, Sepi and Sehotep.

'The war is likely to be terrible,' predicted High Treasurer Senankh, a plump forty-year-old who was a great food-lover but a rigorous administrator. 'Khnum-Hotep is rich, and has built up a formidable army, so his resistance will be more than token. To believe that victory is won in advance would be foolish.'

'I do not claim otherwise,' said General Nesmontu, 'but that is no reason to hold back and leave Pharaoh's work unfinished.'

'Are you certain,' asked the queen, 'that it really is Khnum-Hotep who is wielding the force of Set and killing the Acacia of Osiris?'

'There can be no doubt of it, Majesty,' replied Nesmontu, 'because all the other provincial governors were found to be innocent. He is hungry for power – he wants to rule the whole of the South – but Pharaoh is ruining his plans, so he is seeking revenge by attacking the vital heart of Egypt.'

'He may not be acting alone,' suggested Sehotep.

'That possibility must be considered,' agreed General Sepi. 'Khnum-Hotep has long controlled the trading-routes with Asia, and has made many contacts there. He may have found allies whose interests lie in weakening the throne of the pharaohs.'

'That is merely an assumption,' objected Senankh.

'But easy to check,' said Nesmontu. 'Let us defeat Khnum-Hotep's army, capture him and interrogate him. Believe me, he will tell us the truth.'

'Does His Majesty know the opinion of the member of the Golden Circle who is absent on a secret mission?'

'I shall not speak in his name,' said Senusret.

'I am close to him,' said Sepi, 'and I believe he would favour an attack.'

'Do your reservations signify that you oppose that plan?' the king asked Senankh.

'Certainly not, Majesty. It is that the thought of losing so many lives in a civil war fills me with grief. Nevertheless, I know it is inevitable and I shall do my best to ensure that the country's economy suffers as little as possible.'

'Since the Golden Circle is unanimous,' concluded Senusret, 'let us prepare to attack Khnum-Hotep and to reconquer the Oryx province. The Great Royal Wife and the High Treasurer will return to Memphis to ensure that current matters are properly managed. If I should die during the fighting, the queen will reign as regent until my successor is chosen by the surviving members of the Golden Circle of Abydos and the King's House.'

As bloody conflict loomed closer, Senusret relished the peace and silence of Abydos. Despite the crisis caused by the acacia's sickness, the place still retained the memories of the golden age that had seen the initiates vanquish death through celebrating the Mysteries of Osiris.

It was to save these vital values that the pharaoh must put down Khnum-Hotep's rebellion, make him submit and confess. If Senusret managed to destroy this bastion of Set and reunite the Two Lands, he would have at his disposal a new force which, up to now, he had signally lacked.

On the quayside, the young priestess was standing before the eye recently painted on the prow of the royal ship, reciting the words designed to protect the ship and her passengers on the voyage. Sobek-Khu had himself checked the identity of each crewman, and was now searching the king's cabin for the third time, prior to departure.

'When do you plan to return, Majesty?' asked the priestess.

'I do not know.'

'There is going to be war, isn't there?'

'Osiris, the first pharaoh, reigned over a unified land, all of whose provinces lived in union, without losing their individuality. It is my duty to carry on his work. Whether I return or not, you must finish yours.'

As the ship moved away from the quay, Senusret could not take his eyes off the incomparable landscape of Abydos, fashioned by the eternity of Osiris.

4

Every three months, the guard on the entry-points to the town of Kahun was completely changed. The soldiers were posted at all four corners and the only people they allowed to enter were those who were known and duly authorized to stay there. Certain that he would be arrested, Iker did not even try to get past the checkpoints, but, head held high, made his way to the house of Heremsaf, his overseer.

Before being thrown into prison, sentenced to forced labour, even executed, Iker would tell Heremsaf his deepest thoughts. It would probably be futile, since that high-ranking scribe served Senusret, but he hoped that, if the truth about the tyrant could be spread, people might be won over and another assassin might succeed where Iker had not.

To appear before his judge, Iker had equipped himself with his superb scribe's writing-materials, a gift from his teacher, General Sepi. He would hand over his palettes, his brushes, his graters, gums and inkpots to his accuser. In this way, he would draw a final line under his past.

Heremsaf was eating thinly sliced leeks baked in soft cheese and flavoured with garlic. When Iker appeared, he did not raise his head but concentrated on his favourite dish.

He was a square-headed man, with a small, neatly trimmed moustache, who lived for his work: he rose early and went to bed late, and scorned the very idea of rest. He was one of the leading figures in Kahun, steward of the pyramid of Senusret II and of the Temple of Anubis. Each day he checked the deliveries of meat, bread, beer, fats and perfumes, scrutinized the accounting-scribes' books, checked any additional hours worked by the employees, and ensured that food was shared out fairly.

Iker owed Heremsaf his first post and his subsequent promotions, plus a piece of advice: 'Nothing must escape your vigilance.' In the course of a task entrusted to him by his superior, Iker had found the handle of a knife marked with the name of the *Swift One*, the ship that had been taking him to his death. Simple chance? Or was Heremsaf manipulating him? By refusing to let Iker consult the archives, Heremsaf had proved that he was colluding with the mayor, one of Senusret's henchmen. Yet Iker could make no specific accusations against him without knowing what game he was playing.

Today, he thought, Heremsaf must be going to remove his mask. His true strategy consisted of setting traps for Iker in the hope that he would make a fatal mistake. Now he had decisive information, and would deliver the final blow.

As he ate, Heremsaf said, 'We must talk, Iker.'

'I am at your disposal.'

'You seem rather edgy, my boy. Is something wrong?'

'That is for you to tell me.'

'You are afraid that I am criticizing your work record, is that it? Well, let us look at it closely. You have resolved a delicate matter in the granaries, rid the town of rats, refurbished some of the old storehouses, and reorganized the library at the Temple of Anubis remarkably quickly. Does that summary seem accurate to you?'

'I have nothing to add.'

'Fine achievements, aren't they?'

'That is for you to judge.'

'Even if you are resolved to be unpleasant, you won't change my opinion or my decision.'

'I didn't intend to do that. Here are my scribe's materials.'

Heremsaf at last raised his head. 'Why do you want to part with them?'

Iker said nothing.

'You know very well, my boy, that I do not accept any gifts from anyone. You ought to apologize for doing something so stupid, but that is not your way. Very well, let us forget it – if I uttered the smallest criticism of the most gifted young scribe in Kahun, the mayor would have me punished. The privilege he's granting you appears excessive to me, but I am obliged to accept it. All the same, don't let it go to your head. There will be no lack of jealousy, and you won't get away with the smallest mistake. So be extremely cautious, and don't boast of your good fortune.'

'My good fortune? What do you mean?'

'To your move. The mayor is giving you a new house, much bigger and in a better area. You are now a house-owner.'

Iker was astonished. 'Why is he being so generous?'

'You now belong to the Kahun scribes' elite, my boy, and all the administrative secretariats of the town are therefore open to you.'

'Am I to continue working in the library at the Temple of Anubis?'

'Of course, because new manuscripts will be transferred there this week and you are the best person to file them. I think you will probably soon be summoned to work at the mayor's office as an adviser. Then I shall no longer be your superior, and you will have to manage on your own in the face of officials who have been in their posts for a long time. Be wary of them: they don't like the young, who are liable to try to take their jobs. Now, on a different subject, are you satisfied with your servant?'

'Sekari? I regard him as a friend who works for me on a part-time basis.'

'I am allocating him to you full-time. Your home must be well kept in spotless condition – your reputation largely depends upon it. Enjoy your day, Iker the scribe. You and I have a great deal to do.'

'I had an extraordinary dream,' Sekari told Iker. 'I dreamt I was eating donkey! According to the dream-interpreter I consulted, it's an excellent omen, and means certain promotion for myself or someone close to me.'

'Your dream was a true one: the mayor has given me a big house – to own, I mean.'

Sekari could not suppress an admiring whistle. 'Well . . . You're becoming someone really important in this town. When I think of the bad times we went through, thanks to destiny . . . When do we move?'

'Immediately.'

'Then let's get your things ready.'

'Officials from the mayor's secretariat will see to all that.'

Iker, Sekari and North Wind went to the place indicated by Heremsaf, a neat little street in the best part of Kahun, not far from the mayor's huge house.

'What, this one?' said Sekari in amazement.

'That's right.'

'I can't believe it! It's really beautiful, all whitewashed – with an upstairs. And have you seen the size of the terrace? Will you still be willing to speak to me?'

'Of course, because you'll be living here as my steward.'

'Well! But wait here a moment: we can't go in like savages. I'll go and find what we need.' Sekari wasn't away for long. He came back carrying a bowl of perfumed water, which he set down on the doorstep. 'No one's going into this house without first washing their hands and feet. Owner, the initial honour goes to you.'

That formality completed, the pair went inside. The house had a reception chamber, three bedchambers, brand-new privies and washrooms, an enormous kitchen, a cellar worthy of the name – Sekari was so delighted that he went round the whole place several times.

In the room set aside for the cult of the ancestors, he sniffed the air. 'We shan't be troubled by snakes, scorpions or ghosts,' he said approvingly. 'The walls have been well sprinkled with ground garlic soaked in beer. In fact, there's only one thing missing: the furniture.'

'I think that's it arriving now.'

Several town employees had brought an impressive number of items. Watched attentively by North Wind, Sekari made them wash their feet and hands before setting down their precious burdens in suitable places.

The baskets and storage chests for food, clothes, sandals and toilet articles would have satisfied even the most demanding person. Rectangular, oblong, oval or cylindrical, they were made either of reed-stems bound with strips of palm-leaf, or of wood, and had well-fitting lids tied shut with cords. As for the mats, they were of excellent quality: transverse strips of reed criss-crossed by lengthwise strips of linen, creating squares and diamonds of colour. Some were to be spread out on the ground, others would be hung across the windows to screen out the sun.

The low tables and three-legged stools were all both strong and elegant, but Sekari particularly liked the low, straw-seated chairs. Their feet were square in cross-section and they had slightly curved backs, mirroring the shape of the body. With their strong frames, held in place by sturdy tenon-and-mortise joints, they would last for centuries. And what could one say about the superb lamps, made of a limestone base and a wooden pillar imitating a papyrus stalk, on which a bronze vessel was placed to contain the lamp-oil?

Breathless, Sekari sat down on one of the straw-seated

chairs. 'Have you been appointed the mayor's deputy or something?'

But the biggest surprise was yet to come: three beds, one for each bedchamber, with fittings the like of which Sekari had never seen. He gently touched bed-bases made of skeins of hemp plaited and fixed to a wooden frame decorated with figures of the god Bes and the hippopotamus-goddess Tawaret. Armed with knives, they brandished snakes and guarded the sleeper.

Sekari laid his head on the wool-stuffed pillows, and went into ecstasies when he felt the fine linen sheets. 'Can you imagine sleeping in these, Iker, especially if they're perfumed? The girls won't be able to resist! I can already see them—'

North Wind's braying interrupted this idyllic vision, and the two men hurried outside to see what was up. On the western side of the house, the donkey had discovered a little garden and a small stable roofed with palm-fronds. Comfortable bedding, a manger full of grain, vegetables and that incomparable foodstuff, thistles: it was clear that he was pleased with his change of residence.

As they went back to the front of the house, three sturdy fellows arrived in a heavily laden cart. Sekari hurried over to them.

'Where's the cellar?' asked one of them.

'Why?'

'Delivery of beer from the mayor.'

Sure enough, the cart contained narrow-necked pottery jars, each baked right through and provided with two handles. Clay stoppers ensured that the brew would be of good quality.

Sekari smiled broadly. 'Right,' he said, 'follow me.'

Scarcely had the jars been stored when another man appeared, bearing kilts made of two symmetrical pieces of unbleached linen sewn together down the middle. 'The latest fashion,' he commented. 'This kilt hangs down to the calves and reaches up to the chest. The two longest points of the triangle are knotted around the belt. The smallest must be drawn from back to front between the thighs and tied on the abdomen with the two others. If it works, the fabric should go round the body twice.'

Iker tried one right away and was pleased with the result.

'And I brought this for your servant.' He handed over a broom with long palm fibres, folded and assembled in tufts. Two six-fold bindings kept the handle rigid.

While the servant in question was testing the new tool of his trade, Iker gazed at an unexpected item which ought not to have featured among his things: a woman's face-paint spoon depicting a naked girl swimming; her head was raised and she held an oval cup in the form of a drake. She was the sky-goddess Nut; he was the earth-god Geb. Upon their union depended the circulation of the air and light that made life on earth possible.

Her. This little object made the young priestess seem almost present, yet she was so far away, so inaccessible . . . Was its inclusion in his things a simple error, or a sign from destiny?

'What are you going to do with that?' asked Sekari in amusement.

'You can give it to one of your beauties.'

'You're still thinking about that priestess, but you'll never see her again. I can introduce you to a dozen others, all pretty and very understanding. With a house like this, you'll be one of the most sought-after unmarried men in Kahun.'

Iker thought of the exceptional stone, the queen of turquoises, extracted from the mountain. In the glow from that wonderful gem, he had gazed upon the face of his beloved, whom no other woman could ever replace.

'You're torturing yourself in vain,' insisted Sekari, 'and you don't appreciate your good fortune. A home like this and a job as a high-level scribe – don't you realize how lucky you are?'

'You once mentioned the Golden Circle of Abydos, didn't you?'

Sekari frowned. 'I can't remember, but what does it matter? Everyone's heard of it. It means the people who've been initiated into the Mysteries of Abydos. We aren't among them, and so much the better. Can you imagine life as a recluse, with no pleasures, and deprived of wine and women?'

'But supposing she belongs to the Circle?'

'Forget about her and concentrate on your career. How can you look so miserable when you've got everything you need to be happy?'

'With respect, my friend, you don't understand the reason for this mountain of gifts.'

Sekari sat down on a stool. 'You're recognized as an excellent scribe and you're merely benefiting from the advantages that go with your official position. What's surprising about that?'

'It's an attempt to buy me.'

'Nonsense!'

'People want to stop me continuing my investigations and discovering the truth. A good post, a fine house, material comforts – what more could one wish for, indeed? A clever scheme, but it hasn't worked. No one's going to buy me.'

'Well, if you look at it that way . . . But surely you're exaggerating?'

'In the eyes of Kahun's authorities, I'm dangerous. They're trying to dull my senses.'

'All right, let's say you're right. If you are, why not take advantage of the situation? If the truth you're searching for is going to lead you to disaster, why not give it up and be content with what you've been given?'

'I repeat: no one's going to buy me.'

'Oh, very well.' Sekari got to his feet. 'I'm going to do my first bit of cleaning, and then prepare the midday meal.'

Iker climbed up to the terrace; he didn't feel comfortable

inside the house. By trying to distract him, his enemies would only strengthen his determination. From his kilt, he extracted the knife with which he was going to kill Senusret. He let the sun play on its blade.

5

The widow wanted to ensure that her three children had a happy life. On her isolated lands north of Memphis, she worked hard, growing vegetables with the help of two agricultural workers. The produce was sold in the markets.

As she was piling courgettes into a basket, a hairy and monstrously ugly man suddenly appeared in front of her. Although the widow was not easily frightened, she flinched.

'Greetings, my friend,' said the intruder. 'You have a pretty little estate, I must say. It must bring in a good profit.'

'You're wrong there.'

'Oh no, I'm never wrong.'

'Go away!'

'When people speak to me like that, it annoys me. Don't rely on your workers to defend you – they're in the hands of my men. As for your brats, no one will do them any harm if you prove understanding.'

The widow went white. 'What do you want?'

'A tenth of your income in exchange for my protection. And don't try to cheat. If you lie, or hold anything back, I'll take it out on the youngest girl.'

Crooked-Face's technique was tried and tested. With his band of merciless crooks, he controlled a good number of small farms, whose owners yielded to his blackmail for fear of losing their lives or seeing their loved ones tortured.

The widow proved no exception to the rule.

Because he left no trail of corpses behind him, Crooked-Face had not attracted the attention of the authorities. He now 'protected' enough people to bring in a substantial return. It was a simple beginning, but he congratulated himself on his progress, and hoped that his master would be pleased.

Crooked-Face entered Memphis through the northern district, from where one could just see the ancient white-walled citadel, the work of Menes, 'the Stable One', the very first pharaoh, who had united Upper and Lower Egypt. The town was so crowded that it was easy for Crooked-Face to go unnoticed as he made for the modest lodgings, above a shop kept by loyal followers, where his master, the Herald, had chosen to live.

A criminal since childhood, Crooked-Face had eventually been convicted of armed robbery and sentenced to forced labour in the Sinai mines, from which he had escaped when they were attacked by the Herald and his band, whom he had then joined. Although he usually refused to recognize anyone's authority over him, he had come to realize that he'd never find a better leader than the Herald. The deciding factor was that, providing that he was discreet and that he trained his band of raiders for more serious operations than 'protecting' isolated farms, he could make himself as rich as he liked. The brute revelled in this new life, in which his sole obligation was to come regularly to Memphis to talk with the Herald and bring him his favourite delicacy.

Whatever city might be chosen as capital by one pharaoh or another, Memphis, with its great river port, always remained the centre of Egypt's trade. Here, goods arrived from Minoa, Phoenicia and Asia, to be listed, sorted and then stored in vast storehouses. Countless granaries were filled with grain, the stables housed fat oxen, and the Treasury contained gold, silver, copper, lapis-lazuli, perfumes, medicinal substances, wine, numerous kinds of oil and a host of other valuables. Crooked-Face dreamt of seizing them and becoming the wealthiest man in the land. The Herald encouraged this dream, for it did not hinder his plans.

Crooked-Face was indifferent to beliefs but was afraid of the Herald, whose cruelty surpassed even his own. All he cared about was results. His leader could command, he would have the wealth. And if terror had to be spread by executing all his master's opponents, he'd not lack enthusiasm for the task.

As he approached the Herald's home, Crooked-Face sensed that he was being watched. A network of lookouts spotted anyone showing curiosity and alerted their leader in the event of danger. Here a bread-seller; there a passer-by; over there a street-sweeper.

Nobody stopped him entering the shop, where cheap sandals, mats and fabrics lay in piles. In accordance with their master's instructions, the Herald's followers were honest traders, well liked in the district. Some of them had started families, others were content with fleeting liaisons. They took part in the many festivals celebrated throughout the year, frequented the taverns and thus integrated themselves into Egyptian society. Before striking at their enemies they must learn to pass unnoticed.

'How goes it with you, Crooked-Face?' asked a red-haired fellow.

'Very well indeed, my lad. And you?'

Shab the Twisted, the Herald's right-hand man, was a formidable expert with the knife, and specialized in stabbing people in the back. A cold-hearted criminal, without emotions or remorse, he had absorbed the words of God's envoy with delight and was utterly devoted to him.

He said, 'We're making good progress. Now, I hope you weren't followed.'

'You know me, Shab. I've not lost my touch.'

'In any event, no spies will get this far.'

'I see you're as distrustful as ever.'

'Of course – that why we're going to succeed. The Godless are everywhere, but one day we'll exterminate them all.'

Crooked-Face merely nodded: nothing bored him more than discussions about God.

'The Herald's preaching. Follow me, but don't make a sound.'

The two men went up to the first floor, where about twenty keen-eyed followers were drinking in their master's words.

'God speaks to me,' he told them. 'I, and I alone, have the task of passing on his message. God shows gentleness and compassion to his faithful, but is pitiless to unbelievers, who will be wiped off the face of the Earth. He imposes a terrible ordeal upon you, the holders of the true faith, by forcing you to mix with the Egyptian people, mired as they are in luxury and the worship of false gods. No other way exists to prepare for the great war and impose the absolute and final truth that I bring. All those who refuse to recognize it shall perish, and their punishment will fill us with joy. We shall execute the blasphemers, beginning with the first among them, the pharaoh. Do not believe that our goal is impossible to achieve. Soon we shall rule over this country. Next, we shall erase all borders between countries, to form one single empire covering the whole Earth. Women will no longer be seen in the streets, no debauchery will be tolerated, and God will shower his blessings upon us.'

Always the same message, thought Crooked-Face. Nevertheless, he was impressed by the Herald's vehemence and persuasive power. This leader of men would win over more than a few.

Once the sermon was over, the men withdrew in silence and went back to being bakers, sandal-sellers, barbers and so on.

As always when they met, Crooked-Face was astonished by the Herald's physical power. Tall, rangy, bearded, with deep-set red eyes and fleshy lips, he covered his hair with a turban and wore a woollen tunic which reached down to his ankles. He could terrify even the bravest man with his gaze, which was like that of a bird of prey. His voice was sometimes as sharp as a flint razor, sometimes smooth and enchanting. Each of his faithful followers knew he had the power to dominate the monsters of the desert and feed on their fearsome strength.

'Have you brought me what I need, Crooked-Face?'

'Of course, my lord. Here it is.'

He held out a bag to the Herald, but Shab the Twisted stepped between them and said, 'One moment. I must check it.'

'Who do you think you are?' demanded Crooked-Face angrily.

'The precautions apply to everyone.'

'Peace, my friends,' cut in the Herald. 'Crooked-Face would never dare betray me. I'm right, am I not?'

'Indeed.'

The Herald opened the bag and took out a handful of salt from the oases. He drank neither wine nor beer, nor any other form of alcohol, and very little water, but slaked his thirst with this foam of Set, which formed on the surface of the ground during the great summer heat.

'This is excellent, Crooked-Face,' he said.

'It's the best quality – the seller said it's from the Western desert.'

'He wasn't lying.'

'No one dares lie to me.'

'Are you pleased with the way your "protection" business is going?'

'It's going marvellously. The farmers are so afraid that they do whatever I want.'

'No hotheads among them?'

'Not one, my lord.'

'Has there been any trouble from city or desert guards?'

'None at all. That was a splendid idea of yours, getting me to do this. I'll be able to contribute big profits to the cause.'

'Good. And are your men still training hard?'

'You can rely on it. My lads are stronger than ever, and when you need them they'll be ready.'

'Wait here for me, both of you.'

The Herald left the room, and went to a cubbyhole crammed with chests containing coarse mats. Smiling, he thought of the rebellion he had instigated in the town of Sichem, in Canaan. The Egyptian army thought it had crushed it, not realizing that the fire was still smouldering beneath the ashes. The Herald had been arrested and imprisoned, but had tricked his way out by persuading a simple-minded fellow prisoner to pretend to be him. The Egyptians had executed the man, thinking to rid themselves of the troublemaker. Being officially dead, the Herald could stay in the shadows and foment his plot in peace.

He pivoted a section of the back wall, in which a hiding-place had been created, and took out an acacia-wood box made by a carpenter in Kahun, who had been killed the moment he seemed to be getting too talkative. The box was truly beautiful, worthy to be in the treasury of a great temple. Inside were writings, magical figurines and a glowing green-blue stone, which he handled cautiously.

The Herald went back to the large room and showed the stone to Crooked-Face and Shab the Twisted. 'This is the queen of turquoises.'

The jewel was of unique size and quality. The Herald held it up to the light, to re-charge it with energy. 'With its help, we shall unleash a cataclysm against which Pharaoh will be powerless.'

'I recognize that stone,' said Crooked-Face. 'An informer called Iker brought it out of the belly of the mountain of Hathor. He was killed in the attack on the mine, and his body was burnt.'

'Gaze on it, contemplate its beauty, and enjoy the privilege of doing so – it is reserved for my most loyal men.'

Crooked-Face wasn't interested in contemplation. 'What are your orders, my lord?'

'Increase the number of farms you protect, increase your profits, improve your weapons, and continue to train ruthless fighters. Time is acting in our favour.'

Orders like that suited Crooked-Face perfectly. He bowed in farewell, went downstairs, and emerged from the shop with several pairs of sandals, like any ordinary buyer.

The Herald picked up a fistful of salt.

'According to the latest rumours, my lord,' said Shab the Twisted, 'Senusret is preparing to attack Governor Khnum-Hotep. The fighting's likely to be fierce, and the outcome isn't certain, because the Oryx province has a large, well-equipped army.'

'So much the better, my friend.'

'Perhaps Senusret will be defeated and killed. If he is—'

'If he is, Khnum-Hotep will take his place and will become our new target. It is the whole pharaonic tradition that must be destroyed, not just the individuals who continue it.'

Shab was frowning worriedly. 'My lord,' he asked, 'do you really trust Crooked-Face? If he gets very rich, he might become uncontrollable.'

'Don't worry, he knows better than to betray me – anyone who does will feel the talons of a desert demon sink into him.'

'But he isn't interested in the true faith!'

'Nor are many of our other allies, the simple instruments of God. You are different. My revelation has changed your destiny and you now walk the paths of virtue.'

The Herald's soft voice plunged Shab into a sort of ecstasy. It was the first time his master had spoken to him like this, anchoring his beliefs once and for all. He would follow this fiery-eyed leader to the very end, and would obey him blindly.

'I need to know if our network of Canaanites in Memphis is ready to act,' said the Herald, 'so we are going to entrust them with an important mission. An irritating obstacle is preventing an Asian raiding-party from infiltrating Kahun. The Canaanites are to remove that obstacle.'

6

General Nesmontu's two scouts were seventeen years old, swift as the wind and supple as reeds. They were afraid of nothing. Aware of the importance of their mission, they had had made their minds up to risk everything in order to obtain information about Khnum-Hotep's defence system. The success of the general's attack would depend largely on the information they gave him.

First, they scouted along the Nile. They went unarmed and were dressed in ragged kilts which stank of fish so that they could pass for fishermen. What they saw astonished them: in the port of Menat-Khufu, the province's capital, Khnum-Hotep had massed a veritable war-fleet of assorted vessels, and there were dozens of archers aboard.

When a boat bore down on their small fishing-boat, they were careful not to show signs of alarm.

'Why are you hanging around here?' demanded an officer.

'We're fishing.'

'For whom?'

'For ourselves – we have to feed our families, you know.'

'Don't you know Lord Khnum-Hotep's orders? No boats are allowed on this part of the river.'

'But we always fish here – we live in the village over there.'

'At the moment, it's forbidden.'

'Then how are we going to eat?'

'Go to the nearest guard-post, and you'll be given food. If I see you here again, I'll arrest you.'

The two scouts went off unhurriedly, like two honest fishermen annoyed by the new ruling. They moored outside the guard-post, but instead of going inside slipped into a nearby papyrus thicket, where snakes and crocodiles were known to lurk. Indifferent to the insects biting and stinging them, they reached the edge of the cultivated area.

Here, too, Khnum-Hotep had taken precautions. Hidden by branches covered with earth, deep ditches lay in wait to trap attackers. The occupants of the reed huts were not peasants but soldiers, and it was the same with the farms: the scouts spotted archers perched in the trees. Continuing their exploration, they dived into a canal which led to the capital and swam underwater, now and then surfacing to breathe. A good distance away, they found solid fortifications manned by an impressive number of soldiers. There were no weak points in Khnum-Hotep's defences.

The scouts had got what they came for, but the most difficult part of their mission lay ahead: to get back safe and sound and pass on the information they had gathered.

At that moment, an arrow whistled past their ears.

As soon as Senusret entered his palace, Djehuty, former governor of the Hare province, came to meet him. Djehuty always felt painfully cold, so he was dressed in a voluminous cloak. He tried to ignore his age and his aching joints, and paid homage to the pharaoh whose loyal subject he had become.

'I have been waiting impatiently for your return, Majesty.'

'Why? Is there bad news?'

'I have strengthened the borders of the province and deployed all my troops to isolate Khnum-Hotep, but all the time you were away I feared he would try to force a way through the blockade. His army is larger than mine, so I could not have held out for long.'

'But that has not happened, so we can keep hoping.'

'I am still pessimistic, Majesty. I have doubts about the reliability of my men, because many of them balk at the thought of fighting Khnum-Hotep. And I advise you not to trust the soldiers of the armies that have lately rallied to the Crown: their commitment is only recent, and Khnum-Hotep's reputation frightens them. Most of them think that if there is any fighting he will win. In fact, the only troops you can rely on are your own.'

'Thank you for speaking so frankly.'

'Without a doubt you are the stuff of a great pharaoh – and our country badly needs one – but the difficulties looming up ahead of you seem insurmountable. Even if you win this fight, the wounds can never be healed.'

Djehuty wondered if the king was taking his remarks seriously. Bringing all the rebel provinces – with the exception of Khnum-Hotep's – back into the bosom of Egypt had been a brilliant achievement, but true reconciliation would take time, a lot of time. In demanding total victory, Senusret was risking disaster. But if he procrastinated he would weaken himself as regards Khnum-Hotep, who would not fail to take advantage of the fact.

Sobek-Khu, the athletic and ever-wary commander not only of Senusret's personal bodyguard but of all the country's security guards, had not slept a wink since the king had taken up residence in the Hare province. He had not yet mastered all the elements of security in this vast territory. Moreover, he had to work with Djehuty's soldiers and form mixed teams, which did not inspire him with much confidence. However, he had insisted on posting his best men to keep guard around the king's apartments.

Obviously, Khnum-Hotep would try to kill Senusret before the latter launched an assault, because if they lost their leader the king's troops would probably rally to the enemy. But where and when would the assassination attempt take place?

At Khemenu, the Hare province's capital, the atmosphere was growing sombre. None of the scouts sent out by General Nesmontu from the other side of the front had come back, and Senusret therefore knew nothing of Khnum-Hotep's defensive system. Attacking blindly could only lead to failure.

As soon as dawn broke, Sobek himself searched the palace employees. He even distrusted apparently inoffensive old men, and went to the kitchens, where the cook's assistants tasted the dishes in his presence.

As he was taking a moment to eat a flatcake stuffed with beans, one of his assistants approached hesitantly, looking crestfallen.

'Is there a problem?' asked Sobek.

'No, sir, not really . . . But you ordered us to tell you everything . . .'

'Explain yourself.'

Sobek put down the flatcake. A small dog had been watching it intently for a long time. Seizing his prize, he trotted off to eat it in a quiet corner.

'You see, sir, it was . . .'

'Go on.'

'Well, it was a minor thing. The palace barber went in yesterday evening, a little before sunset, and no one saw him come out again. Normally, he should have finished his work before the midday meal.'

'Then he must be hiding somewhere.'

'Don't worry, sir, I've got his equipment. No one is allowed to walk around the palace with an actual or potential weapon.'

'You fool, he'll have hidden a razor somewhere!'

Sobek and the guard ran towards Senusret's apartments. In the corridor outside them, the guard spotted the barber, who was carrying a small leather bag.

'That's him!'

The man halted in alarm. Sobek leapt on his back and bore him to the ground. The assistant tied his hands and feet with rope that bit into his flesh.

'So, my lad,' said Sobek grimly, 'you wanted to kill the king, did you?'

'No, no, I swear I didn't!'

'We'll soon see.'

Sobek opened the bag. There was no razor inside, only a superb carnelian scarab. 'You stole this, didn't you?'

The barber hung his head. 'Yes, I did.'

'From whom?'

'From one of the royal maids.'

'And you hid in the palace last night, to carry out your crime?'

'I didn't think anyone would notice me. Please forgive me, I—'

'I promise you a long time in prison.'

While Senusret was examining General Nesmontu's plan of attack, Sobek informed them that two scouts had just rejoined the front line of infantry. As suspicious as ever, he asked Nesmontu to identify them before they appeared before the pharaoh.

Both the scouts were wounded – one had an arrowhead in his left shoulder, while the other's right leg was covered in dried blood – but, proud of having succeeded in their mission, they had refused to be treated before speaking to Senusret and Nesmontu, who both listened attentively to their report. When they had finished, Nesmontu congratulated them and promised that they would be promoted to officers, and Senusret embraced them – he had to stoop to do so, because he was a good head taller than they were. The two heroes were moved almost to tears by this signal honour.

When the scouts had been sent off to the army hospital,

Senusret convened his inner council, which consisted of General Nesmontu and General Sepi, Royal Seal-Bearer Sehotep and Sobek-Khu.

Nesmontu gravely summarized the information the scouts had gathered. A long silence followed.

Eventually Sepi broke it. 'Khnum-Hotep's system is impossible to break through,' he said. 'We would need an army three times the size of ours, and even then our losses would be very heavy. In our forces' current state, we stand no chance.'

'I agree that the operation is likely to be delicate,' said Nesmontu, 'but withdrawal is out of the question. I shall take my very best men and we shall break through the enemy defences.'

'If you do,' objected Sehotep, 'you will fight with great flair and courage but you will be killed. When our best soldiers are dead, what hope will we have left?'

'Knowing the enemy's positions gives us a considerable advantage,' said Nesmontu. 'If we make full use of that advantage, destiny may favour us.'

'Vain words!' protested Sobek. 'You yourself have just explained why we're defeated before we even begin to fight.'

'Let us try to negotiate again,' suggested Sehotep. 'I'm sure I could bring Khnum-Hotep over to our side.'

'He'll simply keep you as a hostage,' said General Sepi. 'His head's harder than granite, and he won't negotiate because he won't give up any of his prerogatives.'

No one contradicted him.

'We have no choice,' said Nesmontu. 'Whatever the risks, we must attack. If we don't, the pharaoh's prestige will be fatally damaged.'

'I recommend leaving the situation as it is,' said Sehotep. 'Let us strengthen the blockade and starve Khnum-Hotep into surrendering.'

'That's unrealistic – a mere dream!' snorted Nesmontu.

'His province is rich enough to feed him for months, even years. If we don't act, he will.'

'The king's safety is the foremost priority,' Sobek the Protector reminded him. 'During the attack His Majesty must not be exposed to danger.'

'That is exactly what I intend. And I shall march at the head of my own soldiers.'

Senusret stood up. 'The final decision is mine. You shall know it tomorrow morning, after the celebration of the rites in the shrine of Thoth.'

7

Dressed in a pleated robe with short sleeves and a beige bodice, the young priestess hailed the Tree of Life and played to it on a portable harp, an instrument particularly difficult to make sound harmonious. It was about a cubit long, was made of sycamore wood, and had four strings. The player lodged the bottom edge in the hollow of her shoulder and held it horizontally so as to obtain perfect balance. The harp was decorated with two small protective sculptures, a magic eye of Isis and a head of Ma'at. She played a very slow but rhythmic melody, which soothed anxiety and induced calm.

When the final notes had died away, the Shaven-headed One proceeded with the libation rite. 'The heavens and the stars play music in honour of the Tree of Life, the sun and moon sing its praises, the goddesses dance for it. A true musician knows the Creator's plan, perceives how he orders the universe and makes its component parts resonant. From this order is born a celestial music, whose humble interpreters we can become. May your art be a sacred rite.'

As his boat neared Abydos, Gergu felt tense and depressed, despite his growing wealth and influence. The rich and powerful secretary of the King's House, Medes, whose creature he was, had recently promoted him to the rank of principal inspector of granaries. In this capacity, Gergu had travelled all over Egypt and used his new authority to extort much wealth from landowners, threatening them with reprisals if they did not secretly hand over a share of their possessions to him.

Gergu had a huge appetite for food and drink – he had become somewhat corpulent – and for women. He had been divorced three times, and ought to have gone to prison for beating his last wife. But Medes had got him out of that difficulty, ordering him to use professional whores in future.

A good sailor and an experienced hunter, Gergu hated taking ill-considered risks, but that was just what, by sending him to Abydos again, Medes was making him do – Gergu was in no position to refuse his protector's orders.

The pretext for his visit was bringing the priests supplies of some of the food they were officially entitled to. His real goal was quite different: to re-establish contact with one of the permanent priests at Abydos, corrupt him, and transform him into a reliable ally, in the hope of seizing the temple's legendary treasures.

Following their last meeting, Gergu had thought the plan a workable one. The more he thought about it, though, the more he had a feeling that the priest was setting a trap for him. But no argument could dissuade Medes from his plan, so here Gergu was.

A very superstitious man, afraid of the occult powers of gods and magicians, he never went anywhere without a large supply of protective amulets. He had them with him now, but still, when his boat moored at the landing-stage of Osiris's sacred domain, he felt vulnerable to attacks by invisible forces, and only after several cups of strong beer did he summon up the courage to leave his cabin.

As on his previous visit, he was struck by the number of guards posted to watch over the sacred city. What was going on here? Each new arrival was carefully searched, each boat inspected from top to bottom.

Gergu was not exempted. Seeing an officer and four sturdy soldiers armed with clubs bearing down on him, he started to sweat. They were going to arrest him, throw him in prison and interrogate him!

'Your documents,' demanded the officer.

'Here they are.' Trembling, he handed over a papyrus scroll.

The officer took his time reading it. 'Gergu, principal inspector of granaries, on an official mission with a boat-load of perishable food. Let's check that the cargo conforms with the list.' He paused and looked closely at Gergu. 'You don't look well.'

'I must have eaten something that disagrees with me.'

'There is a doctor on call at the command post. If you get any worse, don't hesitate to consult him. Now, while my men are examining the cargo I shall take you to my office.'

'Why?'

'Because I've had special orders as regards you.'

Gergu thought his legs would give way, but he managed to stay standing. It was clear that his fate was sealed. With so many soldiers around, it would be impossible to run away, so he resignedly followed the officer to a large office where ten scribes were working.

The officer took a wooden tablet from a shelf and handed it to Gergu.

'As you visit Abydos so often, you are to be counted as a temporary priest. Here is your authorization. It has been approved by the scribe in charge of contacts with the outside world, and you must always keep it with you while you are here. It does not authorize you to enter the area forbidden to outsiders, and it does not exempt you from any of the checks, but when someone is known to us it speeds things up.'

Unable to utter a word, Gergu just managed an idiotic smile.

'You will now be escorted to your meeting.'

Still stunned, Gergu was happy to wait at the usual place, because the wait gave him time to regain his composure before his crucial meeting with the permanent priest. But then doubts assailed him again. What if a different priest emerged from the covered temple and accused him of trying to bribe a member of the most closed brotherhood in Egypt? Gergu's throat was so tight that he was barely able to take a sip of water.

The priest appeared: it was Bega again! And he looked as stern and daunting as ever.

Embittered at not being appointed to lead the permanent priests at Abydos, Bega wanted to take his revenge on the principal cause of his disappointment, Pharaoh Senusret. But to do so he needed allies, and he could not find them while he was confined within the domain of Osiris. Gergu's approach had been like a miracle. Gergu himself might be a mere lickspittle, but Bega knew he was the emissary of a powerful man who was determined to discover the Mysteries of Abydos and who had charged Gergu with finding out if there was a crack into which he could insinuate himself.

That crack was Bega. He was determined to sell his services at the highest price possible, and thus would become rich at the same time as getting his legitimate vengeance.

'Your status as a temporary priest,' he said, 'will make contact between us easier. Of course, I shall continue to give you lists of food you are to provide, and you must go on doing this work efficiently.'

Gergu nodded. 'Of course.'

'Before we take our collaboration any further, I should like to know something for certain: can you really provide the necessary networks to distribute what I have to sell?'

'Whatever the merchandise is, there will be no problem.'

'Then you must be a very influential man.'

'No, only an intermediary, but my employer does indeed hold high office.'

'Is he by any chance a member of the pharaoh's inner circle?'

'I am not permitted to tell you any more yet – we must get to know each other better. And, first of all, what do you have to sell that is so precious?'

'Come with me.'

Gergu's stomach tightened. He was sure this was a trap.

'Don't worry,' Bega reassured him. 'I'm going to grant you a favour which is greatly valued by the temporary priests who are given it. You are going to approach the terrace of the Great God.'

With as much fear as astonishment, Gergu followed him along the processional road, which was lined with many small temple-like buildings. Each consisted of a shrine with a courtyard and a tree-filled garden in front, and was surrounded by an enclosing wall.

'Who has the privilege of being buried here?' asked Gergu.

'Actually, nobody has.'

'But then . . .'

'We'll visit one of these monuments and then you'll understand.'

Passing through an open door in the surrounding wall, the two men entered the garden of a large shrine. At the foot of a sycamore tree, consecrated to the sky-goddess Nut, was a pool in which lotuses were flowering. Against the walls were stelae, statues and offering-tables of various sizes.

'No one's body rests here,' explained Bega. 'However, many dignitaries are present at Osiris's side because of these monuments, which they were authorized to send to Abydos and which the permanent priests bring to life, using magic. In this way, the pilgrimage of the soul takes place. To have a stele or a statue near the terrace of the Great God is to be certain of sharing his eternity. My colleagues and I often pour libations known as "divine dew" and diffuse the smoke from incense, "that which renders divine", over these sacred stones. The names of the happy elect are then regenerated.'

Although fascinated by the majesty of the place, Gergu was still nervous. 'That's very impressive, but I don't see—'

'Look more closely.'

Gergu concentrated, but made out only shrines and votive monuments.

'The value of these stelae, these statues and these offering-tables is inestimable,' said Bega, 'because they have been consecrated and impregnated with the spirit of Osiris.'

Gergu dared not understand. 'Surely you aren't planning to—'

'Everything that enters Abydos is strictly controlled, but what leaves is not.'

'To get these works of art out—'

'Not the statues, not the large stelae, not those of the dignitaries sent on missions to Abydos by a pharaoh, but the small stelae. In some shrines there are so many of them that nobody will notice that a few have disappeared. It is up to you to find buyers for these treasures, whose protecting power is unrivalled.'

That won't be difficult, thought Gergu, and I shall charge the highest price I possibly can.

'In the future,' Bega continued, 'I shall have other, even more precious, things to trade, but we'll speak of that later.'

'Don't you trust me?'

'I am playing for high stakes and I don't want to lose. Before going further, let us see how you deal with this first matter.'

'You won't be disappointed. My employer is both efficient and highly discreet.'

'I hope so.'

'But tell me,' said Gergu, 'why are there so many soldiers and guards around Abydos?'

'It concerns one of the pieces of information I shall sell you, about an exceptionally serious matter. Rumours may be circulating, but only the permanent priests and those close to

Pharaoh know the truth, and they have all been sworn to the strictest secrecy.'

'A secrecy you are ready to violate.'

Bega became even icier than usual. 'We shall see.'

The two men walked slowly away from the terrace of the Great God. The silence was so profound that it calmed Gergu's nerves.

'On your next visit,' Bega told him, 'I'll give you the first miniature stele.'

'And then?'

'Don't worry about that. If I'm pleased with our first transaction, I shall want to meet your employer.'

'I don't know whether—'

'You know who I am, and will have certainly told him. I must therefore know who he is, so that our bonds are indestructible and our association lasting.'

'I shall pass on your demands to him.'

'Here is the list of food to be delivered to the permanent priests next time. Do not hurry; be sure to leave a reasonable time before coming back.'

As he walked back to his boat, Gergu found that he was no longer subject to checks. In fact, now that he counted as a temporary priest, he was saluted by the guards, and one of them even carried his travelling-bag for him.

Gergu was astonished by Bega's audacity and determination. He must be full of hatred and rancour to betray his own kind like this, but what a fabulous stroke of good fortune! Even in his wildest dreams, Medes could never have imagined that he'd have the benefit of such an ally at the heart of Abydos.

8

The flamboyant, athletic thirty-year-old Rudi was one of the most feared guards in Memphis. Sobek the Protector had appointed him to a particularly delicate post, that of checking people entering Egypt from Asia, and he did his work with meticulous thoroughness.

Rudi was still finding it hard to come to terms with the Canaanite rebellion in Sichem, during which his best friend had been killed. He had been delighted to learn of the death of the rebels' ringleader, a madman who called himself 'the Herald', but he was nevertheless still very much on guard. Whenever a caravan of foreigners asked permission to enter Egypt, he dealt with the matter personally and consulted each trader's file. If there were any suspicions, he went to the trade-control post to the north of Memphis, where suspects were held, and interrogated them himself.

Rudi disliked Canaanites and Asians, who in his eyes were as bad as each other: accomplished liars, full of deceit and sly tricks. So he sent back as many as possible, convinced that he was helping maintaining the security without which no Egyptian could live happily.

'Sir,' his second-in-command informed him, 'two shady characters have been caught near the Temple of Ptah. They claim they're sandal-sellers, but they've got no sandals with them.'

'I shall deal with them immediately.'

'But sir, it's time for the midday meal!'

'Duty first.'

'The way seems clear,' said Shab the Twisted.

As he led the Herald through the maze of narrow streets behind the port of Memphis, Shab behaved like a hunted wild beast. He was alert to the slightest sign of danger, and no one who tried to follow them would have succeeded in escaping his vigilance. And he greatly appreciated his master's ability to transform himself into a bird of prey and tear his adversary's flesh from his bones.

Shab halted before a dilapidated house and looked around. He saw nothing suspicious.

He knocked four times at a small door. Someone inside answered with a single knock. The Twisted One knocked twice, rapidly this time. The door opened.

Still as wary as ever, Shab stepped across the threshold, into a room with a beaten earth floor, on which two bearded men were squatting. Deciding that there was no danger, he signalled to the Herald, who entered. The door was briskly closed.

'Go and find the others,' the Herald ordered the doorkeeper.

Four men, aged around thirty, swiftly appeared and prostrated themselves before their leader.

He frowned. 'Why have those two let their beards grow back?'

'My lord,' replied the official tenant of the house, 'they have not managed to get used to the way of life in this accursed city. They tried very hard, but seeing all these immodest females moving about freely was more than they could bear. So they prefer to remain here and respect our customs.'

'And what about you? Have you done any better?'

'Not very much better, I fear. I and my companions have become dock-workers, but the Egyptians eye us with suspicion. They drink alcohol, tell licentious stories, laugh very loudly, and amuse themselves with women of ill-repute. How can we possibly become friends with people like that? They disgust us! We want to go back to Canaan, to Sichem, and take up the struggle against the oppressor there.'

Shab the Twisted wanted to spit in the face of this incompetent fool, but it was up to the Herald to take a decision.

'I understand your torments,' the latter said gently. 'Egypt is a depraved land, which must be brought back to the path of virtue.'

Everyone sat down, and the Herald launched into a long sermon, castigating luxury, the scandalous freedom of women, and the pharaonic tradition, which God had ordered him to destroy. Several times the Canaanites nodded in unison. By maintaining his rigid stance, their leader reassured them.

'We shall overcome,' he predicted, 'and you will be the first to do deeds of which all Canaan will speak proudly.'

They looked up at him doubtfully.

'To deal a death-blow to the tyrant,' he explained, 'it is vital that a caravan including our allies reaches Kahun, but they face an insurmountable obstacle, a senior Egyptian official named Rudi. You, my brave disciples, are going to eliminate that obstacle.'

'How?' asked one of the bearded men.

'We shall set a trap for him, and he will not emerge from it alive. And the credit for this dazzling achievement will come back to you.'

The Canaanites listened attentively to the Herald's explanation of what they were to do.

'Until I give you the signal to act,' he concluded, 'you are not to say a single word to anybody about this. If one of you were to talk, we would all be in danger.'

'We shall not move again from here,' promised the other bearded man, 'and we shall obey your orders to the letter.'

The meeting over, Shab the Twisted slipped out of the house and inspected the street. There was no one in sight. The Herald could safely leave the Canaanites' lair.

On their way home, the Twisted One could not keep silent. 'They're nothing but cowards and fools, my lord. In my opinion, you shouldn't rely on them.'

'I agree.'

'But . . . but you've just entrusted them with a mission of the highest importance!'

'Indeed, my friend, but it will be the only one.'

'So,' said Rudi, 'you're sandal-sellers, are you?'

The two suspects knelt down. 'Yes, we are,' replied the older man. 'My brother's dumb, so I'll speak for both of us.'

'If you tell me lies, I'll lose my temper.'

'I swear to you that—'

'I said, don't lie. How did you enter Egypt?'

'By the Ways of Horus.'

'Then your arrival will have been recorded when you passed through one of the border forts. Which one was it?'

'I can't remember.'

'You and your accomplice got into our territory illegally. What were your intentions?

'Egypt's rich, and we're poor. We hoped to make our fortunes.'

'By selling sandals?' said Rudi sarcastically.

'Yes.'

'Which you'd make yourselves?'

'Of course.'

'I'll take you both to a workshop, and you can show me how you make them.'

The man's sighed. 'Very well, We don't know anything about making sandals.'

'Let's start again at the beginning, my lad. And this time not a single lie, or I'll let my men interrogate you in their own way.'

'In Egypt, nobody can be treated brutally,' protested the man.

'When they've finished with you, nobody will even recognize you any more.'

The two brothers shrank in fear. 'If I talk,' said the elder one, 'we'll get into terrible trouble.'

'If you don't, your troubles will be far worse.'

'Well – and this is the truth – I don't know very much, but I don't want any problems. If I tell you everything, will you let me and my brother go free?'

'You ask a lot, don't you? Here's my offer, and it is not negotiable: if you really do tell me everything, I shall have you expelled.'

'Have I have your word on that?'

'You have.'

'Then here you are: my brother and I come from the town of Sichem, in Canaan. We were invited to Memphis by a fellow Canaanite who settled here last year. He promised us work and somewhere to live, but it turned out that in fact he wanted to turn us into criminals.'

'In what way?'

'He was planning to rob one of the port storehouses, and wouldn't have hesitated to kill the guards. We'd never dream of doing something like that, so we're very happy to go home. There, now you know everything.'

'Not quite. I need one last detail: where does this Canaanite live?'

'In a house with a guard behind the Temple of Ptah, opposite three palm trees. But he's very wary.'

'Is there a password?'

'Yes, "vengeance".'

'You and your brother will leave Egypt this very day.'

Rudi knew he ought to inform Sobek-Khu, but he preferred to organize this run-of-the-mill operation himself. By doing so, he could interrogate the Canaanite and obtain the names of all the members of his network. There was no point in disturbing the commander over the dismantling of a band of petty criminals. All the same, he was cautious enough to take five men with him, for the Canaanites were past masters at slipping away, and he did not want to give their leader any chance of doing so.

The house was not difficult to spot. Rudi posted his men and went over to the doorkeeper, who was dozing at the entrance.

He woke him up with a tap on the shoulder. 'Is your employer here?'

'Perhaps. Who shall I say it is?'

'Vengeance.'

'I'll go and see.'

The servant got up slowly, opened the door, trudged along the little sandy path that led to the house, went inside for a few moments, and then reappeared, still dragging his feet.

'He's waiting for you.'

Rudi set off along the path. He was met by one of the shaven Canaanites whom the Herald had brought here the previous day, just before sending two men towards the Temple of Ptah. Their presence there, he had told them, would come to the guards' attention. Rudi would interrogate them and, in response to the information they provided, would investigate in person.

The trap was working marvellously.

'Please repeat the password,' said the Canaanite.

'Vengeance.'

'You're the one who's going to feel that vengeance!'

From behind Rudi, the doorkeeper grabbed him round the waist, while the Herald's other faithful servants sprang out of the house and stabbed him with their daggers. Although on the point of death, he found the strength to shout for help, and his men reacted immediately.

At the end of a fierce fight, only one guard was still alive, and he was seriously wounded. He dragged himself outside, hailed a passer-by and lost consciousness.

According to the agreed code, Shab the Twisted knocked at the door of the dilapidated house. One of the two bearded Canaanites opened it. The Twisted One entered, followed by the Herald.

'Did our men succeed?' asked the other bearded man, who was sitting down drinking a cup of milk.

'Yes. Controller Rudi is dead.'

'Have they already left for Sichem?'

'No, for somewhere much further away.'

The bearded man got to his feet. 'You mean . . . ?'

'They offered their lives to our cause. God will welcome them as heroes, and they shall at last enjoy all the pleasures of heaven.'

'And what about us? Can we leave Memphis at last?'

'Don't you want to become heroes, too?'

Shab the Twisted was already strangling the first man with a leather thong. The second tried to run away, but the Herald's hand came down on his chest.

The Canaanite howled. A falcon's talons sank into his flesh and tore out his heart.

'What shall we do with the corpses?' asked Shab.

'We shall leave them in plain sight, and we shan't close the door behind us. A passer-by will notice them and alert the guards. They'll be delighted to discover the Canaanites' refuge, which they'll probably link with Rudi's killers. A new phase of repression will strike Sichem, and Pharaoh will have Canaan watched more closely than ever, convinced that the source of the evil lies there. We shall be free to act.'

9

From the summit of the hill where his tomb had been excavated, Khnum-Hotep gazed out over at the beautiful province of the Oryx, which, in a few hours or a few days, would be a bloody theatre of civil war.

In his tomb, which was decorated with beautiful, many-coloured birds, a profound peace still reigned. But what would remain of it if Senusret was victorious? He would probably destroy it stone by stone, in order to wipe away all traces of his last adversary. And what would become of the province's capital, Menat-Khufu, 'the Wet-nurse of Khufu', birthplace of the illustrious builder of the Great Pyramid?

But Senusret did not hold victory in the palm of his hand! No, he did not yet reign over the cultivated plains of this province, over its pretty villages with their small white houses, over its palm-groves and its irrigation pools. He did not control the caravan routes winding into the Eastern desert, he did not command the large, well-trained army. The soldiers would fight fiercely, and not a single one would throw down his weapons.

'Fan me,' he ordered two servants, who immediately began to wave two lotus-shaped fans. The men knew their master's tastes, and adopted the speed he liked best.

How charming this landscape is, thought Khnum-Hotep, how imbued with gentleness. This dream had become reality through hard work. Why must it end in such a brutal way?

But he could not prolong these all-too-brief moments of meditation, for everyone was awaiting his instructions.

'We shall return to the palace,' he said, and set off down the hill. At the foot of the hill his three dogs, a very lively male and two plump females, ran up to demand caresses, but he was too preoccupied to grant them more than a short moment of affection.

Khnum-Hotep had three travelling-chairs, with backs that could be inclined. The one he was using today had recently been strengthened, to bear his considerable weight. Four strong fellows lifted the chair and, with the dogs trotting alongside, set off back to Menat-Khufu.

When he reached his palace, Khnum-Hotep had himself massaged with his favourite ointment, which was based on purified fat cooked in flavoured wine, then settled himself in a high-backed chair with arms.

A servant hurried to wash his hands, while a second poured some white wine into his favourite cup, one covered with gold leaf. A third opened a sycamore-wood chest and removed two costly wigs, one short with plaited hair, the other long with wavy locks. Khnum-Hotep liked to vary the style of his wig every day and could not bear the slightest defect, for it affected his dignity. Sometimes he liked to have his forehead, ears and neck hidden; at other times heavy tresses amused him.

'No, neither of them,' he told the wig-maker. 'Give me the oldest and most sober.' To confront the enemy, he wanted to look like his ancestors.

A steward announced arrival of the lady Techat. She was the province's treasurer, who controlled its storehouses and managed the governor's personal possessions.

'Your orders have been carried out, my lord,' she said, 'down to the smallest detail. The defensive system is in place, and the soldiers are at their posts.'

'The Oryx province will be the burial-ground of the

invader's troops. They will charge in to the attack and fall into our traps.'

'Forgive my impertinence, my lord, but isn't that a vain hope? You don't believe Senusret is rash, any more than I do. He sent his scouts to spy on us, didn't he?'

'Yes, but we caught them.'

Techat shook her head. 'Not all of them, I'm sure, so the king knows our strengths and our weaknesses.'

'In that case, we shall wipe out the latter.'

'We haven't enough men.'

'Then the women and children shall help defend our territory.'

'They are already doing so.'

Khnum-Hotep's gaze darkened. 'According to you, Techat, we have no chance of winning.'

'Perhaps our courage will enable us to drive back the attacker.'

'Are you advising me to surrender?'

'Indeed not, my lord! But one cannnot fail to realize that this terrible war, whatever its outcome, will leave our province bled dry. I am afraid – afraid of seeing the destruction of everything we love so much.'

Khnum-Hotep had no words of comfort. What could he say to counter his adviser's clear thinking?

Techat said, 'Give me permission to withdraw, my lord. I refuse to be present at this massacre. If we are defeated, they will not capture me alive, that I promise you.'

Khnum-Hotep slumped in his chair. It was here, in this room, that he would be informed of Senusret's offensive. He would then take command of his best soldiers, who would fight so long as there was breath in their bodies.

There was the sound of running feet, and a moment later his steward burst into the room.

'My lord,' the man said in a trembling voice, 'the pharaoh is here!'

'Where did he attack?'

'He has not attacked, but he is here.'

Khnum-Hotep frowned. 'Here? What do you mean?'

'At your palace entrance, my lord.'

'*What?* My army's been wiped out, and no one tells me until now?'

'Oh no, my lord. No one's been killed.'

'Have you gone mad?'

'The pharaoh is alone – well, almost alone: the Bearer of the Royal Seal is with him.'

In disbelief, Khnum-Hotep got up and strode to the entrance of his palace, where he had to push his way through the courtiers who had gathered.

He was confronted by a giant of a man who not only had the Blue Crown upon his head but wore a remarkable kilt covered with hieroglyphs. They encapsulated the function of this sacred garment: to transform the king into active light, to make him victorious over evil and enable him to see the whole of creation.

Khnum-Hotep gaped at the visitor. 'Nobody . . . nobody tried to prevent you from coming here?'

'Who would dare raise a hand against the King of Upper and Lower Egypt?'

'My province is independent,' roared Khnum-Hotep, and he launched into a long discourse in which he traced his family's history in exhaustive detail, stressed the innumerable benefits his rule had brought the people of the province, and boasted of his good government.

Senusret stood motionless. He waited for the end of this interminable speech without showing the slightest sign of impatience, and then, after a long pause, began to speak.

'The man who harangues the crowd in long speeches is a dangerous man, the talkative man is a troublemaker. Stirring up the multitude leads to destruction. A governor should, therefore, be a craftsman of words.'

The courtiers were convinced that Khnum-Hotep, insulted so gravely, would instantly order the arrest of the foolish king. But the governor seemed thunderstruck: he did not react at all.

Senusret spoke again. 'The pharaoh is the gods' spokesman, and he makes a pact with them. He does not work for his own benefit; the creative energy he guards is destined for his people. The harmony of the state is accomplished in a communion between people who do not demand rights but live by their reciprocal duties. May the thoughts of humankind be united with the spirit of the gods, may the King's House be united, may the government insist on each person's capacity to unite and not to oppose and divide. Also, all the provinces must come together in order to bring offerings to the temple and make Egypt one great body, like the sky. Pharaoh is not content just to speak, he acts. What my heart devises, I carry out, with tenacity and perseverance. If you are a man of duty, and truly responsible, do not condemn the Oryx province to isolation.

'But evil is eating away at you, Khnum-Hotep, is it not? Are you the one who stole the gold of the gods? Was it you who put a curse on the Tree of Life, attempting to prevent the resurrection of Osiris?'

Silence fell once more.

This time, thought Senusret, the governor could not remain silent. This was not a verbal joust, it was a matter of accusations so grave that he would have to kill the king, whether it was because the king knew too much or because he had dared to sully Khnum-Hotep's honour in such a way.

The big, imposing Khnum-Hotep did indeed react, but in a wholly unforeseen way: he burst out laughing, so loudly that he could be heard beyond the palace walls.

When at last he stopped, the pharaoh stared intently at him, as if piercing though into his soul.

'Majesty, I know I'm too talkative! I laughed for two

reasons. First, because of myself and my slowness in grasping the arguments you laid out in words which were few yet very powerful. Next, because of the sheer enormity of your accusations. Mining in the Eastern desert has been reduced to a minimum for a long time, and the little gold I have is destined for the temple. As for the Tree of Life, supposing that it isn't merely a legend, I don't know where it is. And I may worship Osiris, the sole guarantor of my soul's survival, but I haven't been initiated into the Mysteries of his resurrection, so I have no power either over him or over Abydos. I am not the criminal you seek, Majesty.

'But this meeting is the most important moment in my life, for it puts an end to our hostility and enables us to avoid a bloody and devastating war. I see and I hear a true pharaoh, whose loyal subject I shall be from this moment on. I place the Oryx province in your hands, Majesty, and invite you to the greatest banquet ever held in Menat-Khufu.'

For Sobek the Protector, who was not yet convinced of Khnum-Hotep's sincerity, the banquet was a real nightmare. In this vast hall, where the province's dignitaries and their wives had gathered, how could he ensure the king's safety? He feared the governor might be play-acting, trying to lure him into lowering his guard.

Nesmontu, who had only with the greatest reluctance squeezed his unwilling body into his ceremonial robes, agreed. He thought Khnum-Hotep perfectly capable of planning to kill the king and his entourage at this grandiose celebration, which saw soldiers from the Oryx province fraternizing with the pharaoh's troops. Every bit as suspicious as Sobek, he had given very strict orders to an elite regiment, who would intervene at the slightest sign of danger.

Sepi and Sehotep were less pessimistic. The former could see that everyone was genuinely relieved to have averted a terrifying war. The latter had been present at Khnum-Hotep's abrupt conversion, and did not believe anyone could dissemble to that extent.

The banqueting-hall was a feast for the eyes, decorated with hundreds of flowers, perfumed, and lit by dozens of lamps.

When Khnum-Hotep's authoritative voice rang out, silence fell.

'Pharaoh has come. He reunites the Two Lands, Upper and Lower Egypt, governs the red earth and places the black earth under his authority, gives life to the reed and the bee. Let all here present bow before him and venerate him.'

Many tough men, beginning with Nesmontu, were unable to contain their emotion. In that moment, Egypt rediscovered unity, peace and cohesion. The spectre of civil war faded away. For this exploit alone, Senusret would count among the greatest pharaohs in Egyptian history.

Khnum-Hotep's cooks had chosen to serve several types of fish, some grilled and accompanied by asparagus, the others with a sauce flavoured with cumin, celery and coriander. The largest perch, four cubits long, weighed more than a full-grown man. Perch were strong fighters and were not usually easy to catch, but they were vulnerable in the winter, when they came closer to the surface. They had brownish-olive backs and silver bellies, and their flesh was very fine. Charged with protecting the prow of the sun's ship, the perch alerted the divine crew to the presence of the monstrous serpent determined to drink the waters of the Nile.

Nesmontu enjoyed a grey mullet with a rounded head and large scales. These fish lived in the salt marshes and the Delta, and were so swift and agile that they often escaped from the nets. Sehotep feasted on the delicate flesh of a barbel, with its shining, silvery-white body. It was caught with triple hooks baited with dates or balls of germinated barley. Sepi sampled a very expensive fish with a short snout and large eyes, usually found at the river's edge, the mormyre. Nocturnal and timid, it rarely rose to the surface, and only seasoned fishermen could catch it unawares. Sobek the Protector hungrily ate a superb citharine, silver-white on its belly and flanks, and bluish-grey on the back. And no one declined when platters of mullet, eels, carp and tench were passed round.

The prepared mullet roes, washed several times in salted water before being pressed between planks, were of exceptional quality. They accompanied the main dishes, which were a great success and complemented the wines. These were labelled 'Eight times good', the highest classification among great wines. Even Nesmontu had to admit that the master-winegrowers of the Oryx were as good as those of the Delta.

After a while, seeing that conversation had begun to flow more freely and the atmosphere was more relaxed, Khnum-Hotep turned to the king. 'Majesty, may I ask why you asked me those terrifying questions?'

'The Tree of Life, the Acacia of Osiris at Abydos, has fallen victim to a curse. If it dies, Egypt will die, too, and only a certain kind of gold can cure it. We must also identify the evil criminal who is wielding the force of Set against Osiris.'

'And you thought *I* was guilty?'

'We suspected each of the provincial governors who refused to submit – after all, combating the country's unity was preventing the resurrection of Osiris. But now the Two Lands are bound together again, and your innocence – and that of your counterparts – has been established.'

'Then who is the real criminal?'

'Until we find out, we shall be in great danger.'

'I shall help you with all my strength.'

'Unfailingly and without rancour?'

'Order and I shall obey.'

It was well into the night when the last course, succulent honey-cakes, was served. When they were finished, Senusret got to his feet. All the guests did likewise, to listen to a declaration they sensed would be vital.

'Provincial governors no longer exist, and hereditary offices are abolished. Upper and Lower Egypt are reunited in the king's heart and hand. I am entrusting the government of the Two Lands to a tjaty. He will converse each morning with me, will give an account of his activities, will be assisted by ministers and subject to supervision by the King's House. His task will be difficult, harsh, unrewarding, and as bitter as venom. He will apply the law of Ma'at without exceeding it, without weakness or excess, will hunt down injustice, hear both rich and poor, will make himself advisedly feared, and will not bow his head before dignitaries.'

Everyone had the same thought: who would be the first holder of this onerous post, a man who would have the benefit of the monarch's trust but would be weighed down beneath a mass of all-important duties?

'I appoint to the office of tjaty your former governor, Khnum-Hotep,' decreed Pharaoh.

10

The sun had just gone down when Iker entered the abandoned house where his secret meetings with Bina were held. It was a bleak place: one wall was threatening to collapse in ruins, and the beams were splitting. Soon it would be knocked down to make way for a new building.

This evening it seemed deserted.

'It's Iker,' he whispered. 'You can come out now.'

Still no sign of life.

Suddenly, Iker wondered if Bina had betrayed him, by denouncing him to the authorities. Was she conspiring with the mayor or Heremsaf in order to bring about his downfall? By unmasking his plans, she would condemn him to the supreme punishment, and the tyrant would continue to destroy Egypt by spreading misfortune.

He prepared to leave, hoping no guards were waiting outside.

Two hands were placed over his eyes. 'I'm here, Iker!'

He pulled briskly away. 'You're mad! Why did you give me such a fright?'

She pouted like a little girl. 'I like having fun – you don't enjoy yourself enough.'

'How could I have the heart to enjoy myself?'

'You're right. Please forgive me.'

They sat down side by side.

'Have you decided yet?' asked Bina.

'I still have to check a few things.'

'Well, I've got excellent news. Our allies need delay no longer – they'll arrive in Kahun soon. They're real warriors and they'll easily be able to take control of the town. The official who was blocking their way into Egypt has left his post, and his successor is less unbending, so the caravan will get through without difficulty.'

'I assume other towns are involved?'

'I don't know. I'm only a humble servant-girl devoted to the cause of the oppressed. But I do know that the cause will triumph.'

'The town authorities have given me a splendid house,' said Iker.

'They want to stifle your conscience. But you aren't one of those ambitious people who can be bribed, are you?'

'No one will buy me. My old master taught me always to search for righteousness and to act in accordance with it.'

'Then kill the tyrant Senusret!'

'As I said, I still have things to check, but I need access to archives I'm not authorized to use.'

'As you wish, Iker. But don't waste too much time.'

As he lay on his bed, Sekari thought of the marvellous time he had just spent in the arms of his new mistress, a servant in a neighbouring house who hadn't been able to resist his funny, increasingly bawdy stories. When he suggested that they should act one out, the mischievous girl had accepted and had thrown herself into the role, playing it to perfection. And what woman worthy of the name would have refused to roll around in soft, scented sheets of fine linen?

Sekari would gladly have repeated their amorous tussles, but he had to feed North Wind, and the donkey could not be kept waiting. Next, he would have prepare a substantial dinner, although Iker had singularly little appetite. Unless the situation altered, Sekari would have to toil devotedly to finish all the food himself.

When he got home, Iker washed his hands and feet, then sat down in an armchair. His expression was even more sombre than the previous evening.

'I'll wager,' said Sekari, 'you won't enjoy either my beans with garlic or my courgettes baked with cheese.'

'I'm not hungry.'

'Whatever your ideal is, Iker, you won't reach it by fading away.'

A familiar voice called, 'May I come in? I am looking for Iker the scribe.'

'It's Heremsaf!' This time, thought Iker, he won't give me a house or promote me. He must have had me followed and knows of my links with Bina.

'I'll go and greet him,' Sekari decided proudly.

'No, leave it be. This concerns no one but me.'

Heremsaf looked serious and inscrutable. He said, 'It's a fine house, Iker. But you seem tired.'

'It has been a hard day.'

'Will you come with me now, and follow me without argument?'

'Do I have a choice?'

'Of course. Either you stay here and rest, or you attempt the adventure.'

Adventure? That was a strange word for prison, thought Iker.

Could he run away? No, impossible. Besides, Heremsaf would be only too pleased to see him thrown to the ground and beaten by guards. Since this was the end of the road, he would at least behave with dignity.

'I'll come with you.'

'In my opinion, you won't regret it.'

Iker did not react to this biting sarcasm. His conqueror would see no sign of weakness in him.

First, he did not see a single guard. Next, he realized that Heremsaf was leading him not out of the town but towards the southern wall.

'Where are we going?' he asked.

'To the Temple of Anubis.'

'What have I done wrong? Have I done my work badly? Is the library not in good order?'

'On the contrary, Iker, on the contrary. You have done your work so well that the priests of Anubis wish to see you.'

'Now?'

'You know, these people have no concept of days or times. But you are free to refuse their summons.'

What kind of trap had Heremsaf dreamt up? As intrigued as he was anxious, Iker walked on doggedly.

On the threshold of the temple, a shaven-headed priest was holding a torch high above his head. One of his colleagues joined him, bearing a papyrus scroll.

He bowed to Heremsaf, who turned to Iker and asked, 'Iker the scribe, do you wish to become a priest of Anubis?'

Caught unawares, the young man replied without hesitation. 'Yes, I do.'

Those few words contained the fire of an insane hope which, suddenly, was perhaps going to become reality.

'Have you been initiated into the mysteries of sacred writing?' asked the bearer of the scroll.

'I know the mother hieroglyphs and the words of Thoth.'

'In that case, read this ritual text. Next, you are to write words of knowledge relating to the good practice of the scribe's art.'

Iker passed this examination by quoting maxims in which Ma'at, righteousness and justice, held the most important place.

'Let us convene our court,' advised the torch-bearer, 'and proceed to evaluate the applicant's qualities. Does our superior agree to preside?'

Heremsaf nodded.

Iker was astounded. Heremsaf, the high-ranking scribe he thought he knew well, was the guardian of the mysteries of Anubis!

The two priests took Iker by the arms and led him into the first hall of the temple. Along the walls were stone benches, occupied by the permanent priests who celebrated the daily rites and ensured the upkeep of the sacred place.

Heremsaf took his place at the eastern end and asked the first question. 'What do you know of Anubis, Iker?'

'He is the ferryman between the worlds and holds the secrets of the rites of resurrection. Embodied in the jackal, he rids the desert of rotting carcasses, which he transforms into energy.'

Fifty other very specific questions were fired at him. Iker replied unhurriedly and without trying to hide the gaps in his knowledge with learned words.

Afterwards, while the court deliberated, he was left on his own in a small, bare-walled room lit by a single lamp. Time ceased to pass, and he let himself drift off into peaceful meditation.

He was brought back to reality when a priest came in and presented him with a long linen robe, which he put on.

'Take off your amulets,' said the priest. 'In the place you are going to, they will be of no use to you. Your judge, your sole judge, will be Anubis. And his decisions cannot be appealed.'

The priest led Iker down into a dark crypt. 'Gaze at the far end of this cave and be patient. Perhaps the god will appear.'

Left alone again, Iker gradually became accustomed to the darkness. Eventually he could make out two surprising creatures, a male and female jackal, standing up on their back legs and facing each other, leaving between them an empty space which irresistibly attracted him.

Indifferent to the danger, he slid between the two wild

animals, which placed their forepaws on his shoulders.* In that instant, Iker felt new energy circulating in his veins. Everything happened as if his body was being renewed, as if his flesh was being recreated with a vigour he had never known before.

Heremsaf entered the crypt, carrying an acacia-wood box. He laid it at Iker's feet and opened it slowly. Inside was a gold sceptre, the *sekhem*. In hieroglyphic language, it was used to write the concepts of mastery and power. The scribe remembered the words of the potter working at the Temple of Anubis, who had told him that the jackal-headed god possessed true power, embodied in this symbol preserved on the site of Abydos. With the moon, the silver disc he wielded during the night, Anubis lit up the righteous; and he also fashioned a gold stone, taking the form of the sun.

Heremsaf closed the box again and left the crypt. Iker followed him up to a pillared hall floored with large stone paving-slabs. The permanent priests listened thoughtfully to their superior, who addressed the new priest.

'Turn your eyes towards the Most Sacred Place, heaven on earth. Never enter here in a state of impurity, never do anything incorrect, steal neither thoughts nor material possessions, tell no falsehoods, reveal none of the secrets you have seen, do not damage the offerings, do not nourish sacrilegious words in your heart, carry out your office according to the rule and not according to your fancy. You have no teachings to impose, no absolute truth to spread, nobody to convert. When you are called to the temple, put on white sandals, and perform your service thoroughly, for God knows the man who acts for him. Are you ready, Iker, to take the oath?'

'I am.'

'Approach the altar.'

Iker did so.

---

*For this extraordinary scene, see *Mélanges Mokhtar*, I (Cairo, 1985), p. 156, fig. 3.

'This is the foundation stone from which this temple was born. If you were to perjure yourself, it would be transformed into a snake, which would destroy you. Repeat these words with me: "I am the son of Isis. I will not betray the seven words hidden beneath the stones of the valley."'*

After Iker had sworn the oath, Heremsaf told him his duties. 'Once a week, you will deck this altar with offerings. During the processions and festivals of Anubis, you will light a lamp. In exchange for your work, you will receive barley and lamp-wicks. Moreover, you will be the Servant of the *Ka* of this temple, its spiritual power. So, during ceremonies, you will speak the words bringing this nourishing force to life. You are welcome among us, Iker. Come, share our banquet.'

The new temporary priest was embraced by his colleagues.

The night was sweet, the food delicious. During the sharing-out of the ritual flat-cake revealing the face of the god, Iker felt closer to the sacred than he had ever been, even if the greatest secrets were still inaccessible.

He, a little apprentice scribe from the small town of Madu, raised to the rank of temporary priest in the Temple of Anubis, at Kahun . . . How could he have imagined such a destiny? He thought of the young priestess, of that sublime woman he loved. Would she have been proud of him tonight?

No, of course not. She probably spent her time with such senior priests that she would not even set eyes on Iker. But all the same, he had entered the sacred hierarchy and had received the protection of Anubis.

'Iker, here is your new amulet,' said Heremsaf, handing him a small 'Power' sceptre made of cornelian. 'Put it round your neck and never take it off.'

In their turn, the servants of Anubis welcomed their new colleague.

*See S. Aufrère, *L'Univers mineral dans la pensée égyptienne*, Cairo, 1991, book I, p. 109.

As he listened to their peaceful words and their urging to discover, little by little, the teachings of the god, the young man asked himself if he was on the wrong path. Ought he to forget his insane plans and be content to live here in Kahun, fulfilling his new duties and studying its books of wisdom? The magic of this ritual, the serenity of these men, the beauty of this place . . . How radiant that future seemed.

But he had already gone too far. Hidden in his bedchamber was the dagger with which he would kill Senusret, and it would not disappear. Bina, too, was very real and reminded him of his true mission. To neglect it, to forget the unfortunates oppressed by a tyrant, would be unbearable cowardice.

'Do you believe yourself truly able to take on your new offices?' asked Heremsaf.

'If that were not so, would you have called me?'

'Life is a succession of new experiences.'

'Is that what you reduce me to, a simple experience?'

'That is for you to tell me.'

Iker was floating in uncertain space. Added to the heat of these ethereal moments, the wine he had drunk at the banquet was mixing up his thoughts. Was Heremsaf a protector who was opening up the way to the mysteries for him, or an enemy who had sworn to destroy him?

However, this was a time not for questions or answers but for brotherly communion with the servants of Anubis. Deep into the night, Iker savoured it like fine wine.

11

When Sobek-Khu flew into a rage, it was wise to keep one's mouth shut and one's ears open, listen to one's orders, and obey them promptly. So the investigation into the death of Controller Rudi was conducted with the proper thoroughness.

There was no doubt about the identity of the murderers: they were Canaanites from Sichem. The rebel town was closely watched, but the precautions had clearly been inadequate because the terrorists had infiltrated Memphis and committed murder there. These deaths must be linked to the discovery of the corpses of two bearded Canaanites in a hovel behind the port – obviously another of the group's bases. But why the murders? Had they killed each other, or had their leader killed them before making his escape? Although partially destroyed, would the network re-form elsewhere? In any case, it was vital to destroy it at its source, and therefore to conduct a thorough search of Sichem and improve the vigilance of the Egyptian soldiers in Canaan.

Such was the substance of Sobek's report. He gave it to Senusret, who on his return to Memphis convened a meeting of the King's House. It included a new member, Tjaty Khnum-Hotep, who had moved into a huge office next to the palace. A good understanding had immediately sprung up between him and his two principal colleagues, High Treasurer Senankh and Royal Seal-Bearer Sehotep. Khnum-Hotep was already becoming known as a rigorous tjaty, devoted to the service of Egypt. With the help of two assistants, he was recruiting elite scribes and building an efficient government. No one envied him his position, for every day he had to deal with a multitude of problems.

'I have sent General Sepi in search of the healing gold,' Senusret told the meeting. 'With a small band of miners and an escort of desert guards, he will explore the sites where we hope to discover it. I hope that our country's re-established unity will slow the Tree of Life's decline, but it will not be enough to save it. And we still do not know the identity of the criminal who has put the curse on the acacia and is trying to prevent the resurrection of Osiris – identifying him remains a priority.

'But we are facing another possible danger. Sobek thinks the Canaanites' assassination of Controller Rudi may mean that a new rebellion is brewing. We must therefore take vigorous action in Canaan and Syria. Until recently that would have been impossible, but we now have the means to do so by creating an army which includes the troops from the provinces that have returned to the Egyptian fold. I am entrusting the command of this national army to General Nesmontu, who will begin work immediately on its organization. This force is not to be the expression of blind brutality. It is to be a means of fighting disorder and rebellion.'

The only person who made light of the glory conferred on him by his appointment was Nesmontu himself. Indifferent to honours and decorations, the old general busied himself with creating his general staff from men on the ground, disciplined and courageous, some of whom came from the former provincial armies. Each regiment was to include forty archers and forty spearmen, under the command of an officer assisted by a standard-bearer, a quartermaster scribe and a scribe in charge of geographical maps. Bows, throwing-spears, clubs, staves, axes, daggers, shields and leather armbands, produced in large quantities by the Memphis workshops, formed the basis of the troops' equipment. And Nesmontu himself inspected all the warships, checking the captains' service records.

The general was working at such a pace that it would not be long before the Egyptian army was fully operational and could make the Canaanites understand that any attempt at rebellion was doomed to failure.

As soon as the royal decree relating to the creation of this new military force had been issued, Medes, secretary of the King's House, had ordered the royal messenger service to deliver a copy of it to every town in the kingdom. As usual, the work would be done quickly and efficently and Senusret would have no cause to reprimand him.

Medes was in the prime of life, and fully indulged his love of good food and wine. He had black hair that lay flat against his round head, a moon-shaped face, broad chest, short legs and pudgy feet. He owned a superb house in Memphis, and was married to a plump, wilful, unintelligent woman who spent all her time painting and repainting her face. He was the very model of a senior dignitary for whom everything was going right, and was becoming one of the most visible people at court.

However, Medes was still dissatisfied and resentful. Fascinated by power and wealth, he did not think his true worth was being recognized and rewarded. So he wanted to seize the gold of Punt, a legendary land which he believed to be real. He had arranged the kidnapping of a young scribe as a propitiatory offering to the perilous sea, but despite this precaution *Swift One*, the ship he had hired, sank during a storm. And his new post, though it gave him access to important information, meant that, for the time being at least, he could not acquire another ship without attracting attention.

Since Senusret had, to everyone's surprise, succeeded in reunifying Egypt, Medes had not been sleeping well. A few months earlier, he had hoped to destabilize the king, even kill him. He had not given up that hope, but he must now be extremely careful.

Medes's main goal was to penetrate the Mysteries of the closed temple at Abydos, but here, too, he had had no success. Despite his skilful bribery and constant flattery, no High Priest had authorized him to enter the most sacred part of any temple. It was from there, particularly from the temple at Abydos, that the pharaoh derived his power. And it was from there that, sooner or later, Medes would draw his.

For the time being, all doors seemed closed. Moreover, Nesmontu's appointment to lead the new national army was another blow. The old soldier was uninterested in wealth or honours, and Medes, despite investigating him thoroughly, had found no means of bribing him.

Medes was roused from his gloomy thoughts by the entrance of his steward, who bowed and said, 'My lord, Gergu, principal inspector of granaries, requests an audience.'

'Take him to the garden pavilion and bring us some white wine.'

Using and controlling Gergu was not difficult, so long as his morale was raised after his periodic fits of depression. He was a drunken, woman-hating hedonist, a perfect egotist, who cared for nothing but his own pleasure. However, he had so far served Medes well.

When Medes reached the pavilion, Gergu had already emptied his first cup of wine and was smiling broadly.

'I have renewed, and even strengthened, contact with the permanent priest at Abydos,' he said proudly.

'Are you really certain this is not a trap?'

'Through him I was given the rank of temporary priest, which meant I could enter the sacred domain of Osiris, where votive shrines, stelae and statues are erected – an impressive place. But the most important thing is that he told me his plans, at least in part. He intends to sell some of these sacred objects, which we are to arrange to have brought out of Abydos.'

Medes was dumbfounded. He even wondered if Gergu was taking him for a fool, but a detailed explanation reassured him on that point.

'How embittered the priest must be,' he said.

'He doesn't radiate contentment, it is true, but what a godsend! You've dreamt of gaining an ally in Abydos, haven't you?'

'A mere dream—'

'It's coming true, and we're only a hair's breadth away from success,' said Gergu, 'but the priest has come up with a difficult demand. He wants to know who my employer is, and to meet him.'

'Impossible!'

'You must understand that he's as wary of traps as you are, and he wants guarantees. If his demands aren't met, he'll withdraw his cooperation.'

'Given my position, I cannot possibly run such a risk.'

'Given his, neither can he.'

Medes was shaken. He could either content himself with his high post and forget his ambitions, or else attempt a venture in which he might lose everything.

He said, 'I need some time to think.'

At dawn, the young priestess went as she did each morning to the sacred lake of Abydos, the resurgence of the *Nun*, the ocean of energy where life had been born. After purifying herself, she took a vase and drew water for the Acacia of Osiris.

Feeling eyes on her bare shoulders, she turned round. Bega was staring at her.

'What do you want?' she asked.

'Pure water. Would you fill these vases for me?'

'Aren't the temporary priests supposed to do that?'

'If you will do it, I am sure the libations will be more effective than usual.'

She shook her head. 'I am not so important.'

'You belong to the college of priestesses of Hathor, and the Queen of Egypt herself respects you. And a great destiny lies before you, doesn't it?'

'All I want is to serve Osiris.'

'Aren't you too young to choose such an arid future?'

'I don't see it as arid, rather as a light that makes fertile everything it touches.'

A look of distress appeared on Bega's face. 'That is a beautiful thought, but what future is there for Abydos? If the Tree of Life dies, the site will be abandoned and we shall all be scattered.'

'There is still hope,' said the priestess. 'After all, one of the branches has grown green again.'

'A very slender hope, I fear. Nevertheless, you are right: we shall fight to the end, each in our allotted place.'

'The temporary priests will fill your vases,' she said with a smile, as she turned to leave.

She went to the sacred acacia and found the Shaven-headed One already there. Before they poured water and milk at the foot of the tree, he told her some news he had just received.

'A royal messenger brought me a copy of Pharaoh's latest decree: the provincial governors have all rallied to the crown, Egypt is reunified, and the Two Lands are firmly bound together.'

A very gentle wind began to blow. The branches of the acacia tree trembled and, watched with great emotion by the Shaven-headed One and the priestess, another apparently dead branch became tinged with green.

'His Majesty has taken the right path,' said the Shaven-headed One. 'I shall inform him immediately. Perhaps the whole tree will come back to life?'

But, alas, in the days that followed there were no further signs of rebirth. The curse had only been damaged, not broken.

'Come with me to the House of Life,' the Shaven-headed One ordered the young priestess. 'If you succeed in passing through its door, you must search through the ancient texts, looking for indications of ways to heal the acacia.'

Next to each high temple in Egypt stood a House of Life, which contained the *Bau Ra*, the 'Souls of the Divine Light' – in other words the sacred archives. Because of their exceptional quality and number, Abydos's *Bau Ra* were extremely precious, and the building was protected by high walls. Only the pharaoh could grant permission to enter, so the young woman deduced that the Shaven-headed One was acting on Senusret's orders.

He handed her a honey-cake and said, 'On this I have written the hieroglyphs for "enemies", "rebels" and "resisters", all people of *isefet*, the negative and destructive force opposed to Ma'at. Make good use of it.'

He pushed open a small door in the wall, revealing a narrow corridor. Immediately a magnificent she-panther appeared, the Lady of the House of Life, its back decorated with four pieces of cloth. The panther's dark eyes observed the intruder for a long time, then it advanced towards her, its body rippling sinuously.

The young woman stood very still.

After sniffing her, the great cat placed its left forepaw on her thigh; although its claws were unsheathed, they did not tear the flesh. The priestess presented the cake to the incarnation of the goddess Mafdet, guardian of the sacred archives. The panther devoured the confederates of *isefet*, then lay down beside the door and went to sleep.

The way was open.

The world in which the young priestess found herself left her speechless for a long time. On the shelves of the vast library lay papyri and tablets dealing with all aspects of the knowledge of the ancients: the great book containing the secrets of the heavens, the earth and the stars' matrix, the book for understanding the speech of birds, fish and animals, the book for interpreting dreams. Then there was the book of the gods' secret forms, the book for pacifying Sekhmet, the terrifying lion-goddess, the book of transformations into light, the book of the Nile, prophecies, the words of wisdom, treatises on alchemy, magic, medicine, the stars and mathematics. Beside them lay the dictionaries of hieroglyphs, the calendar of secret and public festivals, the ritualists' manuals, the book for preserving the divine ship, the manuals of building, sculpture and painting, the inventory of ritual items, the list of the pharaohs and their annals – just reading the titles made her head spin.

But she had vital work to do, and must not let herself be distracted. Guided by both knowledge and intuition, she selected texts dealing in detail with the creative energy, the *ka*, and with the means of safeguarding it.

The Shaven-headed One himself brought meals to the young woman, who was given permission to sleep in a small room near the library. Hardly stopping to eat or rest, she pursued her quest day and night, gathering clues and following each path without ever being discouraged.

At last, she thought she had found something. After checking her ideas with the aid of a manuscript containing the words of resurrection from the Pyramid Texts, she told the Shaven-headed One of her discovery.

He listened closely, and when she had finished said, 'Your idea seems feasible to me, and your arguments are convincing. Tomorrow morning, you shall take the boat for Memphis, and explain it all to His Majesty.'

12

Heavily perfumed and dressed in a long, richly coloured robe which hid his portly body, the Phoenician merchant looked just what he was: a wealthy, voluble trader, interested in any business deal which would bring him a handsome profit while letting his partner think he had the upper hand over the merchant. He had reason to be well satisfied with his lot. Since his move to Memphis, his trade – illegal as well legal – had flourished, and he was now the owner of a large and beautiful house that was discreet but worthy of a leading citizen.

However, he had two reasons for anxiety. The first concerned the delivery of an important stock of precious wood from Phoenicia, under the noses of the Egyptian trade-control officials. The second was that he had terrible tooth-ache, which must be treated immediately – at this critical moment, he needed to keep a clear head. Sitting in his bed-chamber, he peered again into his mirror, trying to see the afflicted teeth.

'Master,' announced his steward, 'the tooth-doctor has arrived.'

By using his trade and social connections, the Phoenician had persuaded one of the best in the city to come at once. But he was disconcerted when the doctor entered: small and thin, the man inspired him with little confidence.

The doctor put down his bag. 'Where does it hurt, sir?'

'Almost everywhere – especially at the top on the left. But also at the bottom on the right. Will the treatment hurt?'

'If you are afraid of pain, I can give you something to make you sleep.'

'But supposing I don't wake up again?'

'That very rarely happens. Please sit down.'

The tooth-doctor settled his patient in an armchair placed in full sunlight. With the aid of a mirror, he inspected the inside of the mouth and took stock of the damage.

'There is no decay yet, but if you continue to overindulge in sweet foods there soon will be. Your teeth are not being cleaned properly, and your gums are inflamed. A few more years of this, and your teeth will fall out. Fortunately for you, I am highly skilled at making false teeth of ivory and at filling tooth-holes with gold. And I wield the tooth-drill as skilfully as the cauterizing-knife.'

'There's no hurry,' said the Phoenician hastily. 'Can't all that be prevented?'

'Yes. You must rub your teeth and gums at least twice a day with a paste containing sea salt. You must also rinse your mouth with a potion of anise, colocynth and cut persea fruit. It's tiresome but effective.'

The Phoenician sighed in relief. 'How much do I owe you?'

'Two jars of wine, a piece of linen and a pair of gilded sandals.'

Although this tooth-doctor was the most expensive in the capital, the patient was reassured by the diagnosis. He ordered a servant to bring the requested fee, then to go and fetch the remedies from the nearest medical workshop.

But there was still the matter of the wood delivery. His first venture in this field had been a great success, thanks to his accomplice, Medes. Without Medes, it would have been impossible to evade the trade-control checks and bring in the illegal cargo. After some argument, the two men had agreed to share the profits equally. The Phoenician acquired the raw materials, Medes dealt with the administrative obstacles and provided a list of wealthy customers, and the Phoenician then took charge of the commercial transactions so that the Egyptian did not have to show himself.

This time, the heavy cargo-boat was transporting cedar-wood, ebony and various kinds of pine. There was enough to make many pieces of furniture and to satisfy a growing list of customers, who were delighted not to have to pay any tax. It was a splendid arrangement – so long as Medes played the game. He had set his best agent to find out all he could about Medes.

His steward entered again and said, 'Master, a water-carrier is asking for you.'

At last, the man he had been waiting for! The Phoenician hurried down to the ground floor.

Being a water-carrier, the spy could go anywhere and gossip with anyone without attracting attention. He had already followed Medes and identified him as the secretary of the King's House, one of the most important men in the country. But the Phoenician wanted more details.

'What have you found out?' he asked.

'Medes does not go unnoticed: my contacts at the palace had plenty to say. His job is to draw up the decrees formulated by the king, then pass them on to the provinces. Everyone says he is very competent, and no one had any criticisms of him. They said he's a meticulous, authoritarian man who won't tolerate any mistakes by his staff. Dismissals are not uncommon, and he recruits only hard-working scribes. He's rich, happily married, and has a fine house – he's the picture of perfect happiness.

'But according to one man I spoke to, a temporary priest at the High Temple of Ptah, one of Medes's ambitions remains unsatisfied: despite several attempts, he has failed to get access to the Mysteries of Osiris. However, this is a minor point, for his career is going so well that he has much more interesting prospects ahead of him. Sooner or later, he should enter the King's House.'

'Did you hear any talk of theft or corruption?'

'None at all. Medes seems to be honesty personified, and he's earned himself a reputation as a responsible, honest and generous official.'

'What about his friendships?'

'He has a network of officials and leading citizens who owe him a great deal and whom he manipulates as he wishes.'

'And is there any news of my cargo-boat?'

'She has arrived at the port of Memphis. The officials there are processing her normally.'

'Go back there. If anything happens, tell me as soon as possible.'

When the water-carrier had gone, the Phoenician stood still and thought hard. The moment of truth was approaching. Either Medes was playing fair and would soon pay the Phoenician a visit, or else he was laying a trap for him, in order to dismantle his smuggling operations, and would send the city guards instead.

Medes did not, of course, know that the Phoenician was an agent of the Herald and charged with recruiting a senior member of the government who could provide as much information as possible about the court, about the king's inner circle, and about the habits of Senusret himself, the enemy who was to be struck down. Although he was beginning to do business with the secretary of the King's House, the Phoenician felt uneasy. Was he trying to catch too large a fish? But then, if Medes did indeed prove to be an ambitious crook, what more could he hope for?

Thinking made him hungry, so he called for food. The

steward brought him a stuffed quail, which his cook had roasted to perfection, and the Phoenician attacked it with gusto.

Medes was very conceited about his two-storey house in the heart of Memphis. It was indeed most agreeable: the courtyard was encircled by high walls, the pool was surrounded by sycamores, and the garden pavilion had green-painted pillars.

While he waited for Gergu to report on the cargo-boat's progress, he decided to have a word with his wife. He found her engaged in her favourite pastime of painting her face in the latest fashion.

She smiled at him and asked, 'Whom are we dining with this evening, my darling?'

'With the officials in charge of the canals.'

'Oh, they're terribly boring people, aren't they?'

'Yes, but be charming and friendly – they might be useful to me.'

'Well, I'll need some pomade for my hair. And I'll also need a pot of special salve. It's made of fenugreek pods and seeds, honey and powdered alabaster, and it gets rid of the signs of ageing as soon as they appear. If I don't get it today, I shan't dare show myself. The problem is the quality of the alabaster – the kind my usual merchant uses simply isn't good enough.'

'Send one of our servants to the royal sculpture workshop. The overseer will give him fragments of the best alabaster, and you can have it crushed into powder.'

She flung her arms round his neck. 'You really are a perfect husband! I shall do it at once.'

Soon afterwards, Gergu arrived. 'Everything's going well at the port,' he told Medes. 'The trade-controllers working for us have turned a blind eye, the falsified documents have been handed over to the government, and the dock-labourers are unloading the cargo into a storehouse I control. The Phoenician wasn't lying: the wood really is worth a fortune.'

Medes smiled. 'You'll have your share. Now, as regards the priest at Abydos, I have reached a decision: I agree to meet him. Despite the risks, the opportunity seems too good to miss. As soon as possible, you are to go back there and arrange the meeting.'

The full moon was shining in the Memphis sky. Medes pulled up his hood and walked faster. Once he was certain that he had not been followed, he made his way to the Phoenician trader's house, which was tucked away in the narrow streets behind the port, and knocked at the door. He handed the doorkeeper a small piece of cedarwood, on which was engraved the hieroglyph of the tree.

The doorkeeper opened the door, allowed the visitor in and then closed the door immediately. A servant led Medes to the reception room, which was cluttered with expensive furniture. On rectangular tables lay bowls of fruit and cakes. Several perfume-burners gave off sweet smells.

'My dear friend, my very dear friend,' exclaimed the Phoenician, 'what a great pleasure to see you again! Please, do take a seat. Try that armchair, there – best-quality cedarwood and deliciously soft cushions. May I offer you some of this excellent wine?'

'By all means,' replied Medes, visibly on his guard.

'I've just bought some very pretty stone tableware,' said the trader. 'There's blue schist, red brecchia, white alabaster, pink granite – a positive rainbow of colours! It seems that good wines have an even better flavour if they rest for a while in a large granite jar. And look at these marvellous rock-crystal goblets.'

The Phoenician prepared to pour the wine.

'Dear friend,' he went on, 'I must say that I'm extremely

pleased. This fine wine is a rare product, which has been awarded the title of "Thrice good". It's smooth, mellow and very potent, and it keeps for years. The ripe grapes must be gathered on a fine day, neither too hot nor too windy. After treading, the juice is poured into a cauldron used only for that wine. It is boiled over a gentle heat and sieved to remove the impurities until a clear liquid is produced, and that liquid is filtered with great care. One of the keys to the wine's success lies in the second heating, which is very delicate. Next—'

'I didn't come here to learn how to make wine,' cut in Medes. 'I came to talk about our new business venture. Your cargo has arrived safely, and I shall soon have a new list of customers for you. As agreed, your crew will sell the goods and deliver them as quickly as possible. Half of the profits will be paid to me at the earliest opportunity. For our third operation, I shall use a different storehouse.'

'A wise precaution,' said the Phoenician with sudden coldness. 'The secretary of the King's House should always use extreme caution when carrying out transactions which are as secret as they are illegal.'

Medes leapt to his feet. 'What does this mean? Have you dared spy on me?'

'One does not deal in such important business matters without finding out about one's partner – you know all about me, don't you? If I behaved like a foolish innocent, would you take me seriously? Sit down, and let us celebrate our success by drinking this exceptional wine.'

Obliged to admit that the Phoenician was right, Medes held out his rock-crystal goblet.

'Our trade in wood will bring us huge profits,' his host promised him, 'but I have other objectives. Alone, I cannot achieve them. With you, the results will be fabulous.'

'What are those objectives?'

The Phoenician almost salivated. 'First, importing some

beautifully painted Cypriot pregnancy flasks, each shaped like a pregnant woman. These talismans are much sought after in high circles here. I can obtain exclusive trading-rights, and therefore charge high prices.'

'Agreed.'

'Next, I am planning to get my hands on the entire Syrian opium harvest. I still have to dispose of two or three competitors, but that is now just a question of weeks. Because of its strong ambergris-like smell, Egyptian perfume-makers like laudanum. But I do not have the sort of distribution network that would enable me to become their sole dealer.'

'That will not be a problem,' Medes assured him.

'I have kept the best and most difficult to the last: oils. Egypt consumes an incredible quantity of them, but I am only interested in two: sesame oil, mainly imported from Syria, and in particular moringa oil, which is colourless, mild and does not go rancid. It is a true luxury product, used by remedy-makers and perfume-makers, and constantly in demand. Now, I have a network in Phoenicia which can provide us with large quantities. But is it possible to gain control of enough sellers and storehouses here?'

'Yes, it is,' said Medes, who was warming to his associate's plans.

'And will it take long?'

'We must allow a few months, so we can be sure no mistakes are made. The chain of corruption must be strong, and each person must know his place in it.'

'Won't you be too exposed?'

'I have a trusted man who can put in place an effective, secure system.'

'Please forgive the question, but why does someone as highly placed as you take such risks?'

'Because I have trade in my blood and I like wealth. My post at the palace may be an exalted one, but it's poorly paid. I am worth more – a great deal more. With your help, I shall make up part of the deficit. Of course, my very dear friend and colleague, we are now bound together for life. And I am counting on your absolute silence.'

'That goes without saying.'

'Above all,' said Medes, 'do not even consider doing business, however trivial, with anyone but me. From now on, I am your only business partner.'

'That was my understanding of the situation.'

'Since we're telling each other everything, I confess I've been wondering about the extent of your networks and your surprising capacity for innovation. I don't wish to annoy you, but I can't help wondering whether you're acting on behalf of someone else?'

The Phoenician took a sip of wine. 'Do you mean you think I have an overall master who dictates his orders to me?'

'Exactly.'

'That's a delicate question, very delicate.'

'The matters we're dealing are very delicate, too. I still fear that I know less about you than you know about me. So, my dear partner, I want the truth. The whole truth.'

'I understand, I understand . . . But you put me in a difficult position.'

'Don't try to play games with me. No one makes a fool of Medes.'

The Phoenician looked down at his feet. 'Yes, I do indeed report to someone else.'

'Who is he, and where is he based?'

'I have sworn to tell no one.'

'I appreciate your scruples, but I am not content with that.'

'There is only one solution,' decided the Phoenician. 'I shall suggest to him that he meets you.'

'An excellent idea.'

'Don't get too excited. I don't know if he'll agree.'

'Advise him strongly to do so. Understood?'

'Understood.'

Medes was now exactly where the Phoenician wanted him to be, and still believed that he was in command of the situation.

13

The voyage from Abydos to Memphis took less than a week.*
The captain was a skilful sailor, so the young priestess was
able to relax and gaze out at the banks of the Nile.

At Memphis, the quayside was all bustle, contrasting
sharply with the calm of Abydos.

The captain contacted the guards and presented his log to
an officer. The officer ordered two of his men to take the
priestess to the tjaty's office. She would have liked to spend
a few hours in the Temple of Hathor and celebrate the rites
there, but her mission was urgent.

Memphis seemed immense and colourful with its granaries,
storehouses, shops, markets, large houses standing alongside
modest ones, and its imposing official buildings. Among the
most important of these were the temples of Ptah, Sekhmet the
Powerful, and Hathor, Lady of the Southern Sycamore. Close
to the old white-walled citadel and the sanctuary of Neith,
whose seven words had created the universe, the administrative district was a hive of activity. Harassed scribes ran
from one department to another, for here, far from the centre
of the cult of Osiris, the major decisions concerning the
country's government were taken.

Tjaty Khnum-Hotep had his offices in a new wing, added

*The distance is about 485 km.

to the royal palace. After passing through two guard-points and answering detailed questions, the priestess was invited to wait in a delightfully cool antechamber.

A few minutes later, a scribe came to fetch her and showed her into a huge office whose three windows looked out on to a garden. The tamarisks there rivalled the sycamores in beauty.

Two plump little bitches and a lively dog surrounded the new arrival, though without barking. She stroked each of them in turn until the imposing tjaty arrived.

'I apologize if they are being a nuisance,' he said.

'On the contrary, my lord, they are very welcoming.'

'I am Pharaoh Senusret's tjaty. Please show me the orders for your mission.'

She handed him a wooden tablet. It was marked with the Shaven-headed One's seal, and on it was written his request that the bearer be granted a royal audience.

'What have you to say to the king?'

'I am sorry, but I am authorized to tell only him – no one else.'

'You're resolute, arn't you? However, you should know that I am His Majesty's first minister and he entrusts me with sorting out as many problems as possible.'

'I understand your position, my lord. Please understand mine.'

'I have the impression that I shall not make you change your mind. Very well, my secretary will take you to the palace.'

The priestess allowed herself to be led out. As soon as she had passed through the entrance, she was taken to the official in charge of security, who alerted his superior, Sobek.

The Protector reacted in his usual robust way. 'No one enters the audience chamber without telling me exactly what their business is.'

'I have come from Abydos,' she replied. 'My superior has ordered me to give an important message to Pharaoh.'

'What is it about?'

'Only Pharaoh may know that.'

'Unless I know, too, you won't see him.'

'What I have to tell him concerns the future of our country, so I beg you not to stop me.'

'You're asking me to break every single one of my rules and regulations.'

'I'm sorry if I'm obliging you to make an exception.'

'One of my guards must search you.'

The priestess submitted to the ordeal without turning a hair. Then she was taken to an antechamber watched over by two armed guards, and waited again.

As Medes emerged from an office and crossed the antechamber, which was reserved for people awaiting a royal audience, he saw the young woman. He was curious: she did not belong to the Memphis court and he had never seen her at the palace. Where had this unknown woman come from, with her radiant beauty, and why had the pharaoh agreed to receive her? He promised himself that he would find out about her.

'Majesty,' said Sobek soberly, 'the priestess is unyielding. She refused to reveal the contents of her message, either to the tjaty or to myself. Not even a humiliating search could shake her determination. You may consider her wholly reliable, and of unfailing loyalty.'

'Send her in and leave us alone.'

She bowed low before the monarch, whose bearing impressed her, as always.

'Majesty, shortly after we received your decree reunifying the Two Lands, a second branch of the Tree of Life grew green again. Moreover, I was fortunate enough to make a discovery in the library of the House of Life: to combat the acacia's degeneration, the pharaoh must emit *ka*. Bringing all the provinces back into the oneness of your being is not enough, for the oneness of Osiris must also be strengthened.

The ancient texts state clearly that "Osiris is the work of Pharaoh, Osiris is the pyramid."* Although the time of the construction of the great pyramids is past, is it not still vital that Osiris be incarnated in that form?'

Senusret was silent for a long time, his thoughts travelling into far-off space in search of an answer. 'An excellent suggestion,' he said eventually. 'But we have still to find the site where my pyramid will be built.'

Accompanied by the young priestess and his personal bodyguard, the pharaoh travelled through the burial-grounds of Abusir, Saqqara, Giza and Lisht, but no sign manifested itself. At Dahshur, south of Saqqara and on the fringes of the Western desert,† stood the two giant pyramids of Pharaoh Sneferu, who had been Khufu's predecessor, and the small pyramid of Amenemhat II, who had died seventeen years before Senusret ascended the throne.

From this site led a stelae-lined track, which wound to the north of Faiyum and emerged at Qasr el-Sagha, where an unusual temple protected an area of quarrying. Another track led to the oases, which were famous for their wine.

The town of the builders, Djed-Sneferu, 'Sneferu is Ever-living', still housed priests charged with feeding the *ka* of the illustrious pharaoh, who was considered the greatest builder of ancient times. They decked the offering-tables and celebrated the cult in the tall temples built before the eastern face of the two pyramids, one smooth-sided, the other stepped.

The sun would be setting soon; they must think about returning to Memphis.

When the shadows of the two huge pyramids stretched out far across the desert, Senusret halted. 'Sneferu's soul is at peace,' he declared. 'It watches over this place, and continues

---

*Pyramid Texts, 1657a-b.
†About 40 km south of Cairo.

to render it sacred. Through its name, "That Which Accomplishes the Divine", it summons us to create. Here, in the shadow of this great king, I shall build my own pyramid.'

Ever since he had settled in Memphis, Djehuty, the former governor of the Hare province, had been unwell. Fortunately, his doctor, Gua, had followed him to the capital, and was getting a good reputation there. Gua was a short, very thin man, who never went anywhere without his heavy leather bag of operating-knives and emergency remedies.

'If you go on like this,' he told his patient, 'I shall refuse to treat you. I've warned you before: you eat too much, you drink too much, and you don't take enough exercise.'

'It's only an attack of aches in the joints,' protested Dhehuty.

'I wish it were only that – a little concentrated extract of willow bark would relieve your pain. But there is worse: your heart is tired. Each evening, before going to bed, you must take five pills containing grapes, valerian, honey and pyrethra. The channels through which your vital fluids flow have become rigid and congested, so I'll try to unblock them and make them flexible again; they all pass through the heart. In other words, it's essential that you rest, otherwise, I can no longer answer for anything.'

Djehuty's steward interrupted the consultation. 'Forgive me, but—'

'Who do you think you are?' demanded Doctor Gua indignantly.

'Pharaoh Senusret is here, and he wishes to see Lord Djehuty immediately.'

The doctor closed his bag. Seeing the king enter his patient's bedchamber, he wondered if he would one day have to treat a giant of a man like that. He said, 'I have only one wish to express, Majesty: do not give my patient with any more work, but send him into retirement immediately.'

Still grumbling, the doctor left.

Djehuty put on a white wig. 'Old age is getting nearer,' he admitted, 'but I am still keeping it at a distance. That dear doctor has been promising me imminent death for many years, but his treatments keep me alive.'

'Have you had any news from General Sepi?' asked the king.

'His expedition is likely to be long and difficult, because such maps as exist are vague. And he must assemble the most expert miners and people who know the deserts well.'

'Despite what your doctor said, would you accept a new office, to which I attach considerable importance?'

Djehuty grew solemn. 'Majesty, I am your servant. I wish to work to my last breath for the greatness of Egypt.'

'Djehuty, I appoint you mayor of the pyramid town I am going to build at Dahshur. High Treasurer Senankh will take care of financing the construction.'

In the benevolent shadow of Sneferu's monuments, Senusret mentally viewed the plans for his own, whose principal elements he dictated to Djehuty.

'When a pharaoh founds a temple,' said Seal-Bearer Sehotep, 'he recreates Egypt. By building, he prolongs the creation of the first morning. May these living stones become one of the foundation stones of your reign.'

On a rough stone, turned golden by the last rays of the sun, the young priestess poured water drawn from the sacred lake of the Temple of Ptah.

'The name of this domain shall be Kebehut, "Cool Celestial Water",' announced the king. 'We shall surround it with a fortified curtain-wall on the model of Djoser's pyramid at Saqqara. Because the pyramid must give off *ka* as soon as possible, we shall dig down to the rock and place upon it a core of raw bricks, which will then be covered with limestone from Tura. Within this core – which shall be called

Hotep, "Sunset", "Peace, "Amplitude" – will be traced the soul's journey to the "provider of life", the sarcophagus, place of regeneration for the body of light.'

As the monarch explained his vision, Djehuty drew it on papyrus.

'To the north of the pyramid,' added the king, 'is Khnum-Hotep's house of eternity. The other, more modest tombs of court members will be inspired by those of the golden age. Inside will feature texts written during that period.'*

At Abydos, the young priestess had realized why the building of houses of eternity was necessary. Only this symbolic architecture, magically brought to life, could transform initiates into *akh*, the radiant being able to enter into contact with all the energies flowing around the universe. Beyond physical death, the reborn individual remained active on earth and transmitted the light in which he lived a new life. Around the pharaoh's pyramid, his faithful servants would form a supernatural entourage, charged both with protecting him and with spreading his blessings.

'The builders' houses will be ready very soon,' said Djehuty. 'First thing tomorrow, they will begin to prepare the ground. I am relying on Senankh for the transport of materials and equipment.'

As he wrote the decree relating to the building being done at Dahshur, Medes was struck by the huge size of the project, and by the extensive means being deployed so that it would be completed as quickly as possible. Senusret was complementing his government of the country with spiritual creation, increasing his prestige still further. Was it really possible to strike down an adversary of such stature?

Postponing that question until later, Medes tried to find out about the young woman who had requested an audience. By

*The Old Kingdom, 2686–2181 BC.

gathering snippets of information, he eventually learnt that she was a priestess from Abydos, and had brought the king a confidential message. Clearly she was a minor figure, of no importance. But why had the priests sent her to Memphis? Perhaps Gergu would find out at his next meeting with the permanent priest.

14

Fishing in the weeks before the annual flood was a tall order: the Nile was at its lowest, the heat was overwhelming, and the fish were wary. However Sekari, as Iker's good servant, wanted fresh food, full of *ka*, so he did his best in the hope of bringing back a few good catches. Alas, fishing with a line ended in utter failure. With a landing-net, which took quickness of hand and eye, he felt sure he'd succeed. But the fish had no sooner entered the net than they swam out again. The only thing left to try was a trap-net hidden in the reeds. Mullet and silurids ought to have swum into it and then found they could not get out again, but . . . How was it that they always spotted the trap-net?

'Not a very impressive catch,' he admitted to North Wind, who was carrying the pathetically empty baskets. 'With such cunning little creatures, you need patience.'

The donkey blinked his big brown eyes, and cocked his right ear as a sign of agreement. Because of the tuft of reddish hair on the back of his neck, the sign of the strength of Set, as a young foal he had been abandoned and condemned to certain death. Purified by the ibis of Thoth and saved by Iker, the foal had grown into a huge animal, and he would be faithful for ever to his rescuer.

'To be honest,' Sekari went on, 'your master worries me. He's lost all his good humour and his zest for life, and he wallows in black thoughts that lead nowhere. Have you tried to talk to him?'

North Wind cocked his right ear again.

'And did you get anywhere?'

The donkey raised his left ear.

'That's what I was afraid of. Even you no longer have any influence over him. He picks at his food, he can't tell the difference between good and bad wine any more, he goes to bed too late and gets up too early, he doesn't laugh at my best jokes like he used to, and and he gets carried away with his absurd plans. But I refuse to give up hope. He's a good fellow at heart, and we'll get him out of this rut eventually. In the meantime, we'd better stop off at the fish-stall and buy something to eat.'

The mayor of Kahun rarely emerged from his huge house. It was always bustling with activity: day and night scribes, brewers, cooks, bakers, potters, carpenters and other skilled people busied themselves bringing this hive to life. They were paid well, and were given increases according to merit.

Although confined to his office, where he had to get to grips with complex files, the mayor was kept informed of everything that happened in his town. Nobody was promoted without his agreement, and no administrative errors escaped him. Those who appeared before him did not know if they would be blamed or praised. In the latter case, it was advisable to keep a cool head, for compliments were inevitably accompanied by extra work, usually more difficult than before. Iker was therefore unsure what the mayor's summons would bring.

'You have covered a lot of ground, my boy,' said the mayor. 'Becoming a temporary priest at the Temple of Anubis at your age: that's quite an achievement. As for your management of the library, everyone agrees that it's a real miracle. Even your more experienced colleagues, despite their jealousy, recognize your qualities and don't know how to harm your reputation. Your only fault is that you're too austere. Why don't you ever rest? Or why don't you marry some pretty girl who'd be happy to give you fine children?'

'I came here to become a scribe of the highest rank.'

'And you shall, my boy, you shall. However . . . Your private life is your own concern; your public life, on the other hand, depends on me. Heremsaf never stops praising you, and I'm surrounded by too many incompetent people, so I am appointing you to my council on town affairs.'

'I am honoured by your trust in me, but I'm very happy in my present post.'

'In Kahun, my decision in such matters is final. You've shown that you're hard-working and efficient, and I intend to make the most of your abilities. Don't think for a moment that your promotion is due to the goodness of my heart, because I have none. Pharaoh has charged me with making this town prosperous and creating the best scribes' school in the kingdom, and that is what I am going to do. You may go.'

Iker did not believe a word of this speech. By promoting him, the mayor was merely hoping to trick him. Overwhelmed by his new responsibilities, flattered by professional courtiers, well housed and well fed, he was supposed to doze off in comfort and forget both his past and his ideals.

It was a clever plan, but it would not work. Instead, Iker would turn it to his own advantage. His behaviour would be exemplary: he would pretend to fall into line, and would perform his duties with the greatest zeal and competence. Neither the mayor nor Heremsaf would guess his true intentions. And they would even provide him with a weapon, which he would not hesitate to use.

A house like this was a real joy. For Sekari, looking after it was not work but pleasure. He usually whistled a popular tune as he wielded his broom, and he could not bear to see a kilt carelessly thrown on to a chair. The kitchen and washroom were always spotlessly clean, and the other rooms were models of order and comfort. He loved the strong, elegant furniture: baskets, storage chests, seats and low tables, all of which would easily last for generations. And meals certainly tasted better when eaten from plates and bowls of good quality.

Sekari was painting the front doorframe red, to drive demons away, when a voice behind him asked, 'Is your employer at home?'

It was the scribe Long-Hair, a noted repeater of malicious gossip; he was as loose-tongued as he was lazy.

'I suppose you're bringing bad news, as usual,' growled Sekari.

Long-Hair lived up to his reputation. 'It isn't good, I admit, but that isn't my fault, is it? I must speak to Iker.'

'Wash your feet before you come in, and sit down in the first room. I'll go and fetch him.'

Eager to be rid of his unwelcome guest as quickly as possible, Iker did not offer him refreshments but merely asked, 'What is it, Long-Hair?'

'The mayor's office sent me, as a matter of urgency. They've just received the prediction for the annual flood, and it's rather worrying.'

'Too weak or too strong?'

'Too strong. You'll have to organize the strengthening of the banks and retaining-walls straight away.'

'I'll see to it.'

'Will you have me in your team?'

'If there's going to be a disaster, it's probably as well to have you on my side. Go to the entrance to Faiyum and ask for a detailed report on the state of the retention pools.'

'I'll leave at once.'

Iker himself went to the building that contained the state archives he so badly wanted to examine.

The curator, a reserved and pernickety man, greeted him with deference. His attitude was very different from that when Iker had first visited the place.

'How can we help our new councillor, whose well-deserved appointment I applaud unreservedly?'

'In order to evaluate the dangers of the annual flood, I should like to consult the documents relating to water in the region.'

'Of course – all the archives are at your disposal.'

But Iker did not limit himself to the water documents. At last he had access to the register of boats built in Faiyum province, and to the names of the sailors in their crews. He began to search through them.

There was no trace of *Swift One* – as in the province of Thoth, all the records had been destroyed. Nor was there a single mention of an expedition to Punt.

But one piece of proof still existed, and it was more than sufficient: Turtle-Eye and Sharp-Knife were listed as sailors in the pharaoh's trading-fleet. So it was indeed the tyrant Senusret who had ordered Iker's death.

'Where are you hiding, Bina?' asked Iker, looking around their meeting-place.

'Behind you. I shan't show myself until I know your decision.'

'It is irrevocable.'

'Will you attack the monster?'

'I shall kill him.'

'Then I can show myself.'

When he saw her, he did not recognize her: it was like looking at a different woman. Her face was carefully painted, and her eyes were lined with kohl. A broad wig hid most of her face.

'Is it . . . Bina, is it really you?'

'I knew your answer would be yes, so I'm going to take

you to meet our friends. No one who sees us in the street must be able to identify me, so I'm in disguise. Have you got your dagger with you?'

'Yes.'

'I'll lead the way, and you must keep a good way behind me. When I enter a workshop, follow me.'

A few lamps lit the workshop, where knives and daggers were being made, some for domestic use, others for the security forces.

The craftsmen who were crouched there in the half-light regarded Iker with hostility.

'Don't worry,' said Bina. 'These men are friends. They steal a portion of what they earn, for use by the liberators. Soon our ranks will swell. Kahun is promised to us, Iker, but nothing will be possible while the tyrant wields absolute power. Show us the weapon that will dispense justice.'

Iker did so. Bina took it, handed it to the overseer, and said, 'Sharpen it well. Let its blade cut as keenly as death.'

Although preparing for the dangers of the flood took an enormous amount of work, Iker was equal to the task. With a team of scribes and specialists, and labourers hired for the occasion, he had the canal banks raised, using earth embankments. Every retaining-wall was reinforced, every retention pool strengthened. He calculated and recalculated how strong they needed to be, and the amount of earth to be moved and then heaped up to prevent them leaking or collapsing. Even if the flood was monstrously high, the towns and villages would not be drowned.

He also dealt with the transport of forage to the places where animals would be gathered together, safe from the floodwaters. And he did not forget to draw up a list of the many boats that would enable the population to move about.

Everyone marvelled at the young man's incredible

capacity for work. Although he was by no means a huge man, he seemed inexhaustible and determined to control everything by himself. Sometimes Iker felt that the mayor had given him far too great a responsibility, but he persevered. When exhaustion and discouragement threatened to overtake him, he thought of the young priestess, who was always there in the back of his mind. And then a ray of light appeared in a cloudy sky, his energy was renewed, and he was ready for the fight again.

But the outcome of that fight remained uncertain.

As the five days 'above the year' drew near, putting an end to one cycle of three hundred and sixty days and heralding the next, everyone held their breath. In the country's great temples, the priests spoke the words designed to pacify the terrifying lion-goddess Sekhmet, so that she would not send out her emissaries and bad spirits to bring misfortune and sickness to the people of Egypt. On the first of these five momentous days, the birth of Osiris was celebrated, for the annual flood symbolized his resurrection. The second was consecrated to his son Horus, protector of royalty. But the third could provoke catastrophes and cataclysms, for it saw the birth of Set.*

Her face again so heavily painted that she was unrecognizable, Bina met Iker in a small, palm-shaded square.

'The whole town is talking about you,' she said. 'They say you've prevented a disaster.'

'Everyone has given of their best. The Nile will decide.'

'I can't wait for the Day of Set. I pray that he'll punish this accursed country!'

'"Accursed country"? What do you mean?'

She realised she'd made a mistake. 'I meant the damned

---

*The days 'above the year' were inserted into the calendar to bring the length of the year up to 365 days; the other deities whose birthdays were celebrated were Isis and Nephthys.

tyrant who's leading the country to its downfall and causing misery among its people. You haven't changed your mind, have you?'

'Do you think I'm that unreliable?'

'Of course not.'

'Then fear and worship Set. If he kills Senusret himself, that's all to the good. But how can you be glad of the prospect of the farmlands being laid waste, reducing thousands of people to poverty?'

'Don't get the wrong idea! I was just hoping that the god's strength would advance our cause.'

On the Day of Set, the tjaty's office did no business. The king remained in the temple, and everyone stayed at home. The endless hours crawled by. At at last the Day of Isis came, followed by the Day of Nephthys. Thanks to the benevolent sisters, the new year had a harmonious beginning.

Although the turbulent floodwater ran fast and high, it caused only slight damage to the banks and retaining-walls, and no one was drowned. The Kahun authorities congratulated Iker on his excellent work. All his calculations had proved correct, and the town and the surrounding area were unscathed. There were even predictions of rich harvests, which would enable the granaries to be filled and reserves to be accumulated in case of bad years.

At the end of the new year celebrations, Iker was at last able to take a few hours' rest.

'You don't look happy,' observed Sekari. 'I hope the mayor won't go on squeezing you like a sack of grapes.'

'Don't delude yourself: I have a report to write on Kahun's storage facilities. The archives will make the task easier, but all the same I shall have to check everything, because the experts have an annoying tendency to copy their own mistakes.'

'About the archives . . . Have you found your famous proof?'

'I'm no longer in any doubt about what I must do.'

'You're clever, intelligent and cultivated. Me, I'm an unsophisticated man, with little or no education, but I trust my instinct and it's seldom wrong. Why dwell on your misfortunes just when happiness is beckoning?'

'Happiness won't be possible until I've achieved my aims.'

'Well, remember what the sages say: Pharaoh knows everything that happens. There's nothing he doesn't know about, either in the heavens or on the earth.'

'However much he knows, justice will eventually strike him down.'

Sekari lowered his eyes. 'I'm embarrassed to say this, but . . . don't rely on me to help you. My life hasn't always been easy, and I've taken a lot of hard knocks. Here, I feel really at home.'

'I understand, and I had no intention of asking you for help. But will you swear not to betray me?'

'I swear it.'

15

Early in the morning, Medes's beautiful house was filled with hysterical cries from his wife, who was having an attack of nerves because of a succession of inexcusable catastrophes. First, the braids that decorated the neckline and sides of her winter tunic had come unsewn, as if the garment had been made by a set of incompetent fools. Next, her usual hairdresser had had the bad taste to be ill, and had sent a replacement so clumsy that she couldn't even fix false tresses on to a wig – all she had to do was lift up a tress of the wig, roll it round a large pin, hook on the false tress and put the other one back in place, concealing the artifice. In rage, Medes's wife had thrown her mirror on the ground and sent the stupid girl away without paying her.

Then a terrible headache began. She tried to soothe it by rubbing her head with a pomade of dill, bryony and coriander seeds, but this time the remedy didn't work.

She burst like a fury into her husband's bedchamber. 'Darling, I'm terribly ill! Send for Doctor Gua – he's the only one who can cure me.'

'Deal with it yourself, and don't wake me up like this again. I work for a living.'

She stormed out and slammed the door.

Medes got up and went into the washroom. Usually, he enjoyed his morning routine, which was followed by a copious breakfast. But he had slept badly, disturbed by too many cares.

When would Gergu at last return from Abydos, and what would the results of his visit be? Medes still could not believe that he would soon have an ally on the inside. How could a permanent priest betray his community like that? If it was an attempt to manipulate the situation, the person behind it would not be easy. But was Medes being too suspicious?

And then there was another problem: Khnum-Hotep's remarkable success. The tjaty was an excellent administrator and was ensuring perfect cohesion between central power and the provinces. Like many people, Medes had expected disagreements, clashes and protests, but nothing like that had happened. With the help of the King's House, none of whom envied him his job in the least, the tjaty was in firm control of an effective, hard-working government. Fortunately, Khnum-Hotep was already old and so would not serve for long. But Medes saw his own influence diminishing while he waited for the old man to die, so he must take care to maintain his networks of useful friends and courtiers.

A number of doors were closing, and opening them did not seem likely to be easy. Today, Medes's greatest hope was called Abydos.

The prospect of meeting the Phoenician trader's superior excited him. What criminal had been skilful enough to secure the trader's services? A man like that must be interesting, and Medes was definitely planning to make use of him.

As he finished dressing, his wife reappeared. 'Doctor Gua can't come until this evening,' she moaned. 'You must use your influence to make him cancel his appointments and give me priority.'

'In the first place, Gua is a cantankerous man and will never bow to pressure. In the scond, your headache doesn't seem mortally dangerous. Go back to bed and sleep until midday. Then your friends' visits and prattle will set you back on your feet.'

The arrival of Gergu interrupted the conversation. Feeling tense, Medes led his henchman into his office and carefully closed the door.

'The news is excellent,' said Gergu with a broad smile. 'What a fellow that priest is! He understands your caution and wants to prove his willingness to cooperate, so he's given us the means of doing business without him.'

Astonished, Medes wondered if Gergu was under the influence of drink.

'First,' Gergu went on, 'here is a seal of Abydos. It can be applied to all sorts of materials, and that means we can create certificates of authenticity for fakes we will make ourselves, and then sell them as coming from the sacred site of Osiris. That is my idea, anyway, and I've found a craftsman who's willing to do the work.

'And here is our new ally's second gift, and it's even more precious than the first: the sacred words evoking the warm welcome given to the righteous in the other world: "May he sail in the ship of Osiris and handle its oars; may he travel wherever his heart desires; may the Great Ones of Abydos welcome him in peace; may he participate in the Mysteries of Osiris, and may he follow him on pure paths in the sacred land." We can engrave the text on some of the items we produce, and sell them at exorbitant prices!'

The wine-trader, who came from a modest family, could feel his health failing, so his thoughts turned to the great journey that lay ahead. He was wealthy enough to afford a fine sarcophagus, but he envied the privileged folk whose names were engraved for all time on a monument at Abydos, near Osiris and under his protection. Could there be any better assurance of a happy eternity?

When he saw Gergu appear, the wine-trader immediately

wondered how large a discount the villain was going to demand on his next order. But it was necessary to be on good terms with him, because he had many contacts at the palace, so the wine-trader put on a smile.

'My dear Gergu, I've just received a new vintage. Would you like to sample it?'

'Certainly I would. But first, can we speak privately?'

'Of course. Come down into the cellar.' The trader's throat tightened. What new blackmail was about to be inflicted on him?

To mollify Gergu, he gave him a cup of an exceptionally fine wine.

'Not bad,' said Gergu, 'but a little sweet for my taste.' He put the cup down. 'You've ordered a sarcophagus of the highest quality, I understand.'

'One must think of the afterlife.'

'Abydos: what does that mean to you?'

'Abydos? I don't understand.'

'I can obtain an authentic stele for you, bearing the sacred words. All you will have to do is engrave your name upon it and then you can spend your eternity at the foot of the Great God's staircase.'

The trader was so deeply moved that he almost died. 'Are you . . . joking?'

'The price will have to be high, because of my expenses.'

'Whatever you want!'

'Before committing yourself, come with me and I'll show you the stele.'

The wine-trader was trembling with emotion as Gergu led him to a warehouse and, once there, showed him the stele.

'I'll take it,' stammered the trader.

'And there you are!' Gergu told Medes triumphantly. 'Your wine cellar and mine well filled in exchange for a pretty sculpted stone which will never go anywhere near Abydos and which our craftsman will destroy tonight – don't worry, I paid him well. We needn't go to Abydos, either, and we can get by without that fine priest.'

'You are wrong,' said Medes. 'I don't deny that I'm interested in your method – though it must be used sparingly – but there are better things to do, much better. Real stelae will interest the very wealthiest people in Memphis, and we can fix high, non-negotiable prices.'

These arguments shook Gergu. 'So we won't leave the priest out of the affair . . . ?'

'That would be a big mistake, because we need his collaboration in two ways. First, he will help us do excellent business deals. Second, he can give us information about Abydos and can help us penetrate the secrecy of the great Mysteries. His help is providential. Arrange my meeting him as soon as possible.'

Wah-sut, the town Senusret had had built at Abydos, was coming to life. It housed the builders of his temple and his tomb, the priests charged with bringing these monuments spiritually to life, and the administrative staff, with their families. Each house had several rooms, an internal courtyard and a garden. The streets were narrow – only five cubits wide – and were laid out at right angles to each other. On the desert side, there were luxurious houses. At the south-western corner of the town was the mayor's official residence, which also housed the administrative offices and a number of workshops.

It was in one of them that permanent priest Bega was due to meet temporary priest Gergu and his 'assistant'. Gergu was now well known to the guards at Abydos, and had explained that his work had become so arduous that he needed an assistant if he was to keep up the high standards the priests at Abydos expected. Medes had easily passed through the security checkpoint under a false name.

When Bega entered the room, Medes felt an icy chill. He had not imagined that someone initiated into the mysteries of Abydos could be so ugly and cold: tall, ramrod-stiff, with a prominent nose.

Bega sat down some way from the other two men and, not deigning to address Gergu, asked Medes, 'Who are you?'

'My name is Medes, and I am the secretary of the King's House. Pharaoh Senusret dictates decrees to me and I send them out into all the provinces.'

'That is a very important post.'

'Your own is not unimportant.'

'No, but I had hoped for better – much better. Perhaps you feel the same?'

'The seal and the sacred words have enabled us to make our first business deal – you will of course share in the profit. From now on, let us help each other achieve the standing and wealth we deserve.'

No smile lit up Bega's disagreeable face, but nevertheless Medes could see that he was pleased.

'Did your friend Gergu pass on my proposals?' asked Bega.

'Yes, and they suit me perfectly. We shall undertake the manufacture and sale of false stelae, which the buyers will think are destined for Abydos. But you need not fear that any of them will actually arrive here, because we shall destroy them ourselves. On your side, how will you manage to get genuine pieces away from the site, and how should we arrange their transport to Memphis?'

'As I explained to Gergu, people and goods coming into Abydos are checked very thoroughly, but it is easy to get out. I have acquired the help of one of the security guards, who's posted every ten days to guard the Great God's staircase, on the desert side of town. There is a good hiding-place there, where I shall put small but extremely valuable stelae. You must have someone trustworthy ready to collect them. Then all you need do is to follow a path I'll show you. It will take you back to the Nile, where a boat will be waiting.'

'That seems an excellent plan. But tell me, why are you doing this?'

'I might ask you the same question.'

'As we're both running so many risks,' said Medes, 'it would be stupid to lie to each other. I'm paid far less than I am worth, so I'm proving my true value to myself by using all the means at my disposal. But you, a man of the inner temple . . .'

'For a long time I believed that the spiritual dimension was enough for me and that my desires had dwindled to the minimum. Senusret's intervention changed everything. Instead of appointing me High Priest, he has taken charge of Abydos himself and is reorganizing the colleges of priests. His unwarranted assumption of power means I am denied the privileges due to me, so I decided to take my revenge. To achieve it, I need a great deal of wealth.'

'Let us be clear, Bega. What exactly do you mean by "revenge"?'

'I shall kill the man who's ruining my career.'

'Do you know Senusret? I see him all the time, and there is nothing I don't know about his ability to act. Believe me, he's more fearsome than a wild bull and more ferocious than a lion. I'd like to see him dead, too, but how can anyone undermine such a powerful man?'

'Have you given up the fight, then?'

'I'm wondering what methods to employ. The king is surrounded by faithful friends, and his tjaty is unanimously praised.'

'However strong they appear, human works end up being broken. It is up to us to join forces and identify his weak points.'

'Tell me, why are there all these soldiers guarding Abydos?'

Bega became very still. 'That is a state secret.'

'Now that we've come this far,' said Medes, 'you might as well tell me.'

'One of the Mysteries of Abydos is the Tree of Life,' said Bega. 'It is gravely ill and is in danger of dying. Intervention by Senusret and the ritual priests is slowing its degeneration, but for how long? Curing it requires a particular kind of gold, which may never be found.'

The gold of Punt! thought Medes, greatly excited by these revelations. Aloud, he asked, 'What or who has caused this curse?'

'We don't know. The king has launched several investigations to try to find out who is responsible.'

'Are there any suspects?'

'Not one. If the acacia dies, the Mysteries will no longer be celebrated and Osiris won't be reborn. It will be the end of Egypt.'

'Let's talk about these famous Mysteries. Surely they're just a legend, aren't they?'

'If you knew even the tiniest thing about them, you wouldn't say that.'

'As a permanent priest, you enter the secret heart of Abydos and perform the rites reserved for initiates.'

Bega said nothing.

'I want to know everything,' insisted Medes. 'I've been trying for years to get access to the covered temple. The temple of Abydos is the largest and most vital of all, isn't it?'

The priest smiled strangely. 'I have sworn not to betray the secret.'

'Every man has his price. You possess several extremely valuable pieces, and I'll pay you a fair price for them.'

'We'll have plenty of time to discuss that.'

'You're right: too much haste would lead to failure. Let's put our collaboration on a firm footing first, and build up our war-treasury. Then we can go on from there.'

Bega looked hard at Medes for a minute. 'Let's put each other to the test. If all goes well, we can go on from there.'

Medes nodded. 'One last question: at Memphis, I noticed a young woman who said she'd come from Abydos with a confidential message for the king. Do you know her?'

'Describe her.' Bega listened attentively. 'She's one of the priestesses of Hathor who live here. Our superior, the Shaven-headed One, opened up the library of the House of Life to her so that she could carry out research into the ancient texts.'

'No doubt she was taking the king the plans enabling him to build a pyramid. Does this woman play a key role here?'

'No, she's an underling and was only the Shaven-headed One's messenger. She's a dreamer, a mystic, so we have nothing to fear from her. I won't say the same for my colleagues, but I am going to take certain precautions. What about you, Medes? Will you be careful enough?'

'I am not in the habit of making mistakes.'

16

On the return voyage to Memphis, Medes went over all the arguments in favour of breaking up the nascent alliance with Bega. None of them withstood scrutiny. The priest did indeed seem the ideal accomplice. He was embittered, full of envy and hatred, motivated by a twisted intelligence, tenacious, and wholly lacking in that basic sensibility which prevents people from committing evil. Also, he knew secrets that Medes had always wanted to learn. He would have to be cajoled, flattered at the right moment, and led to believe he was the most important of the three men, but Medes was sure he could do all that.

And Medes had not forgotten the gold of Punt. At the moment, he could not hire a crew without someone noticing. Later, he would get control of a warship boatyard and use his wealth to acquire the treasure.

When he and Gergu reached his house, the outside guard at the entrance saluted his master by bowing very low, and alerted the inner guard, who immediately opened the heavy door. On the path that led to the house they met Doctor Gua, who was clearly in a hurry.

'Is my wife ill?' asked Medes.

'It's only a headache caused by idleness – I've prescribed a salve and a light sleeping-draught. But there is a more serious matter.'

'Tell me, please.'

'She's too fat. If she goes on nibbling cakes all day she'll get seriously obese. Food, that's the secret of health. Anyway, I have more serious cases to treat.'

Medes and Gergu were served beer, hot flatcakes and dried meat, then shut themselves away in Medes's office.

'Assassinating Senusret seems impossible,' said Gergu. 'He's too well protected, and nobody will dare raise a hand against him. If we employ an assassin, he'll be arrested and will denounce us.'

'Probably, but nevertheless there is one thing we can do: weaken the king by attacking those close to him. If we undermine foundations he considers indestructible, we can isolate him, and then he'll be within our reach. Let's begin with the man you know best: High Treasurer Senankh.'

'Yes, I do know him well, but unfortunately I have nothing interesting to tell you. He's an honest man! His only fault is an excessive fondness for good food. And there isn't a single woman, however alluring, who can transform him into a helpless lamb.'

'I agree. So, since we can't corrupt him, we'll entrap him. I work at the Trade secretariat, don't forget, and I know exactly how it works. This is what we'll do – my wife's special talent is going to be very useful.'

The kingdom's High Treasurer, head of the Double White House, was a vigorous forty-year-old with plump cheeks and a round belly. He looked like a friendly, warm man who enjoyed good living. In reality, he was an implacable, feared leader of men, intransigent by nature, with no sense of tact, and ruthless with good-for-nothings; flatterers and weak men did not last long in his employ. Charged by the pharaoh with the just distribution of Egypt's wealth, Senankh considered that keeping the state's accounts properly was vital if Ma'at and civilization were to be maintained. In the event of widespread waste, debt or negligence, the fabric of society would tear itself apart and the door would be open to all kinds of abuse.

As he did each week, the High Treasurer went to see Tjaty Khnum-Hotep, to discuss the needs of the least prosperous provinces. By improving their lot, every day the tjaty did more to consolidate the country's rediscovered unity, in accordance with the king's wishes.

The two dignitaries were as frank and direct as each other, and had an excellent understanding. Without Senankh's help, Khnum-Hotep might not have succeeded in overcoming the thousand and one mean tricks of central government. Neither man was driven by ambition; they were content with the responsibilities the king had entrusted to them.

'Any particular problems?' asked the tjaty.

'Some granaries urgently need to be rebuilt, taxes on river travel have been increased without my consent, ten complaints against tax inspectors who are behaving like tyrants, delays in the delivery of jars to Thebes, two work-shy fellows I've just dismissed . . . I'll spare you the rest. And what about you? Are you in good health?'

'The tjaty is worn out, but Egypt is well – at least, almost well.'

Senankh knew that, in Khnum-Hotep's mouth, such shades of meaning led one to assume there were grave problems. 'Can I help?'

'Most of all, I hope you can help yourself. The just sharing-out of wealth is your foremost duty, isn't it?'

'I never forget that.'

'Several senior scribes think otherwise.'

'Why?'

'I have received ten extremely embarrassed reports, accompanied by letters bearing your seal and ordering somewhat surprising distributions of grain. In summary, three-quarters is to go to rich landowners and the rest to modest families and to villages in difficulty, which therefore won't receive enough food. The people will soon find out, and they'll protest vigorously and lodge complaints with the judges. The judges will come to me, and I shall be obliged to punish the culprit. I shall have to leave the King's House, and you, Senankh, will end up in prison.'

'Do you mean you take these accusations seriously?'

'I've been losing sleep over the problem, but I have no right to destroy these documents.'

'If you committed such a crime, you would be unworthy of your office. Show them to me.' Senankh read them attentively.

'Is that really your seal?' asked the tjaty.

'Anyone would swear it was.'

'And your writing?'

'They'd swear that, too.'

'In that case, what is your explanation for all this?'

'I should like to give it in the king's presence.'

'His Majesty would demand as much, so let us waste no time.'

Khnum-Hotep got wearily and stiffly to his feet. He could well have done without this scandal, which would gravely weaken the King's House; he would never have dreamt Senankh would succumb to corruption. The High Treasurer's calm was astonishing. How could he stay calm when faced with such weighty accusations? Still, when faced with Senusret, his façade was bound to crumble.

Under the pharaoh's piercing gaze, Khnum-Hotep set out the details of the case.

The king showed no emotion. 'It is all false, of course.'

'Of course,' confirmed Senankh.

'Majesty,' objected the tjaty, 'you have the proof in front of you.'

'My seal and my writing have been copied perfectly,' said Senankh.

'Is that not a rather feeble defence?' asked Khum-Hotep anxiously.

'It would be, if I could not prove my innocence.'

The tjaty began to hope again. 'How?'

'It occurred to me some time ago that forgery might be used against me in official correspondence, so I always take precautions against it. First, I indent the third and fifth line of my letters. Next, when I write the "lock" hieroglyph for the sound *s* for the eighth time in a document, I clearly lengthen the right side; and the second time I write the "leg" hieroglyph for *b*, I make the foot smaller. Lastly, I arrange three very small black dots in a triangle in the middle of the text. If you examine the forged letters closely, you will find none of these signs.'

The tjaty was still not fully reassured. 'How can I be sure you have not just invented them?'

'If you go to the archives and look at some of my official letters, you will find that these signs always appear. In addition, what I have said can be confirmed by a trustworthy witness who knows the secret.'

'And who is that witness?'

'The Pharaoh of Egypt.'

Khnum-Hotep swallowed hard. 'I'm glad, very glad indeed, and I shall immediately inform your accusers that they have been deceived. But what malicious person could have committed such a crime?'

'Someone who wants to get rid of me legally and without violence. The idea was a clever one, and thwarting it seemed impossible at first. Imitating a seal and writing-style like that is quite an achievement. Everything leads me to believe that I have a determined adversary at the heart of the upper levels of government.'

'Perhaps even within your own secretariat,' suggested the tjaty. 'Seek him among those men who are jealous and disappointed, and aspire to taking your place. And I advise you to be extra-cautious from now on. Change your code and do not tell anyone except His Majesty the new one.'

For the tenth time the Phoenician trader tried, and for the tenth time he failed. How could he possibly resist smooth white wine, slow-stewed beef, beans in goose fat, honey-cakes and fig jam? True, the Herald had advised him to eat and drink less, and advice from that quarter amounted to an order. But what use was wealth if one had to live in a way which removed all the joy from life? The Phoenician had bought more voluminous robes, which he hoped would hide his extra weight, and he resolved that in the Herald's presence he would behave like a fasting ascetic.

To his best agent, the water-carrier, he offered only dried figs.

'Medes is back in Memphis,' said the spy.

'Where from?'

'Abydos, according to my informants.'

'Abydos?' exclaimed the Phoenician. 'But Abydos is the sacred domain of Osiris, and is barred to all but a few initiates. Whyever did he go there?'

'I've no idea.'

Intrigued, the Phoenician dismissed his agent, had himself bathed and massaged, and put on a fringed robe which was so soft that when he stretched out on some cushions he fell asleep.

His steward woke him to inform him of a visit from his captain, an excellent sailor who was in charge of transporting wood from Phoenicia.

The captain had a deeply lined face, and his hair was dishevelled. He spoke slowly, in a deep, rough voice. 'The new new cargo has arrived safely, sir. And the rest, too.'

'Any problems with the trade-control officials?'

'Not the slightest – the system's working perfectly. As regards transport, there's no problem, but there's still some trouble with the internal network. Since reunification things have got better, though, because people can move easily from one province to another. I now have contacts in every port, and information circulates quickly. But there's a blockage at Kahun.'

'Why?'

'A local scribe is refusing to give our caravan final authorization. It has safe-conduct passes from the government in Memphis, but that isn't enough for him. The fellow wants checks done on the identity of every new arrival and on all consignments of goods, and he wants to do them himself.'

'That's annoying, very annoying. What is his name?'

'Heremsaf.'

'I'll take care of him.'

Rather like a dog turning up its nose at tainted food, Heremsaf did not like the smell of this caravan. The case seemed perfectly clear, and the merchants had all the necessary authorizations, so he ought to have opened the gates of Kahun and welcomed the foreigners without a second thought. And yet his instinct told him to carry out one last check. He might be wrong, but at least he would have no cause for self-reproach; over-caution was better than laxity. It would not be the first time a caravan harbouring undesirables and trans-porting dubious goods had tried to enter Kahun. Recently, a Syrian had tried to sell second-rate papyrus, claiming it was of superior quality.

And tomorrow, Heremsaf decided, he would also talk to Iker; it was some time since he had last done so. The young man was enjoying a meteoric rise in his career, which would take him beyond his wildest imaginings, and since his remarkable work to avert devastation by the Nile flood many people called him 'the Saviour'. So why was he always so sad and troubled? Something bad was eating away at him. What could it possibly be?

The only way to get honest answers was to ask direct questions. Yes, first thing tomorrow, Heremsaf would definitely summon Iker and at last find out the truth.

His secretary informed him that a young woman was asking to see him.

'Very well, show her in.'

She was a pretty brown-haired woman, her face attractively painted. She presented him with a dish of beans with garlic, in a herb sauce. 'This is one of Iker's cook's special recipes. Iker thought you might like to try it.'

'A kind thought.'

'Eat it while it's hot, to enjoy it at its best.'

As he had had no time to eat at midday, Heremsaf needed no further prompting, particularly since the dish was delicious.

While he ate, Bina walked away, a smile on her lips.

Heremsaf felt the first spasms in the middle of the night. At first he thought it was food poisoning, but the pain became so fierce that it took his breath away and he could not get out of bed.

Before long his muscles stiffened and his heart stopped beating. The Phoenician poison had had the planned effect.

17

'Long-Hair is asking for you,' Sekari told Iker, whom he'd had to shake awake. 'He seems very upset.'

'What bad news has he brought this time?'

'He won't tell anyone but you.'

Iker hastily rinsed out his mouth, then went downstairs. 'What is it, Long-Hair?'

'It's Heremsaf . . . He died last night.'

'Heremsaf? Are you certain?'

'Unfortunately, yes.'

'What was the cause of death?'

'His heart gave out. He'd been overworked recently, but he refused to rest. Although you're much younger than he was, this ought to teach you a good lesson. You work too hard, too.'

Iker went to the Temple of Anubis, whose new High Priest would conduct Heremsaf's burial rites. He placed himself at the High Priest's disposal, so that the ritual would lack nothing.

The dead man's work was taken back by the mayor's office and shared out among various officials. The scribe who dealt with the delayed caravan saw nothing abnormal about it, and so gave it permission to enter Kahun.

*

Wakha, the former governor of the Cobra province, was dead. As usual, Senusret had not let his feelings show, but the news had affected him profoundly. At the start of his struggle against the rebellious provinces, Wakha had been the first to support him and swear fidelity to him. When the country might easily have toppled into civil war, Wakha's support had proved decisive. His death might be a crucial turning-point. How would his family, his inner circle and his advisers react? Would they submit to Tjaty Khnum-Hotep, who had been sent to the Cobra province for the funeral ceremonies, or would they rebel and try to set up a new provincial governor? If they rebelled, the king would be obliged to use force. Well, Khnum-Hotep would be back at any time, so he would soon know.

These sombre thoughts were joined by a persistent worry: who had placed the curse on the Tree of Life and wanted to prevent the resurrection of Osiris? The pharaoh now knew that it was not one of the provincial governors formerly opposed to reunification. Logically, the wicked magician ought to be a rebel Canaanite, whose only goal was the destruction of Egypt. Perhaps General Nesmontu's scouring of Syria and Canaan would result in the criminal's identification?

Khnum-Hotep reached Memphis that evening, and went immediately to see the king. 'No one is contemplating re-establishing a local governor, Majesty,' he said with obvious relief. 'I have set up a new provincial government, which will be supervised by one of my own men.'

'He must permit neither weakness nor excess. The Cobra province, like all others, must be run according to Ma'at, none of its inhabitants must suffer from hunger, and all injustice must be severely punished. I am responsible to the gods for the happiness of my people. And you are responsible to me.'

'I was in the forefront of those who witnessed your great

work of reunification. Now it is part of my being, and my dearest wish is to help consolidate the unity whose guarantor you are. The provinces will cause you no more concern.'

'But what if we fail to heal the Acacia of Osiris? What will remain of Egypt?'

'What, nothing? demanded Medes, pacing angrily up and down his office.

'It's true: nothing at all has happened to him,' confirmed Gergu. 'Senankh is still High Treasurer.'

'No punishment at all?'

'No. The tjaty still trusts him.'

'The pharaoh does, too, it seems – I'd hoped he was just play-acting in order to save face and preserve the reputation of the King's House. I don't understand it. My wife imitated Senankh's writing perfectly, and every detail of the seal was copied accurately.' Suddenly, realization dawned on him. 'A code – Senankh uses a code! There's no other possible explanation. That's why he was able to prove his innocence so easily.'

'If we study the archives, we'll find out what it is.'

'There's no point. He'll have changed it.'

'Someone else must know the secret, surely?'

'Yes, of course: the pharaoh himself.'

Gergu gave way to gloom. 'Then Senankh is still untouchable.'

'For the moment, my friend, only for the moment. But there are easier targets to hit.'

Medes told his new plan to Gergu, who thought it excellent and set off immediately to put it into action.

This failure had taught Medes a great deal, and did not discourage him in the least. The King's House was like a strong fortress, which he could not knock down in one day. But now he had an ally at Abydos, an ally who would enable him to touch the heart of the great Mysteries and acquire a power equal to the pharaoh's.

The Phoenician used several mirrors to check his appearance. His voluminous robe with its vertical stripes made him look much thinner. Nevertheless, when the Herald entered the reception chamber, he could not meet his visitor's eyes.

The Phoenician hastened to offer the Herald a drink of cool water, but the offer was refused.

'Would you like something else, my lord?'

'Only a detailed, honest report.'

There were no cakes or fruit on the low tables; the Phoenician hoped the Herald could see what efforts his host was making.

'My lord, our trading prospects are excellent, and the forthcoming business transactions should bring us substantial profits. My arguments convinced Medes, and I do not doubt his value as a collaborator. As planned, I am making him wait to meet my . . . my superior. His curiosity has been aroused, and he is bound to ask me again.'

The Herald gave a faint smile, which was more worrying than reassuring.

'As regards my network of informants,' the Phoenician went on, 'it is working better and better. With only a small number of agents, information circulates rapidly. Senusret's unification of Egypt is more than just a word; no province now opposes the central power, and travelling throughout Egypt is becoming easy.'

'And what about the caravan travelling to Kahun?'

It was the Phoenician's turn to smile. 'That proves how efficient my network is! My best agent there, a young woman named Bina, discovered that a senior scribe, a suspicious, cantankerous man called Heremsaf, was blocking the caravan's authorization and refusing to let it enter the town.

So I supplied Bina with a powerful poison used in Phoenicia for getting rid of inconvenient people. She has carried out her mission successfully: Heremsaf is dead, and the mayor's office at Kahun has removed the last obstacle to our people's arrival.'

'You have done well.'

The Phoenician blushed. 'I'm doing my very best, my lord. Harming Egypt gives me great pleasure.'

'Although you have got even fatter, you will be forgiven a great many things.'

When the long caravan neared Kahun it was stopped by the town guards, who checked its authorizations in minute detail.

Bearded and bare-chested, the Asians were wearing orange kilts and black sandals. Some were laden with mats, others played the eight-stringed lyre. The women wore rings round their ankles, many-coloured tunics and leather boots.

The guards inspected the donkeys' burdens: baskets, vases, throwing-spears, face-paints made with malachite from Sinai, and metalworkers' bellows.

'Who is your leader?' asked the scribe in charge of the checks.

'Ibcha,' replied a cheerful-looking boy.

'And where is he?'

'At the rear of the caravan.'

'Go and fetch him.'

The boy ran off and soon returned with Ibcha, a sturdy fellow with a bushy beard.

The scribe asked, 'Why are there weapons in your baggage?'

'Bows and arrows would have enabled us to defend ourselves if we were attacked. Several of us are metalworkers and know how to make metal-tipped throwing-spears.'

'Since you are setting up in Kahun, I am confiscating your

135

weapons. I shall question you one by one, and you will give your names, ages, family situation and professional skills. Then I shall allocate you a place to live.'

The Asians cooperated docilely.

Once the formalities had been carried out, the scribe turned to Ibcha again. 'Strict security rules are in force in Kahun. If anyone commits even the smallest crime, he and his family will be expelled. We will not tolerate any fighting between you, and we demand absolute obedience to the mayor's instructions. Follow me.'

He took Ibcha to the workshop that produced knives, which were piled up on shelves. It was here that Iker's dagger had been sharpened.

'Production here is too low,' explained the scribe. 'The mayor wants to provide the town's guards and soldiers with brand-new, high-quality weapons. The neighbouring forge has been enlarged, and stocks of metal have just been delivered. Of course, each item produced will be checked and numbered. You may have two days' rest while you settle in. Then you will begin work, and your wages will be those of skilled workers. You and your people will be able to get everything you need here. A pair of sandals will buy you two jars of oil, or twenty loaves, or twenty-five jugs of beer. You are welcome among us.'

Bina watched the arrival of the caravan. The first part of her mission had been successful, and she would continue to exploit the Egyptians' foolish belief in the effectiveness of their checks. For every ten weapons they made, the Asians would secretly make another, which would be hidden away. Little by little they would build up a store big enough to arm the city's future masters. If Iker succeeded in killing Sensuret, the revolution would be swifter than expected.

'My allies have arrived at last,' Bina told Iker. 'Soon we shan't have to hide in this horrible house any more.'

Still shocked by Heremsaf's death, Iker had paid no attention to the caravan's arrival. 'What is their plan?'

'I don't know, but you can trust them. They hate the tyrant as much as you and I do, and they'd gladly sacrifice their lives to defeat him.'

'At Kahun,' he reminded her, 'foreigners are always closely watched. What are they going to do?'

'I told you, I don't know.'

'And what will your role be?'

'Oh, I'm only an ignorant servant-girl, so I'll just get food and clothing for them. But they've given me a very pretty gift. Would you like to see it?'

Without waiting for an answer, she showed Iker a small, hemmed triangle of linen. 'You pass one corner between your legs,' she explained in a sugar-sweet voice, 'and knot it into a garment with the two other corners. Will you help me?'

She took off her tunic and stood naked in the half-light for a moment. Then she moved closer to Iker. 'Will you help me?' she repeated.

'Forgive me, but I . . . I'm too preoccupied.'

The temptress fought back her anger. 'Another time,' she conceded.

The Festival of Bes was in full swing. Everyone in Kahun took part, wine flowed freely, and music was played in every part of town, in the hope that the bearded and lion-masked god would dance by on his thick legs. Bes drove away demons and cut up evil spirits with his long knives, which was why craftsmen depicted him on beds, bed-heads, lamps, chairs and toilet utensils. When he stuck out his red tongue, Bes uttered the purifying word; when he banged his tambourine, he gave out positive waves of sound. It was his task to watch over the birth of ordinary children in the birthing-room and of initiates in the temple.

There were lit torches everywhere; in a blaze of light,

Kahun gave itself up to the joy of living, to laughter and to the pleasures of good food and drink.

After drinking a few cups with the mayor's other councillors, Iker excused himself, saying that he had a slight fever and a headache.

Despite himself, his steps took him towards the workshop where the Asians had sharpened his dagger. On this night of revelry, it was the quietest place in town: no music, no songs, no laughter, only a faint light coming from the place.

Iker went closer. The windows were screened by curtains, but one of them was torn and he was able to peep inside. He saw Bina reading a document in a low voice to ten men, who listened closely. Then she picked up a brush and started writing a letter.

Stunned, Iker withdrew. So she had lied when she said she couldn't read or write! The poor, ignorant servant-girl, oppressed and bullied, was in reality the leader of this group of terrorists.

Feeling sick, Iker headed for home.

'Iker, wake up!' called Sekari. 'It's late!' He winced and clutched his head, which was still clouded from the celebrations.

There was no reply, so he pushed open the door of Iker's bedchamber. The room was empty. So was the washroom. Incredulously, Sekari searched the whole house, but without success. Then he went to the stable, where he found only North Wind peacefully munching his fodder.

'Surely he wouldn't have abandoned his closest friend and confidant? Oh, I know what's happened. He had too much wine and he's sleeping it off somewhere. But where?'

Sekari scoured Kahun and asked everyone he saw, but in vain. It seemed that Iker had left town.

*

As the boat sailed swiftly towards Memphis, the only thing the young scribe regretted was leaving North Wind behind. But there was a good chance that Iker wouldn't come through this adventure alive, and he knew Sekari would take good care of the donkey.

The instant he realized that Bina had lied to him, Iker had decided to sever all contact with the Asians, whom he no longer trusted as allies. He did not care what their real aim was. He must act alone.

18

In the middle of the night Bina summoned the metalworkers to an urgent meeting.

'Iker has left Kahun,' she told them.

'He'll denounce us all!' exclaimed their leader, Ibcha.

'If he'd wanted to do that, we'd already be in prison.'

'Then why has he run away?'

'His nerves have snapped,' explained the young woman. 'He wants to act alone and strike down the tyrant when he thinks the moment is right, and he wants to do it without telling anyone, not even me.'

'He doesn't stand a chance!'

'He's no ordinary man. Inside, he burns with an unquenchable fire, so I don't think he is beaten in advance.'

'Can you imagine how many obstacles he must get past before he reaches the king?'

'He's overcome a lot of obstacles already. Besides, I convinced him that Senusret is a pitiless monster, who must be killed by any means possible in order to save Egypt.'

'And the foolish boy believed you?'

'Iker knows that evil exists and he thinks Senusret is its source. If he has to sacrifice himself to destroy that source, he won't hesitate.'

'Well, I still think he'll be killed, but if he succeeds it'll be all the better for us.'

'There is another cause for concern,' said Bina, and she told them about the unidentified man who had tried to kill Iker and whose body had been eaten by crocodiles.

'If he was sent by an organized network,' said Ibcha, 'they won't leave it at that. Has anything else happened since then?'

'No, and in Kahun the affair caused little interest – anyone would think nothing had happened.'

'Are people jealous of Iker?'

'Indeed they are, because of his capacity for work and his rapid rise to success.'

'Then we need look no further: it was a simple settling of scores, and Iker got rid of an inconvenient rival. I find that rather reassuring. If he knows how to fight, he has slightly more chance of success.'

At the age of thirty-two, Sehotep had the reputation of being one of the most accomplished seducers in Memphis. The only son of a wealthy family, an exceptional scribe, with a quick, dynamic mind, and always dressed in the latest fashion, Sehotep gave people entirely the wrong impression. He was generally considered to be a lover of life's pleasures, disinclined to work for hours on end. That view failed to take account of his eyes, which glinted with intelligence, and his remarkable ability to assimilate complex matters with equally remarkable speed. As Bearer of the Royal Seal, he oversaw all the king's works, and was charged with seeing that the secrecy of temples was respected and that livestock was treated well. He met these onerous responsibilities head-on, in an apparently casual manner which concealed meticulous thoroughness.

The courtiers loathed Sehotep, whose life resembled a succession of easy successes. He himself gave credence to this reputation, by letting it be known that he never encountered the slightest difficulty and easily overcame any and all problems. Of course, he never missed any of the capital's great social events or the sumptuous banquets given by the leading citizens. People were happy to talk there, while Sehotep listened and gathered as much information as possible.

Memphis's new school of dancing was being inaugurated, and the Bearer of the Royal Seal honoured the ceremony with his presence. The teacher was as excited as her young pupils, who wore kilts short enough not to hinder their performance.

A pretty brown-haired girl offered Sehotep her most beautiful smile. He returned it. Then she joined the other dancers, who executed a breathtaking series of acrobatic moves. Keeping her torso completely upright, each girl extended one leg forward, raising it until her foot was level with her shoulder. The dancers then bent and sprang with stunning speed. Next, they executed a succession of perilous jumps, their bodies arched, successively supporting themselves on their hands, with the fingers stretched out, and on the tips of their toes. Sehotep had the impression that they formed a circle, but his gaze was increasingly fixed on the pretty brunette.

When the demonstration was over, the teacher asked Sehotep anxiously, 'Are you satisfied?'

'A remarkable performance. I should like to congratulate the dancers.'

'What a great honour!'

Sehotep lingered with his favourite. 'What suppleness and rhythm you showed. I assume you have been learning the art since you were very young?'

'Indeed, my lord.'

'What is your name?'

'Olivia.'

'And how old are you?'

'Eighteen.'

'You must be betrothed.'

'No . . . at least, not really. The director of dance is very strict.'

'Perhaps we could perhaps dine together? Let's see . . . This evening?'

The oasis wine was smooth, strong and aromatic. It accompanied a delicious and intimate meal, and Olivia displayed a good appetite as she spoke of the difficulties of her craft. After the meal Sehotep dismissed his servants.

When he gently took her hand, she did not withdraw it. Desire shone in his eyes. He led her to his bedchamber, where he slowly undressed her.

'We neither of us want a child, do we?' she said. 'Be good, and use this preventative salve.' She spread it over her lover's manhood. It was made from crushed acacia thorns, and was smooth and scented.

Olivia cared little for the preliminaries, so Sehotep wasted no time in interminable caresses. Guessing her tastes, he busied himself satisfying her, thinking only of the beautiful girl's pleasure. And in this way they executed a dance in which each rivalled the other in talent.

Afterwards, lying side by side, they savoured the sweet moments following shared ecstasy.

'What does a Bearer of the Royal Seal do?' she asked.

'If I described all my tasks to you, you wouldn't believe me. Do you know, for example, that I am dealing with the next arrival of fat oxen for the Temple of Hathor? A great ritual is being arranged with a view to initiating new priestesses, and it will end with a feast. I am also overseeing the restoration of the temple's doors and shrine.'

'Are you a master-builder, then?'

'No, but I employ all the master-builders in the kingdom and I oversee all the sites, especially in exceptional circumstances.'

'Are the circumstances exceptional now?'

'I also make sure that the secrecy of the temples is respected,' said Sehotep with a smile.

'Is that really so important?'

'If you knew the size of the treasure that will be delivered to the shrine of Neith, you wouldn't doubt it.'

'I love treasure! What will this one be?'

'That's a state secret.'

'You're making me even more curious! Can't you tell me even a little bit about it?'

'It includes something so precious and important that the gods themselves will be enchanted by it.'

Olivia's caresses soon reawakened her lover's desire, and they launched themselves into a new dance of love.

At its end, the young woman jumped out of bed. 'Shall we go out on to the terrace? The view must be wonderful.'

Sehotep acquiesced.

Their naked bodies entwined, they gazed at Memphis, lit up by the full moon.

'How beautiful it is,' she murmured. 'I wouldn't have believed there were so many temples. That enormous one, over there, is that the Temple of Ptah?'

'That's right.'

'And the other one, to the north, who does that belong to?'

'To Neith.'

'The temple that's going to receive the treasure?'

'Well, actually it will only house it temporarily.'

'And then where will it go?'

'Somewhere inaccessible to outsiders.'

'Is it far from here?'

'In Abydos.'

'The sacred domain of Osiris! Do you know it?'

'No one can boast of knowing Abydos.'

She pressed herself against him. 'Tomorrow evening we're dancing at a banquet, but I'm free the evening after that.'

'Unfortunately, I'm not.'

'Then can we meet next week?'

'I am leaving to examine the oxen for the ritual. When I return, the treasure will be housed in the Temple of Neith, and I shall have to accompany it to Abydos. After that we'll be able to see each other again.'

She kissed him passionately.

For the third time in less than an hour, Olivia submitted to Gergu's assault. He paid her well, but he was fat and brutal. She would much have preferred to make love with the subtle and inventive Sehotep – she would always remember that delicious night, when she had been treated like a princess.

'Finished?' she asked.

'You've worn me out, my beauty! A man is never disappointed with you.'

'When will your superior get here?'

'He won't be long. Now, remember to tell him absolutely everything, not leaving out a single detail. If he's pleased, you'll be paid more than you were promised.'

When Medes entered the room where Gergu brought his conquests, Olivia thought him fat and ugly. But then, after Sehotep few men would find favour in her eyes.

'So, young lady,' said Medes, 'you seduced the Bearer of the Royal Seal, did you?'

From the tone of his voice, Olivia guessed that the questioner was dangerous. With him, she must take no chances. 'Gergu promised me some beautiful clothes.'

'And Sehotep gave you a warm welcome?'

'Warmer than I'd hoped.'

'He can't have put up much resistance to a girl as pretty as you. Did you get him to tell you anything?'

'After making love, some men like to boast about their work. Fortunately, Sehotep is one of them.'

'I am listening to you, my pretty. You'll be paid according to the value of your information.'

'He talked about the various things he has to oversee: the great construction sites, the—'

'I know all that. Did he say anything more specific, about something he'll have to do in the near future?'

'He's leaving Memphis to examine some fat oxen and then bring them back here.'

The detail interested Medes, because there were no large celebrations planned for the immediate future. 'What are the oxen going to be used for?'

'For the celebration of a ritual and a banquet at the Temple of Neith.'

'He told you nonsense, little one. The temple's being refurbished.'

'Sehotep's supervising the work. And I know why the banquet's being arranged.'

'Then tell me.'

Olivia smiled. 'Can we agree on my payment first?'

Medes seemed amused. 'You're skilful and intelligent, but don't try your luck too far.'

'If you threaten me, you won't find out any more.'

'What is your highest ambition?'

'To have a fine house in the centre of town.'

'That's exorbitant!'

'I don't think so.'

'Well, let's see what you have to sell. If the merchandise is of high enough quality, I'll agree to the house.'

'I proceeded in stages, so that Sehotep really trusted me. He's vain, and proud of his own importance, and he couldn't resist the temptation to impress me. If I'd shown no curiosity at all he'd have been surprised, and asking too many questions would have made him suspicious. As it was, we reached a comfortable understanding, and he relaxed and told me about a great treasure which is soon to be placed in the shrine of the Temple of Neith – that's when the banquet will be held.'

'A treasure? What kind of treasure?'

'He said there's something in it "so precious and important that the gods themselves will be enchanted by it" – those were his exact words.'

Sehotep never spoke lightly, so Medes was surprised by these solemn words. He asked, 'And he said nothing more specific about it?'

'It will arrive in Memphis next week.'

'Probably a statue to adorn the temple,' said Gergu, disappointed.

'Definitely not,' said Olivia.

'How can you be so sure?' asked Medes.

'Because it will stay there for only a short time.'

'Do you know its final destination?'

'About my house: I'd like to have a document proving it's really mine.'

'Gergu, bring me a papyrus.'

Medes dictated to Gergu a certificate in the correct legal form, in the name of Olivia the dancer. 'Will that do?'

'Well . . . you haven't put your seal on it.'

'You haven't told me where the treasure's going.'

The young woman sensed that she must not go too far. 'Abydos.'

Medes suppressed an exclamation. 'Are you sure?'

'Yes. Sehotep even said that the treasure would be inaccessible to outsiders there.'

Gold! thought Medes. It was the gold that could heal the sacred acacia. Olivia's discovery was worth a lot more than a fine house in Memphis. 'When will you see him again?'

'When he comes back from Abydos, after delivering the treasure.'

Medes had to pace up and down to calm himself. 'Good work, Olivia, very good work.' He tore up the papyrus.

'What are you doing?' she cried. 'You promised—'

'The house is already yours, and you shall live in it from

this very evening. And that is only the first part of your payment.'

'You're making fun of me!'

'Gergu will take you to the house, but you must keep working for me if you want to earn your property certificate. There will be other benefits as well.'

'What more do you want?'

'I want that treasure, and you're going to help me get it.'

'How?'

'By passing yourself off as a priestess of Neith and entering the shrine.'

'But what if I fail?'

'You won't.'

'And what will my payment be?'

'Enough to feed and clothe you for many years; also a manservant and a serving-woman paid by me and entirely at your disposal.'

The dancer began to dream of a life of luxury. 'I'll find out when the treasure is to be deposited in the temple, and I'll tell you at once.'

'Then you can act.'

'Alone?'

'No, one of my men will accompany you and deal with any . . . problems. And he, not you, will remove the treasure from the shrine.'

'All the same, it will be very risky.'

'No more than the career of a dancer. One serious injury, and your future is shattered.'

Olivia understood the threat. She could no longer draw back. 'Then I'll wait to hear from you – in my new house.'

'Take her there, Gergu. It's the second house on the first street at the north-eastern corner of the Temple of Ptah – there's a knife painted in red on the door. The doorkeeper of the house opposite will give you the key. Tell him you're acting on behalf of Bel-Tran.'

Under this Syrian name, Medes owned several houses in Memphis, which he used as storehouses for goods from his various illegal trades. This one, his most recent acquisition, was still empty.

When Olivia and Gergu had left, Medes sat for a while, enjoying the moment. Sehotep's lust had proved his undoing. Senusret would hold him responsible for the theft of the treasure, and the King's House would fall apart. A happy consequence of the plan that was going to make Medes the owner of the healing gold.

19

Though he thought constantly of the treasure, Medes could not neglect his affairs. He had to meet the Phoenician trader again, to check that his business partner was keeping his promises. Taking the usual precautions, he went to the Phoenician's house late at night.

His host welcomed him warmly. The low tables groaned under the weight of delicous cakes, and the wine he gave Medes to drink was excellent.

'I've just received it,' said the Phoenician, pouring some for himself, 'and I'm glad you're the first to taste it. Egypt's wonderful. A marvellous climate, superb wines, cooking which makes losing weight impossible – here, even the gloomiest man abandons his dark thoughts.'

'Your philosophy is not without interest, but I'd like to know if our plans are bearing fruit.'

'Do me the honour of tasting this spiced tart with date wine. My pastry-cook says it's the best in Memphis.'

Medes accepted; he thought the cook was probably right.

'The Egyptians love cedar-wood furniture so much that our stock is almost exhausted,' the Phoenician went on. 'A new consignment, bigger than the previous ones, is on its way. Any problems on your side?'

'No.'

'The pregnancy flasks will arrive in two weeks. According

to my correspondent, they surpass anything on the market in beauty and strength. Also, the opium harvest is the best for ten years, and I've bought it all: my competitors have been . . . eliminated. The same is true of the sesame and moringa oil. How many storehouses are available?'

'You're outstripping me,' admitted Medes.

'I can be patient.'

'I confess that you've surprised me.'

'Coming from you, that's a great compliment, and I shall work non-stop to continue to earn your esteem. But I haven't yet finished the good news: my superior has agreed to meet you. Will the next new moon be convenient for you?'

'It will. In Memphis?'

The Phoenician looked embarrassed. 'No, further south.'

'Where, exactly?'

'Near Abydos.'

'Abydos? That's forbidden territory.'

'He said you know a permanent priest there. He wants to meet you, Gergu and the priest.'

Medes turned pale. Who could know about his alliance with Bega? 'Tell me his name.'

'He'll tell you himself.'

'Be careful, Phoenician! You know very well who I am, so don't make me angry.'

'I've had strict orders, and I must obey them. I'm sure you understand that.'

'I shall not go to this meeting.'

'It would be inadvisable to miss it.'

'Is that a threat?'

'No, no, that isn't my way! I simply believe the meeting will be very beneficial to you.'

Medes was livid with anger. How dare this damned thief try to tell him, the secretary of the King's House, what to do? He said icily, 'Unless you stop spying on me, I shall end our partnership.'

'Wouldn't that be a mistake, when it offers so much?'

'What do you know about Abydos?'

'Me? Nothing at all.'

'But your employer—'

'He merely asked me to suggest this meeting to you.'

The Phoenician seemed sincere. And supposing his mysterious employer was another Abydos priest, hoping to supplant Bega?

'I'm not interested in trying to entrap you,' added the Phoenician, 'and neither is my employer.'

'I must think.'

Losing his position as controller of the game . . . the thought appalled Medes. But sometimes one must pretend to lose in order to win a greater prize later on.

All the permanent priests of Abydos began their duties as soon as dawn broke. The priest who watched over the wholeness of the great body of Osiris checked that the seals on the door of the tomb were in perfect condition. The priest whose actions remained secret because he saw the Mysteries assisted him, before helping the priest who poured the libation of fresh water on to the offering-tables. By celebrating the ancestors, the Servant of the *Ka* was re-establishing the link with the beings of Light, the protectors of Abydos. And the seven female musicians who served Hathor enchanted the divine soul.

Since he had no criticisms of their work, the Shaven-headed One summoned them to Senusret's tomb, which was now finished. He led the procession and passed through the open portal at the centre of the northern part of the surrounding wall. From there, a roadway led to the temple, a vast rectangular building surrounded by a courtyard bordered by a portico with fourteen pillars. Service doors opened off the portico, providing access to the storerooms where offerings and ritual items were kept. Beyond was the pillared hall.

Using water from the temple pools, the Shaven-headed One purified the officiating priests one by one. Then they passed before the statues of Pharaoh and the Great Royal Wife, who, in the serenity of the shrine, celebrated the Mystery of the sacred marriage for all eternity.

On the ceiling of the covered temple shone gold stars. On the walls, the king was depicted communing with the gods, notably Osiris.

In the name of the king the Shaven-headed One offered Ma'at to the Invisible power.

'This temple was built by Osiris to resemble the land of Light,' he intoned. 'Its pillars are the supports of the cosmos, the sacred symbols lie in their rightful places, the perfume of the world beyond is present. Let the ladies of the acacia sing and play music for the Tree of Life.'

The priestesses' voices mingled in a slow chant, which, for as long as it lasted, brought back the harmony that Abydos had known before the acacia's sickness.

Then it was time to return to reality.

'Only two branches have grown green again,' the Shaven-headed One reminded them. 'The pyramid of Dahshur may prevent any further degradation, but I must emphasize the vital necessity of carrying out our tasks rigorously. In the current circumstances, no dereliction of duty will be tolerated.'

It was the turn of the young priestess and Bega to clear the altars and share out the offerings among the temporary priests. After the gods had savoured their intangible aspect, they could nourish human bodies.

'Did your mission to Memphis go well?' asked Bega.

'I gave the pharaoh the message from our superior.'

'Did you like the capital?'

'It is a great city,' she said, 'very lively, and the temples are superb, but I wouldn't like to live there. I prefer the calm of Abydos.'

'The royal court seethes with intrigues and ambitions.

153

Christian Jacq

Here the kingdom finds its real balance. Preserving Abydos is the pharaoh's essential duty, and I am convinced that the construction of this pyramid will be a decisive step.'

'We all hope so.'

Her duties completed, the priestess remained inside the temple for a long time, walking around it and gazing at its adornments. Each carving, each painting, each symbol, radiated an energy that fought against *isefet*, the tendency to destruction and chaos. By creating this sacred dwelling, Senusret was contributing to establishing the heavens on Earth. The priestess felt a vital need for this universe, in which the abstract became perceptible, in which the divine laws illuminated the senses.

Near the gateway in the surrounding wall, she stopped. At her feet, an enormous scarab beetle with a shining carapace was fashioning a ball out of cow-dung by rolling it over and over. When the ball was completed, the master-potter rolled it along with its back feet, moving backwards, from east to west. Then it buried the ball in the loose earth.

'To know the outcome of this work,' said a deep, serious voice behind her, 'you will have to wait twenty-eight days.'

The priestess looked round and saw Senusret.

'Abydos is the city of the divine scarab,' he went on. 'At the end of a moon's cycle, the old Osiris contained within the ball will have confronted the ordeal of death. If righteousness has been respected, the light will emerge from the earth and he will be reborn. A new sun will rise, life will spread into every space. How many people can divine such a mystery by observing this insect, which the non-believer crushes so easily underfoot? It will take many more long hours of work and research for you to perceive this message. Are you determined to pass through another door?'

'It is my dearest wish, Majesty.'

'Are you aware of the danger?'

'I have already discovered so many riches that they would

154

be sufficient fulfilment for an entire lifetime. But to back away from running a risk would be unforgivable cowardice.'

'Then follow me.'

Senusret set off along the paved ramp, fourteen hundred cubits long, that led from his temple to his strange eternal dwelling. It, too, had just been completed. It stood on the edge of the desert, not far from the burial places of the pharaohs of the First Dynasty, and it was protected by a surrounding wall and a temple of welcome.

'We are going to enter the stellar matrix,' the pharaoh warned her. 'Osiris, the creator of the rites and the rule of the temples, is permanently regenerated there. However, a great misfortune has struck him. The universe is subject to crime and death, the night becomes dark, the day disappears, our world falters. Do you wish to experience this ordeal, whatever it costs you?'

The young priestess nodded.

'I have warned you: the way is dangerous, the shadows thick, and the weak heart will not withstand it. Do you still wish to go on?'

'Yes, Majesty.'

In the courtyard were two wells. One was vertical, the other sloped relatively gently, allowing access to a corridor which ended in a chamber with limestone-clad walls and a ceiling imitating wooden roundels with remarkable accuracy. To all appearances, the tomb ended there.

But Senusret entered a section containing quartzite, sandstone and granite. By becoming impregnated with the special fire hidden in the heart of these stones, the young priestess experienced the stages in the alchemical work.

Some blocks were missing from the ceiling. Using this opening, which would later be blocked off, the pharaoh and the priestess slipped into a very narrow chamber, some twelve cubits high.

'We are changing level and world,' explained the pharaoh.

'That which seemed closed and ended was not. By passing upwards, through the limitless spirit, we are opening the door to the hidden Light.'

With the aid of a rope, they helped each other to climb up and reach a horizontal passageway ending in a chamber similar to the one they had just left. Descending the wall with the aid of another rope, they reached the ground again.

The look in the young woman's eyes had changed. She could see the brightness at the heart of the stone.

'We have come back to the same level,' said the king, 'but it is different. By passing through the door of the stellar matrix, you gaze upon the other side of life. Here, human perceptions come to an end. That is why the block of granite you are gazing at will be hidden under limestone cladding and lined with another block. If I wanted to spare you, we would go no further. But I warned you that terrible ordeals await you. You can still choose another destiny, so long as you do not go beyond this limit.'

'I wish to know the Invisible.'

'The price to be paid is very high, and the effort demanded almost superhuman.'

'Is that not the Rule? May Your Majesty continue to guide me.'

They followed a corridor about forty cubits long. When the tomb was closed, blocks of granite would conceal its entrance.

And they came upon the small quartzite-lined chamber of resurrection. In it stood a granite sarcophagus and a chest with canopic jars, illuminated by a gentle glow.

'The sarcophagus is the ship of Osiris,' said Senusret. 'Its lid will hide him from human eyes and destructive spirits, and he will sail peacefully through paradise. The four canopic jars correspond to the four sons of Horus, and are charged with continuing the work of their father Osiris; they will be hidden in the walls of the chamber. A descendant of Ra, Osiris fashioned the Light as he emerged from his mother, the sky. Creation was born out of his body. So he dwells in all provinces and all shrines. It is happiness to love him, for he protects those of just voice and the reborn. Since you want to know him, climb into his ship.'

She hesitated. What the king was proposing was inconceivable. How, in her lifetime, could she undertake such a journey?

But nothing would make her draw back. Leaning on the king's arm for support, she stepped over the edge of the sarcophagus and lay down inside, her eyes gazing up at the stone sky.

'See, journey and know,' ordered Senusret's solemn voice, whose echoes seemed never to fade away. 'Then you shall understand Egypt's greatest secret: those who are initiated into the Mysteries of Osiris can come back from the dead.'

20

After travelling along the Mouth of Peker, a canal leading to the tomb of Osiris and lined with three hundred and sixty-five offering-tables, the members of the Golden Circle of Abydos met far from prying eyes and ears, under the protection of Sobek, whose guards kept watch on the surrounding area.

The royal couple presided over the meeting. Present were the Shaven-headed One, Royal Seal-Bearer Sehotep, High Treasurer Senankh and General Nesmontu.

'Unfortunately, two of our number are absent,' said the king. 'General Sepi is continuing his exploration of the gold mines – so far without result. Our other spiritual brother is carrying out the delicate mission I entrusted to him, and no one suspects his true identity.'

'Majesty,' ventured Sehotep, 'I propose welcoming Khnum-Hotep into the Circle. He is working tirelessly, and everything he does strengthens the unity you restored. He lives according to Ma'at and loyally applies it in every idea he submits to you. By initiating him into the mysteries of the Golden Circle, we will broaden his vision still further.'

'Does anyone oppose his initiation?' asked the pharaoh.

The only answer was silence.

'Since all are agreed, Khnum-Hotep will soon be among us. We must now take stock of the situation frankly.'

'Planting four acacias at the cardinal points is providing

the Tree of Life with good energy,' said the queen. 'It now stands in the centre of a field of power which cannot be crossed by miasmas or sicknesses. But this is only a defence, not a cure.'

'The door of the heavens is closing,' the Shaven-headed One reminded them gravely. 'The ship of Osiris no longer sails normally through the Invisible world, and little by little it is degenerating.'

'Building the pyramid at Dahshur will help us fight,' said Senankh. 'The construction is under way, and the craftsmen's working conditions are excellent. Djehuty is devoting himself unstintingly to the work so that not a moment is lost.'

'But the main question,' the king reminded him sombrely, 'is still unanswered: who put the curse on the Tree of Life?'

'The situation in Syria and Canaan is improving,' said General Nesmontu, 'and my men have questioned a huge number of suspects, including village magicians. So far we have learnt nothing but trifles, yet I have the feeling the attack came from that area.'

'It's possible that the criminal is a courtier from Memphis,' said Sehotep, 'but my investigations in that area have produced nothing. I never miss a social gathering, in the hope that a boastful comment will put me on the right track.'

'And scrutinizing the administrative scribes,' said Senankh, 'has brought no results, either.'

'I have no reason to suspect any of the priests and priestesses of Abydos,' said the Shaven-headed One. 'They perform their duties with complete commitment.'

Senusret could not exclude the sinister possibility that the evil might be coming from the sacred territory of Osiris itself. But the young priestess, who was charged with watching for the smallest sign, had said nothing.

'We are fighting a formidable enemy,' said the king. 'He is intelligent, cunning and endowed with dangerous powers, and he leads a team who are extremely well hidden. Neither the tjaty's men nor Sobek's have managed to see through the fog concealing the enemy.'

'It's frightening,' said Senankh. 'The monster is weaving a web whose threads we cannot see. When we do eventually see it, will it be too late?'

'Is it already too late?' asked the Shaven-headed One worriedly.

'Certainly not,' said Senusret firmly. 'In however small a way, our actions have hindered his. The Acacia of Osiris is still alive, and we are producing the energy necessary to keep it from dying.'

'Yes, Majesty, but the enemy knows that,' Sehotep pointed out, 'so he is likely to do something new, in order to break down our final defences.'

'The site of the pyramid will be protected with the greatest care,' the king assured him, 'and the security measures around Abydos will be strengthened.'

'We cannot remain on the defensive for ever,' said the queen. 'Making weapons capable of fighting such an enemy takes time, but the Golden Circle must never yield to despair. Since we are in a position to save Egypt's spiritual source, that is the only thing we must think of.'

Jutting-Chin awoke with a start. He'd been half asleep, but the sound of footsteps jolted him out of his doze.

This was the tenth night in a row that he had huddled at the corner of a narrow street and watched the little side door of the Temple of Neith. The main door was being refurbished, and was only opened for major ceremonies.

Jutting-Chin liked darkness. He knew all the bad places in Memphis and had robbed more than one unwary traveller. Twice already, his dagger had plunged into the belly of a victim who tried to resist, and the guards wouldn't catch him any time soon, because he had the protection of his employer, Gergu, who wielded a lot of power.

His orders this time were to watch the temple all night and see if anyone took anything into it. Jutting-Chin would be paid well for his reports. He'd treat himself to two or three high-class whores in the best ale-house in the city.

He'd been watching so long that he'd begun to believe nothing would happen. But now there were these footsteps. He peered cautiously out and saw two men carrying something which looked quite heavy. They were whispering, and he caught snatches of sentences: 'Careful . . . very precious . . . Nobody around? . . . it in the shrine . . . split up . . . silence.'

If he had emerged from his hideout, Jutting-Chin would have been intercepted by a third man, who was walking some distance away from his companions, apparently guarding them. The job was soon done, the door was locked with a large key, and the three men dispersed.

Jutting-Chin waited a good while before leaving his post. He took a roundabout way, one which was free of guards, to the meeting-point, and gave Gergu a detailed report.

''The treasure has arrived,' Gergu told Medes. 'A chest carried by two men.'

'That little girl Olivia really has done her work well. When a statesman like Sehotep talks too much, he commits an unpardonable crime. Have you found out about the guards patrols around the temple?'

'Two extra patrols at night, no more. Sobek does not wish to attract attention to the building because, as it's being refurbished, there's normally nothing there to steal.'

'How did the bearers get in?' asked Medes.

'Through a side door. One of them had the key.'

'We must have it, too.'

Gergu smiled. 'Jutting-Chin took a clay impression. We shall have a key tonight.'

'Do you trust that rogue?'

'He's efficient.'

'Has he killed anyone before?'

'He seriously wounded two of his victims.'

'So killing Olivia shouldn't pose him any problems.'

'For the right payment, no.'

'Tell him to leave the slut's corpse there, to compromise Sehotep. The investigation will show that he is both imprudent and guilty.'

'I don't want to do this any more,' said Olivia, with a disdainful pout.

Gergu couldn't believe his ears. 'What do you mean?'

'My career is dancing. I've got a lovely house now, and servants, and I want to devote myself to my art. I don't want to be mixed up in your schemes any more.'

'You're losing your head, girl. Have you forgotten our bargain?'

'I've done my job.'

'You haven't finished it yet. You must go to the temple tonight, pass yourself off as a priestess if you have to, and bring back the treasure – this friend of mine will help you.'

Olivia cast a suspicious eye over Jutting-Chin. 'I don't like him.'

'Nobody's asking you to like him. He's the one who'll help you and spare you any difficulties.'

'You can't make me do it.'

'As you wish, little girl. But don't expect me to get you out of the filthy Memphis ale-house where you'll spend the rest of your miserable life.'

Suddenly frightened, Olivia gripped her protector's arm. 'You're joking, aren't you?'

'My employer never forgives a betrayal. You'll be expelled from your dance troupe, and no one will ever dare employ you again – except me.'

She stepped away. 'All right, I'll do it. But promise me you'll leave me alone afterwards.'

'I promise.'

The reason why Jutting-Chin had escaped the guards for so long was that he knew his ground perfectly and was extremely cautious. So, before going to fetch Olivia, he had spent a long time walking round the Temple of Neith like an ordinary visitor. Stone-cutters worked there until sunset, then the guard patrols began. Jutting-Chin spotted nothing unusual.

He repeated the exercise around Olivia's house. There, too, everything seemed peaceful. So he knocked on the door, using the agreed code. The young woman appeared, dressed in a sober green dress. Round her neck, she wore an amulet in the shape of two crossed arrows, the symbol of Neith.

'You look so respectable that anyone would take you for a real priestess.'

'Let's dispense with personal comments.'

'We're not in a hurry, my pretty one. Wouldn't you like to enjoy a relaxed moment or two with me?'

'Not in the least.'

'You don't know what you're missing.'

'I'll get over it.'

'We won't walk side by side. You follow me, a good distance behind, and if I start running you're to go straight home, because that will mean I've spotted trouble. If you aren't sure, hum to yourself and change direction.'

Nothing untoward happened.

When he reached the side door of the temple, Jutting-Chin used his key. 'It works – come here quickly.'

Olivia ran up and was first to enter the building, which was full of the smell of incense. Ten lamps dimly lit the pillared hall, but the offering-tables were empty. Scaffolding stood against the walls.

'Let's go to the shrine,' whispered Jutting-Chin.

'I'm scared.'

'Scared of what?'

'Of the goddess. With her bow and arrows, she can fire on intruders.'

'Don't talk nonsense, girl.' He gave her a push in the back.

As they reached the threshold of the innermost shrine, a woman's voice hailed them: 'What are you doing here?'

They turned and saw an old priestess, so frail and tiny that a gust of wind could have knocked her over.

Impressed, Olivia bowed to her and said, 'I am a servant of the goddess, and I have come all the way from the provinces to pray to her.'

'At this hour of the night?'

'My boat leaves very early tomorrow morning.'

'How did you get in? And who is this man?'

'My servant. We came in through the side door.'

'The guard must have forgotten to lock it. Have you brought with you the invocations to Neith, creator of the world?'

'They are in my heart.'

'Then compose yourself, and may her seven words illumine your consciousness. I'm tired and I'm going back to bed.'

The old priestess disappeared – fortunately, for Jutting-Chin had been on the point of knocking her out. He waited until he was sure nothing else was going to disturb the calm of the place, then picked up a lamp and ventured into the shrine, followed by Olivia.

An acacia-wood chest stood on a granite plinth.

'There's the treasure!' whispered Jutting-Chin. 'Help me carry it.'

Another voice, a man's this time, rooted them to the spot. 'Good evening, Olivia. So you're nothing but a contemptible little thief, are you?'

'Sehotep! But what . . . I mean, how . . . ?'

'I love women, and I don't dislike quick conquests and brief liaisons, but I am first and foremost Bearer of the Royal Seal. That is why I never talk in bed, except when I have the feeling that someone is setting a trap for me. What better solution than to set one in return?'

Several guards emerged from the darkness.

Jutting-Chin had always scrupulously fulfilled his contracts, an essential condition of being re-employed. So, before turning to run, he slit Olivia's throat as planned.

'Don't kill him!' ordered Sehotep.

One of the guards leapt forward to catch Jutting-Chin, and got a deep wound from a slash of the killer's knife. To save his own life, he plunged his short-sword into Jutting-Chin's heart.

Sehotep did not reproach the guard, for Jutting-Chin had reacted much faster and more fiercely than expected. Unfortunately, neither he nor the dancer could now give him the name of the person behind their crime.

'What shall we do with the chest?' asked the officer commanding the detachment.

'Take it home. It's empty.'

21

Since his appointment as head of all the guards forces in the kingdom, Sobek-Khu had not been sleeping much. Consumed by the need to keep Senusret safe, he complained that the king moved around to much and took far too many risks – Sobek would have preferred him never to leave his palace. But Senusret ignored advice to be careful, and the Protector had to accept the situation, however worrying it might be.

Despite the burden of his office, Sobek continued to train for at least an hour every day with the hand-picked soldiers who guarded the king's person. There were only a few of them, but they were extremely efficient; they never left the king's side when he was on his travels, and knew how to react instantly to any threat.

This morning, Sobek was in a bad mood. He knew it was not easy to set up a good information network in a reunified Egypt, particularly in the provinces that had formerly been hostile to Senusret; but why had the guards learnt nothing about any of the rebels? Criminals never stayed huddled in the shadows for long, because they loved to have people talk about them. Endangering the country by attacking its spiritual centre was surely an exploit they would want to boast about. And yet . . . nothing.

Sobek badly wanted to be able to tell the king he had a lead, so he often summoned the commanders of the various security and investigation forces and told them to redouble their efforts. Even if the criminal or criminals were the accomplices of demons, they could not be invisible.

Following the incident at the Temple of Neith, Sobek and Sehotep met at Sehotep's house.

'Did you know Olivia,' asked Sobek, 'before you met her at the school of dance?'

'No. And she succumbed to my charms so quickly that I immediately suspected she was working for someone. Have you questioned the dancing-mistress?'

'Yes, and all the other dancers. None of them knew anything. You take too many risks. Suppose she'd intended to kill you?'

Sehotep shook his head. 'No, that wasn't her style. Anyway, after Senankh's problems, I was sure someone would make me a target, too, and try to discredit me, so I was on my guard. I think our enemy has decided to attack each member of the King's House and destroy the pharaoh's inner circle. So tell me, what have you found out about Olivia?'

'Nothing interesting, I'm afraid. She really did want to make dancing her career.'

'Did she have an official lover?'

'No, only brief relationships. We've found the last two men, but their interrogation yielded nothing useful. To all appearances, Olivia was just an ordinary girl.'

'Only in appearance – someone was certainly using her.'

'I know,' said Sobek. 'And people don't collaborate by chance with a hardened criminal like Jutting-Chin.'

'That one certainly wasn't acting on his own initiative.'

'Of course not, but it's impossible to identify his employer. Jutting-Chin worked for whoever paid the most.'

'He'd been ordered to kill Olivia, don't you think?'

'Probably.'

'In every gang of evildoers, there's always a weak link.'

'In this case, I'm beginning to doubt that more and more.'

*

'Both dead? You're sure?' asked Medes anxiously.

'Absolutely sure,' replied Gergu.

'Did the guards have time to learn anything from them?'

'To judge from Sobek's anger, definitely not. As a good professional, Jutting-Chin honoured his contract and killed the dancer, and then he himself was killed while trying to escape. If you want my opinion, we came dangerously close to disaster.'

'I underestimated Sehotep,' conceded Medes. 'How was I to guess that he'd lay such a cunning ambush for us?'

'Senankh and Sehotep – two failures,' said Gergu bitterly. 'The King's House are difficult targets.'

'The pharaoh didn't choose them at random, and they've just proved their worth. But they're only men. We'll find their weak points eventually.'

Gergu sank into a low armchair. 'We're rich, well-respected and influential. Why don't we content ourselves with what we've got?'

'He who does not go forward goes backwards,' said Medes. 'Don't let these setbacks dishearten you. Destabilizing the king is vital.'

Gergu poured himself some wine. 'From now on, everyone close to him will be on their guard.'

'Then we must be cleverer than they are. I know where to deliver the decisive blow.' Medes set out his plan. It would require a lot of work, but nothing unreasonable. If it was successful, Senusret would indeed be greatly weakened.

Yet again Sobek's meeting with the guards commanders had produced nothing: none of them had any serious leads. In the streets and taverns, none of their informants had heard anyone boasting of deeds that might put the kingdom in danger.

One of the commanders seemed embarrassed. 'Several

annoying complaints have reached me,' he said. 'They come from four provinces, one in the North, three in the South.'

'Who are the plaintiffs?'

'Some itinerant traders who were apparently unjustly arrested, and a businesswoman from Sais and a Theban farmer who were roughly treated by guards officers.'

'They're unimportant.'

'Well, perhaps, sir, but incidents like those are normally very rare, and this sounds almost like an epidemic.'

'Launch an official investigation. If offences really have been committed, I shall punish the guilty parties.'

As he left his office, Sobek bumped into one of Khnum-Hotep's scribes, who said, 'Commander, the tjaty wants to see you urgently.'

Perhaps he has an important clue, thought Sobek.

He would have preferred to find it himself, but this was no time for professional vanity. Valuable information would be welcome, wherever it came from. But when he saw the tjaty's grim expression, he realized the news was not good.

'His Majesty holds you in high esteem,' said Khnum-Hotep, 'and so do I, but—'

'But I haven't produced any results, and I deserve to be reprimanded. All the same, I assure you that my men are searching everywhere, relentlessly.'

'I know, and I'm not criticizing you about that.'

'Then what is it?'

'You are responsible for the free movement of people, aren't you?'

'That's right.'

'I've just received several detailed complaints about instances of unjust curtailment of that freedom.'

'They're trifling matters.'

'On the contrary, since the reunification of Egypt there are no longer barriers between the provinces and everyone must be able to go from one place to another in safety. The guards' role is to reassure people, not to impose unnecessary controls. The number and seriousness of these complaints show that your men are becoming too authoritarian, which is deplorable.'

'I have ordered an investigation.'

'Please see that it reaches its conclusions as quickly as possible, and that the resulting punishments will be a warning to others. I shall overlook these offences, so long as they do not happen again.'

On the boat taking him to Memphis, Iker was wary of all the passengers, from the captain down to a hirsute peasant slumbering on his bundles. The young man did not even notice the beauty of the landscape, so obsessed was he with his goal of killing the tyrant.

He was glad now that he had undergone military training during his stay in the Oryx province, for at the fateful moment he would need strength, courage and determination, like a soldier in battle.

Iker felt incapable of killing a human being in cold blood. But the man he must kill was no ordinary human being. Senusret was behaving like a bloodthirsty tyrant and leading his country to misfortune and ruin. How many murders had he committed to consolidate his vile power?

A voice beside him roused him from his thoughts: 'I say, friend, are these fine writing-materials yours?' An old man was peering at the scribe's equipment that Iker had laid at his feet.

'Yes, they are.'

'Then you can read and write! I dreamt of learning to, but there was the land, marriage, children, the flock – in short, life passed in the blink of an eye and I didn't have time to study. Now I'm a widower and have passed my land on to my sons. I've settled in a little house in Memphis, near the port. Are you going there, too?'

'Yes.'

'I bet you have a job there. You're very lucky. It's the most beautiful city in the land. You know it already, I take it?'

'No, I don't.'

'So it's your first stay in Memphis. I remember mine – I was struck dumb by it. Prepare yourself for a thousand and one discoveries. I say, would you be kind enough to do something for me?'

'That depends.'

'Oh, nothing complicated. I have to write a letter to the authorities about my taxes, which ought to be lowered now that I'm retired, but I don't know the right words.'

'There are public scribes who—'

'I know, I know, but as we're here and you have the time, it would be simpler. Look, I'm not an ungrateful man. If you help me, you can stay with me in Memphis, free of charge, until you find somewhere better.'

The proposition was attractive, but might it be a trap set by the guards? No, Iker couldn't see them using an old man like this, so he decided to take a chance.

'All right,' he said, 'I accept.'

'Thank you. You'll make my life much easier. Shall we begin?'

Iker opened his travelling-bag, and took out a piece of papyrus and a brush. After diluting a little black ink, he listened carefully to the old man's request, asked him for the exact details and wrote a letter incorporating the kinds of phrases the tax authorities liked. When the tax inspector saw that it was written by a scribe who knew the appropriate laws and practices, he would almost certainly grant the old man's request.

'You write extremely well, my boy,' said the old man. 'I'm very lucky, too. If you like, I'll show you the city – I know every corner of it. But perhaps you'll be too busy?'

'No, I have a few free days before I take up my post.'

'You won't regret it. I'll turn you into a native of Memphis.'

Wisely, the old man had Iker write a second letter, addressed to his tax-collector's superior. It was a tricky letter to compose, because Iker had to find words which would persuade the official to keep an eye on his subordinate, but which would not annoy either of them.

The old man was an inveterate chatterbox. He loved to talk on and on about his perfectly ordinary life, giving a host of details which were of interest to nobody but himself, and never once repeated himself.

As they approached Memphis, he seemed rejuvenated. 'Here we are. Look at the port, with its never-ending quays and its hundreds of boats. All kinds of riches end up here. And the storehouses are the largest in Egypt. Watch the dock-labourers – it's fascinating.'

The place was like an anthill.

'I live not far from here. Can you carry my baggage?' Briskly, the old man forced a way through the crowd.

Iker followed him. Alone in a strange city, how would he have managed? Destiny had come to his rescue.

His companion lived in a humble district where small two-storey houses alternated with smarter ones. Children were playing in the street, housewives were exchanging recipes and gossip, and a seller of flatcakes was hawking his wares.

'This is it,' said the old man. He pushed open a door on which a bearded, laughing Bes was painted in red, to drive away evil spirits.

On the threshold, Iker stopped dead: he could hear that there was someone inside. He put down the baggage. How many men were waiting for him? Would he manage to escape from them?

A sturdy sixty-year-old woman appeared, broom in hand.

'My cleaning-woman,' said the old man. 'When I'm not here, she looks after the house.'

'Is this one of your sons?' she asked suspiciously.

'No, a scribe who's taking up a new post in Memphis. He'll be staying here for a while.'

'I hope he's clean and well-brought-up and won't make everything dirty.'

'I promise I won't,' said Iker.

'We'll see – I prefer actions to words.'

'Your room is upstairs,' said the old man. 'Settle yourself in, and then we'll go and have dinner at a good tavern.'

As soon as he was alone, Iker took the dagger from his tunic, laid it on the bed and gazed at it for a long time. Nothing was going to make him forget his mission.

22

The captain of the grain-boat was enjoying a midday meal of some chickpeas pounded with garlic. In less than four hours he'd be in Memphis and reunited with his wife, an uninhibited woman who loved sailors' stories.

'Sir, there's a river guards' boat coming,' his second-in-command informed him.

'Are you sure?'

'They're ordering us to dock.'

Furiously, the captain abandoned his food and headed for the prow. A fast boat with about ten armed men on board was indeed barring the way.

'Compulsory inspection,' shouted the officer.

'On whose orders?'

'Commander Sobek-Khu's.'

Given the commander's reputation, the captain knew it was best not to argue. So he docked immediately and allowed the guards to come aboard.

'What's going on?' he asked.

'The rules for river travel have been changed,' replied the officer. 'You must wait until tomorrow to return to the capital.'

'You're joking! I have to get there at the specified time.'

'What's more, we must inspect the cargo.'

'My documents are all in order,' said the captain.

'That's what we're going to check – without any obstruction.'

'That's not my way.'

'Then show them to me while my men do their work.'

The captain obeyed.

At sunset, the verdict was reached. 'You are in breach of the law,' said the officer. 'Your boat is in poor condition and overladen, and your crew is too small. You will be permitted to travel on, but you will have to pay a heavy fine.'

When the river guards had gone, the captain punched the hand-rail. 'This is outrageous! Sobek has no right to change the rules whenever he likes. I'm going to complain to the tjaty's office.'

The old man never stopped talking, but he was an invaluable guide. There was now nothing that Iker did not know about Memphis. He'd explored the port area, the centre of the city and the outer northern and southern areas; he had admired the temples of Hathor, Ptah and Neith, strolled in Ankh-tauy, 'the Life of the Two Lands', and seen the shrines to the memory of the dead pharaohs; he had travelled by boat along the canals, walked round the ancient white-walled citadel and dined in the best inns; and all this in exchange for some business letters written for the old man and his relations.

Several times, Iker and his mentor had gazed at the palace. They could not get very near it, because the many soldiers guarding it prevented them.

'Is the pharaoh afraid of being killed?' asked Iker.

'Egypt is stable and at peace again now, but that doesn't please everyone. The families of the former provincial governors don't like the king much, because they've lost many of their old privileges. But Tjaty Khnum-Hotep has them well under control, and ordinary people think Senusret's wonderful. A king like him is a great boon to the country.'

Iker realized that he could not criticize the tyrant in any way, because the old man was one of the people under his spell.

'Sobek-Khu's work must be very difficult,' he ventured.

'That's what we all think, my boy, but he's got broad shoulders. Besides, if you so much as set eyes on him you're ready to confess everything, even crimes you haven't committed. So as long as the king's protected by Sobek, he has nothing to fear.' The old man paused and licked his lips. 'I'm thirsty. Are you?'

He had a remarkable capacity for drink, and Iker had difficulty keeping up with him. Fortunately, alcohol made him talkative, so Iker was becoming extremely well informed about Memphis.

That night, as almost every night, the same memories mingled in Iker's dreams: being tied to *Swift One*'s mast, the shipwreck, the Island of the *Ka*, the snake asking if he would save his world, the legendary land of Punt, the false guard who'd tried to kill him, his old master talking to him of an undecipherable destiny, and then the young priestess, so beautiful, so radiant, so inaccessible.

He awoke with a start and gripped the handle of the dagger to reassure himself. He knew what his future would be.

'Why aren't you eating this morning?' asked the old man. 'A good breakfast is very important.' Certainly, his own appetite never flagged.

'Forgive me,' said Iker. 'I'm not hungry.'

'Don't you like my cooking?'

'It's excellent, but I've a knot in my stomach.'

'I think I know why. There's a delay in granting you your new post, isn't there?'

The young man's silence spoke volumes.

'Don't worry too much; the authorities always move slowly. You're earning your living the right way, writing letters for the local people. But tell me, what exactly are you hoping for?'

Iker had foreseen this question. 'I'm not only a scribe but also a temporary priest, so I must apply to the temples.'

'Ah, I see. You'll soon become someone important, and you think I'm very unimportant.'

'Oh no,' said Iker, 'it isn't that at all. On the contrary, I don't know how to thank you for your hospitality.'

'You saved me a lot of trouble with the tax authorities, and it's thanks to you that I'm enjoying my retirement. It's been a great blessing and a great stroke of luck having the benefit of your skills, but I know it won't last for ever.'

Iker went to the Temple of Ptah, which was surrounded by administrative buildings, workshops, storehouses and libraries.

A guard escorted him to the steward, who asked, 'What is your name?'

The young man decided to be honest. 'Iker.'

'And your rank?'

'Scribe and temporary priest of the Temple of Anubis at Kahun.'

'Hm, that is worth quite something. What are you hoping for?'

'I've been working as a librarian, and I'd like to complete my legal training while making myself useful.'

'Do you need lodgings?'

'If possible.'

'I'll introduce you to the priest in charge of recruitment; he will test your skills.'

The test included several pitfalls, but in General Sepi's classes Iker had learnt how to avoid them, so it was a mere formality. He was taken on for a period of three weeks, followed by two rest days. If he gave satisfaction, he would be taken on again.

Surrounded by books again, Iker felt a kind of peace.

Plunging once again into the basic texts, whether religious, literary or of new learning, gave him profound joy. His task was to check an old inventory, correct any errors and add the new acquisitions, and as he worked he came to appreciate the great wealth of the library. From time to time, he felt the assessing gaze of the overseer on him, weighing up the new scribe's abilities, but he enjoyed his work so much that he soon forgot about it.

When the overseer tapped him on the shoulder, Iker jumped.

'The working day is over, my boy.'

'Already?'

'Working beyond normal hours requires special authorization, which I cannot give you. Besides, if you work too hard and too quickly, you'll make your colleagues jealous. You should keep to your place.'

Without a word of protest, Iker got up and left the library.

The overseer led him to the building reserved for temporary priests, and showed him his room. 'Tomorrow,' he said, 'you will take part in the sharing out of the offerings after they have been consecrated. As it's past the time of the evening meal, I shall wish you good night.'

Iker slid a hand into the bag containing his scribe's materials, which never left him, withdrew the dagger and clasped it to his chest. He did this every evening, to strengthen his determination.

Shaved, purified and perfumed, Iker was handed some round, golden-crusted loaves by a permanent priest, and offered them to each of the officiating priests at the morning ritual. He was the last to taste the food, which was accompanied by fresh milk.

'You're new, aren't you?' said a slightly stooped man aged around thirty. 'What is your speciality?'

'Law.'

'Where did you learn it?'

'In the province of the Hare.'

'The city of Thoth provides excellent training, but you'll have to relearn a lot, now that there are no longer any independent provincial lawgivers. The tjaty heads the legal process, applying the law of Ma'at.'

'Where can I study?'

'At the lawyers' school, near the palace and the tjaty's offices.'

'I take it that I'll need a recommendation?'

'If you do your work well, you'll get one.'

In the weeks that followed, Iker's behaviour was exemplary. He merged into the mass of temporary priests, and worked neither too little nor too much. Armed with a recommendation from his superior, he went to the school, where the prevailing atmosphere was one of great studiousness. His fellow students showed neither friendliness nor hostility to the newcomer, who attended the classes assiduously. It was immediately clear that he had reached the required level of knowledge, and so would not be sent away as a good number of applicants had been.

One day, during a meal break, a thin, lively-looking student came over to Iker and asked, 'Are you a native of Memphis?'

'No, I'm from the Theban region.'

'That's a beautiful area, they say.'

'Thebes is much smaller than Memphis.'

'Do you like it here?'

'I came to learn.'

'You won't be disappointed. The teachers give us a hard life, but they train us extremely well. The best students will enter the highest levels of government, but that won't mean an easy life, because the tjaty has reorganized all the state secretariats, which now have to prove that they're efficient. No one has a job for life any more, and there's no question of lolling about in one's office, or resting on one's laurels. It's as well not to make Khnum-Hotep angry, and the pharaoh's just as strict, so one can't count on leniency from anyone.'

'Does the king spend much time in Memphis?'

'Oh yes, a lot. Every morning, the tjaty reports to him on important matters concerning the country's government – and since unification there's no shortage of them.'

'Have you ever seen Senusret?'

'Twice, when he was coming out of his palace. You can't miss him: he's the tallest man in the whole of Egypt.'

'Why are there so many guards and soldiers round the palace?'

'Because of Sobek the Protector, the man responsible for the pharaoh's safety – a real maniac! He probably thinks disappointed dignitaries will take against His Majesty. Besides, the situation in Canaan is getting more and more venomous. General Nesmontu seems to have things under control, but you can never tell with terrorists. One of them might be mad enough to try and kill the king.'

23

'Kindly explain these, Sobek,' demanded Tjaty Khnum-Hotep, showing him the complaints that had been piling up on his desk for several days.

Sobek examined the documents. Captains of cargo-boats were protesting vigorously about the arbitrary change in the rules governing river travel, the unjustified increase in taxes and the unacceptable behaviour of the forces of order.

'I gave no such orders,' said Sobek.

'But you are in charge of all the kingdom's guards forces, and you are responsible for river travel?'

'I don't deny it.'

'Then you are not in proper control of your men. That is serious, Sobek, extremely serious. Because of their inexcusable conduct, Pharaoh's reputation is in danger of being damaged – even the process of unification could be called into question. If local forces make the law, intercept cargo vessels and hold them to ransom, what will be the end of it all? We might even see the return of provincial governors.'

'For the moment, I have no plausible explanation.'

'That is a most alarming admission. Do you think you're still worthy of your office?'

'I intend to prove it to you. These regrettable incidents will soon be explained.'

'I shall await your report – and concrete results.'

Sobek-Khu rushed about like a whirlwind, and his inspectors carried out detailed investigations. He himself questioned all the captains and compared their statements. The information he gathered made the truth plain, so he went to see the tjaty again.

'My men have not violated the travelling regulations,' he said, 'except in one case where they were deceived by false documents.'

'What do you mean?'

'That a gang of skilful criminals is trying to cause trouble.'

'Have they been arrested?'

'I'm afraid not.'

'Are you serious?'

'Unfortunately, I am.'

'Is the civil peace at risk?'

'We mustn't exaggerate,' protested Sobek. 'I'm certain now that it was a small, well-prepared, very mobile group, not an army. From now on there will be two river guards aboard every cargo-boat, and in addition I shall alter my command code. It is your task, Tjaty, to make it known that the rules of navigation remain unchanged and that no captain must react to provocation if someone tries to convince him otherwise.'

Khnum-Hotep grew calmer. 'Could these bandits be linked to the attacks on the acacia?'

'There's no proof of it, but this isn't the first instance of this kind of troublemaking. The measures I'm suggesting will restore calm, and of course the hunt has begun and the criminals will end up in prison.'

'These two successive scandals have caused a great deal of hostile gossip about you, Commander.'

Sobek shrugged. 'I don't care.'

'Well I do! If you're found to be incompetent, I shall be forced to take steps. Don't forget that you're also in charge of Pharaoh's safety.'

'Do you think His Majesty is under threat?'

The tjaty didn't answer the question, but said, 'I shall continue to support you, but I will not tolerate any further regrettable incidents.'

Iker divided his time between work as a temporary priest at the Temple of Ptah and law classes at the school, where his quiet conscientiousness made him respected by all. At the temple, he had contact with the priests' superior, the guardian of the Mysteries, the official in charge of clothing, the ritualists, the accounting-scribes, and the officials in charge of the grain stores and livestock. But none of these grand individuals, who were distant with young scribes, would tell him what he wanted to know: the king's daily habits and the way to approach him. The best solution seemed to be not to rush anything and to wait for the right opportunity. But how long would he have to wait?

At the end of a law class on the King's House and its responsibilities, the teacher announced a piece of news which made Iker's heart leap. The whole class was to put forward proposals for reforms which would help to simplify the legislative process. The three whose proposals were judged the best would have the privilege of being presented to the Bearer of the Royal Seal, who usually brought them before the pharaoh in order to demonstrate the high quality of their teaching.

As his subject, Iker chose the management of the grain stores, stressing the necessity to build up reserves in the major towns and to facilitate their distribution when the annual flood was inadequate. But many of the relevant documents were out of date, and this negligence meant that unfair arrangements were being allowed to continue. Iker cut his hours of sleep and rest to a minimum, and worked furiously hard on his proposals.

The day came when the results were to be announced. The

two first names spoken by the teacher were not his. But the third and last . . .

A student elbowed him in the ribs. 'Are you asleep, Iker? Anybody would think you didn't care, but we were all dreaming of it. And here you are, one of the chosen who are going to meet the pharaoh!'

The unlucky ones were good losers, and congratulated the winners. Iker accepted their good wishes distractedly, for he was already thinking of the moment when he would rush at the tyrant and stab him.

Each dressed in an impeccable kilt, an immaculate tunic, a good-quality short wig, leather sandals, the three apprentice lawyers gave an impression of sober elegance, but had difficulty hiding their nervousness.

As he slid the dagger into the folds of his clothing, Iker had pondered. Weren't visitors searched, whoever they were? If the weapon was found, he would immediately be arrested and imprisoned. But without it he could no longer strike down the tyrant, so he would have to seize a guard's sword and act at lightning speed. In the end, he returned it to its hiding-place.

The search took place without incident. A secretary and a palace guard escorted the little group to Sehotep's audience chamber.

'Be concise,' the teacher advised them. 'The Bearer of the Royal Seal has only a very short time available.'

The great man made a deep impression on the students. The first stammered, the second forgot a key point in his argument, and Iker set out his ideas with relative confusion.

'Interesting . . . My departments may perhaps retain a few elements,' said Sehotep. 'I hope your pupils will continue to study and learn better control of themselves.'

'When will you present them to His Majesty, my lord?' asked the teacher.

'That custom is no longer in force.'

*

Iker had two problems to solve: getting into the palace with his dagger, and then being admitted to the king's presence. They both seemed insoluble, but he would not let himself give up. So far, fate had smiled on him: he had thought settling in Memphis would be very difficult, but doors had opened to him.

He decided the best course was to continue being a model student and an exemplary priest. When his teacher suggested a long training-course, he accepted immediately; and when the High Priest of the Temple of Ptah asked him to assist the star-watchers by spending nights observing the sky, he obeyed without question. Star-watching offered a special advantage: from the roof of the temple, you could see the royal palace. Iker did not only note the positions of the stars; he also studied the guards' comings and goings, in the hope of finding a flaw in the security system.

His hopes were dashed. There were just as many guards at night as there were during the day, and they were relieved with a precision and speed that ruled out any intrusion. Sobek was highly skilled, and so were his men.

Iker thought of questioning the official responsible for security at the Temple of Ptah, in order to learn more about the habits of the king's personal guard, but abandoned the idea because it might have aroused suspicion. How could he glean information about the palace and find out exactly where inside it the pharaoh lived?

Getting into the building seemed impossible, so the only other option was stabbing the tyrant outside, if Iker could find out the dates of his movements. But how?

Gergu had spent the evening in an ale-house. A Syrian prostitute had been docile, and the wine was good: when he emerged, he had difficulty walking in a straight line. He managed to find the way to Medes's house, but the door-keeper made him wait while his name was sent in.

When he staggered into Medes's office, Medes immediately said, 'You'd better sit down.'

'I'm thirsty.'

'Have a cup of water.'

'*Water?* To celebrate our success? The news I've got for you merits wine – and the best wine, at that,'

Medes gave in. Gergu's expression suggested that he was still in possession of his wits. Besides, this optimistic mood must not be broken.

'It's working splendidly,' declared Gergu, draining his wine-cup. 'The rumour's spreading wildly and feeding off itself. I didn't believe it, but you were right to attack Sobek.'

'Have you seen to it that the false river guards were paid properly?'

'I used third parties – all very satisfactory, and no one will be able trace them back to us. However, we can't make further use of that system, because Sobek has taken radical measures. There are some of his men on every single trading-boat, and all the checks have been strengthened.'

'That doesn't matter. We've achieved what we wanted: we've tarnished Sobek's reputation. I hear that the tjaty himself is beginning to doubt his competence – and even his honesty.'

Gergu poured himself more wine. 'I can just imagine his rage! He thought he was untouchable, but he must be having nightmares now.'

'Then we'll move on to the next phase,' decided Medes.

'Wouldn't that be . . . unwise?'

'If we stop now, we'll have wasted all that time and effort. It isn't enough to weaken Sobek. We must get rid of him altogether.'

Suddenly, Gergu didn't feel like drinking any more. 'Let's be patient. The tjaty may dismiss him.'

'There aren't yet sufficiently serious charges against him, and Sobek is still close to the king. What we must do is to provide proof of his unworthiness.'

'I don't see how.'

'You have a few reliable men who can lie confidently, haven't you?'

'No problem.'

'Then we'll get rid of Sobek by dealing him a crushing blow in a way which will turn the tjaty's suspicion into certainty.'

Every time the Phoenician met the Herald, his stomach clenched so tightly that he momentarily lost his appetite. The elusive falcon-man both terrified and fascinated him. Ever since the falcon's talons had almost killed him, leaving indelible marks in his flesh, the trader had known that he would always work for him and would never escape from him. Making the best of his lot, he was making as much profit as possible from it, and being entirely honest with his formidable master. As soon as he had new information he passed it on to Herald straight away, because neither delay nor negligence would be forgiven.

There were no cakes set out on the tables, there were fewer cushions on the chairs and couches – in fact the whole room was notably more austere. The Phoenician tried everything he could think of to avoid being reprimanded.

'Give me some salt,' ordered the Herald.

'At once, my lord.'

The Herald glanced disdainfully round the room. What was the use of all this luxury? Once the true faith held sway, it would be eradicated.

The trader held a bowl out to him. 'This is the very best from the oases, my lord.'

The Herald quenched his thirst with the foam of Set. 'What news have you for me?'

'Only rumours, my lord, but they're so persistent that they can't be unfounded. People say that Sobek-Khu is suspected of restricting people's free movement and of arbitrarily altering the rules of river travel. Everything's been hushed up, but relations between him and Tjaty Khnum-Hotep are said to be getting worse.'

'In your opinion, can this man Sobek be bought?'

'Definitely not. He's a dedicated, hard-headed officer, and he's incorruptible. Someone's trying to compromise him so that he'll lose his post.'

'Do you know who?'

'No, my lord. I'm trying to find out, but I can't say where my inquiries will lead. Anyone who dares attack Sobek the Protector must be as dangerous as they are cautious.'

'Will the tjaty be deceived by false accusations?'

'It's unlikely, but Khnum-Hotep oversees the proper application of the law, and his reputation for thoroughness is well deserved. If he's given real proof, something really plausible, he'll have to dismiss Sobek. Once the Protector's out of the way, the whole security system will fall apart, at least for a while. And then Senusret will be vulnerable.'

24

Iker loved the early mornings at the temple. After the dawn purification, taking part in the offering-rites brought him a calm which surprised him each time. As he gazed upon the sacred lake, he forgot his worries and his terrifying plan. Life once more became harmonious and peaceful, as if evil no longer existed. But when the rites ended he was faced with reality again.

'You look tired,' observed the High Priest. 'It's time you stopped helping the star-watchers. I have a new task for you. It may not be to the liking of a lover of books and the law, but a scribe should be trained in all disciplines.'

Iker bowed. 'I am at your service.'

'I consider obedience a major virtue, Iker, and you have it. From today, you are in charge of checking meat.'

The decision, which could not be disputed, distressed Iker deeply because he couldn't bear seeing animals killed. He always thought of North Wind, whom he'd had to leave in Kahun in Sekari's care.

Pale-faced and heavy of limb, Iker went to the sacrificial slaughterhouse and butchery, with their staffs of strong men – complainers and weaklings had no place in this team. Accustomed to dealing death and to the dying looks of the cattle, which knew their fate, they kept to themselves and did not willingly mingle with the priests and scholars in their immaculate linen robes.

Iker arrived at the time of their midday meal break. With healthy appetite, the butchers were enjoying grilled cuts of beef. They did not interrupt their meal, but looked up suspiciously at the intruder.

'Who are you?' asked the master-butcher, a sturdy fifty-year-old with white hair and a barrel chest.

'My name is Iker. I've just been appointed to check the meat.'

'Another petty scribe who takes us for fraudsters! Have you eaten?'

'I'm not hungry.'

'Don't you like grilled meat?'

'Yes, but . . . not just now.'

'Our work disgusts you, is that it? You aren't the only one, my boy, but someone has to kill the animals and provide good food for the meat-eaters – which means everyone.'

'I don't in the least despise your work – though I confess I couldn't do it.'

The butcher tapped him on the shoulder. 'Don't worry, we won't ask you to. Go on, eat. Then you can write down the names and number of the pieces we've cut this morning.'

Iker had to learn to identify fillet, sirloin, spleen, liver, offal and all the other parts of a cow's body. He recorded the findings of the animal-doctor who, after examining each animal's blood, guaranteed its purity. He got used to the particular atmosphere of the place, and ensured that the strictest cleanliness was observed. But he never watched the slaughter, which was carried out by at least four men, led by the master-butcher, who was the only one who could cut the victim's throat with one slice of his knife, so that the animal suffered as little as possible.

Gradually, trust and respect grew up between Iker and the craftsmen. He did not go out of his way to find fault or inconvenience them; they were a little less rough and ready.

One evening, at the end of the day's work, the master-butcher and the scribe sat down side by side for their meal of beer and dried beef.

'Where did you learn your trade?' asked the butcher.

'In the province of the Oryx and then at Kahun, where I became a temporary priest of Anubis.'

'Anubis the jackal cleanses the desert by ridding it of carrion, which he transforms into vital energy. It may surprise you, but we're colleagues: I'm a priest, too, and so is every other master-butcher in Egypt, because slaughter must be a ritual. There's no cruelty in my heart or my hand. I thank the animal for giving its life to prolong ours. The priestesses of Hathor sanctify our work – which is not without its dangers.'

'Do you mean the animals' unexpected reactions?'

'No, we know how to immobilize them with ropes. I mean the confrontation with the fearsome Set himself.'

'When does that happen?'

'Every time we touch the left foreleg, the strongest one. Look up at the night sky and you'll see it.* The priests present this leg to the gate of the world beyond, so that it will open and allow the souls of the reborn to enter. If the rite wasn't performed, it would stay closed and the fire of Set would destroy Egypt.'

Iker was astonished. He asked, 'The souls of the dead pharaohs dwell in the stars that surround the Pole Star, so are they placed under Set's protection?'

'They feed on his strength, as the living pharaoh does on the meat I take him.'

'You . . . you know Senusret?'

'"Know" is a very big word, but I do indeed have the privilege of seeing him once a week, when he's in Memphis.

*A reference to the Great Bear.

On those evenings he likes to take his evening meal alone. I and my assistant present him with meat rich in energy.'

At that moment, Iker knew he had at last found the right way to get close to the tyrant. He must keep calm, he told himself, and show neither impatience nor enthusiasm.

'That's a heavy responsibility,' he said, 'because it would be unthinkable to disappoint him.'

'It's just a matter of doing my job properly.'

'I've heard that the king isn't an easy man.'

'You can certainly say that! He towers over everyone, and no one can meet his eyes. When he speaks, his deep voice penetrates right into your soul and you feel tiny. And then there's his almost inhuman calm, which nothing ever seems to disturb. And I haven't mentioned his authority – the sages who chose him as pharaoh chose well.'

'Fortunately,' ventured Iker, 'he is extremely well protected.'

'Under Sobek's security arrangements, Senusret really has nothing to fear. Only known individuals get through the checks. Even I and my assistant are searched several times before we're permitted to enter His Majesty's apartments.'

Iker thought he now knew enough to construct a plan that might have a chance of success. But for fear of making the master-butcher suspicious he changed the subject. 'A lot of people think there may be war in Canaan. Do you?'

'Not at all. The king's right to act firmly in Canaan, because the place is full of potential rebels. They think of nothing but making trouble, even when it harms their own people. Only a general of Nesmontu's stamp can break them. What do you think of this grilled meat?'

'I've never tasted better.'

'It's the king's favourite food.'

'You really are very lucky to meet him.'

'If you became my assistant, you'd have that luck, too.'

'I'm only an accounting-scribe. I couldn't possibly carry out the craft of a butcher.'

'You wouldn't need to if you were merely going to accompany me to the palace and carry the dish of meat. If my current assistant chooses another profession, I'll gladly take you with me at least once. His Majesty will be happy to meet a young and highly skilled scribe.'

Slender-Nose had just finished mending the sail of his boat so that he could go and sell his stock of pottery in the nearest town, about an hour downriver. In his village, two days' voyage from Memphis, the housewives had all the pottery they needed, but there was a shortage of strong, good-sized boats.

Two men in the uniform of river guards came towards him along the riverbank. 'Are you Slender-Nose?'

'I am.'

'And you're the village potter?'

'As far as I know, there isn't another one.'

'Does this boat belong to you?'

'Yes.'

'You and your boat are requisitioned for compulsory work.'

'Compulsory work? What compulsory work?'

'You'll soon see.'

'I won't see anything of the sort! I'm a craftsman, and I only have to do compulsory work in emergencies, like when the dykes have to be repaired before the flood. And it isn't that time of year.'

'We have our orders.'

'From whom?'

'From Sobek the Protector, head of all the guards forces in the kingdom.'

'And what does he want, your Sobek?'

'I told you, you'll see.'

'It's out of the question.'

'If you disobey, we'll seize your boat.'

'Just you try it!'

With a blow from his club, one of the guards knocked Slender-Nose's legs from under him. The other threw himself on top of him and immobilized him.

'Keep quiet, my lad, or I'll smash your skull.'

They bound Slender-Nose's hands and feet, then boarded the boat and raised the sail. As Slender-Nose watched his boat disappear downstream, anger overtook his fear. He might have been attacked, wounded and robbed, but he swore to himself that he'd fight back.

After a long conversation with the pharaoh, Khnum-Hotep returned to his office. When he saw the mass of business to be dealt with, he felt momentarily overwhelmed. Setting up the new government, fighting corruption, getting the best from everyone, ensuring a decent life for every Egyptian, ensuring that no province was at a disadvantage: these were only a few of the tasks Senusret regarded as priorities. The king himself dealt with a considerable volume of work, as well as with his daily ritual obligations. The tjaty took care of the rest – all the rest – with the help of the King's House.

Anyone who thought that holding high office was pure pleasure was a fool or hopelessly ignorant. As the saying went, it had all the bitterness of venom. But Khnum-Hotep felt a profound joy when he succeeded in making the Law of Ma'at reign or in handing down true justice regardless of the social rank of accuser or accused.

'How many requests for audiences today?' he asked his secretary.

'About twenty.'

'Anything serious?'

'I don't think so. Well, except perhaps for one craftsman, but his story's so bizarre that the poor fellow's probably lost his wits.'

'Send him in first. If he is a madman, at least the conversation will be short.'

Slender-Nose was so nervous that he didn't dare enter the tjaty's office, and the secretary had to push him in.

'What is your name?' asked Khnum-Hotep.

'Sle . . . Slender-Nose.'

'And your profession?'

'Potter.'

'According to the report I have here, the headman of your village said he could not deal with your complaint himself and advised you to approach the provincial court. But that court also declared itself unable to deal with it, so the tjaty's court is your last resort. I therefore take it that this is an exceptionally serious matter.'

'It . . . it is, my lord.' Slender-Nose knew he wouldn't get a second chance, so he took a deep breath and spoke at top speed, sometimes running his words together. 'Iwasattacked and they beat me and stolemyboat two of them armedwithclubs they threatenedtokillme if I resisted and all because of compulsorywork but it's the wrongtimeofyear so I refused and—'

'Who were these men?'

'River guards.'

'River guards? Are you sure?'

'Yes, my lord. They said they were acting on the orders of Sobek the Protector.'

The tjaty's face became openly menacing. 'Will you repeat that statement, and swear on the name of Pharaoh that you are telling the truth?'

Slender Nose repeated it and swore the oath.

'Which way did they go?'

'Northwards. Are you . . . are you going to give me justice?'

'The state will give you a new boat, and some wheat, beer, oil and clothing. You will be taken to a doctor who will examine you and treat you. My office will defray the costs of your travel and your lodgings here.'

'Will that man Sobek be punished?'

'Justice will take its course.'

Armed with the description of the stolen boat, whose sail bore Slender-Nose's name, scribes went to the part of the port reserved for the river guards' vessels.

At the entrance they were stopped by an overseer.

'What are you doing?' he asked gruffly.

'Oh, it's just a general inspection.'

'Have you got a written order from Commander Sobek?'

'No, but we've got one from the tjaty.'

'I don't obey orders from anyone but Commander Sobek.'

'And he obeys the tjaty. Let us pass or we'll have you arrested.'

Reluctantly, the overseer stood aside.

It took only half an hour to find Slender-Nose's boat: it was hidden between two vessels belonging to the river guards.

25

'What is it now, Tjaty?' demanded Sobek-Khu.

'This time it is really very serious. A potter, Slender-Nose, was attacked and robbed by two river guards who were acting on your orders to conscript him for compulsory work.'

'This isn't the time of the flood, and anyway I never gave any such orders.'

'I have proof.'

'What proof?'

'The thieves stole their victim's boat, and we have just found her at the river guards' docks.'

'That's ridiculous – and impossible!'

'The facts are plain, Sobek: there are at least two criminals among your men. I would like to believe that you have been deceived, but the culprits must be arrested, and quickly. If not, you will be considered fully responsible for this serious crime.'

The Protector turned on his heel and stormed out. Once back in his own office, he abandoned all his other work and began a detailed investigation of all the guards forces.

Their foreheads were low, their eyes were dull and they had dock labourers' shoulders, but they were rich. Gergu had just handed each of the two bogus river guards a leather bag full of semi-precious stones, which would fetch high prices.

'Good pay,' conceded the older man, 'considering how easy the job was. Hitting the potter, frightening him and stealing his boat – we've known worse.'

'Mooring her at the river guards' quay was risky, though,' said the younger.

'Well, it was a moonless night and the watchman was drunk, so we didn't have to try too hard. I don't suppose you have any other jobs as lucrative as this one?'

'I'm sorry,' said Gergu, 'but it's better that we don't see each other again. At Sichem, on the other hand, a friend of mine has a splendid surprise for you.'

'Even more profitable?'

'Much more.'

'We won't get through the King's Walls without the right documents.'

'Here's a tablet for you to show the border officials. You'll pass without difficulty.'

'We can't read, but I suppose it's all right.' The man slipped it into his tunic. 'What's your friend's name?'

'When you get to Sichem, go to the mayor's office. He's expecting you.'

The bandit understood: it was the mayor himself, rotten to the core like so many others. Working for Gergu was certainly taking them a long way, but for pay like this it was worth it.

Gergu slid behind a clump of bushes, and from their shelter watched the two men walking calmly towards the border guard-post.

When they showed the tablet to a soldier, things changed abruptly. A brawl ensued, and the criminals were greatly outnumbered. As they turned to run, several archers took aim: they did not miss.

Gergu smiled. On the tablet he had written: '*Death to the Egyptian army! Long live the rebellion in Canaan!*' Now that the men were dead, no one would be able to establish a link between Slender-Nose's attackers and these crazy rebels.

'You were asleep, were you?' demanded Sobek furiously.

'Yes, sir.'

'And you slept all night instead of watching the port?'

'Not all night – well, not quite all, sir. I couldn't have suspected . . . After all, it's the river guards' quay, so there was nothing to—'

'Had you been drinking?'

'Some date wine, and it was good stuff!'

'Who gave it to you?'

'I don't know, I found it in my hut. I tasted it and then, well, sir, you know how it is. You get bored, it gets cold . . . I must say, though, I usually hold my drink better than that.'

The fool was drugged, thought Sobek. The author of the plot wasn't stupid and he'd left nothing to chance. The trap would close on Sobek unless he could identify the corrupt river guards. But were they real guards or impostors?

The Protector immediately began a series of particularly unpleasant interrogations, and his loyal subordinates carried out in-depth investigations to find any black sheep.

Before long, the rumour spread that serious problems were undermining the guards forces.

The drunken Syrian climbed on to the tavern table and started dancing, kicking up his heels with all the grace of an elephant. The drinkers applauded.

'I've beaten Sobek!' he crowed. 'He thought he was stronger than the others, but hahaha, one good kick in the ribs, and he collapses! I'm the strong one.' A spate of incoherent words followed, drawing peals of laughter from the other drunkards.

The Phoenician's water-carrier agent paid close attention to these ravings. He drank very little because, here and in the other taverns he'd visited, he was seeking information which would enlighten him about Sobek's misfortunes. This was probably just drunken boasting, but the water-carrier was a meticulous man. So when the tavern closed and the Syrian lurched out into the night he followed.

In a darkened alleyway, he closed up on the Syrian, and caught him as he was about to fall over.

'Thank you, friend,' said the Syrian. 'Fortunately there are still good fellows around – not like that man Sobek. But I got the better of him, I did.'

'Did you indeed? All by yourself?'

'Yes, by myself – well, almost . . . A small team, very small indeed. And if you want to know, we pretended to be river guards. You should have seen the grain-boat captain's face! He took us for the real thing, us, who hate those fellows! We laughed our heads off. And we were well paid, as long as we didn't say a word. So listen, friend: I've told you nothing, absolutely nothing.'

'I haven't heard a thing. Do the others say the same as you?'

'They've all disappeared. We were supposed to get together again to celebrate Sobek's downfall, but they didn't come.'

'Where do you live?'

'That depends . . . I don't like being pinned down.'

'Who employed you, you and your team?'

The Syrian stood up stiffly, his finger pointing at the sky. 'That's more secret than secret. But he can't be a pauper.'

Evidently, the petty criminals used to compromise Sobek were being killed after their work was done, so that they couldn't reveal the truth and thus prove the commander innocent. But the job had not been done properly, because one of them was not only still alive but drunk and talkative. Meticulously, the water-carrier eliminated the problem before setting off for the Phoenician's house.

*

How could he possibly resist quails in a golden-brown, richly spiced sauce? This dish came after a few appetizers, some fish and another meat dish, and preceded a new dessert created by his cook. The Phoenician trader forgot his diet and abandoned himself to the unequalled pleasures of food, while thinking over the water-carrier's latest report.

There could be no further doubt: someone was indeed plotting against Sobek-Khu. That was very good news, all things considered, but the man behind it must still be identified without alerting him and attracting his wrath. The Phoenician's spies would have to take the greatest care – their own lives might well be at stake.

A meal of this quality, accompanied by a red wine which delighted the palate and regenerated the blood, necessarily opened the mind. In the mass of information accumulated by his agents, one detail caught the Phoenician's attention: the boats intercepted by the false river guards had all been carrying grain. Who would know their movements and where to intercept them?

There were only two possible answers. The first was the man in charge of the river guards. But he had been appointed by Sobek, so why should he wish to harm him? The second candidate was much more interesting: Gergu, principal inspector of granaries. Behind Gergu stood Medes, secretary of the King's House. Could Medes possibly be the the the instigator of the plot? If so, it was vital to inform the Herald before doing anything else.

'No doubt, Commander,' said the tjaty, 'you asked to see me in order to give me the results of your investigation. I hope they are positive.'

'From my point of view, yes.'

'What are the names of the culprits?'

'I don't know, but I do know they aren't river guards.'

Khnum-Hotep's voice hardened. 'This attempt at evasion is both pointless and ridiculous. The evidence is overwhelming. If you persist in shielding your men, you will be considered solely responsible for their offences.'

'I am not shielding anyone. Rigorous inquiries were made, and no one was spared investigation, but the only result was low morale and an atmosphere of distrust.'

'You leave me no choice. I am obliged to to dismiss you from your offices and to charge you with these crimes.'

'I am the victim of a conspiracy and your decision is unjust.'

'If I did not punish you, I would be insulting justice and the royal power would be considerably weakened.'

'You are making a grave mistake, Tjaty.'

'Before your trial you will have time to prove your innocence, because you are no longer in charge of the guards forces. And I also think it advisable that the king's safety is no longer entrusted to men chosen by you.'

Sobek was aghast. 'Why?'

'Supposing the criminals belong to that group of men? You set it up and control it, and you hand-picked its men, so it would hardly be wise to leave it free to act.'

With an enormous effort, Sobek kept his temper. 'Understand this: a criminal is trying to destroy me precisely in order to make the pharaoh vulnerable.'

Khnum-Hotep reflected for a long time, then said, 'That is one of the possibilities, indeed, and I shall take the necessary measures to ensure that His Majesty is in no danger. But there is another possibility: that men loyal to the commander of all the kingdom's guards forces thought they could commit crimes with impunity because the commander would shield them. Such disgraceful conduct would be a clear sign that Egyptian society is becoming debased. My principal duty is to prevent it.'

'Am I permitted to see the king?'

'An audience would lead people to assume that he sanctioned your actions. Now, the pharaoh never interferes in matters of law.'

'I have a great regard for you, Tjaty,' said Sobek. 'You don't know me well, and you are wrong.'

'I sincerely hope I am.'

'We've done it!' exclaimed Gergu triumphantly. 'The tjaty has charged Sobek with assault, theft of a boat, illegal use of compulsory work, and abuse of power. That should go a long way, don't you think?'

'Khnum-Hotep will want to make an example of him and prove to the people that the state is not corrupt,' said Medes. 'But Sobek hasn't been convicted yet, don't forget.'

'He has no chance of escape. The proof is overwhelming, and the potter will maintain his accusations. My two little bandits did their work well.'

'And I take it there's no danger from that quarter?'

'None at all. The border guards killed them, as we planned, and I've made sure to leave no traces behind me.'

'Sobek will try to prove his innocence.'

'He won't succeed, I promise you. The problem called Sobek-Khu has been solved – eliminated.'

'The tjaty will probably appoint several officers to head the different forces and will take overall control of them himself. In the early days things will be very disorganized, and we must take advantage of that to carry out our plan.'

Gergu's enthusiasm waned somewhat. 'Wouldn't it be better to attack the rest of the King's House first? Sobek's downfall will alarm them and—'

'Without him, Senusret is vulnerable. His personal body-guard, which is loyal to the Protector, won't be replaced immediately. So it is inside the palace itself that we should strike.'

'Neither you nor I can possibly do it!'

'Are you drawing back, Gergu?'

'Killing the pharaoh . . . It is too risky.'

'As soon as Sobek's men have been dismissed we'll buy the right replacements, and then the way will be open.'

'Don't ask too much of me, sir.'

Medes was under no illusions: Gergu knew how to work away in the shadows, but he would never have the courage to kill Senusret. 'You are right,' he said. 'Neither you nor I must do anything so dangerous. We shall recruit someone who is afraid of nothing.'

'Whom are you thinking of?'

'I don't know yet. Your task is to find him, Gergu, by searching through the taverns, the docks and the poor districts. Find me a hot-head who can't resist the prospect of becoming very rich in a single night.'

'But if he fails he'll denounce us.'

'Whether he succeeds or fails, he won't live to denounce anyone. Either the guards will kill him before he escapes from the palace, or we'll kill him ourselves when we pay him.'

26

Medes's predictions were coming true in every respect.

Isolated and depressed, Sobek prowled up and down like a caged lion, fearing he would never again be free. Doors were closing one by one, and he felt deprived of the breath of his life: the pharaoh's support. 'No smoke without fire,' people whispered, even in the ranks of the guards forces. So the incorruptible Protector wasn't incorruptible after all, they said. He'd been given too much power and had overstepped the boundaries of the law, thinking himself untouchable.

Sobek did not know where to look: he had nothing but vague suspicions, not the slightest lead, no means of investigating. All he could do was protest his innocence while his good name was dragged through the mud. Moreover, at his trial people would invent new grievances and encourage jealous, disappointed and embittered men to testify against him. He would be given a heavy sentence.

Faced with such injustice, he should probably have tried to leave the country. But Sobek would not behave like a coward, and in any case running away would only convince people of his guilt. All that was left was to hope for a miracle.

Wounded to the quick, he saw the work he had accomplished over several years being destroyed. Khnum-Hotep had done as he said: the king's personal bodyguard had been transferred to other units and replaced by ordinary soldiers who had had no training in dealing with terrorist attacks. Moreover, the rivalry between their commanding officers, who were all vying for the tjaty's favour with a view to promotion, disrupted the patrols, their rounds and their watch over the palace. Sobek feared the worst.

Iker and the master-butcher were getting along marvellously. Although he now understood the difficulties and the ritual aspect of the work, he knew he could never carry it out. But all that was asked of him was that he kept meticulous account of all the meat, none of which must be diverted from the service of the gods.

One day every week, the master-butcher was away from the slaughterhouse, taking part in ceremonies at the Temple of Hathor, along with the ladies of the House of the Acacia, whose superior was none other than the queen.

Over their midday meal of beef, Iker summoned up the courage to question him. 'Do you ever talk to the queen?'

'When she's in Memphis, she leads the ritual – she hasn't got time for idle talk.'

'How is it that you're linked to the priestesses?'

'I bring them the strength of Set, which only they know how to master and integrate into a harmony of celestial origin. Don't you know that Horus and Set dwell together in the same being – that is, Pharaoh? The queen is the only seer who can discern the unity of this dual nature. In gazing upon the king she creates him, and in creating him she enables him to reconcile that which cannot be reconciled.'

Iker wanted to declare that in the tyrant Senusret Set had got the better of Horus, but he managed to hold his tongue.

'The burden of the queen's duties seems very heavy,' he ventured.

'Especially at the moment.'

'Why? What's happening?'

'She is performing more rites than ever, so as to protect

king. There's a crisis in the guards forces because their commander, Sobek-Khu, is accused of abusing his power. It's a very hard blow for the pharaoh, who trusted him completely. The tjaty's reorganizing the security forces, but it will take time.'

'But surely the palace won't be left wide open?'

'Almost. The system devised by Sobek has been utterly destroyed. Yesterday evening, when I and my assistant took the king's meal to the palace, many of the usual checks weren't made.'

One fact was becoming clear: Iker must take the place of the butcher's assistant. Sobek's downfall offered him an unhoped-for chance to act.

After savouring his ration of salt, the Herald fixed his falcon's gaze on the Phoenician. 'What have you to tell me, my friend?'

'Some excellent news, my lord. The tjaty has dismissed Sobek the Protector from all his posts, probably as a result of Medes's machinations. I can't prove that conclusively, but I don't think it would be wise to push my investigations any further.'

'Who has replaced him?'

'Nobody. He had so many responsibilities and skills that his dismissal has left an enormous gulf. The tjaty's trying hard to fill it, but without much success, so the king isn't as safe as he used to be . . .'

'Why did Khnum-Hotep do it?'

'He's a rigorously honest man, and he feels that the application of the law comes before all other considerations. Rumour has it that he has overwhelming evidence against Sobek.'

'A sort of settling of accounts . . .'

'Probably. Khnum-Hotep used to be governor of the Oryx province, and it must please him to humble an old adversary.

I assume he won't stop while things are going so well, and will soon take action against other men close to the king.'

'Can we buy information about the interior of the palace and Senusret's private apartments?'

'While Sobek headed the guards services, I would have said no. But it's different now, because the guards and the palace staff aren't subject to such strict discipline.'

'Try to find out the times when the king is at his most vulnerable.'

'You think . . . ?'

The Herald spoke with extreme gentleness. 'Destiny may enable our cause to move forward much more quickly than I foresaw.'

The taverns were full of petty criminals ready to commit one more offence – within reasonable limits. True, Sobek-Khu's dismissal had encouraged some of them to take up their activities again, but most were well known to the city guards and had no wish to return to prison. The tjaty took the safety of people and their possessions very seriously indeed. Murder and rape carried the death penalty, and theft was also a serious crime because a thief showed himself to be greedy, and greed was one of the main manifestations of *isefet*, the destructive power opposed to Ma'at.

To find the rare bird who would risk stealing again, Gergu would have to take advantage of the period of flux while Khnum-Hotep was reorganizing the guards forces and appointing their new commanders. But he was not very hopeful.

The taverns? People there talked a lot – in fact, far too much. Unearthing the sort of men he usually used, and then ensuring their permanent silence, was easy. They wouldn't be missed and would soon be completely forgotten. But a pharaoh's murderer would need to have a certain stature. In all the ale-houses he'd visited, Gergu had not spotted a single potential killer.

Methodically, he explored the humble areas of Memphis, but even there he found an atmosphere of joy in living. No one suffered grinding poverty, and Senusret's popularity was growing all the time. Thanks to his reforms, everyone had enough to eat, and medical treatment when necessary; they lived in peace and no one was afraid of the future any more. When the pharaoh was a good pharaoh, they all agreed. everything went well. Gergu heard nothing but praise for the king, so he gave up and decided to look elsewhere.

The only other likely place was the docks. This place offered two big advantages. The dock-workers had great strength, which would be essential for killing the king; and the docks employed men from many countries. It would benefit his and Medes's plans if the murderer was a foreigner.

Gergu discreetly investigated the workforce, taking a particular interest in those who worked in handling grain. As principal inspector of granaries, he had access to all the administrative documents. After several days' research, he found an interesting detail. On quay number two, the ten-strong team of labourers included a Syrian and a Libyan.

In fact, there were eleven of them, but legally the eleventh worker did not exist. Secretly observing the team's comings and goings, Gergu noticed that, from time to time, a big fellow with a badly scarred chest stole a sack and hid it in a nearby storehouse. Each time he did so, he exchanged a few words with the Libyan.

When night fell, the Libyan appeared, leading two donkeys, loaded up the sacks and left the port. Gergu followed them to a quiet outer area of the town. There the Libyan unloaded his booty, which he hid in a hut near his home.

As the Libyan crossed the threshold of his house, Gergu showed himself.

'Stay calm, my friend, the house is surrounded. If you try to run, the archers will shoot you down.'

'Are you . . . the guards?'

'Worse than that: fraud investigation department. With us there is no judgment, no court, just instant punishment. I know all about your illegal trade. Stealing grain – that means forced labour for life. But we might perhaps come to an arrangement.'

Terrified, the Libyan stammered, 'W-what kind of arrangement?'

'Let's go inside.'

The house was quite attractively furnished, Gergu noted. 'Your little business is obviously bringing you a nice profit.'

'You must understand, I only wanted to earn a little more. I won't do it again, I swear!'

'Who is your accomplice?'

'Nobody . . . I haven't got one.'

'One more lie and it's the end of your freedom.'

'All right, there is someone who gives me a hand. He's my brother.'

'An illegal worker?'

'Sort of.'

'Why didn't he enter Egypt legally?'

'He couldn't.'

'I want the truth – now!'

The Libyan hung his head. 'He killed a guard who insulted him – it was my duty to save him. As he isn't listed among the salaried dock-workers, we get by. The others agreed not to say anything.'

'Where does he live?'

'In a miserable little house near the port.'

Gergu demanded the details so that he could find it easily. 'And what's his name?'

'Scarred-One. To be honest, he's always been a bit of a fighter.'

'No doubt he's killed more than one guard, your charming brother.'

'He had to defend himself! Are you going to arrest us?'

'That depends,' replied Gergu enigmatically.

'Depends on what?'

'On how well you cooperate, you and your brother.'

'What must we do?'

'You must keep your mouth shut and work normally, and tell your colleagues your brother's gone back to Libya.'

'Then you *are* going to arrest him!'

'By no means. I'm going to offer him a mission in the interest of stamping out fraud,' said Gergu. 'If he carries it out well, he will earn permission to remain here and a permit to work. You will both have proper legal status and can stop behaving like thieves. On the other hand, if he refuses your future looks very bleak.'

'Can I talk to him?'

Gergu pretended to hesitate. 'That would be rather irregular.'

'Trust me, I beg you! Scarred-One may react badly if I don't prepare the ground.'

'You're asking a lot, but all right. Tomorrow, you are to steal no more sacks. You are to speak to your brother, and in the evening I shall meet him at his home. Try to be persuasive.'

'You can rely on me.'

27

Crooked-Face liked Memphis very much. He dreamt of
ransacking its storehouses and becoming very rich.
Unfortunately, that seemed likely to be much more difficult
than the discreet pillage of the isolated farms under his
'protection'.

The farmers were so afraid of this huge, unshaven,
immensely strong man that they kept silent about his raids
and paid what he demanded with perfect regularity. As a
result, Crooked-Face's little fortune was growing nicely.
When he visited Memphis, besides giving an account of his
activities to the Herald, he spent some of it on the pleasures
of life.

The district where the Herald lived was patrolled by men
loyal to him, who very quickly spotted a new face or anyone
showing curiosity. Crooked-Face entered a shop run by a
rebel fighter with a friendly face. He sold sandals, mats and
coarse fabrics to the common folk. With a look, he gave the
new arrival permission to go upstairs.

At the top of the stairs, Shab the Twisted blocked his way.
'I must search you.'

'Stop it, will you? It's me, not a stranger.'

'Those are the Herald's orders.'

'Be careful, Twisted One, or I'll lose my temper.'

'Orders are orders.'

The two men had never been friends. Shab regarded Crooked-Face as a depraved bandit who thought of nothing but his own interests, while Crooked-Face detested the Twisted One, who was as devoted to his master as an abandoned dog given a home.

'I never carry weapons when I come to Memphis, so if the guards search me I don't have to worry.'

'Let me check anyway.'

'If it amuses you . . .'

Crooked-Face had told the truth: he was unarmed.

'Follow me,' said Shab.

The Herald was seated in the centre of a darkened room. Mats covered the windows, allowing only a single ray of light to enter.

'How are you, my good friend?' he asked.

'Very well, my lord. Business is flourishing – I've brought my contribution to the cause.'

'In what form?'

'Two of my men are following me. When they reach the shop they'll leave there some precious stones bought with the contributions of the people I protect. You can trade them for weapons.'

'I hope you aren't taking any risks.'

'None at all, my lord. I find promising new farms, I threaten, I use force if necessary, and I take the price of my protection on the spot – no delay permitted.'

'Thanks to me, Crooked-Face, you are now rich.'

'Well, let's not exaggerate, my lord. The upkeep of my band costs a fortune.'

'Don't your warriors tend to get unfit dealing with nothing but farmers?'

'Certainly not, my lord. They train regularly, and no man holds back.'

'Sobek-Khu is no longer head of all the guards, and the forces are being reorganized. The resulting confusion is

213

favourable to us. I shall soon have information that will enable us to act inside the palace. I need a good man who is both willing and able to kill Senusret.'

'All my men are like that, but there's one I particularly recommend, a Syrian. He's so fast and vicious that no one has yet succeeded in knocking him down, and he hates Egypt so bitterly that he'd gladly ravage the entire country. For him, killing the pharaoh would be the greatest pleasure life could offer.'

The place was totally dark. If Gergu had not explored it during the day, he would have had serious difficulty in finding it now, in the early part of the night. The area would soon be demolished to make way for new buildings, better designed and larger.

'Show yourself, Scarred-One.'

There was no response.

Suddenly, Gergu felt afraid. What if the dock-worker robbed him? Bearing in mind the fellow's impressive muscles, Gergu would not fare well in a hand-to-hand fight.

'Show yourself, or I shall leave.'

'I'm over here,' said a hoarse voice.

Gergu stepped forward and made out the Libyan in the darkness. Arms folded, he was leaning against a wall.

'Your brother spoke to you?'

'He did.'

'And do you accept?'

'Certainly not. Nobody forces me to do anything.'

'That's too bad for your brother.'

The Libyan unfolded his arms. 'And what does that mean?'

'It means that the anti-fraud secretariat has arrested him, and his fate depends on your agreement.'

'I'll break your bones!'

'That won't save your brother. Unless you obey me, he'll die.'

The Libyan spat. 'What do you want from me?'

'Since you've already killed several men, you won't hesitate to do so again.'

'That's possible.'

'Your previous exploits were small beer, Scarred-One. Will you undertake to kill someone important?'

'Important or not, what does it matter? It'll only be one fellow the less.'

'Even the pharaoh?'

The Libyan flattened himself against the wall. 'The pharaoh? But . . . he's a god!'

'No more than you or I.'

'Go away! I don't want to hear any more!'

'You must choose between the king and your brother. If you refuse, your brother will be executed before morning.'

'But the king's protected by strong magic.'

'He used to be, but the situation has changed.'

'Oh? What's happened?'

'Sobek the Protector has been dismissed, and without him the magic won't work. The king is now just a man like any other.'

'What about his personal guard?'

'The men Sobek trained have also been dismissed. We'll find a way of getting you into Senusret's private apartments.'

'When? And what weapon will I have?'

'We'll provide you with the right weapon. When it's time, I'll let you know. From now on, just stay indoors and wait.'

'What about my brother?'

'We'll hold him prisoner until you've done your work. Then you'll be rich, both of you, and you won't need to steal, won't need to hide or to work. You and your brother will be heroes. You'll be able to buy a fine house and employ a whole army of servants. But of course you're free to refuse.'

'I accept.'

*

The master-butcher's assistant was a jovial, hard-working lad who, sensibly, was learning the trade slowly and thoroughly and who followed his instructor's directions to the letter. Thanks to these skilled craftsmen, the butchery at the Temple of Ptah was one of the best in the land.

'I have wonderful news,' he told Iker during the midday meal. 'I'm getting married soon. I can't tell you how pretty she is! Her parents weren't easy to persuade, but she's made her mind up, so they had to give in.'

'I wish you much happiness.'

'Aren't you going to get married?'

'Not yet.'

'Aren't you a bit too . . . serious?'

'For someone from the provinces, settling in Memphis isn't at all easy, and first of all I want to make progress in my studies. Then we'll see.'

'Well, in the meantime you can always visit prostitutes.'

When the assistant went back to the butchery, Iker's thoughts turned to the young priestess whose face haunted his dreams. If he had not been committed to a mission which he knew he would not survive, he would have begun searching for her. But what was the use? He'd never find her, and even if, by some miracle, he did see her again, she'd probably burst out laughing at the stupid words he stammered out. With her, he could have built another life. But feeding on dreams and illusions led nowhere. Iker knew the destination of his final journey: the royal palace.

While he wrote his weekly report, which was as favourable as all the previous ones, he debated how to overcome the last obstacle. He could falsify the accounts and throw suspicion on to the assistant, but that would mean betraying Ma'at and destroying an honest lad's career. Complaining to the master-butcher about him would be equally unjust.

Iker was so close to his goal, yet he felt powerless. A criminal would have disposed of the inconvenient assistant without a second thought, but he, Iker, was no criminal. He simply wanted to deliver Egypt from a murderer and a tyrant. He alone must pay the price.

As he drew hieroglyphs with a steady hand, Iker sought desperately for a solution.

After checking that nobody was watching him, the water-carrier entered the Phoenician's house in the middle of the night. The doorkeeper had orders to let him in at any time.

While a servant went to wake his master, the unexpected guest made the most of the pastries laid out on the tables. As he was constantly on the move, he never had any problems with his weight.

The Phoenician soon appeared, wrapped in a voluminous robe and still half-asleep. 'Couldn't it have waited until tomorrow?'

'I don't think so.'

'Very well, I'm listening.'

'I've become the lover of one of the palace washerwomen. She's a feather-brained little thing but she has one priceless virtue: she never stops talking. She's so proud of her job that I don't even need to ask questions. As of this evening, I know practically all the security arrangements.'

The Phoenician was no longer sleepy: the water-carrier had never been boastful. 'Go on,' he said.

'Experienced soldiers, very sure of themselves and their skills, have replaced the guards trained by Sobek. They're highly disciplined, and unquestioningly obey their officers, who are rotated every six hours. Sometimes the king stays alone in his office and takes his evening meal there while he reads through cases. And note this: there are no guards on duty in his private apartments. Now, he will be having one of these solitary evenings the day after tomorrow.'

'Good work!' said the Phoenician warmly. 'But there are still those guards.'

'Not if we lure them away.'

'How?'

'My charming mistress told me the name of the officer who'll be on duty tomorrow, from the first hour of the night. We must intercept him and substitute one of our own men, who will order the soldiers to leave the palace for an external operation. Then the way will be clear.'

The one-eyed man punched the ground in acknowledgement of defeat. The Syrian ought to have stopped strangling him, but instead he tightened his grip ferociously.

'That's enough! Let go of him!' roared Crooked-Face.

The Syrian turned a deaf ear, and Crooked-Face had to pull him up by the hair until eventually he let go.

'The one-eyed man asked for mercy,' said Crooked-Face angrily.

'I didn't see – and anyway if he did it was a trick. He's crazy, that one. He pretends to give up and then counter-attacks.'

The one-eyed man was still lying on the ground, his one good eye wide open.

'Come on, man, get up.' Crooked-Face's order had no effect.

'He looks dead,' said the Syrian.

'Yes, he is. You've killed him.'

'He's no great loss – he was fighting less and less well.'

'Go and wash and get dressed,' ordered Crooked-Face. 'You're leaving on a special mission.'

The Syrian's eyes sparkled with excitement. 'That's more like it! And who am I to kill?'

'The Pharaoh of Egypt.'

28

The master-butcher was preparing the offerings for the morning ritual when he heard the bad news: the future bridegroom was suffering from a high fever and was therefore unable to come to work.

He called to Iker, who was busy diluting some ink. 'This evening,' he said, 'the king will be alone, and I'm to prepare his meal. Would you be willing to work extra hours and replace my assistant, who's ill?'

The scribe suppressed a surge of enthusiasm. 'I'm afraid I may not have the necessary skills.'

'Don't worry, there's nothing complicated about it. I'll carry the first dish, and you carry the second.'

'Nobody knows me at the palace. The guards won't let me in.'

'Yes, they will, because they all know me. Besides, security isn't nearly so strict now, so you'll get in without any difficulty, believe me. Are you afraid of seeing the king?'

'I must confess that—'

'Don't panic! I'll knock on his door. When he says, "Enter," in that deep voice of his, we go in, with our heads lowered, and lay the dishes on a low table on the right. Either the king will be absorbed in his work and we'll leave immediately, or else he'll ask me if everything is in order at the butchery. He's bound to notice that I've got a new assistant, so I'll introduce you. Mind you, I can understand your being nervous. Even sitting down, the king looks as tall as a giant, and he has a way of looking at you which strikes you dumb. And even when you know him he makes the same impression on you. Anyway, that's enough talk: back to work. Note down the number and quality of the pieces destined for the temple. Then we'll have a bite to eat.'

As the master-butcher walked away, Iker spilt some ink. His hands were shaking. He was so close to his goal, but would he have the courage to see things through?

The Libyan dock-worker could not keep his mind on his work. To make matters worse, his colleagues were giving him the cold shoulder. Two of them, with whom he was unloading a cargo of grain, disliked his country, he knew, but they'd always worked together without problems. He dared not asked them why they had suddenly taken against him, and he agreed to carry heavier loads than usual, all the time thinking about his brother. Would he really cooperate? The strange man who was blackmailing them hadn't been joking: they'd had no choice but to do as he said.

Yet another sack, so heavy that he almost collapsed beneath its weight. 'Hey, lads,' he protested, 'there ought to be at least two of us to carry this.'

'When you raped the little girl you did it on your own, didn't you?' demanded one of his colleagues, fixing him with a look of hatred.

'What are you talking about?'

'We know everything, you piece of filth.'

'You're wrong. I haven't attacked anyone.'

'We know everything, I tell you. Scum like you don't deserve a trial. We're going to carry out the sentence now,' and he threw the Libyan into the water. Unable to swim, the Libyan struggled in vain. When he called for help, a full sack was dropped on his head, knocking him out, and he vanished under the water.

'Justice is done,' commented his colleague.

Gergu had witnessed the scene from a distance. He'd planted the story the previous night, and had paid the workers well to kill the 'rapist' and make it look like an accident. The men had done their work with commendable zeal. As Medes had ordered, Gergu was covering his tracks carefully.

At the end of the meeting of the King's House, Sehotep passed on to Medes the information he would need to draw up the new decrees. They improved the situation of craftsmen and softened the rigid rules hindering trade between the provinces.

'His Majesty wishes to see these laws disseminated quickly,' said Sehotep. 'In other words, it is more than urgent.'

'I'll have a plan ready to present to the king this evening.'

'No, not this evening. He'll be dining alone and working on matters of state. Tomorrow morning, after the dawn rites, would be a good time. Don't confine yourself to a mere plan, and you'd better forget that the night is generally used for sleeping.'

'I was warned,' Medes conceded with a smile, 'so I've no reason to complain.'

'You haven't the easiest of jobs, but the king is pleased your work.'

'Serving one's country is the greatest satisfaction of all. But please forgive me, I haven't a moment to lose.'

Medes went home and sent a servant to fetch Gergu from the granaries inspection office, where he was strutting around in front of his subordinates. Abandoning his demonstration of authority, he uttered a few well-chosen words on the laziness of his officials and hurried to Medes's house.

'We must act this evening,' said Medes. 'Senusret will be alone in his office.'

'What about the guards?'

'The change of guard will take place at the first hour of the night, and then, for a few minutes. the corridor leading to the king's private apartments will be unguarded. Have your Syrian enter by the servants' entrance and make straight for his goal.'

'What if he comes across an unexpected obstacle?'

'Tell him to break it down. Show him this plan of the inside of the palace and have him engrave it on his memory, then burn it. Has his brother's case been dealt with?'

'Once and for all.'

'Contact your brute and give him his orders.'

Gergu did not like this district at all. The atmosphere here was oppressive, very different from Memphis's habitual gaiety. A pestilential stench rose from a heap of steaming filth. Stray dogs roamed in search of food. Bricks lay scattered on the ground, as if the building they had been destined for no longer had any chance of seeing the light of day. Even in the sunshine, Scarred-One's lair was sinister.

'Come out,' demanded Gergu.

The door remained closed.

Nervously, he went closer. 'Come out immediately!'

A few paces from Gergu, rats seethed menacingly. As he was picking up a broken brick to throw at them, two hands grabbed him round the neck and lifted him right off the ground.

'I want to strangle you!' roared Scarred-One.

'Stop!' croaked Gergu. 'I've brought you your first payment.'

The dock-worker put him down. 'If you're lying, I'll smash your head.'

Gergu fingered his neck: the fool had almost broken it!

'Well, where is this payment?' growled Scarred-One.

Gergu congratulated himself on his prudence. Foreseeing

this imbecile's reaction, he had come armed with a little leather bag containing a magnificent lapis-lazuli. He showed the stone to Scarred-One and said, 'It's worth a great deal. And it's only a small part of the total fee – on condition that you act tonight.'

The Libyan fingered the treasure. 'Never seen anything like it . . . Tonight, you say?'

'I'm going to show you a plan of the royal palace and explain how to get in. If you succeed, you'll have a life beyond your wildest dreams. Now, here's the short-sword you'll use.'

The officer commanding the palace guards for the next six hours used his own methods rather than Sobek's, which he thought were too rigid. He sent a junior officer to tell the guards when they would be relieved, and they all left the palace, one by one, in the reverse of the order they had arrived in. As they did, the officer could identify and count them. Next, he put his own men in place.

The soldier guarding the servants' entrance was glad to leave his post. His back was aching so much that he could hardly stand upright.

Scarcely had he left when Scarred-One entered the palace, ready to kill anyone who crossed his path.

The person who was most surprised to see him was the Syrian. As a good raider trained by Crooked-Face, he had been watching the area for more than an hour, awaiting the diversion to be organized by a fake soldier, before he entered the place in his turn. This fellow was not, the Syrian was sure, a palace guard. Who was he and what did he want? With his short-sword and his brutish face, he looked thoroughly dangerous.

Then the Syrian realized: he must be a guard in disguise. And supposing there were others hidden inside? The only way of knowing was to kill this one, then find out for himself.

Suddenly orders rang out, followed by the sounds of running feet. It was the planned diversion: the officer had just been informed of an attempt to break into the tjaty's offices. All the guards must intervene as a matter of urgency.

Scarred-One moved slowly along the corridors, remembering the plan he had learnt by heart. His work was proving so easy that it made him smile.

At that moment a long blade slit his throat, with both ferocity and precision. In his last spasms of life, he thrashed the air with his sword, hoping to hit his attacker. But the Syrian had stepped away and, satisfied, was watching the death throes of the supposed guard.

Then he continued on his way.

No guards, no soldiers. As he had been told, this part of the palace was empty for a short period.

At last, he reached Senusret's office. A short time from now, the pharaoh would have ceased to live. The Syrian would boast of his deed until the end of his days.

Just as he was preparing to push open the door, a head as hard as stone butted him in the belly. All the breath knocked out of him, the killer fell backwards. With a kick, his opponent broke his right arm, making him drop his weapon.

Hours and hours of training had taught the Syrian how to react in even the worst situations. Despite the pain of his broken arm, he got to his feet and, with his left fist, struck the man in the side as he tried to knock him down. Then, making the most of his advantage, he sprang forward, head first. But the other man had foreseen his move, and in any case was faster: he dodged aside and grabbed the Syrian by the neck. If the raider had not not been injured, he would easily have freed himself from this grip, but this time he could not. The fight ended with the sinister cracking of his shattered neckbones.

With a sigh of relief, the victor dragged the corpse to a storeroom where dirty laundry lay in heaps.

*

Outside the main gate of the palace, the fuss was dying down. Although the changing of the guard had been disturbed following a false alarm, the officer had never lost control of the situation.

'Can we go in?' asked the master-butcher, who was waiting outside with Iker. 'His Majesty won't like it if his meal gets cold.'

'Go in,' ordered the officer, who did not want to draw the king's wrath for being too zealous. The guards were not yet posted in the corridor leading to the royal apartments, but everyone knew the butcher.

Iker's heart was thumping wildly, and he saw nothing of the palace he had entered so easily. His eyes were fixed on his guide's back. The butcher walked briskly along, leading Iker to the goal that he had for so long believed inaccessible. Perseverance and good luck had eventually overcome all the obstacles.

'Here is the king's office,' said the master-butcher.

Before ridding Egypt of the tyrant, there was one formality to carry out. Once more, Iker was glad of his military training. His arm was perfectly steady as he raised the alabaster dish and neatly knocked out his companion.

Hidden among the vegetables spread across the floor was his dagger. Even if he had been searched, who would have thought of looking in the food? Iker cleaned his weapon and halted before the door. He must forget all sensitivity, think of his vengeance, regard himself as killing not a human being but an evil demon. He must act quickly, very quickly, giving the king no time to react.

As he opened the door, a deep voice stopped him in his tracks.

'Come in, Iker. I have been expecting you.'

29

Bathed in the gentle light of many lamps, the king's office looked enormous. Senusret was seated on the floor like a scribe, an unrolled papyrus on his knees, gazing fixedly at the young man.

'Come in,' he repeated, 'and close the door behind you.'

Terrified, Iker obeyed.

'If you want to kill me, you will need another weapon.' The monarch rolled up the papyrus and stood up – he loomed over Iker like a giant. 'Do you think you could kill a pharaoh with that miserable dagger? Take this one, which is wielded by the guardian spirits of the otherworld.'

Iker dropped his dagger and, with a shaking hand, accepted Senusret's gift.

'Now,' said the king, 'choose your office: servant of Ma'at or accomplice of *isefet*? Companion of Horus or of Set? Do you desire the fire of life, which regenerates and transmutes, or the fire of death, in which criminals burn?'

Senusret was nothing like the tyrant Iker had hated for so long. There was nothing dishonest or furtive about him. He stood there, unarmed, less than two cubits away, while Iker held a razor-sharp weapon more than capable of killing him.

'Make up your mind, Iker. Some doors open only once.'

'Majesty, how do you know my name?'

'Have you forgotten that our paths crossed once, during a

226

country festival? I asked one of my loyal friends not to lose sight of you.'

Sekari emerged from a dark corner of the room.

Iker was almost speechless. '*You?* But . . . you . . . prison and the mines . . . my servant . . . cleaning and cooking!'

'My work requires all kinds of skills. You weren't easy to track – I even had to climb a wall and frighten the lady Techat into letting you leave the Oryx province. But it was worth all the effort.'

'So you knew about all my meetings with Bina?'

'Your meetings, yes, but not what you talked about. If you become a faithful servant of Pharaoh, the only guarantor of Ma'at, you will tell him what is afoot in Kahun. I'm convinced that Heremsaf, to whom you owe your rise to the dignity of temporary priest of Anubis, was murdered. You are at the centre of a terrifying conspiracy, Iker. Until now your enemies have been using and deceiving you. Open your eyes and see the truth.'

Iker was overcome by dizziness.

'Come and sit down,' advised the king. 'Sekari, does security appear to have been re-established?'

'The guards are at their posts. The master-butcher will have a fine headache, but before he lodges a complaint against Iker Sehotep will explain to him that it concerns an affair of state, in which his assistant of one day is in no way implicated.'

A veil was being torn away. Here, at the heart of the palace, in the presence of the Lord of the Two Lands, Iker was beginning to experience the benefits of a radiant power. Weak, stupid, unseeing . . . How many failings he had shown!

'Majesty, I—'

'No excuses and no regrets, Iker. You had to face up to adversity and unwittingly follow a merciless training programme. That past offers nothing of interest unless you draw lessons from it. The only future that interests us, you and me, is Egypt's. Let us therefore consider the real problems. Thanks to Sekari, I have certain information, but I lack vital details. How was your life suddenly changed?'

'Majesty, I come from the village of Madu, where I was the pupil of an old scribe – sadly, he's dead now – who taught me to read and write. I was kidnapped from there by pirates, who took me to their ship, the *Swift One*, and tied me to the mast; the captain said I'd be sacrificed to the sea-god. The pirates were planning to find gold in the land of Punt.'

'Did this captain tell you who was to receive the gold?'

'No, but he said the voyage was a "state secret".'

'What was his name?'

'I don't know, Majesty. I know only the names of two sailors, Turtle-Eye and Sharp-Knife, but all traces of them have been removed from the records.'

'Evidently the sea-god spared you.'

'There was a terrible storm and the ship sank – I was the only survivor. When I recovered consciousness, I found myself on a beautiful island, the Island of the *Ka*, where a giant snake appeared to me in a dream and told me it was the lord of the divine land, the wondrous land of Punt. "I could not prevent the end of this world," it declared. "Will you save yours?" The island sank into the sea but a ship rescued me, and also salvaged some chests of perfume. I know all this seems unbelievable, but it's the truth, Majesty, I swear it is.'

'I do not doubt it, Iker,' said Senusret gently.

'But my rescuers were pirates, too, and they handed me over to a false desert guard, who tried to kill me.'

'The one I had to kill at Kahun,' put in Sekari.

'Majesty, I have never stopped trying to find out why I suffered so many misfortunes. Everything I learnt led me to believe that a single person was responsible: yourself. This was borne out by the fact that a vessel of *Swift One*'s size – a hundred and twenty cubits – must have belonged to you and the crew must have been under your orders.'

'Did you find proof?'

'I was hoping to find it in the archives of the Hare province, but Djehuty said that all the documents relating to the *Swift One* had been destroyed. The ones at Kahun have been destroyed, too.'

'You are right, Iker: a ship of that size must necessarily belong to the royal warfleet.'

The young man shivered. If he was right on that crucial point, he must indeed be in the presence of the despot determined to kill him.

'However,' said Senusret, 'none of my seagoing ships is called *Swift One* – her construction must have been secret and fraudulent. That is a serious act of piracy, and first thing tomorrow I shall see that a detailed investigation is begun. There can be no doubt that the author of that crime is also the person who hired the fake desert guard to kill you. But he has failed. What he wanted to avoid at all costs has just happened: you have told me the truth. When he knows you are alive, you will be in grave danger again.'

'Majesty, I never leave Iker's side,' Sekari reminded him.

The king rewarded him with a smile, then turned to Iker again. 'What else have you discovered about the gold of Punt?'

'Nothing, unfortunately. But I remember some words from the *Book of Kemit*: "May the good scribe be saved by the perfume of Punt." Could the legendary land actually be real?'

'Do you know what has become of the queen of turquoises, which you extracted from the mountain of Hathor?'

'No, Majesty. The killers who laid waste the site stole it.'

'They were probably Canaanites, perhaps even the ones who inspired the Sichem rebellion and whom General Nesmontu silenced when he took back the town. The day will come when we shall wish we had that stone.'

Sekari sensed that a new mission was in prospect. With what means and in what direction?

'There was something else, Majesty,' said Iker. 'At Kahun an old carpenter called Plane told me about an acacia-wood box he'd made, and said it was destined for a long voyage. I wondered if the pirates were planning to hide the gold of Punt in it. But Plane's dead now, I'm afraid, and he didn't tell me his customer's name.'

Senusret turned to Sekari. With a look, the spy indicated that he knew no more.

'Now, Iker,' commanded the king, 'tell me everything that you did in Kahun, and do not try to hide anything.'

Iker knew that by speaking he was condemning himself to death, but he owed total honesty to the pharaoh he had unjustly suspected. He took a deep breath.

'A young Asian girl convinced me that you were a bloodthirsty tyrant, indifferent to the distress of both Egyptians and the foreigners under your yoke. Her concerns mirrored my own. I was under a spell, obsessed by a single idea: to avenge myself by killing you and, in doing so, to give the people back their freedom.'

'You, a priest of Anubis, were prepared to commit murder?'

Iker looked down at his hands. 'I tried to persuade myself that I could, but now I'm waking up after an interminable nightmare. I admit I conspired against you, Majesty, and that's an unforgivable crime. Before I was kidnapped, all I wanted was to become a good scribe. Then these incomprehensible things happened, one after the other, and I lost my reason. But nothing excuses my blindness, I know that.'

'Does the Asian girl lead a faction?'

'She lied to me and said she was a poor servant, and hadn't been allowed to learn to read and write. The truth is that she wants to seize control of Kahun, with the aid of some fellow Canaanites who have succeeded in infiltrating the city. I couldn't bear being deceived, so I broke off all contact with her and decided to act alone.'

'Was one of their allies waiting for you in Memphis?'

'No, Majesty. I thought it would be impossible to get near you, but circumstances served me well.'

'The kind old man who took you in, the law classes, the Temple of Ptah,' Sekari reeled off, 'the master-butcher, his assistant's illness. Are those the circumstances you mean?'

'You . . . you knew everything all along?'

'I told you, the king ordered me not to lose sight of you.'

'But then why did you let me get in here?'

'His Majesty wished it.'

Again, Iker felt dizzy.

'This evening,' said Sekari, 'you weren't the only danger. Under cover of a false alarm, which disrupted the change of guards, two men got into the palace. They can't have been accomplices, because one of them killed the other, a man whose chest was covered in scars. I then dealt with the victor. From the way he fought, it's clear that he'd had intensive training. In my opinion, they were a Syrian and a Libyan, and I'd have preferred to take them alive and learn the names of their leaders. If the king permits, I should like to withdraw now, because the palace guards will be here at any moment and I must continue to work in secret.'

Senusret agreed.

When Sekari had gone, there was a long silence. Iker did not doubt what the king's judgment would be: here and now, he would plunge the guardian spirits' knife into Iker's heart. An attempt to kill the pharaoh fully deserved death.

'Hide that weapon in your clothing,' ordered Senusret.

He seized the dagger with which Iker had hoped to murder him, and broke it. Then he opened the door, in front of which stood the officer and ten guards.

'Majesty, we have just found the dead bodies of two unknown men, and the master-butcher has been knocked unconscious. As soon as he regains consciousness, we shall question him and—'

'He is innocent. Take him to Royal Seal-Bearer Sehotep. As for the bodies, try to identify them.'

'The guard has been doubled, Majesty, and nobody is

231

allowed near the palace. First thing tomorrow, we shall search the servants.'

'A little late, don't you think? The systems devised by Sobek are to be used again, exactly as before.'

The officer stared in astonishment at Iker. What was the master-butcher's assistant doing here? But he swallowed his amazement, bowed and withdrew.

The king crossed the corridor and indicated a room. 'You will sleep here, Iker.'

30

Iker could not sleep. Lying on his luxurious sycamore-wood bed, he relived every moment of that incredible night, during which so many thick veils had been torn away.

The young scribe was floating between two worlds, the first that of his stupid illusions and the second that of reality, which in the morning was bound to destroy him. Even if he had had an opportunity to run away, he would not have done so, for he deserved his punishment. The king would make an example of him. As the only survivor of the three would-be assassins who had converged on the palace at the same time, he, too, must die.

How Bina must have enjoyed making a fool of him! The only thing in which he could take even a little pride was that he had not succumbed to her poisonous charms. Because of the memory of the young priestess, he had at least not offered the Asian girl that pleasure.

Dawn was breaking. In the temple, the pharaoh was celebrating the first ritual of the day.

Iker washed and shaved in the washroom next to the bedchamber. Everything set out for his use was worthy of a prince, but how could he enjoy this luxury when he knew he was living his last moments? Still, at least before dying he had met the pharaoh and been given the chance to realize how wrong he had been. The king would ensure that Egypt did not leave the path of Ma'at.

Someone knocked at the bedchamber door. 'Open up. It's the guard.'

Resigned, Iker obeyed.

A fully uniformed officer whom he had not seen before stood there. Snapping a crisp salute, the officer said, 'His Majesty is waiting for you. Follow me.'

Iker did so. The bright light illuminating the corridors reminded him of a passage from a scribes' training text: *'The palace is like the horizon. The pharaoh rises and goes to bed there like the sun.'*

The officer led him to a large room, lit by several windows, where the king was being served his early-morning meal of milk, honey and various sorts of bread.

'Sit down, Iker,' the king said, 'and eat some of this food. You will need *ka* in order to confront the day.'

It was impossible to bear the king's gaze, even briefly, without faltering. Added to the solemnity of his voice and his authoritative appearance, the depth of his gaze made the observer feel very small indeed.

But why, Iker wondered, was he enjoying the incredible privilege of sharing this moment instead of huddling in a prison cell?

'I am looking for a man with a nimble heart,' said Senusret, 'a man capable of perceiving, understanding and filling his mind with righteous thoughts, an ingenious man, reserved, effective in speaking, a man who knows how to brave his fear and track down the truth at risk to his own life. Are you that man, Iker?'

'I would like to be, Majesty, but—'

'You thought you were fighting for Ma'at, but in fact her deadly opponent, *isefet*, was deceiving and making use of you. Nevertheless, your intentions were pure. Freeing a country from a tyrant's yoke: what could be nobler than that?

And you have done something truly remarkable. You have freed yourself from your mental bonds by fully recognizing your faults.'

'Majesty, I deserve—'

'You deserve a task which matches the level of your desire. I ask you this question one last time: do you want to be the man I have described?'

Iker bowed before the pharaoh. 'With all my heart, Majesty, I will try.'

'You will succeed if your heart is honest and undivided. You will need it thus if you are to accomplish the perilous missions that await you. You wanted to become a great scribe, didn't you? Then let us go and pay homage to your ancestors. You will have great need of their help.'

When he emerged from the palace, a wonderful surprise awaited Iker: North Wind, bright of eye and jaunty of appearance, carrying his master's writing-materials. After an emotional reunion, the donkey proudly followed his master and the pharaoh, who were guarded by a company of archers.

Fascinated, Iker discovered the immense sacred territory of Saqqara, over which towered Pharaoh Djoser's stepped pyramid, a gigantic stairway to the heavens.

The king entered a house of eternity where several illustrious scribes were depicted.

'Listen to the words of the ancients, Iker, gather their teaching, read their books.* Man dies and his body becomes dust, but the works enable his being to endure. None of us is superior to the man who can pass on a vital thought through writing, for writings are active.'

---

*This respect for writers, who do not speak on their own behalf but are vehicles for words of wisdom, was still very much present in the New Kingdom. In a tomb of that era (see D. Wildung, *L'Age d'or de l'Egypte, le Moyen Empire*, Paris, 1984, p. 14, fig. 4) great authors like Ptah-Hotep, Ii-Meru, Ptah-Chepses, Kaires and Neferti are honoured.

Seated in the scribe's position, facing the sculpted wall, Iker noted down the king's words.

'The scribes, in their great wisdom, did not plan to leave behind them perishable heirs, children of flesh who would preserve their names. They created for themselves, as successors, books and teachings. They turned their texts into priests who would serve their *ka*; their palettes into their beloved sons; wording into their pyramids. Their powerful magic touches their readers. If you want destiny to favour you, Iker, remain reserved and silent, and avoid idle chatter. Above all, do not be greedy and do not yield to the whims of your belly. The glutton and the greedy man are heading for their downfall. The fire of the man who rages destroys him, whereas the truly silent man searches for places where harmony reigns. He resembles the tree that grows peacefully in the garden, grows green and gives fine fruit with matchless flavour. Its shade is benevolent, and it ends its days in paradise. The sage scrutinizes the meaning of the ancient writings, teases out its complications, teaches his own heart, surpasses what he achieved yesterday and is always moderate in action. As for him who, on this earth, has knowledge of the words of transformation into Light, he will emerge into the daylight in all the forms he desires and will return to his rightful place.'

As he wrote, Iker experienced a moment of radiant happiness. He remembered what General Sepi had said about the qualities needed by the scribe who wished to reach the sphere of creation: listening, understanding and mastery of the fires. Today, on this magical morning, it was from the pharaoh himself that he was receiving a lesson designed to build him.

'The goal of the sage,' Senusret went on, 'is to attain the completeness that the hieroglyphs symbolize by the offering-table, *hotep*, a word synonymous with "sunset", that ineffable moment when work is completed before the beginning of a

ew journey. We are very far from that serenity, Iker, and we
must leave the peace of this house of eternity to confront a
very disturbing reality.'

As he put away his materials, Iker thought of the prediction
made by the captain of the *Swift One*: 'Your destiny is to
become a sacrifice.' He had escaped from the sea-god, but did
even more fearsome ordeals still await him?

The king led him a little way into the desert.

'Egypt is under threat of death,' said Senusret. 'There is
even a danger that her spiritual message will disappear if the
Mysteries of Osiris are not celebrated. A curse has been
placed upon the Tree of Life, the Acacia of Abydos. By a
variety of measures, we have stopped the process of decay
and even made two branches grow green again. But this
inadequate result may only be temporary. We know that we
must find the healing gold, for it is the only thing that can
save the acacia. I have therefore sent General Sepi to search
for it.'

'My teacher?'

'A great scribe is complete only if he is also a man of
action and practical experience. Despite our efforts, we have
not yet succeeded in identifying the criminal who is wielding
the strength of Set against the Tree of Osiris. That demon of
darkness is determined to destroy Egypt, and has proved to be
an adversary as fearsome as he is effective.'

'Might he be Bina's superior and the one who sent those
two men to kill you last night?'

'Those are good questions which deserve good answers.
No doubt other serious incidents, such as the murder of a
border-post controller and the disturbances in Canaan, are
also crimes committed by this demon. Have you ever heard of
the Herald?'

'No, Majesty.'

'He is the man who induced the town of Sichem to rebel.
He was arrested and put to death for sedition, but it seems the

fire is far from out. Thanks to our new national army, General
Nesmontu is managing to maintain order, but I am concerned
that there may be attacks by small, well-trained groups,
which are difficult to spot. For a long time, we believed that
the demon in the shadows was one of the provincial
governors; now we suspect Canaanites or sand-travellers.
The latter think of nothing but looting caravans, and it is
difficult to predict, and therefore reduce, their raids, but we
must do so. And we must see if among them there may be one
or several leaders who have succeeded in misappropriating
Set's fire.'

Iker was expecting to be entrusted with a specific,
dangerous mission. Senusret's next words struck him like a
bolt of lightning.

'I appoint you royal scribe, in the direct service of
Pharaoh. This title will enable you to become a member of the
court.'

Memphis was abuzz with rumours, most of them as mad as
they were contradictory. Some claimed that the king had been
assassinated by an apprentice butcher, others that Canaanites
had attacked the palace, and yet others that armed bands were
still fighting with the guards in the king's apartments themselves.

It took an appearance by Senusret, on the forecourt of the
Temple of Ptah, to silence this gossip. Not only was the king
very much alive but he was celebrating the midday ritual
himself, assisted by a new royal scribe.

The master-butcher, his head comfortingly bandaged, was
delighted to see his one-time assistant promoted. Convinced
that he'd been knocked out by one of the bandits who were
trying to get into the pharaoh's office, he believed that the
young man had run to the king's aid and had been rewarded
for his courage.

The deployment of the forces of order and the arrival of

several ministers, including Royal Seal-Bearer Sehotep and High Treasurer Senankh, led the people to believe that something exceptional was about to happen. Curious people and passers-by jostled one another at the temple entrance in the hope of learning the news as quickly as possible. When the tjaty arrived, too, nobody could doubt that whatever was going to happen was imminent.

In the great open-air courtyard, permanent and temporary priests and senior officials wondered what the king was going to say. First of all, was he completely unharmed? Next, what kind of repression would he decree? Almost certainly, a harsher occupation of Canaan, perhaps the establishment of a curfew in Memphis – and then there was the punishment of the guards and soldiers who had failed to ensure the palace's security. Lastly, had the criminal or criminals been identified and arrested?

When Senusret emerged from the temple, all eyes converged on him. He was even taller than usual, for he was wearing the Double Crown symbolizing the union of Upper and Lower Egypt. There was no trace of a wound, no sign of weakness.

'Let Iker the scribe approach,' ordered Pharaoh.

Hesitantly, the young man walked towards the king and knelt.

'Let Tjaty Khnum-Hotep raise him to his feet.'

The tjaty took Iker's hand, surprised to see him again in such circumstances.

'I appoint Iker the palace's only ward,' declared the pharaoh. 'He shall receive the title of Royal Son.' And he strode across the courtyard, followed by the Khnum-Hotep and Iker.

The tenor of this declaration and its brevity stunned the watching throng. Indeed, one of them almost fell over backwards.

Medes, secretary of the King's House, couldn't believe his

eyes or his ears. This couldn't possibly be Iker, the insignificant little scribe kidnapped from Madu to serve as a sacrifice! How could this lad with no family, whose existence was known only to a few uncouth peasants, have managed to survive and follow a path which led to the pharaoh? One of Medes's henchmen, the sham desert guard who had later disappeared, had sworn to him that Iker was dead.

If this really was some kind of miracle, what would he say to the king? The kidnapping, the voyage towards Punt, the shipwreck, the attacks, the wanderings . . . No, none of that was dangerous, because Iker didn't even know Medes existed and certainly knew nothing that might lead back to him.

Iker, a contemptible little man with no future, the Royal Son! There was only one way to dispel the nightmare, and that was to destroy him by any means possible.

31

The tjaty had not been able to bring the king good news. First, the investigation into the two attackers had produced no useful results. None of the guards and soldiers posted around the palace recognized them, so, as Sobek could not be asked to search the Memphis underworld, they would probably never know where the would-be murderers had come from. Next, the inquiries concerning the *Swift One* had also led nowhere: no ship of that name had been built in Memphis.

'And yet they must have bought wood, employed shipwrights, forged the documents and engaged a crew,' said Senusret. 'Such activities cannot have gone completely unnoticed.'

'Once again, Majesty,' said Khnum-Hotep, 'I acknowledge that we miss Sobek-Khu a great deal. But by covering up his men's offences, he put himself in a very delicate position. If I had not charged him, I would have been betraying my office.'

'I am not criticizing you, Tjaty,' said the king.

'To my mind, there are two possibilities as regards the *Swift One*. Either she was built on the coast by a clandestine ship-owner, and we shall never trace her; or else an Egyptian warship yard built her, but in great secrecy. If the latter is the case, there must still be clues somewhere.'

The king summoned Iker and Sekari.

'Majesty,' said Sekari, 'I have gathered some scraps of information while trawling the quays. From the description I gave, a dock-worker identified the scarred man as an illegal Libyan worker, whose brother had got him the docks job and was protecting him. The fellow was strong and didn't balk at lifting even the heaviest loads, so the other workers tolerated him.'

'And the brother?'

'He's disappeared. His house is empty.'

'Another dead end,' said the tjaty.

The king turned to his adopted son. 'You said the *Swift One*'s crew were definitely Egyptian, didn't you?'

'There was no doubt about it, Majesty.'

'Dig deep into your memory. At some moment or other, did you not learn a detail, no matter how small, about her construction?'

Iker thought for a moment. 'Plane, the carpenter in Kahun, said that parts of her were made in Faiyum. I didn't have time to investigate there.'

'I think we should,' said Sekari. 'I'll leave straight away.'

'One moment,' said the king. 'Iker, accompany the tjaty to his office. He will set out your duties as royal scribe.'

The two men withdrew.

'I've missed the Golden Circle of Abydos badly,' admitted Sekari, 'and I'd very much like to regenerate myself there. But something tells me there are more urgent matters to deal with.'

'I should also like us all to gather in the city of Osiris, but when Egypt is in such grave danger our personal preferences are of no account. Nevertheless, if you feel your forces are weakening, I will do what is necessary.'

'I am still strong, Majesty.'

'Are you taking too many risks, Sekari?'

'Nesmontu and Sepi gave me an excellent training.'

'The way Sobek was trapped worries me. It was the work

of a well-organized group controlled by a man who knows how to use our own laws against us. The unfortunate Protector is struggling like a wild animal in a cage, with no chance whatsoever of proving his innocence. Go and see him, Sekari, and try to find a way of re-opening the investigation.'

As they entered the wing of the palace set aside for the tjaty's departments, Khnum-Hotep and Iker met Medes.

He bowed to them and said warmly, 'I am delighted to meet the hero of the hour. What His Majesty has done is justice and recognition of your exceptional talents. Allow me to congratulate you, Iker, and to wish you a warm welcome at the Memphis court.'

Iker confined himself to a polite acknowledgement.

'This is Medes, secretary of the King's House,' said Khnum-Hotep. 'He is one of the most important people in the state, in charge of writing the official decrees and disseminating them throughout the kingdom. It's difficult work, but he does it extremely well.'

'Such a compliment goes straight to my heart, but I know it must be earned anew every day and that if I make mistakes I shan't be forgiven.'

'That is very clear-sighted,' said the tjaty.

'If I can be useful to the Royal Son, he must not hesitate to ask for my help. I am unfortunately in a hurry, for the official in charge of message-carrying is ill and I must replace him within the hour. Please excuse me.'

Iker and his host climbed up to a terrace from where they admired the centre of the city. In the sunshine, the official buildings and temples seemed safe from chaos and misfortune.

'You did not waste your time in the Oryx province,' said Khnum-Hotep, 'and I don't regret training you. At the time, I even regarded you as my probable successor, for I was distancing myself from my abysmally stupid descendants, who were wholly incapable of governing. Then the king arrived, this king who is truly a pharaoh. He taught me to laugh at myself, my vanity and my illusions, and made me pay for them dearly by appointing me tjaty.' To Iker's surprise, Khnum-Hotep laughed resoundingly again. 'I ruled over my little realm as an absolute despot, and here I am in the service of others without a single day's rest! Who but Senusret could have imagined it? Obey him, Iker, revere him and be loyal to him, for he is the guarantor of Ma'at and the Light acts through him. He is the only one who can confront the forces of darkness without trembling. If we are defeated, Egypt's civilization will disappear – well, the pharaoh has told you how serious the situation is.'

'I am entirely at your service.'

'Normally, a royal scribe becomes a zealous administrator of the kingdom's riches. But in your case you must not expect to strut about at the head of an army of underlings. The king has other things in store for you. He told me to speak to you so that I can put you on your guard against the many dangers that lie in wait for you here at court. From those close to Senusret – that is to say, Generals Nesmontu and Sepi, Royal Seal-Bearer Sehotep and High Treasurer Senankh – you have nothing to fear. They are all totally devoted to His Majesty.'

'Does Medes not belong to the King's House?'

'Sooner or later he will enter it, if he remains hard-working and competent. But there are others – envious dignitaries and disappointed or embittered courtiers – and there are many, many of them. Your sudden rise to the highest rank has occasioned resentment and hatred of an intensity you cannot imagine. Dozens of second-rate men have already sworn to bring about your downfall, and they will proceed with infinite caution so as not to draw down one of Senusret's thunderbolts. Luckily, Sekari is watching over you. You will live in a palace apartment and will be guarded night and day. However, knowing you, I am sure you want to start work at the principal library without delay.'

'You know me well,' agreed Iker with a smile.

'Above all, do not forget your vocation as a scribe and a writer. Passing on the words of power is vital to ensure that Ma'at is present here on earth.'

Sobek the Protector was half mad with rage. If he had still been in his post, with his methods being followed and his security system in place, the pharaoh would not have been the target of a threefold attack.

He had had to leave both his official residence and the barracks where he had trained the members of the king's personal guard, and now lived as something of a recluse in a small house. The place was permanently watched by two guards; they had only recently been enlisted and refused to speak to him. For news he had to rely mainly on his cleaning-woman, which meant it was not easy to separate gossip from reality.

When a strange, rather jolly fellow came to see him, Sobek wondered how he was going to be manipulated this time.

'My name is Sekari,' said the visitor, 'and my mission is highly confidential.'

'Who sent you?'

'The pharaoh.'

Sobek scowled. 'He refuses even to see me!'

'Since a court case is in progress, he cannot converse with the principal accused, on pain of being accused of favouritism. If he were, it would make things much worse for you.'

Sobek shrugged. 'I suppose so. Does the tjaty know you're here?'

'Certainly not.'

'My two jailors will soon tell him.'

'No, they won't, because they've just been relieved. Their replacements have served under you and support you unreservedly.'

Sobek leant out of the window: Sekari had told the truth.

'Well, so you really are the king's envoy. What exactly do you do for him?'

'I obey his orders.'

'And what has he ordered you to do?'

'He is certain of your innocence but he cannot violate the law, and the evidence against you is extremely strong.'

'The truth is that Khnum-Hotep wants my hide.'

'No, he doesn't. The truth is that, given the weight of the evidence, he can't do anything else.'

'Someone is trying to drown me while the real criminal lurks in the shadows.'

'So that everything is clear between us,' said Sekari solemnly, 'I want a firm and final answer to one question: are you shielding guards who have committed crimes?'

'Absolutely not! If there had been criminals among my men, I'd have identified them and then, believe me, they would not have remained in the guards much longer.'

Sekari was convinced by Sobek's obvious sincerity. He said, 'Then the king is right, and you are the victim of a plot. I'll tell the tjaty so.'

'I'm glad to hear it, but what does that change?'

'You're stuck here, but I'm not. Give me some leads, and I'll follow them.'

'Unfortunately, I haven't got any. Has my replacement been appointed yet?'

'No. Instead of one overall commander, there are now several, and their working relationship leaves something to be desired.'

'They'll tear each other apart and the pharaoh's safety won't be ensured. What exactly happened at the palace?'

'An illegal Libyan dock-worker and an unidentified raider got in. Both were killed, but we have no clues as to who sent them. There's only one thing we're sure of, and it isn't encouraging: they weren't from the same source. In other words, two different networks want to kill Senusret.'

'Libyans, Syrians, Canaanites . . . You must search among the scum of those peoples. But my cleaning-woman said there were *three* attackers.'

Sekari smiled. 'The case of Iker the scribe is a truly remarkable one. Certain scheming people tried to use him, telling him he would be a righter of wrongs. However, the king had seen Iker at a countryside festival and been struck by his special character. His Majesty ordered me to follow him closely, and not to let him out of my sight. Doing that was both useful and instructive. I uncovered an embryonic terrorist network in Kahun and saved Iker's life – a false desert guard had been ordered to kill him.'

Sobek's expression hardened. 'You're really sure about this Iker?'

'The king has officially designated him the sole palace ward and Royal Son.'

'But what if those schemers you mentioned are still trying to use him?'

'When you know him better, you will know that he's seen the error of his ways and is ready to give his life for Pharaoh.'

Sobek's face fell. 'If the tjaty sends me to the copper mines, I shan't know anyone but criminals and bandits.'

'You're innocent, so don't lose heart.'

'The court investigation is continuing, the trial will take place soon, all the circumstances are against me, and I haven't even the shadow of the beginnings of a lead. My enemies are numbered by the score, and the one who brought me down is still invisible.'

'Have you had any trouble with officials recently?'

'Dozens of times. Those fellows can't bear talk of repression. They want security – but without any guards being present.'

'Do you suspect anyone?'

'The whole court! In my head I've run through what happened, over and over again. But no matter how often I do

it, I get nowhere. In the end, I concluded that the tjaty was
dismissing me so as to put the king at risk.'

'I repeat: Khnum-Hotep is a loyal servant of Senusret.'

Looking sceptical, Sobek flopped into a chair.

'I'm taking matters in hand again,' said Sekari, 'and I shall
get you out of this mess.'

This time, he had the distinct feeling that he was making
the future seem brighter than it really was.

32

Dressed in a superb white robe of royal linen and a ritual wig, Iker accompanied the king to the festival of the goddess Useret, the Powerful One, which the priestesses of Hathor were celebrating under the queen's direction. He felt as though he was living in a dream. He, a humble villager destined for a career as a public letter-writer serving the illiterate, was walking beside the Lord of the Two Lands, watched with admiration and jealousy by the court. However, he knew that this respite would probably be only brief, so he made the most of these exciting hours, performing his duties with an unassuming naturalness which disarmed those watching him.

Many people would have liked to mock him by treating him as a peasant and a clodpole, but Iker had the bearing of a royal scribe brought up in the palace. So a new rumour began to circulate: the boy must be Senusret's natural son, whose existence the king had – for mysterious reasons – concealed until now.

As for Iker himself, he waited eagerly to be told what it was that the king wanted him to do. Whatever it was, it would no doubt be dangerous and he might lose his life, so while they waited for the rites to begin, and at the risk of annoying the pharaoh, he tried to clarify some uncertainties.

'Majesty,' he asked, 'does the Golden Circle of Abydos still exist?'

'Who told you about it?'

'During a regeneration ritual for Djehuty, when he was still governor of the Hare province, I saw light pouring out of two vases, and General Sepi said, "You who wished to know the Golden Circle of Abydos, see it at work." Sekari seems to know about it, too.'

'The Golden Circle is the emanation of Osiris. When one belongs to it, one no longer belongs to oneself, for the only thing that counts is the vital function entrusted to each member. Their role is not to preach or convert or impose revealed truth and dogmas, but to act righteously.'

The pharaoh took his seat on the dais that had been built before the temple, and gestured Iker to a chair on his right.

'You have been initiated into the first mysteries of Anubis. What do you know of divine power?'

'The Invisible One is unique, more distant than the far-off sky, too mysterious for his glory to be revealed, too great to be perceived,' replied Iker. 'If anyone spoke his secret name, they would immediately die of terror.'

'A salutary terror,' said the king, 'but not enough to attain the Golden Circle. Have you observed the centre of the sky?'

'Set reigns there, over the deathless stars.'

'The cosmos is the body of the Great God, and his soul is the energy that gives it life. Set is restricted to a part of this cosmos, his strength being manifested in the thunder, the lightning, the tempest and the rainstorm. As for Osiris, he is the entire universe, traversed by creative powers so numerous and so varied that human thought cannot conceive of them. When they become concentrated, they form an energy beam of particular intensity. What we call a divinity then appears. Each one, in his or her specific function, is transformed into spiritual substances which can be assimilated by our hearts and consciences. The creative act is One. By becoming Two, it accomplishes the impossible marriage. Then it is unveiled in the form of the Three, before being multiplied into millions, while still remaining One.'

'Why is the hieroglyphic symbol for divinity a mast with a banner flapping in the wind?'

'Because its reality is transmitted in the radiant light, stimulated by the breath of the world beyond. It is embodied in an axis which must be protected, and is therefore bandaged like the mummy, carrier for the body of light. The whole of Egypt is the beloved dwelling of the gods. You can encounter them in the temples, in country prayer-places, in humble shrines or at festivals. Learn to discern their true nature and to understand how they weave the harmony of the universe. If the parts of this totality are assembled, it is because Osiris remains pure and spotless, for he does not become involved in the disorder or calamities provoked by the human race. His Mysteries do not become impaired, in either the visible or the Invisible world.'

Iker would have liked to question the king for hours, but the rites were about to begin and silence fell.

Assisted by priestesses of Hathor, the queen raised minerals towards the sun, then laid a golden boat on an altar. At the prow stood Userhet, the Powerful One, who could vanquish the darkness thanks to her four faces. '*Userhet*' meant the neck, the axis, that which holds the head, but also the torture stake to which the confederates of *isefet*, the destructive force, were tied.

A priestess hailed the rebirth of the light, rendered effective by the Powerful One in the boat of millions of manifestations. Then a gold disc was inserted, the feminine sun, which also took the form of the uraeus, the female cobra spitting its fire in order to clear the pharaoh's path.

Iker was no longer listening to the sacred songs. He was not even interested in the ritual any more. He could not take his eyes off a young priestess standing near the queen. It was she: the young woman who was always present in his thoughts and his dreams, she with whom he was hopelessly in love. He drank in every movement she made, every step she took, hoping that their eyes would meet, even for an instant. But she was concentrating solely on her part in the rites, and appallingly soon the ceremony came to an end.

A sudden hope flooded into him: he was no longer an obscure, petty provincial scribe, but the adopted son of Pharaoh Senusret. As such, he might speak to her. But the surge of hope soon faded. Anything he said would be ridiculous, colourless and uninteresting. But if he showed too much emotion she would turn him away.

The king's solemn voice dragged him away from his torments. 'Did you clearly understand the importance of the ritual?'

'I don't think so, Majesty.'

'Always be as honest as that. If you are not, I shall stop teaching you. Know that I had to strengthen you before sending you on your mission. The radiance from the golden disc and the fire from the uraeus have entered your body and your soul.'

'Majesty, do you know the young priestess who assisted the queen?'

'She usually lives at Abydos.'

'What is her name?'

'She bears an illustrious name, that of Isis, Osiris's wife. She has devoted her whole life to the temple and its Mysteries.'

The revelation plunged Iker into despair: beautiful Isis was as far out of reach as ever.

One of Sekari's main characteristics was determination, especially when it was a matter of establishing the truth – and, in this case, exonerating an innocent man. Nevertheless, Sobek's future looked extremely grim.

Sekari followed a simple line of reasoning: the men who had succeeded in disgracing Sobek must be extremely proud of their achievement, so they would show themselves in some way, perhaps noisily. But it was a tenuous thread, so he asked the tjaty to give him the reports on all the incidents, however small, that had occurred since the Protector was charged. He almost gave up when he saw the mass of documents. He enlisted the aid of two skilled scribes, and asked them to sort the documents according to the seriousness of the events: tavern brawls, thefts at markets, marital disputes leading to formal legal complaints, disagreements about field boundaries . . .

Sekari began his investigations with the worst ones: a murder in Memphis, and the killing of two foreigners who had been trying to cross the north-eastern border illegally. The murder had resulted from a violent quarrel between two cousins over the ownership of a three-hundred-year-old palm tree. The one who was more skilful with a club had broken the other one's head. Clearly, there was no connection with Sobek's case.

On the other hand, the attempt at crossing the border included an interesting detail: the foreigners were trying not to enter Egypt but to leave. Sekari went to the fort to consult the officer who had signed the report. Being armed with official written orders from the tjaty, he was well received.

'Please give me the facts, officer,' he said.

'The two fellows approached the fort without any apparent hostility, but my men didn't like the look of them – and their instincts are good. The men were clearly Canaanites, so I asked them where they were going. "We're going home, to Sichem," they said. "Our documents are in order," and they quite confidently – even arrogantly – showed me a tablet. But when I read it, the tablet said, "*Death to the Egyptian army! Long live the rebellion in Canaan!*" The situation immediately became heated, the Canaanites tried to get away, and the archers brought them down. Two rebels fewer.'

Sekari frowned. 'Either the rebels wanted to die or else

they couldn't read. Someone gave them the tablet and told them it was a safe-conduct pass, so that the border guards would execute them perfectly legally. Did you find out their names?' he asked, not very hopefully.

'Unfortunately not, but I like drawing, and as that was the most serious incident that's happened here I made sure to draw them both.'

Sekari sat up very straight. 'Please show me the drawings.'

'They're only the work of an unskilled artist, I warn you.'

But in fact the officer's pictures were remarkably lifelike. 'I'll take them with me,' said Sekari.

When he saw the guards coming, Slender-Nose, who had moved to a humble district of Memphis, snatched up a big stick and brandished it in the air. 'Don't you come near me,' he shouted, 'or I'll knock you down!'

'Don't be afraid. The tjaty sent us. He wishes to see you urgently.'

'Who says you aren't false guards like the others?'

'I do,' declared Sekari.

'And who are you?'

'Pharaoh's special envoy. No member of the forces of order will lay a hand on you in my presence.'

The potter relaxed a little. 'What do they want with me this time?'

'To check something important, in the tjaty's presence.'

'The tjaty himself? In person?'

'He is waiting for you.'

Although still wary, the potter agreed to go to the palace with them. When Sekari showed him into Khnum-Hotep's office, he realized that there was no deception this time, but nevertheless he was determined to show at once that he would not be browbeaten.

'If you're asking me to renounce my complaint, I refuse. They attacked me, beat me and stole my boat. The criminal behind them may be the head of Pharaoh's guards, while I'm only a simple potter, but I demand justice.'

'That is precisely my duty,' Khnum-Hotep told him. 'Whatever the plaintiff's social status, justice does not vary. Sobek the Protector has been charged and is confined to his house until the trial.'

'Good. I trust you.'

'Now, please look at these pictures.' Khnum-Hotep laid the officer's drawings on the table in front of Slender-Nose.

The moment the potter looked at them, he exclaimed, 'Them – it's them! The two guards who robbed me. So, you've found them at last. I want to see them immediately. They'll listen to me, the dirty pigs!'

'They're dead,' said the tjaty. 'They were Canaanites who prentended to be two of Sobek's guards, so that he would be blamed for what they did. Please tell me formally: are the men in these pictures your attackers?'

'Of course they are! It's them – couldn't be anybody else.'

While a scribe was still writing out the deposition in the correct legal form, Sekari ran to Sobek's house.

33

'Is there any news from General Nesmontu?' the king asked Sehotep.

'The army is deployed throughout Canaan, Majesty. Nothing worrying has happened.'

'And the Dahshur construction project is progressing well,' said Senankh. 'Djehuty is doing remarkable work: the craftsmen are well housed, the materials delivered without delay. I regret to say, though, Majesty, there has been no word from General Sepi. He must have encountered serious difficulties.'

'His silence is not necessarily cause for alarm,' said Sehotep. 'He is a cautious and wary man, and he probably won't contact us until after he has found the gold.'

'Not only are people trying to kill me,' the king pointed out, 'but they are also attacking those close to me, to discredit them and isolate me. You, Senankh, escaped the net, and you, Sehotep, foresaw the trap and used it against those who had laid it. But Sobek was almost destroyed, so you must all exercise extreme vigilance, for there will be other attacks.'

'And we still have not the slightest indication of who is behind them,' said Senankh angrily.

'Majesty,' Sehotep asked, 'have any courtiers or dignitaries recently asked you for promotion?'

'No.'

'A pity. I thought the master-criminal might have succumbed to vanity and his hunger for power, and made the mistake of revealing something of himself. He is even more devious than I thought.'

'He might be a foreigner, not an Egyptian,' suggested Senankh.

'That is possible,' admitted Sehotep. 'But in that case would he have set up networks in the very heart of Memphis?'

'Now that Sobek has been restored to all his offices,' said Senusret, 'he will investigate again in his own way – he is already taking the palace's security back in hand. After Iker's revelations, the most urgent thing was to warn the mayor of Kahun. I have ordered him to keep a close watch on the rebels who have infiltrated the town, in the hope that, one way or another, they will lead us to their master.'

'Supposing they try to take control of the town?' asked Sehotep worriedly.

'With the benefit of surprise, they might have succeeded. But now we shall nip any attempt in the bud. And, speaking of Kahun and Iker, how is the court reacting to my adoption of him?'

Senankh smiled. 'As you predicted, Majesty: they are stunned and jealous. The many candidates who think themselves equal to him, or better, will pursue him with their hatred. But the boy seems as solid as granite to me. Neither criticism nor praise seems to touch him. All he is interested in is the path to be followed, and nothing will stop him.'

'What about you, Sehotep? What is your opinion of Iker?'

'He is almost as astonishing as the successful reunification of Egypt, Majesty. Anyone would swear that that humble little scribe had always lived in the palace. He has a natural instinct for the right gesture and the right behaviour, without losing a jot of his personality. Of course, there are rumours that he is of your blood.'

'Well, and has he not become my son? I am going to send

257

him on a dangerous mission, which may enable us to find out where a ship was built in great secrecy; she then sailed for the land of Punt.'

'But, Majesty, those who envy him will think you are sending him away from court, and they will be delighted,' said Senankh.

'Forgive my impertinence, Majesty,' ventured Sehotep, 'but is he really battle-hardened enough to be sent on such a dangerous venture?'

'Iker's destiny is not like any other man's. What he must accomplish goes beyond the limits of reasonableness, and no one could act in his place. If he fails, we shall all be in great danger.'

It was advisable not to annoy Sobek, even about a minor matter like a kilt belt or a regulation leather wristband. The Protector was working night and day to re-establish the security system his successors had been in such a hurry to dismantle.

He summoned each man, officer or not, who had made mistakes during the horrible night of the attempts on the pharaoh's life. His anger made the walls of his office tremble. Even his most trusted officers quaked in their sandals as they waited for the storm to die down; some of the more stupid men would spend many years in provincial garrisons, where their most demanding task would be to count cows and oxen. Then the Protector checked that the pharaoh's personal guard had regained all its old efficiency, and its members did not balk at the exercise.

When Sobek sought out the king to present the results of his work, he found him with Iker.

'You have not yet met my adopted son,' said Senusret. 'Iker, this is Sobek the Protector, commander of all the guards forces in the kingdom.'

'Hail to your *ka*,' said Iker.

'And to yours,' replied Sobek tensely. 'At the risk of annoying a Royal Son, Majesty, I would like to speak with you alone.'

With the monarch's agreement, Iker withdrew.

'Majesty,' the Protector went on, 'three men tried to kill you. Two are dead. The third was Iker.'

'I am neither surprised nor shocked that you are still supicious of him. However, you may be certain that I have nothing to fear from him.'

'All the same, let me have him watched.'

'I was going to order you to do so, since his life – like mine – is still threatened.'

Sobek did not hide his pessimism. 'Getting rid of me was part of a carefully worked-out plan to set up rebel networks in Memphis and, no doubt, in other Egyptian towns, beginning with Kahun. That necessarily requires involving many of the common people, and perhaps even leading citizens. Some may not be aware that they are being used, but there will be others who wish to overthrow you. I have been out of touch, I am considerably behind, and I am groping along like a blind man. If I am no longer good enough for the job, Majesty, I beg you to replace me.'

'That is exactly what our enemy is hoping for,' said the pharaoh. 'Do you think I am going to give him that satisfaction?'

At the end of a long morning's work with the tjaty, Iker was walking in the palace garden with the king. Sycamores, tamarisks, pomegranate and fig trees provided agreeable shade. Here, the world was all gentleness and beauty.

'Khnum-Hotep says he finds your work satisfactory, Iker. Even those who hate you are obliged to keep silent, because you do not behave arrogantly and you shun worldly concerns.'

'There is so much to discover, Majesty! Khnum-Hotep

guides me wonderfully well, but one only truly assimilates what one experiences personally. As regards the management of the livestock—'

'I have another mission for you.'

By immersing himself in administrative work, Iker had tried to forget that the king would utter those words sooner or later. For a while, he had slept in the false calm of a privileged life.

'I am setting you several goals, all of which are difficult to attain,' said Senusret. 'First thing tomorrow, you will leave for Faiyum with Sekari. You will have the seal of a Royal Son, but use it only as a last resort. Try rather to pass unnoticed, for we do not know who our enemy is or where he is hiding. Through research done in the library of the House of Life in Abydos, we have learnt that many, many years ago an acacia dedicated to Neith was planted somewhere in Faiyum. If you can find it, we shall attempt a graft on to the Tree of Osiris. Next, try to find the warship yard where the *Swift One* was built. Lastly, go to Kahun, question the Asians and destroy their plans.'

A painful thought passed through Iker's mind. 'Majesty, the death of Heremsaf the scribe—'

'Was probably murder. I considered him a faithful servant. When he asked my permission to initiate you into the first mysteries of Anubis, his reasons for doing so were very convincing.'

'Is the mayor of Kahun an ally or an enemy?'

'When he was appointed he seemed motivated by the best intentions. But power often changes men. It is up to you to detect his true nature.'

'You have always known everything about me, Majesty, my desires, my worries and my hopes. That is the truth, is it not?'

'Spend a quiet afternoon in this garden, my son. And come back as soon as you can.'

As Senusret walked away Iker stood still, speechless. It was the first time the king had called him 'my son'. Those two words, so ordinary, so simple, suddenly took on a formidable resonance. Another world opened before him, a world in which he would be fighting not for himself but for his father, the Pharaoh of Egypt.

Although the garden was delightful, Iker had no wish to linger there and dream. His bags must be packed, and he must obtain the most detailed map of Faiyum he could find, one which gave the locations of its sacred sites.

As he was leaving the peaceful garden, a southerly wind began to blow, so gentle and so sweetly scented that he stopped in order to enjoy it.

He saw a vision: Isis was coming towards him with the southerly wind, which she embodied in a ritual designed to bring back the regenerative water and make life grow. On the narrow gold band round her head were buds of blue and white lotus, from which a golden light emanated. How could he describe her almost supernatural beauty?

Iker closed his eyes, then opened them again. She was still there, and now a little closer.

'I am afraid I am disturbing you,' she said, in a voice so enchanting that it made him stammer.

'No, no . . . not at all. I . . . I was thinking.'

'I like this pomegranate tree very much,' said Isis, pointing to the oldest tree in the garden. 'It flowers the all year round, it is equally beautiful in all seasons. When one flower withers, another grows immediately.'

'Unfortunately that is not the case with the Acacia of Osiris.'

The priestess's face became tinged with anxiety. 'If I had to give my life to save it, I would not hesitate.'

'The king is sending me on a dangerous mission: I am to go back to Faiyum, suppress a rebellion and find a remedy which will heal the acacia.'

'A branch of the Acacia of Neith.'

'How do you know about it?' Iker was astonished.

'I am the one who does the research in the archives at Abydos. But Neith's tree, if it ever existed, must have been dead for a long time.'

'If it is still alive, I shall find it.'

His enthusiasm made her smile.

He would not – could not – hide anything from Isis: she must know the truth about him. 'I intended to kill Senusret,' he confessed, 'because I thought he was a tyrant, the originator of all my misfortunes.' In a few jerky sentences, he told her his adventures, not concealing his mental torment.

'But the pharaoh has adopted you as his Royal Son,' she said when he had finished, 'so he must believe that you are honest and upright.'

'What about you? Can you forgive the wrong I have done?' Even as he asked the question, Iker felt that he had made a mistake, perhaps an irreparable one.

Isis smiled again. 'His Majesty has given his verdict. Why should mine be different? Your sincerity touches me and even, coming from such a high-ranking man, honours me.'

'I'm only a scribe from Madu,' protested Iker.

'You are the Royal Son, and I owe you respect.'

Iker felt as if his tongue were cleaving to the roof of his mouth. He could not find the words to tell her of his feelings and tell to her that she, and she alone, had so often saved him. All he could manage was 'Will you be returning to Abydos soon?'

'First thing tomorrow.'

'It is an extraordinary place.'

'I am forbidden to speak about it. I always wanted to live there, as close as possible to the source of our spirituality.'

'Will you . . . will you ever come back to Memphis?'

'I am under the command of the pharaoh and the superior of the permanent priests.'

For a moment, a too-brief moment, he thought he detected a shy glimmer of interest and understanding in her eyes, regarding what he was attempting in vain to express. But she was going away. How could he hold her back?

'Perhaps you could enlighten me regarding a strange thing that happened during the ritual of Userhet,' he ventured. 'In a pool, I saw a woman with magnificent hair and very smooth skin. Which goddess does she embody?'

'Userhet herself, the Powerful One, lady of the uraeus and feminine sun,' replied Isis. 'It is a privilege to have seen her, but you put yourself in great danger by not uttering the words of pacification. But perhaps, as she was revealed during the ritual you attended, there is no need to fear her. May she help you to accomplish your mission.'

'Perhaps we shall see each other again?'

'That is for destiny to decide.'

34

Medes was unsure of the best thing to do. Should he attack the Royal Son with the most extreme caution, besmirching his reputation little by little? Or should he be content to ignore him? At first he had thought that Iker, aware of his new importance, would occupy a considerable position at court. Later he had noticed that the young man was working under the tjaty's direction like any other royal scribe, that he did not attend any society dinners or mix socially with the dignitaries, and in fact occupied quite a minor position.

Both astonished and suspicious, Medes had invited him to lunch in order to weigh him up. Was this provincial lad so content with his lot that he preferred to remain in the shadows, or was he following a strategy whose results would be visible only in the long term? All in all, the most likely answer was that Iker was behaving this way because the king had told him to. Knowing that his 'sole ward' had no standing, Senusret was restricting him to a career as an administrator, where he would be no hindrance to anyone.

'My lord,' his steward informed him, 'Iker, the Royal Son, cannot honour your invitation.'

'Why not?'

'He has left Memphis.'

At the palace, Medes tried to find out more, but learnt only that Iker had boarded a boat heading south. He was travelling alone, except for his donkey. This far from glittering departure looked like a disgrace. Senusret must be displeased with him, and so was sending him back to his province; no one would hear of him again.

Reinvigorated, Medes unrolled his letters. One, written in code, came from the Phoenician trader. Buried in a hotchpotch of polite sentences there was one important one: '*I must see you as a matter of urgency.*'

'A cup of wine, my dear Medes?' suggested the Phoenician.

'I had to cancel a dinner to come here. I hope I shall not regret doing so.'

'My employer has confirmed the meeting near Abydos, aboard a boat which belongs to me.'

'Here are my conditions: Gergu will be on board before we leave Memphis, and I shall arrive at the agreed place by my own means.'

'As you wish.'

'Will you be there?'

'My employer does not wish it,' replied the Phoenician smoothly. 'Our business affairs keep me here – they are flourishing, I am happy to say.'

The look in Medes's eyes was menacing. 'Are you preparing to play a trick on me, dear colleague?'

'I'm not mad enough to do that. Thanks to you, I am making a fortune and leading a most agreeable life.'

'And is your employer, too?'

'He is different. Each unto his own pleasures.'

'He is a most mysterious man.'

'He does not like me to talk of him.'

'If he tries to harm me, he will regret it.'

'He has no intention whatsoever of doing so,' said the Phoenician. 'He merely wishes to meet you in order to strengthen our cooperation.'

*

As soon as they set eyes on each other, Gergu and the captain who worked for the Phoenician trader took a liking to each other. Gergu liked this kind of coarse, rugged fighter with dishevelled hair, capable of killing without feeling the least emotion: and Gergu's bulky, brutal appearance pleased the sailor.

'I must inspect your boat from top to bottom,' said Gergu.

'You can do it with a cup in your hand, can't you?'

'I can indeed,' confirmed Gergu.

'I've got some some wine – it's a bit rough, but it goes down well.'

Gergu emptied a first cupful. 'If anything, I find it a little young.'

'It will improve as we travel down the Nile.'

The joke much amused them, and the inspection took place in a relaxed atmosphere. Gergu found nothing out of the ordinary. The crew comprised ten unarmed men, and the cargo was flatcakes, dried fish and jars of wine.

'Are you reassured?' asked the captain.

'Cast off the mooring-ropes, Captain.'

During the trip, the two new friends drank constantly. Gergu praised Medes's merits, and the captain replied by praising the Phoenician's. He congratulated himself on the way the illegal traffic in precious woods was organized, then spoke of his plans for a fine farm with oxen – he'd eat meat every day.

'The only thing wrong with your boat,' said Gergu, 'is that there are no women aboard.'

'I'd have liked to bring a whore along,' confided the captain, 'but the Phoenician forbade it.'

'Doesn't he like women?'

'He does, but it seems the great leader isn't the amorous sort.'

'Do you know him?'

'Never seen him.'

The boat pulled in to the side of the river and moored well before reaching Abydos. As she was hidden by a thick mass of reeds growing along the bank, nobody would notice her. If the river guards saw and checked her, which was highly unlikely, the captain would claim that he'd stopped to make repairs. According to the Phoenician, the great leader himself had chosen this ideal place.

'I shall leave you now,' said Gergu. 'I'm going to fetch my own employer.'

The captain lay down on the deck and fell asleep.

Bega was intrigued. 'Why are you insisting that I accompany you to this meeting, Medes?'

'To seal our agreement once and for all.'

Temporary priest Gergu and Medes, who was again posing as his assistant, had passed through the checkpoints without difficulty, then asked to speak Bega as usual, to take his new order. This was what they always did, and the security guards no longer paid the two men any attention.

'Who is this "great leader"?' asked Bega.

'Someone who will help us become wealthier without our attracting attention. Your presence will show the extent of our collaboration. I shall not hide my secret hope from you: that it will enable us to overthrow Senusret very soon.'

'What if he is nothing more than a common bandit?'

'The Phoenician is a smuggler of the highest sort, and his leader can hardly be a nonentity. Can you leave Abydos easily?'

'Permanent priests are not recluses,' Bega reminded him. 'But I am not yet reassured. This mysterious man might be laying a trap for us.'

'Gergu has inspected the boat where the meeting will take place, and his men are keeping watch on the area. If there is any sign of danger, they will intervene. Believe me, Bega, I am in control of the situation. And I am convinced that we are taking a decisive step forward together.'

*

In a small boat, Gergu rowed out to the vessel. Everything seemed quiet.

'Captain? It's Gergu.'

He listened carefully, and heard snoring. Climbing aboard, Gergu found the captain and his crew dead drunk. Meticulously, he searched the vessel one more time, again without finding anything alarming.

Climbing back into his own boat, he rowed to Medes's vessel, which was moored a little way off. 'All is well,' he said.

'Are your men in position, Gergu?'

'Our security is assured.'

Medes woke the captain with a kick in the ribs. He groaned and opened one eye.

'Do you know when your employer will arrive?' asked Medes.

'No,' said Gergu. 'But I don't mind waiting.'

'Captain, clean the cabin.'

The captain shook his crew awake. Grumbling, he restored the boat to some semblance of cleanliness.

Suddenly, pushing aside the reeds, a hooded man appeared on the bank.

'Come, Bega,' Medes urged him. 'There's nothing to fear.'

Rather awkwardly and with much hesitation, the priest ventured on to the gangplank. Afraid that he might fall in, Medes hurried to support him. It was clear that physical activity was not Bega's strong point.

Out of breath, he sat down on a three-legged stool. 'Is everyone here?' he asked.

'Our host hasn't arrived yet.'

A long wait began. Bega kept his face lowered; Gergu drank in secret, behind the cabin; Medes paced up and down the deck.

Eventually, infuriated, he hailed the captain, who was

slumped against the handrail. 'I do not permit people to make a fool of me. I am leaving now. You will pay for this insult!'

A voice at once smooth and menacing rooted Medes to the spot. 'Why this pointless anger? I am here.'

He was standing at the prow. Nobody had seen him arrive. Tall, bearded, with an emaciated face, he wore a turban and a woollen tunic which reached to his ankles. His eyes were red, and set deep in their sockets.

Gergu dropped his cup, Bega stiffened, Medes stood open-mouthed.

Eventually Medes recovered enough to ask, 'Who . . . who are you?'

'I am the Herald. You three will become my faithful followers.'

A madman – he's a madman! thought Medes, and he signed to Gergu to unleash his men.

'There is no point in becoming agitated,' advised the Herald. 'Your boat is under my control. The petty crooks employed by Gergu were no match for my men.'

Springing out of the reeds, Crooked-Face and Shab the Twisted threw severed heads and hands on to the deck.

'Let me leave,' begged Bega in a quavering voice.

'No one will leave this place before receiving my orders and promising to obey me,' said the Herald gently.

Despite this, Gergu tried to throw himself into the water, but the talons of a falcon sank into his shoulder. Howling with pain, he was forced to his knees.

'If you do that again, I shall rip out your liver,' promised the Herald. 'What a ridiculous death, when you could be making your fortune.'

'You really are the Phoenician's employer?' asked Medes, fascinated.

'He has learnt, in his flesh, not to betray me and to be obedient. May he serve as your example, for together we shall bring great plans to fruition. All three of you have good

Christian Jacq

intentions, but you have come up against formidable enemies and up to now have achieved only disappointing results. Senankh, Sehotep, General Nesmontu and Sobek the Protector all emerged unscathed from the snares you set for them. And then there is the pharaoh. By sending an unskilled man against him, you made the expert charged with killing him fail. Now Sobek has been exonerated, and Senusret is once again under close protection.'

'You want to kill the king, too?' asked Medes, slightly reassured.

'Individual efforts condemn us to failure. That is why I have decided to coordinate them. You, take off your hood and tell me your name.'

The priest had not the courage to resist. 'My name is Bega and I am a permanent priest at Abydos.'

'A fine prize, Medes,' commented the Herald.

'The secrecy of the Mysteries of Osiris must be penetrated,' said Medes, 'but Abydos remains the centre of Egyptian spirituality and the source of the pharaoh's power.'

'Do you think I don't know that?' said the Herald scornfully. 'Bega, tell me about the Tree of Life.'

The priest raised stunned eyes. 'You . . . you know?'

'Answer me.'

'The Acacia of Osiris has fallen gravely ill, the victim of a curse.'

'Has it not completely dried out?'

'No, it has regained a little life. A first branch grew green again when the temple and tomb of Senusret were built. They give off *ka*, and the priests toil daily to fix it within the tree. A second branch grew green when the decree of Egypt's reunification was proclaimed.'

'What else is being done to try to heal the tree?'

'Senusret is having a pyramid built.'

'Where?'

'At Dahshur,' replied Medes.

'Who holds the Golden Palette?' demanded the Herald.

Bega was dumbfounded. 'Do you know all our ritual treasures?'

'Answer me.'

'Pharaoh himself. Our superior, the Shaven-headed One, does nothing without the king's explicit agreement.'

'What about you, Bega? What do you desire?'

'To be rid of that despot and obtain the post that is due to me. Because of my experience and age, I should be ruling over Abydos.'

'And why have you formed this alliance with Medes?'

Seeing Bega's embarrassment, Medes stepped in and gave a full explanation of the trading plans he and Bega had made.

'Those are excellent ideas,' nodded the Herald. 'You are to continue in that way. We agree on many points, but you lack scope. I, the Herald, am the guardian of the truth. I shall draw up a definitive law. Not one word of it can ever be changed, for God will dictate it to me. It will apply to all of humanity, and those who oppose it will be slaughtered. But first we must destroy the principal obstacle, Pharaoh and the pharaonic tradition, and seize control of Egypt. When we are masters of this land, the centre of the world, the conquest of the others will be mere child's play.'

Medes had not planned to go so far, but why not? As for Gergu, he would follow Medes. And Bega was so terrified that absolute obedience seemed to him to be the only way to survive.

'We shall sow terror among the unbelievers,' prophesied the Herald, 'we shall execute the blasphemers, we shall wipe away borders, we shall force women to stay in their homes and serve their husbands, we shall seize the gold of the gods and we shall prevent Osiris from being reborn.'

35

The Herald's voice sent shivers through those who heard his words. He took three pieces of red quartzite from the pockets of his woollen tunic.

'The light has not damaged these stones of Set,' he explained, 'so they still contain the destructive fire that will help us to combat our enemies. All three of you, hold out your left hand.'

The Herald laid a stone in each man's palm. 'Now, close your hand and hold the stone tightly, very tightly.'

Medes, Bega and Gergu all cried out at the same time. The quartzite was burning them but they could not relax their grip.

The Herald stretched out his hands, and the pain instantly disappeared. 'Now, you bear the mark of Set in your flesh. You are his allies and his confederates, and you will obey me without question. If do you not, your bodies will burst into flame and you will die in appalling pain.'

The quartzite had disintegrated. Like his co-conspirators, Medes saw in the hollow of his hand a minuscule head of the god, with his okapi's snout and his large, erect ears.

Bega was almost choking. He, the servant of Osiris, was now the disciple of Set, his murderer!

'Now nothing can separate us,' added the Herald. 'Our pact is sealed.'

'What troops will we use to attack the pharaoh?' asked Medes.

'Has he not just created a national army?'

'Yes, and General Nesmontu commands it. It has fearsome strength and power.'

'A frontal assault would inevitably turn to our disadvantage,' conceded the Herald, 'for I can counter it only with a band of boastful, snivelling, cowardly Canaanites. There is only one solution: terrorism.'

'With what weapons?'

'My people in Kahun are making them. Officially the weapons are for the Egyptian forces, but my people are stealing some for our use. We shall organize quick, bloody actions which destabilize the pharaoh and spread fear through the population.'

'Won't innocent civilians turn against us?' asked Gergu anxiously.

'There are no innocents. People will be with us or against us. To submit to the pharaoh and respect the Law of Ma'at is to be guilty. From now on, each in your own place, you will trample upon it ceaselessly. I want to know everything about Abydos, Senusret, his government, his army and his guards. Now we shall go our separate ways.'

Bega pulled down his hood again and was the first to leave. Staggering, he made his way down the gangplank and disappeared into the reeds.

'Is it true that Senusret has made an extraordinary decision?' asked the Herald, gazing into the distance.

'Indeed,' replied Medes. 'He has adopted a son.'

'What is his name?'

'Iker.'

'Is that not the young man from Madu whom you were to sacrifice to the sea-god?'

Once again, Medes was stunned. 'Yes, but . . . how do you know?'

273

'Who told you the sacrificial victim's name?'

'A local informant.'

'He was acting on my orders. I saw in that boy remarkable capacity to resist the forces of evil. By sacrificin him, we would have gathered them to our benefit. B escaping from the shipwreck, he gained additional strength.

Crooked-Face emerged from the cabin. 'Would that Ike be the informer? I thought he was burnt alive in the mountai of turquoises.'

'He survived the fire and continued on his way, unaware c the power that guided him. Today, he sits beside the pharao and receives his teaching.'

'Don't worry,' said Medes. 'He's left Memphis – h proved so inadequate that the king has discreetly got rid c him.'

'Where has he gone?'

'To the South. He's probably going back to his hom village, where he can parade for a while as a hero befor resting on his privileges. In the capital, we will hear no mor talk of him.'

In their turn, Medes and Gergu left the boat.

The Herald turned to the captain. 'Leave for Faiyum once. Keep your eyes and ears open, and if you spot Iker ki him.'

None of Iker's maps mentioned the Acacia of Neith. Th archives had provided the information that it stood on the Is of Sobek in Faiyum, but unfortunately the map-makers ha not given the Isle's location. By questioning the inhabitan of the province, however, the young man might manage find it.

Ever since he left Memphis, Sekari had been watchir Iker. The two men pretended not to know each other, ar never talked to together, but if danger arose Sekari wou react as vigorously as necessary.

He had thought two peasants looked suspicious, especially hen they sidled up to Iker. But they only wanted to talk, and thing amiss had happened by the time they arrived at the port rving Henen-nesut, the Town of the Royal Child,* where ilders were enlarging a temple in honour of the ram-god eryshef, 'He Who Is on His Lake'. He was responsible for the od in Faiyum and for the province's proper irrigation by the eat canal that wound through its fertile land.

Work was going on everywhere: drying out some of the arshland, founding villages and temples, constructing small ms, locks and drainage channels. A large part of the region oked like a vast forest, a paradise for plants and animals.

Enjoying his journey, North Wind walked with a light step. fter making the usual fuss, snorting and rolling about on the ound so that Iker could not trim his hooves, which were as rd as ebony, he got up and stood proudly again, drawing any admiring looks.

'You know perfectly well that your hooves must be filed wn three times a year,' said Iker reproachfully.

The donkey chose not to answer, and carried on his way as r as the trade-control post at the entrance to the Town of the yal Child.

'Have you any goods to declare?' asked the official.

Iker showed his scribe's writing-materials.

'That's all right, you can pass.'

'I'm looking for a very ancient sacred site, where an acacia dicated to Neith grows. Do you know anyone who might be le to help me?'

'The person who knows most about the region is the erseer of dykes.'

The official told Iker where the overseer's house was. As he understood the route better than the Royal Son, North nd set off in the right direction.

erakleopolis Magna.

275

The overseer was enjoying the fresh air in his garden, the shade of a canopy. Iker greeted him, introduced himse and explained what he was looking for.

'The Acacia of Neith? Yes, I've heard of it. It grows in forgotten corner where only a few shepherds and wild beas venture from time to time. Go north-west, leaving the obeli of Senusret I on your right – on the top of it there's a sol disc symbolizing the birth of the light from the primordi waters. Why are you interested in the sacred tree?'

'I am identifying the ancient sites of the province to no them on a map.'

In the evening, at the ale-house, the overseer natural related this conversation to his friends. The description Iker and his donkey came to the ears of the captain who ha been sent by the Herald. He resolved not to let his pr escape.

The luxuriant greenery was not all good. If they had not had t protection of an ointment which repelled mosquitoes, Iker a North Wind would have given up and gone back to Hen-nes

In a tiny village they met an old man who told them that t goddess's tree was not much further, but they must be caref when walking alongside the lake as it was full of monstro crocodiles, one of which was eighty years old and liked bask in the rays of the setting sun.

Iker wondered if Sekari was still following him at distance through this maze. He pushed his way through tangle of tamarisk branches and came upon a lake hidd among the trees, its far end lost in a forest of willows.

Further along the bank, a shepherd was cooking a fish.

Iker went up to him. 'Is the Isle of Sobek far from here?

'Maybe, maybe not.'

'I am Iker the scribe, and I am looking for the Acacia Neith.'

The captain's disguise was thoroughly convincin

Dishevelled and unshaven, he looked just like one of those ill-tempered, solitary men who have little fondness for human company but know every cubit of their territory.

'The Acacia of Neith,' he repeated. 'What do you want with it?'

'To put it on my map.'

'Maps are useless. Better to trust your nose.'

'All the same, will you help me?'

'Have to finish my meal first. Are you hungry?'

The two ate in silence. Then the 'shepherd' stood up.

'The Isle of Sobek is at the far end of the lake,' he said. 'We'll take my boat.' He parted the reeds and untied the mooring-rope. 'Hold my arm,' he advised Iker. 'With all the crocodiles around here, it's best not to fall in.'

Choosing a moment when Iker was off balance, the captain shoved him hard in the back. Iker hit the surface of the lake hard, sending up a spray of water. In the time it took him to recover his wits and swim towards the bank, he saw the old crocodile who ruled the place bearing down on him, a monster the weight of ten men. Seizing Iker, it dived down beneath the water.

'Mission accomplished!' guffawed the captain.

The murderer had no time for further celebrations, because Sekari leapt out of the undergrowth and hurled him into the lake.

'Help!' screamed the captain. 'I can't swim!'

Sekari could not have helped, even if he had wanted to. Two more crocodiles were already dealing with this writhing prey. The first clamped its seventy razor-sharp teeth round his neck, while the other's jaws closed on his left leg. Eagerly, the huge creatures tore the Herald's envoy to pieces.

Sekari reproached himself without mercy. 'I thought he was a real shepherd,' he told North Wind angrily. 'Even if I'd suspected him, I'd have thought he wouldn't attack Iker before he'd taken him to the acacia.'

North Wind stared at the lake, which was reddened wit[*] the captain's blood.

'I can't abandon Iker. I'm going in after him.'

North Wind stepped in front of him and cocked up his le[*] ear.

'What do you mean, no? He may only be wounded Perhaps . . .'

In the donkey's big eyes, Sekari read unfailing deter mination, but not despair. Despondently, he sat down on th bank. 'You're right. All I'd do would be get myself eaten.'

Now many more crocodiles had joined the fight, each on trying to seize a morsel of the feast.

Sekari was in tears. 'I couldn't save my best friend. It[*] because of me that he's dead.'

North Wind cocked his left ear again.

Sekari stroked his neck and said, 'Your kindness warm my heart, but I hate myself. Come on, let's leave this place.

The donkey stepped in front of him again.

'It's over, North Wind. Everything's over.'

But the donkey's left ear disagreed with that statement.

'You want to wait longer?'

Now North Wind's right ear was raised towards the sk[*] with great emphasis.

'All right, we'll wait. But for what?'

North Wind settled himself comfortably on the ground, h[*] eyes fixed on the lake.

36

he crocodile had moved so fast that Iker had no time to be
fraid of dying. As the enormous creature slid under him he
lung on to it, and they plunged together towards the bottom
f the lake.

After passing through a turbid, grey area, he saw a watery
orest, lit by a gentle sun. The magic words of a sacred song
ritten to appease the fury of the crocodile-god came
aturally into his mind: 'You who rise up in the primordial
ater and dispense brightness from the waves, cause it to be
eborn on earth, be the fertilising bull, lord of foods, search
or your father Osiris and protect me from danger.'

Entranced by the beauty of the many-coloured plants,
hich swayed gracefully in the water, Iker forgot about
reathing. The old crocodile rose to the surface again and laid
s burden on the edge of a small, sunny island which rose
ently up from the lake to form a central mound.

Iker could not understand how he had survived, but he had
e sensation that he was equipped with a new weapon, the
rength of the great fish.*

Before him lay an extraordinary mummy: the head of
siris's body emerged from the body of a bronze crocodile,

This strength was called *at*. The Egyptians classified the crocodile as
fish.

which had gold teeth and was sheathed in a mantle of coppe
and other metals.* The master of the waters was presented a
an indestructible boat, offered to the deceased to trave
through the wide stretches of the world beyond. In the pas
few minutes, completely forgetting himself, Iker had
experienced the rebirth of the Light, which had emerged from
the bottom of the primordial lake.

At the centre of the island, on the mound, was an acacia tree

Alas, someone had set fire to it, and so recently that the
ashes of its branches and leaves were still smoking. On the
charred trunk, the name of the goddess Neith had been
defaced with red ink.

'Tell me again,' demanded Sekari.

'That's ten times,' protested Iker.

'Because of you, I thought I'd made a fatal mistake. And
in any case, your story seems so mad that each time you tel
it I have to memorize every detail and tell myself that you
aren't making up new ones when you repeat it.'

'And am I?'

'Not so far, no, but one can't be too careful.'

'The evil criminal has destroyed the Acacia of Neith. It'
strange he should have done it now. Anyone would think h
knew what we were going to do.'

'One more reason to go immediately to Kahun, arrest Bin
and dismantle her network.'

'Yes, but first we ought to make sure the mayor's honest.

'Make your entry into the town as public and official a
possible,' advised Sekari. 'If he throws you in prison, I'
ensure that the army takes action. Let's hope the town isn'
already in the Asians' hands.'

*The association between man and crocodile is attested by a mumm
conserved in the storerooms of the Topkapi Museum in Istanbul.

*

Bina felt ready. In three days' time, the Asians in Kahun would collect the weapons they had hidden, and attack the guard posts during the night. With Ibcha, who was as determined as herself, she would kill the scribes, in order to terrify the population and make them understand that their new masters rejected the ancient culture.

After the fall of Kahun, Bina would undertake the conquest of the other towns and villages in Faiyum – none of them would be able to withtand her forces. Other Asian caravans would arrive as reinforcements, and Senusret's army, immobilized in Canaan, would take a long time to react. Next, it would suffer an exhausting guerrilla war.

Such were the Herald's instructions, and she would follow them to the letter.

She would owe her victory to her charm. Every three months, the mayor entirely renewed the Kahun guard. Bina had seduced the official in charge of the next transfers. As much by her caresses as by her fiery declarations, she had persuaded him to rally to her cause, promising him a senior post in the future high command. Through this foolish fellow – he would be one of the first to die – she knew the exact number of soldiers and their positions. The Asians would annihilate them within minutes.

'Name and office?' demanded the officer guarding the main gate of Kahun.

'Iker, scribe and temporary priest of the Temple of Anubis.'

'Any items to declare?'

'My writing-materials.'

The officer searched North Wind's panniers. 'You may pass. I'll soon have finished with this damned work! The day after tomorrow I'm being relieved at last, and I'm going back to the Delta.'

'Is the town calm?' asked Iker.

281

'Yes, there's been no trouble at all.'

Led by North Wind, who of course knew Kahun well, Iker headed for the mayor's huge residence, which also contained the workplaces of many scribes and craftsmen.

One of the messengers recognized him. 'Iker! Where did you disappear to?'

'Is the mayor in his office?'

'He never leaves it. I'll announce you.'

The young man settled North Wind in the shade of an inner courtyard and had some fodder brought to him. A scribe led the visitor into the house.

The mayor raised his head from from a mass of scrolls. 'Iker, is it really you? According to a decree I've just received, you've been appointed Royal Son, but that can't be true, surely?'

'I'm afraid it is.'

'When you disappeared, I decided not to launch an investigation – even though you deserved a severe punishment! But I felt that something strange was going on, for you were really too different from the other scribes. I'll wager you've come back on official business, haven't you?'

'I want to know what master you serve.'

The mayor gripped the arms of his chair. 'What does that question mean?'

'Someone tried to kill the king. And there are rebels hiding here in Kahun; they will make their move soon.'

'Is this some kind of joke?'

'I know a few of the leaders. Most of the rebels are Asians employed as metalworkers.'

The mayor seemed stunned. 'You cannot be talking about Kahun, my town!'

'Unfortunately, I am. Either you are in league with the terrorists or you will help me wipe them out.'

'Me, on the side of those bandits? Have you gone mad? How many soldiers do you want?'

'We must arrest them all at the same time, which means we

must take care not to alert them. Poorly prepared action would lead to much bloodshed.'

'Then what does Royal Son Iker suggest?'

'Summon all the officials concerned, and we'll organize a series of well-targeted raids. When the conspiracy has been destroyed, be so good as to obtain for me a list of all the boatyards in Faiyum, including those that have been closed down, and not forgetting the one where the dead carpenter known as Plane used to work.'

'It will take time to put together but you shall have it.'

'May I stay in my former house?'

The mayor looked terribly embarrassed. 'I'm afraid that won't be possible.'

'Have you allocated it to someone else?'

'No, it isn't that . . . Well, you'll see for yourself.'

The blacksmith employed in the annexe to the mayor's house pretended to have unbearable backache and left the forge in his assistant's hands, saying he must consult a healer urgently. In reality, he had recognized Iker and must immediately warn his leader, Ibcha, foreman of the main workshop where weapons were made.

Ibcha sent for Bina, who immediately stopped cleaning the luxurious house of the Keeper of the Archives, her latest employer. The trio shut themselves in a storeroom.

'Iker has come back,' said the blacksmith.

'You're sure? Really sure?' asked Bina.

'I'm very good at remembering faces.'

'This is disastrous,' said Ibcha.

Bina did not contradict him. She knew that the man sent by Crooked-Face to kill the king had failed and that Iker had become sole palace ward, in other words the pharaoh's faithful servant. However, she had recently been informed that Iker had fallen into disfavour and had had to leave the court. He was said to have gone to the South, and was not

283

expected to live very long because one of the Phoenician'
agents was preparing to kill him.

'The pharaoh still trusts Iker,' she concluded, 'and ha
charged him with destroying us. There is only one solution
we must escape immediately, taking as many weapons a
possible with us. Our weakest elements can be sacrificed
we'll order them to create a diversion and fight for as long a
they can.'

Ibcha protested, 'But we're only a few hours away from
taking Kahun!'

'If the Royal Son has gone to see the mayor, it can only b
to organize our arrest. He wants us alive. Don't forget that h
knows the location of the weapons workshop and the true rol
of the Asian metalworkers. We have not a moment to lose. I
we delay, we are lost.'

Although devastated, Ibcha had to accept his leader's wa
of thinking. 'What sort of diversion have you in mind?'

'An attack on the mayor's house.'

Iker and North Wind were devastated. All that was left of th
beautiful house and its fine furniture were ruins, bearing th
marks of a fierce fire.

'We could not save anything,' explained Long-Hair, who
characteristically, had appeared to explain and describe sa
events. 'The fire began in the middle of the night; and it wa
no accident.'

'How can you be sure of that?'

'Because there were at least ten different fires and the
were all lit at the same time, which is why nothing could b
done. An old woman saw several men running away, Yo
know, Iker, I like you a great deal, but there are jealou
people and evildoers in Kahun.'

'Do you suspect anyone in particular?'

'Not really, no . . . Is it true that the pharaoh has adopte
you as his son?'

'Yes, it is.'

'Well, will you help me obtain promotion?'

'That is a decision for the mayor to make.'

'The mayor doesn't like me very much. If I got you some important information, would you support me?'

'Get the information and we'll see.'

'Where are you going to stay?'

'At the Temple of Anubis.'

The donkey led the way to the temple, where the permanent priests gave Iker a mixed welcome. Some were glad to see him again, but others reproached him for abandoning his post as a temporary priest without warning anyone.

He offered his apologies to the priests, who thanked the Royal Son for honouring the temple with his presence. They offered him the best room, but he first wanted to see the library where he had listed and classified so many remarkable manuscripts dating from the age of the great pyramids.

His stay in the library did not last long, however, for a message was brought to him that Long-Hair was asking for him. Iker received him in his room.

'I've got it – your information, I mean. Will you speak to the mayor?'

'Yes, I will.'

'Well, here it is: one of the fire-setters was the Asian blacksmith whose forge is in the mayor's house. When he saw you this morning, he suddenly left the forge, complaining of pain in his back. But his assistant says that's a lie, because he ran off like a hare.'

So Iker had been spotted by one of Bina's men. Either she would launch an attack almost at once, or else she and her men would try to get away. As the guards' operations had not yet been fully planned, she had a definite advantage.

'Quickly, Long-Hair,' said Iker. 'We must warn the commander of the city guards.'

As the two men were running towards the barracks, shouts rang out.

'Someone's attacking the mayor's house!' shouted a jar-seller, dropping his wares.

37

Soldiers and guards raced towards the mayor's house. While confusion reigned in the town, Bina, Ibcha and most of the Asians made their escape, carrying heavy baskets full of weapons.

'Keep out of the crowd,' Sekari warned Iker. 'In that ruckus, I couldn't protect you – you might be hit.'

The main fighting was on the hill of Kahun. The 'weakest elements' chosen by Bina had killed several unarmed servants, but the town's craftsmen were defending themselves with the tools of their trades. And when the soldiers arrived, some of the Asians forgot their vow to give their lives for the cause, and fled like frightened sparrows. Others, on the other hand, fought fiercely but eventually succumbed to weight of numbers.

A hunt throughout the town for any remaining terrorists then began, ending a good two hours later when the last few were caught and killed. The mayor put aside his shock and anger, and did his best to comfort the wounded.

Iker and Sekari tried to find out how many Asians had escaped and what direction they had taken. Sorting through the statements, which were a mixture of exaggeration and fear, was not easy, but it seemed most likely that some had fled towards the north of the province, the rest towards the Nile.

'We'll track them down later,' decided Sekari. 'The most urgent thing is to identify their accomplices in Kahun itself. If we don't, there's a risk of another murder.'

Only one suspect was unwounded: the blacksmith who had warned the Asians. He claimed that he was a victim, but no one believed him.

An officer grabbed him by the hair. 'Let me question him my way. He'll tell me everything, believe me.'

'No torture,' decreed Iker.

'In the circumstances, the end justifies the means.'

'I shall question the prisoner myself.'

The officer let the blacksmith go. Disobeying a Royal Son could have serious consequences.

Iker asked the blacksmith, 'Did you often see Bina?'

'Yes, but so did lots of other people in Kahun.'

'What was her plan for seizing control of the city?'

'I don't know anything about it.'

'That's hardly likely,' said Iker, 'because, working in the mayor's house, you were in an excellent position to observe everything that happened there. You were supposed to kill him during the fighting, weren't you?'

'I was just working at my forge.'

Sekari sat down next to the prisoner. 'I'm neither a soldier nor a city guard, my friend. The Royal Son who's questioning you so nicely has no influence over me, because he can't affect my career. The amusing thing is that I am rather an expert on interrogation. Between you and me, I can even admit that I find it entertaining. On your side, though, it wouldn't be so funny.' He showed the blacksmith a sharp-pointed piece of wood. 'I always start by putting out one eye. It's very painful, apparently, especially when you haven't got the right tool for the job. But that's just for amusement. Afterwards I set to work in earnest. Perhaps the Royal Son would like to leave now, if he doesn't want to see this painful spectacle . . .'

Iker turned and began to walk away.

'Don't go!' cried the blacksmith. 'Stay, please, and stop this madman torturing me. If you promise not to let him, I'll talk.'

Iker turned back to him. 'Very well, I'm listening. But tell just one lie and the torture will begin.'

'Bina wanted to take advantage of the change of the guards tomorrow. Once the soldiers had been killed, she'd easily have conquered the town.'

'So she had an accomplice among the soldiers?'

'Yes, but I don't know who.'

'You're lying, aren't you?' said Sekari.

'No, I swear I'm not!' He was so terrified that it was clear he was telling the truth.

Iker and Sekari rejoined the mayor, who was happy and relieved to see order re-established.

'Who is in charge of changing the guards tomorrow?' asked Iker.

'Captain Rechi.'

'Where can I find him?'

'In the barracks outside the city, beside the canal.'

The barracks was empty, for all the soldiers had gone back to Kahun to ensure its security. The only man left was a solitary sentry.

'I am looking for Captain Rechi,' said Iker.

'Who are you?'

'Royal Son Iker.'

'Oh! Rechi's watching the canal from his boat, my lord.'

'In that case, he must surely have seen the fugitives. Take me there.'

'My lord, the captain ordered me not to leave my post, and—'

'I'll take full responsibility.'

'Thank you, my lord. It's this way.'

The two men hurried to the canal. Half hidden in the reeds they saw a good-sized boat with a central cabin.

'Are you there, Captain?' shouted the soldier.

The only response was that a cloud of annoyed lapwings fluttered away.

The soldier frowned. 'It's odd that he didn't answer. I hope nothing's happened to him. Let's go aboard and see.'

They boarded at the stern, where there were two harpoons used for hunting hippopotamus. As Iker pushed open the cabin door, he had a sudden premonition and dodged to his left. If the blow had landed on his head he'd have been knocked out. Instead he was hit on the shoulder and felled to the deck.

'He's too curious, this busybody!' exclaimed Rechi, seizing a harpoon.

Iker rolled frantically aside to avoid the weapon's hooks, which sank into the deck a finger's breadth from his head.

Rechi was preparing to strike again, with the second harpoon, when a knee thudded into his back. His arm was twisted savagely until he dropped his weapon, and a chop to the throat deprived him of air: he lost consciousness.

'That coward doesn't know how to fight,' said Sekari contemptuously. 'Are you all right, Iker?'

'I'll have a nasty bruise, I think. Let's wake him up.'

Sekari ducked the captain's head in the canal.

He soon came round. 'Don't kill me!' he begged.

'That will depend on your answers. We already know that you're a traitor and in Bina's pay.'

'Our cause will triumph. We're oppressed and—'

'Your cause doesn't interest us, and your plot's failed. Where have the rest of the Asians gone?'

'I can't tell you. I—'

Sekari ducked his head in the water again and held it there for a long time. When he pulled it out again, Rechi had difficulty getting his breath back.

'I'm running out of patience,' said Sekari. 'Either you talk or your miserable life will end here and now in this canal.'

The captain did not take Sekari's threats lightly. 'They split up into two groups. The first took the track leading to Birket Qarun, the great lake, and the other took a boat for Memphis.'

'Who are they to join there?'

'I don't know.'

'Another little ducking?' suggested Sekari.

'No, don't, not that! Have mercy! I swear I've told you everything.'

'We'll take him back to Kahun,' said Iker.

Although exhausted and feeling as if he'd aged ten years, the mayor was gradually regaining his spirits. Now that the rebels and all traces of the fighting had been removed, Kahun was once again becoming a quiet, attractive city.

'I'd never have imagined such a terrible thing could happen here,' he confessed to Iker.

'That's what the terrorists were counting on, that and our lack of foresight,' said Iker, 'and they're far from being destroyed.'

'Before you leave,' said the mayor, 'please attend the festival of Sokar. Then I'll have time to assemble the information you want about the boatyards.'

Iker recalled that this mysterious god featured in the song of the men who carried travelling-chairs: 'Life Is Renewed by Sokar'.

As a temporary priest of Anubis, he joined the procession carrying the god's remarkable boat. It embodied the force of the deep, bringing the souls of the righteous on to the path of resurrection. At the prow was the head of an antelope, the animal of Set, whose capacity for destruction had been mastered, sacrificed, then used in favour of harmony. Near it were a fish, whose task was to guide the god of light in the darkness of the abyss, and some swallows, who had come from the world beyond. At the centre of the boat, the cabin symbolized the primordial mound where life had manifested itself in the 'first time', which was brought to life again each day. From the cabin emerged the head of a falcon, an affirmation of royal power and of the victory of celestial brightness over the darkness of chaos.

'Is Sokar linked to Osiris?' Iker asked the priest who was leading the ceremony in the shrine of Senusret II.

'The boat drives his enemies away and offers Osiris a place of change and nourishment. So at the end of the festival it will be taken to Abydos.'

Abydos . . . The sacred site haunted Iker's thoughts. Might his new office enable him, at some point in the future, to be admitted there and meet Isis again? He was in reflective mood as he fervently took part in the entry into the temple, away from the eyes of outsiders. Would Sokar grant him the help he needed?

'There is no doubt now about Sharp-Knife and Turtle-Eye,' the mayor told Iker. 'They did indeed belong to the trading-fleet at one time, but they were expelled for theft. When they were hired for the *Swift One*, they were mere outlaws. The rest of the crew, including the captain, were probably no better.'

'A ghost ship and a ghost crew,' commented Iker. 'What about the list of warship yards?'

'I sent scribes to question the overseers and craftsmen at the yards currently operating in Faiyum, and they found nothing untoward. On the other hand, I have no information on a site that was closed last year, near Birket Qarun.'

'That's where some of the Asians were going!'

'If you wish to go there yourself, I'll provide you with an escort. I thought the place was peaceful, but . . .'

'Send a messenger to Memphis within the hour, to inform

His Majesty as quickly as possible about what happened here.'

Iker doubted that the Asians could be caught before they reached their hideouts, which would have been established a long time ago. It was up to Sobek the Protector to dismantle the networks of spies and traitors, whose numbers and scope were still unknown. What the enemy had begun at Kahun, he would try to continue in Memphis.

38

With his little team of miners and desert guards, General Sepi explored the lands on either side of the Nile Valley, then entered Nubia. The maps he had been given had so far proved accurate, and he had not once lost his way. From the gold-mining sites, most of them now abandoned, he had taken a few samples, which one of his men would take back Memphis and pass on to Senankh.

The region seemed safe enough, but the miners were reluctant to go any further south.

'What are they afraid of?' Sepi asked the desert guards' commander. 'After all you and your men must have crossed and re-crossed this land hundreds of times.'

'Yes, sir, but the miners know I'd rather not take on the Nubians. The tribes around here are always causing trouble.'

'Surely we can deal with a few Nubian bandits?'

'They're fierce fighters, sir, and their cruelty's legendary. We'd need reinforcements.'

'That's impossible – we'd be spotted easily, and my orders are that we go unnoticed.' 'Is there a specific enemy that bothers you?'

The officer hesitated. 'Well, sir . . .'

'One of the desert monsters, is it that? Don't worry. If it appears, I have the necessary incantations to stop it in its tracks.'

Since Sepi was not given to idle boasting, the officer felt somewhat reassured.

'Why hasn't Elephantine warned the pharaoh about the trouble caused by the Nubians?' asked the general.

'When the province was independent, the governors acquired bad habits. Changing things will take time.'

As soon as he returned to the Nile Valley, Sepi decided, he would rectify this problem once and for all. The great Southern province might have rallied to Senusret, but its governance was still thoroughly unsatisfactory.

The little force set off along a track that ran eastwards, along the dry bed of the Allaqi wadi. Unfortunately, for the first time Sepi's map did not correspond to the terrain around them.

The guards officer did not recognize the area. 'You see, sir,' he told Sepi, 'the winds often move the dunes, and fierce rainstorms fill the dry riverbeds and sometimes change the rivers' course. But this is really strange. Anyone would think that giants have moved the rocks around. We'd better retreat.'

'On the contrary,' said Sepi, 'we must not ignore such a sign. We'll go as far as our water reserves permit. Perhaps we'll find a well.'

At the end of three days' march they saw some dry-stone buildings which marked the location of a mine.

One of the miners went into a narrow gallery, to see if it contained any seams which were still viable. Hardly had he entered when the roof collapsed. His companions immediately tried to rescue him, but after several hours' work all they managed to retrieve was his dead body.

The other entrances to galleries looked accessible, but Sepi was taking no more risks. He picked up a large stone and threw it into a downward-sloping passage. A few seconds later, there was a loud crash. That roof, too, had fallen in.

'The whole mine has been set with traps,' he concluded.

'We'd better return to Egypt,' advised the officer.

'That's exactly what the enemy wants us to do. But he doesn't know me very well.'

'But, sir, there aren't any mines beyond this one.'

'You, stay here with the men; I'll take one volunteer and go on a bit further. If we do find another mine, we'll come back and fetch you.'

Sunburnt and dry-mouthed, the desert guard was beginning to regret having volunteered. However, he'd been travelling the desert tracks for a long time. The heat, the burning sand, the sore eyes, the mirages, the insects – none of these was anything to be frightened of. But he was having trouble breathing. The wind strengthened suddenly, whipping his skin, then died away just as quickly and was replaced by an all-consuming sun which had never seemed so hot before. Fleas were biting his legs, and this was the third, very aggressive, horned viper that he had driven off by pelting it with stones.

'We'd better give up, General,' he said hoarsely.

'Just a little further, soldier.'

'It's hell here – just the desert, the snakes and the scorpions. No trace of gold.'

'I'm sure that isn't so.'

The volunteer wondered where Sepi got so much energy. Step by step, he followed him.

Suddenly, Sepi saw an apparition: a tall, bearded man, his head covered with a turban. Astonished, Sepi went towards him. 'Who are you?'

'I am the Herald and I knew you would dare venture this far, General Sepi. But it's a futile deed, and no one will never know about it. Now you must die.'

Sepi drew his sword and charged at the strange man. He intended to plunge his blade into the Herald's belly, but a falcon's talons sank into his arm and forced him to drop his weapon.

Rooted to the spot in horror, the volunteer saw terrifying monsters emerge from nowhere and rush past him. An enormous lion, an antelope with a horn on its forehead and a griffin charged at the general, who was soon brought down and torn to pieces.

The soldier tried to run away, but a powerful hand knocked him to the ground.

'To you I shall grant life. Tell your comrades exactly what you have seen.'

'The poor lad's completely mad,' said the officer. 'The sun's scorched his brain.'

'But desert monsters do exist,' objected a miner.

'I'm more inclined to believe it was a Nubian attack. He probably panicked and ran, leaving General Sepi to die. Deserting his post . . . If he wasn't in this state, that would earn him severe punishment.'

'His whole body's badly burnt,' said the miner, 'and he's on the point of death. Reaching here must have taken incredible courage. And don't forget, sir, you're also afraid of those monsters.'

'Well, perhaps . . . In any case, we can't just leave General Sepi's body in the desert – if he really has been killed.'

'You mean we must go and find it?'

'If we go back to Egypt without the general, and can't explain why, we'll have serious problems.'

The miner knew the officer was right but, at the thought of confronting creatures which crushed people's bones and drank their blood, his legs almost buckled under him.

'We are all going,' decided the officer, 'and we'll stick close together.'

The little force met nothing out of the ordinary. When they found Sepi's body, it was in a terrible state, torn apart by huge claws. Only his face was undamaged.

'We'll dig him a tomb at the head of the Allaki,' said the

Christian Jacq

officer, much moved, 'and cover it with stones so that animals can't get at his remains.'

As soon as he received the gold brought by Sepi's emissary, Senankh went to see Khnum-Hotep. Abandoning their work, the two dignitaries requested an audience with the king.

'Summon Sehotep and Djehuty,' said the pharaoh. 'I shall inform the queen, and we shall all leave for Abydos. In our absence, Sobek will ensure the safety of Memphis. Where is General Sepi now?'

'In Nubia,' replied Senankh. 'We should have more news soon.'

'We must check these samples as soon as possible.'

'Should I not remain at my post, Majesty?' asked the tjaty.

'The time has come to enlarge the Golden Circle of Abydos,' said Senusret. 'Under the protection of Osiris and in his sacred territory, you and Djehuty will undergo his ritual. It will increase the weight of your responsibilities still further, but will strengthen our unity in the face of our enemies.'

As recommended by Sobek, who was growing increasingly gloomy and suspicious, each of the illustrious travellers took a different boat, escorted by two river guards' vessels. However, despite the Protector's protests, the pharaoh insisted on leading the flotilla.

As soon as they arrived at Abydos, the site was entirely closed off. Not even the temporary priests who had come to work for the day were admitted.

Accompanied by the priestesses and permanent priests, the Shaven-headed One bowed before the pharaoh. The priest who watched over the wholeness of the great body of Osiris ensured that the new arrivals were not wearing or carrying anything made of metal.

As he watched, Bega wondered why Pharaoh, the Great Royal Wife, the tjaty and the most senior ministers in the state had come to Abydos. Something exceptional must have happened to justify such a spectacular journey.

'Majesty,' said the Shaven-headed One, 'the ship of Osiris has been halted, and no longer travels the universe gathering the energies needed for resurrection. But the Tree of Life is still resisting the curse.'

'I have brought some gold. Perhaps it will cure the tree.'

Bega ground his teeth. Had the pharaoh's faithful servants at last achieved the impossible?

'Let us go to the acacia,' ordered Senusret.

The procession took place in silence.

Hoping that the gold would be effective and dispel the nightmare, Isis was first to enter the magical area demarcated by the four young acacias planted round the Tree of Life and corresponding to the four points of the compass. At the foot of the Tree of Life, she poured water and milk.

Then the king approached and touched the trunk with gold from the desert of Kebet. There was no reaction, and no warmth spread through the acacia's veins. Nor was the gold sent by General Sepi any more effective.

Distress spread though the throng. Bega rejoiced so much at this setback that he had difficulty looking grief-stricken.

'Majesty,' the Shaven-headed One reminded the king, 'we need regenerative gold not only to heal the tree but also to make the ritual objects without which the Mysteries of Osiris cannot be righteously celebrated.'

'The search in Nubia has only just begun, and if any man can find the gold that man is General Sepi. Now, let us initiate two new followers of Ma'at into the Golden Circle of Abydos. Let Khnum-Hotep and Djehuty retire into a cell in the Temple of Osiris and meditate there.'

It was a long time since all the members of the Circle had been brought together, around the four offering-tables marking its members' unchanging resolve to devote their lives to passing on the spirituality of Osiris. Senusret thought of Sekari, charged with ensuring the Royal Son's safety, of General Nesmontu, busy maintaining peace in Canaan, of General Sepi, whose mission was proving even more difficult than expected.

The three men were grievously missed, but the king knew they would approve unreservedly of the initiations of Khnum-Hotep and Djehuty, two former opponents who were now loyal not only to him personally but to the pharaonic tradition, the only guarantor that Ma'at would be maintained on Earth.

Despite the dangers threatening the country and the profound disappointment caused by the failure of the gold, the two ceremonies took place in serene tranquillity, as if the participants were outside time. Khnum-Hotep took his place at the north, with Senankh, and Djehuty at the west, near the Shaven-headed One.

The ensuing feast was nearing its end when a soldier announced the arrival of an officer from the Nubian force. The king immediately left the reception chamber and received the man in a nearby office.

The officer would rather have fought fierce warriors than appeared before the king, whose eyes he dared not meet.

'Majesty, I am the bearer of very bad news.'

'Tell me, and hold nothing back.'

'The gold mines of Nubia are all inaccessible, exhausted or full of hidden traps. Worse still, General Sepi is dead.'

This was the first time Senusret had had to mourn the death of a member of the Golden Circle of Abydos. Never again would Sepi's chair be occupied; no one would replace him. He had carried out his sacred duties unfailingly and trained Iker by opening his mind to the many dimensions of the scribe's profession. Exceptionally intelligent, courageous to the point of recklessness, Sepi had played a key role in the reunification of Egypt by preventing Djehuty from making war on the king.

As usual, the king did not allow his feelings to show. He merely asked, 'How did he die?'

'He told us to remain where we were while he, with one volunteer, explored further towards the Great South. The volunteer got back, and before he died of sunstroke he told us a strange and confused story about General Sepi being killed by desert monsters. In my opinion, it was more likely Nubian looters who destroyed the mines. But the region is far from secure, and we have no chance of finding the general's murderers.'

'You are wrong,' said Senusret. 'I shall arrest them and I shall punish them. Did you take proper care to protect his body?'

'Of course, Majesty. We buried him at the head of the Allaki wadi.'

'Return there with an embalmer and bring Sepi back to the province of Thoth.'

39

Bina was furious, but she had to obey orders. She thought she would have been much more useful in Faiyum than hiding in Memphis. But nobody, not even she, could question a decision made by the Herald.

After the disastrous flight, the journey down the Nile had gone well. Bina's prompt action meant that her best men had been saved, and only the weakest and most inexperienced had been left to face certain death. She blamed herself bitterly for underestimating Iker – she'd never make that mistake again. Although she knew he was fiery and determined, she'd thought him malleable enough to control. That was a shattering misjudgment.

By becoming Royal Son, Iker had declared himself an implacable enemy. Far from being sent away from court and banished to his home province, he was one of Senusret's most trusted men. He had even been entrusted with destroying the rebels in Kahun, which was far beyond the reach of normal legal procedure.

And to think that Iker's intervention had come only a few hours before the town was to be taken by the Asians! The Herald would probably hold Bina responsible for that misfortune, in which case her days were numbered. However, she was not afraid of confronting him or of explaining herself.

She would even accuse her allies in the capital of a lack of foresight.

A red-haired man with a villainous gleam in his eye greeted Bina at the port of Memphis. In accordance with security instructions, the Asians had split up before entering the city, for the guards would be on the watch for groups of foreigners.

'You look like the portrait that was drawn for me, little girl.'

'I am not a little girl any more. And hide your flint knife properly – anyone with eyes in his head can see it.'

A rictus grin appeared on Shab the Twisted's face. 'Walk a few steps behind me, little girl, and don't lose sight of me. This is no time to make eyes at the men.'

Given the number of passers-by strolling through the streets of Memphis, it was not difficult to pass unnoticed. Bina slipped into the crowd and followed her guide, ever on the alert.

When he entered a shop, she did likewise. The door immediately closed behind her.

'I have to search you, little girl,' said Shab with a leer.

'You will not touch me!'

'It's a vital precaution – no exceptions allowed.'

Without lowering her gaze, Bina took off her tunic and underclothes. When she was naked, she sneered at Shab, 'As you can see, I'm not hiding any weapons. Give me my clothes.'

He threw them at her, and she dressed slowly.

'Go upstairs,' he ordered acerbically.

Bina's sarcastic smile disappeared. The next man she spoke to would be much more dangerous than this voyeur.

The room upstairs was in almost complete darkness. Frozen to the spot, the young woman felt a presence.

Two red dots glowed in the darkness. 'Welcome,' said the Herald's soft voice. 'You can see only my eyes, but I can see you very clearly. You are beautiful, cunning and brave, but you have not yet given your all.'

'I was not responsible for the failure in Kahun, my lord, for I was not warned of Iker's return or of the reasons for it. It was impossible to seize the town according to the agreed plan. I chose to save our best men rather than see them die in a fight they could not win.'

A long silence followed. Bina awaited the verdict, her fists clenched and shaking.

'I do not blame you in any way, young lady. In difficult circumstances, you proved your initiative and saved most of the weapons made in Kahun. Our people here are now well armed, and we can better help our Canaanite brothers.'

Bina breathed more easily, but was not content with this. 'My lord, my place is not here. I would have been more useful by going to the temple near Birket Qarun. The next part of our enterprise is going to be very difficult, and I am not sure that Ibcha is capable of carrying it through, despite his determination.'

The red eyes flamed. 'Your talents must not lead you into disobedience. It is I who command, Bina, and I alone, for no one else hears the voice of God. It gives me the breadth of view necessary to conduct our strategy according to His will. You, like my other followers, must bend to it without question.'

Bina had never allowed a man to control her. With the Herald it was different. He behaved like a true leader, inspired by a higher force which, after ravaging Egypt, would extend over all the world. Killing, destruction and torture did not worry her because there was no other way of achieving success for the cause to which she had devoted her life. In this way she would avenge her humiliated people.

'It is here that you will be most useful to me,' went on the Herald, 'for I am going to endow you with new powers. Up to now, you have fought only with your own abilities. They will not be enough in the face of our formidable enemies. Come here.'

For a moment she wanted to run away. But it would be utterly shameful to panic when so close to the supreme master. She stepped forward.

The red eyes flamed more brightly. Suddenly, Bina had the impression that a falcon was sinking its beak into her forehead and its talons into her arms. But despite the intensity of the attack she felt no pain. She could have sworn that warm blood was flowing through her whole body, from her head to her feet.

'My flesh is now in your flesh, my blood in your blood. Thus you have become the queen of the night.'

Still incredulous, Medes and Gergu gazed at the minuscule tattoos, depicting the head of Set, on the palms of their hands.

'So we weren't dreaming,' said Gergu, draining a cup of strong beer. 'Surely the Herald can't be a mere man? He's a demon who's emerged from the heart of the night.'

'He's more than that, my friend, much more,' said Medes. 'He is evil itself, that evil which has always fascinated me and which the law of Ma'at attempts to stifle. We've already taken great steps forward together, and the alliance with Bega showed us glimpses of a fine future. But the Herald has otherworldly powers. With him, we'll achieve miracles.'

'Well, I'd gladly leave him to succeed alone.'

'He needs us. However powerful he may be, he has to lean on reliable men, who know the country and its government well, so our role will be extremely important. The Herald didn't choose us at random: we'll occupy the highest positions in Egypt's future government. No matter how great the risks, he'll kill Senusret – and then we'll taste the fruits of victory.'

Although less optimistic than Medes, Gergu was so afraid of the Herald that he would obey him without question.

'Go to the port,' said Medes, 'and try to find out when the pharaoh's ship is due.'

Medes found it incomprehensible that the royal couple, the tjaty and the government's most senior ministers had all left Memphis at the same time. Sobek the Protector was ensuring the city's safety in the meantime, and he no doubt knew a lot about why they were away and how long they would be gone. Questioning him would have aroused his suspicions, though, so Medes had to content himself with acting like the perfect secretary of the King's House, hardworking, competent and discreet.

Suddenly, the palace flew into a frenzy of activity and all the staff emerged from their torpor. From the window of his office, Medes watched the return of Senusret and his ministers.

The King's House was immediately convened, and its secretary had to give a detailed account of his management. The tjaty asked him many questions, but no one had any criticisms to make. Medes noted that each man's face was very solemn and bore the marks of profound sorrow.

'Well? What did you find out?' Medes asked Gergu.

'It's strange how sailors always need to talk about their journeys. The pharaoh has been in Abydos.'

'Go and see Bega. He'll tell us what happened.'

'I know already that the king made a stop at Khemenu, capital of the Hare province, to celebrate the funeral rites of General Sepi, whose body had been brought by boat from the South.'

'Senusret has lost a valuable man. Do we know the cause of his death?'

'Apparently he was killed by Nubians. Miners and desert guards attended the funeral rites, and Sepi had an exceptionally fine sarcophagus.'

'Nubia, miners, desert guards . . . Sepi was searching for the healing gold! Only Bega can tell us if he found it.'

Following the usual procedure, Gergu went to Abydos to deliver produce to the permanent priests and receive Bega's order for supplies. Bega had thought it best to wait for things to return to normal before resuming the traffic in stelae. While the king and his ministers were there, the doubling of military and guards numbers had made any transaction impossible.

Bega's information made Medes rejoice. None of the gold sent back by Sepi had healed the Tree of Life. Besides this disheartening failure, the general's death was weakening the king, who, according to Bega, had to be content with magically protecting the Acacia of Osiris: he could not heal it.

Egypt was more and more like a giant with a sick heart. By forcing it to make exhausting efforts, the Herald would sooner or later provoke a fatal seizure. Then the door of the temple would be wide open, and Medes would seize its Mysteries.

He gazed again at the palm of his hand. He, the ally of Set, would triumph over Osiris.

'Have you anything to report?'

'No, Majesty,' said Sobek-Khu. 'Everything has been very quiet – and I don't like it.'

'Why not? It's because of your own efficiency.'

'The mayor of Kahun's messenger brought a warning from Lord Iker that rebels were heading for Memphis, but my men didn't catch a single one. There are three possibilities: that the Asians were skilful enough to get into the city without being spotted; that they went somewhere else; or that Iker lied.'

'Your last possibility is a serious accusation.'

'Forgive me, Majesty, but I can never forget that he tried to kill you.'

'You're wrong, Sobek. The man whom Iker wanted to see dead was not me but a criminal and bloodthirsty tyrant who was determined not only to kill Iker but to plunge the whole Egyptian people into despair. A master of the darkness, acting through cunning agents, made use of the boy. I knew Iker would come that night. I also knew, having met him once at a country festival, that his heart is large and righteous. And Sekari had kept me fully informed about the adventures that strewed the road leading him to the palace.'

The explanation shook the Protector. 'You took an enormous risk, Majesty!'

'No reasoning would have persuaded Iker to give up his plan to hand down justice. Only meeting and conversing with me could tear down the veil that blinded him.'

'So you truly do trust him?'

'The title Iker bears is not merely honorary, for his duties are many and onerous. Many more ordeals lie in store for him, and, whatever affection I feel for him, I cannot afford to treat him gently.'

'If I understand rightly, you think my first possibility the most likely.'

'Unfortunately, I do.'

'It has very worrying implications. The rebels must have accomplices among the Egyptian population. They now have safe places to live in Memphis, and a organization which has so far been infallible – none of my informants has succeeded in infiltrating it. What is even more surprising is the silence. No one talks, no one congratulates himself on outwitting the authorities.'

'That shows that all the members of this network are afraid, deeply afraid, of their leader, because they know he will instantly kill anyone who does not hold his tongue. He is the monster who was using Iker, and Iker is bound to meet him along the way.'

'Why has the Royal Son not come back to Memphis?'

'Because you are watching over the capital and he is following a different track. Kahun no longer has anything to fear, but some of the Asians have probably not left Faiyum. Iker must find out why.'

40

Preceded by North Wind, Iker set off for Birket Qarun. Despite repeated objections from Sekari, who was following him at a distance and, like a guard dog, was constantly on the alert, the young scribe wanted to explore this lead.

Iker was confident that Kahun was safe. He knew the mayor would never be so trusting again, and would keep a careful watch on his town. On the other hand, he did wonder why some of the Asians had fled in this direction.

Equipped with the amulet representing the 'Power' sceptre, endowed with the swift strength of the crocodile, and armed with the knife of a guardian spirit given to him by Senusret, the Royal Son had no fear of danger. His only weakness was to think too often of Isis.

Stupid, timid, inconsistent, he had not been able to tell her of his feelings. And his new status, although unhoped-for, was no advantage as regards her. She had been visibly unimpressed by his title, and was interested only in Abydos.

He had so often dreamt of that meeting, so often gone over what she had said and done. The truth was that it had been a fiasco. He could not forget Isis; quite the reverse. He had been near her, had been able to speak to her, look at her, breathe in her perfume, hear her voice, admire her grace . . So many causes for happiness, but all so fleeting.

The appearance of two strong fellows brandishing clubs

brought him back to harsh reality. North Wind halted and pawed the ground, a signal that this was a dangerous encounter.

The two men advanced. One was bearded, the other clean-shaven.

'This is a forbidden area,' said the bearded man. 'What do you want?'

'I'm looking for an abandoned warship yard.'

The men looked puzzled. 'A warship yard? We've never heard of one here. Who sent you?'

'The mayor of Kahun. I'm making an accurate map of the area, showing all the public buildings and other sites.'

'The problem is, we've orders not to let anyone through.'

'Whose orders?'

The bearded man hesitated. 'Er, the mayor of Kahun's, actually.'

'In that case, there's no problem. Let me through, and in my report I'll say that you scrupulously obeyed your orders.'

'We can't let you pass, even so. Orders are orders.'

'Are there only two of you to watch the area around the lake?'

The question left the two guards lost for words.

'Very well, I'll go back,' said Iker, 'but I shall take a different route. Besides, your tour of duty will be over soon, and soldiers from Kahun will come to inspect the area.'

'Oh? What's happening?'

'The mayor must make sure there are no fugitive Asians hiding around here.'

The clean-shaven man's hand tightened round the handle of his club. Neck stretched out, North Wind stared at the bearded man.

'This is beyond us,' he said. 'We're going back to our post to wait for reinforcements.'

'About the boatyard, is there anyone who'd know about it?'

'No idea. Well, anyway, no one around here.'

'Then I shall try in another direction.'

Iker walked off slowly, feeling the two guards' unfriendly gaze weighing heavily on him.

When he was out of sight, Sekari joined him. 'They scampered off like hares,' he said. 'I was afraid they'd beat you.'

'Their explanation was absurd,' said Iker. 'They're in league with the Asians – in fact, they were keeping watch and have gone to warn their leader.'

'Then the place can't be too healthy for us. We'd better get out of here.'

'On the contrary, we're almost at our goal. North Wind will easily follow their trail.'

'Yes, but our army consists of only two fighters.'

'And my donkey.'

'Three against an armed band? Aren't those rather poor odds?'

'We just need to be careful.'

Knowing how obstinate Iker was, Sekari did not persist. 'Well, we must go slowly.'

'If there's danger ahead, North Wind will warn us.'

The waters of the great lake of Birket Qarun, as brilliantly blue as the skies above, filled them with wonder. Fishermen were resting and eating grilled fish. They were friendly men, and invited Iker to share their meal. After watching for a long time, Sekari joined them. He was welcomed, too, and enjoyed the food.

As they ate, the fishermen talked of their methods and of the intelligence of certain kinds of fish.

'Didn't there used to be a warship yard near here?' asked Iker.

'It's a strange story,' replied one of the fisherman. 'There used to be one, sure enough, about a hundred paces from here – they made big boats and even ships there. One day a carpenter called Plane arrived, and brought some disagreeable workmen with him. After that, access to the yard was forbidden. They made enormous sections of hull, as if they were building a ship for the open sea. Then they took them away, and must have assembled them somewhere else. Shortly afterwards there was a big fire. I actually saw Plane setting fire to some branches. After that the yard was abandoned.'

Iker knew he had found the place where *Swift One* had been created. But, disappointingly, his discovery had brought him no information about the person who had ordered her to be built. Although Plane had held an important position, he had not paid the craftsmen.

'Have you by any chance noticed a band of wandering Asians around here?' asked Sekari. 'They stole some equipment from us, and we'd like a few words with them.'

'We haven't seen anything on this side of the lake but they might be hiding near the temple with the big stones – nobody would disturb them there.'

'Why not?'

'Because the place is haunted. Once priests and about thirty guards and their families lived there, and workmen worked in a nearby mine. The shrine was the arrival point for caravans from the Baharia and Siwa oases, and there's a road from it to Lisht and Dahshur. But demons drove everyone away.'

Iker and Sekari looked at each other.

'We'd like to take a look at this shrine,' said Sekari.

'Don't even think about it. Those who've ventured there lately haven't come back.'

'What's the best way to get there?'

'You'd have to cross the lake to reach the landing-stage, but . . .'

'If you take us across,' said Iker, 'I'll ask the mayor of Kahun to give you new boats.'

The fisherman gaped at him. 'You know him? The mayor?'

'I am the Royal Son and a palace scribe.'

313

*

The crossing was a new delight for Iker. The fisherman was nervous, but he handled his boat skilfully, sending her skimming over the water. North Wind, balancing easily on his strong legs, sniffed the breeze. Iker and Sekari enjoyed this moment of communion with the sky, air and the lake, but kept their eyes constantly on the bank.

As they got nearer, they saw that the place looked deserted. Nothing and no one was stirring.

'I'm going to row to the bank, you get off very quickly, and then I'm leaving,' said the fisherman, whose hands were shaking.

A magnificent paved roadway led to the temple,* which was set back a little from the north bank of the lake. Standing sentry at the edge of the desert, protected by a curtain wall, with a courtyard in front and ancillary buildings to the sides, the temple was built of enormous blocks of sandstone, obliquely cut, somewhat like those used by the builders of the great pyramids at Giza. In the middle of the south side, a narrow door gave access to the one interior chamber, a sort of wide corridor off which opened seven shrines, vertical, roofed niches.

North Wind stayed outside, and would warn the two men if danger threatened.

'Everything's been looted,' observed Sekari. 'The thieves made people believe the place was haunted so that nobody would discover their crime.'

There were no scenes or inscriptions. The temple resembled a relic-holder in which the power of the number Seven was celebrated, an expression of the mystery of life. Not a single ritual object remained, but Iker found a few pieces of pottery and some mats.

'People have been sleeping here,' he said.

*Qasr el-Sagha.

Sekari was particular interested by the exterior wall, to the right of the entrance. He set off down a narrow passageway cut into the thickness of the building. At its far end, a hole made it possible to spy on people coming and going. On the ground lay a multicoloured tunic and some black sandals.

He showed them to Iker. 'These are Asian. A lookout was stationed here, and the rest of them hid inside the temple. But where have they gone?'

The two companions searched the rest of the temple and the outlying buildings, where they found other traces of the intruders' presence.

'Let's follow the paved roadway,' suggested Iker. 'It probably leads to where the miners and guards used to live.'

'And that's probably where the Asians have set up camp. We mustn't take any risks. I'm used to moving around unseen, but you'd better wait for me here. If North Wind shows himself, I'll come back.'

Sekari was not boasting. In any surroundings he knew how to move soundlessly and slip past the most vigilant guards. His experience saved him, for an Asian was indeed watching the road. It ended at the settlement of miners' houses, which were arranged in a geometrical fashion, and guards' houses, which were divided into four districts containing some thirty dwellings.

A bearded man with thick arms was haranguing a group of well-armed men. Sekari could not hear what he was saying, but dared not risk trying to get closer.

He returned to the temple and told Iker, 'I've found our fugitives. There's no sign of any miners or guards. What are the Asians likely to do? I should think that either they intend to escape to Libya through the desert, or else they're planning something nasty.'

'Is there somewhere where we can watch them without being seen?'

'The temple roof would be ideal. If the Asians make a

move, we'll see what happens. As for the two of us attacking
them, don't even think about it. I don't know exactly how
many of them there are, but they've got spears, swords and
bows.'

'That sounds like a small army. They must be preparing for
an attack.'

'Certainly not against Kahun. The mayor won't be caught
unawares again.'

'We must find out their target,' said Iker.

'All right, but in the meantime go and get some sleep. I'll
wake you when it's time for your turn as lookout.'

Iker hesitated a moment, then asked, 'Sekari, why did you
speak to me about the Golden Circle of Abydos?'

'I don't really know.'

'You've been initiated into the Mysteries, haven't you?'

'Me? How could a country fellow like me be admitted to
brotherhood like that? My honour consists of serving the
pharaoh the best way I can. I leave secrets to other people.'

They did not have to wait long. As dawn broke, a column of
Asians emerged from their camp. Iker recognized their
leader, Ibcha, with his bushy beard and thick arms, but did not
see Bina. Had she gone to Memphis with the other group?

Sekari opened his eyes. 'Are they all leaving?'

'It looks like it.'

A few minutes later there could be no doubt that the rebels
were leaving their Faiyum lair. Their choice of route would
provide important information. If they headed west, towards
the desert, it would mean they were running away. If they
went east, they were on the attack.

'They're taking the eastern track,' said Sekari worriedly.

'We must follow them,' said Iker.

41

General Nesmontu hated not only the town of Sichem but all Canaan and all Canaanites. If he could have sent the entire population further north and transformed the region into a haven for wild plants and game, he would have achieved peace in Canaan, something which was currently only an illusion. For the old soldier was not deceived: the calm that his troops had imposed was as thin as a sheet of papyrus. Every Canaanite family contained at least one rebel who longed to wipe out the Egyptians.

For the tenth time, he had tried to set up a local government with responsibility for running Sichem and the surrounding villages. But, in the general's view, as soon as a Canaanite had power, no matter how little, he immediately thought of setting up his own system of corruption, making a mockery of his fellow countrymen's wellbeing. As soon as he had proof of misdemeanours, Nesmontu threw the culprit into prison and chose a new official – who soon proved to be as dishonest as the previous one. The general also had to deal with innumerable clans which were perpetually at loggerheads as they tried to wring as many advantages as possible out of the protectorate.

If he had been listened to, Nesmontu would have made a clear-cut decision. But he was carrying out the orders of the pharaoh, who was concerned to ease tensions, and who said that a lasting peace could only be built on prosperity.

The old general did not believe that. With the Canaanites, there was no respect for a man's word or a contract. Yesterday's best friend became tomorrow's enemy. Only one rule was constantly applied: falsehood. Nesmontu managed from time to time to get his hands on petty thieves, but had not yet gathered any information on whoever had attacked the Tree of Life.

'General,' said his personal servant, 'here is a message from the pharaoh.'

The text was coded and was indeed in Senusret's hand. The few lines plunged Nesmontu into profound sadness, for they told him of the death of General Sepi. Sepi had been at the heart of the Golden Circle of Abydos, and had always showed clear-sightedness and determination. When reunification had seemed far off, even impossible, he had committed himself to the fight without a qualm, certain that Senusret would be a great pharaoh.

Deprived of the healing gold, the Acacia of Osiris remained very fragile. Sepi had given his life to save it, and Nesmontu was determined that his sacrifice should not be in vain: his spiritual brothers would continue the struggle, whatever it cost them.

'General,' his servant added, 'there are disturbances in southern Sichem. A rebel has burnt down several houses and taken refuge in an empty grainstore.'

'I shall go there.'

It was a long time since there had been such a serious incident. Was it the prelude to an attempted uprising? If so, Nesmontu would nip it in the bud.

At the head of a troop comprising forty archers and forty spearsmen, he hurried to the area in question. The youngest men had difficulty following the pace set by the general, who forgot his age as soon as he went into action. As the soldiers went by, doors and windows closed.

The fire had utterly destroyed the miserable houses. On a

heap of filth nearby lay the dead body of a man employed by the Egyptian government.

'He'll pay for this!' vowed Nesmontu, climbing the granary's grainstore's stairs three at a time, while his men took up their positions.

As soon as the general opened the trapdoor, the Canaanite inside threw his dagger. Crooked-Face had promised him that Nesmontu would be the first on the scene and that he would be able to kill him easily.

The general saw the flash of the dagger as it flew from the man's hand, and instinctively flung himself aside. The blade grazed his shoulder, leaving a bloody furrow.

The Egyptian archers surrounded the general and took aim at the attacker.

'Don't fire!' shouted Nesmontu. 'Get that coward out of his hole, and check that there are no others in the area.'

Fearing he would be beaten, the Canaanite let out a howl.

'Don't damage him,' ordered the general. 'I shall interrogate him myself.'

While an army doctor was treating Nesmontu, the old soldier observed the man who had tried to kill him. He was short, with reddish stubble covering his cheeks and chin, and was glaring at the general with hatred. An officer checked that his feet and hands were securely shackled.

'You're an incompetent fool,' said Nesmontu. 'At that distance, I wouldn't have missed my target. And your employer's even stupider than you are. If you try to kill the commander of the Egyptian army, you use someone competent.'

'You won't live much longer,' snarled the Canaanite.

'Longer than you will – you'll be executed before the doctor's finished bandaging my wound.'

The Canaanite's eyes opened wide in astonishment. 'Aren't you even going to question me?'

'What's the use? Either you won't answer or you'll lie. Anyway, even if you wanted to tell the truth, a miserable wretch like you wouldn't know anything important.'

'You're wrong, General. I am a true resister of your vile occupation, and hundreds of others will continue the just fight.'

Nesmontu burst out laughing. 'You can't even add up, can you?'

'The numbers aren't important. In the end we'll drive you out of Canaan.'

'What always surprises me about pathetic wretches like you is your vanity – mind you, that makes my work easier. You're cowardly and timid, so you'll never be able to put up a real fight.'

'The Herald will lead us to victory!'

Nesmontu's expression hardened. 'Your Herald is dead.'

The Canaanite sniggered. 'That's what you Egyptian dogs think.'

'I saw his body with my own eyes.'

'Our leader is very much alive. Soon you will be carrion without a grave, and he will triumph.'

'Where is he hiding, your great leader?'

'I'll never tell you that, not even if you torture me.'

With one hand, Nesmontu seized the Canaanite by the throat and lifted him off the ground. 'If I had my own way I'd hang you on a butcher's hook to help you talk more easily, but Pharaoh demands humanity, even for lice like you. So I shall hand you over to expert interrogaters.'

But the only names the Canaanite gave were those of his parents, who had been dead for a long time, and of a rebel killed during the first Sichem rebellion. A search of his home produced nothing.

The execution took place in the city's largest square, in the presence of a large crowd. The Canaanite's body, bleeding from many arrow-wounds, was buried without funeral rites.

Nesmontu's speech was brief and to the point: the first stirrings of rebellion would be punished with the utmost severity.

The investigators were unanimous: the Canaanite was an unbalanced man who had been acting alone, without the support of an organized band. But the old general was not so sure. His instinct told him that the incident must not be taken lightly.

It did not surprise him that someone had tried to kill him, and it would certainly not be the last attempt. On the other hand, what the attacker had said interested him. This was the first time since Sichem had come under his control that a rebel had mentioned the Herald, the madman who had stirred up the first rebellion. Did it mean that another lunatic had taken up the torch? On the face of it, that was unlikely. But then, the appearance of the Herald had also been unlikely.

Nesmontu summoned his senior officers and ordered them to place their troops on alert throughout Canaan and to question all suspects in depth. Reports were to be sent directly to him, and any suspects to be questioned further were to be brought before him immediately.

'The Asians haven't moved for two days,' grumbled Sekari. 'You'd think they're waiting for reinforcements.'

'Perhaps they aren't sure which route to take?' suggested Iker.

'I'd be surprised if they aren't. I think they're following a specific plan. Here, halfway between Faiyum and the valley, they're making sure they haven't been spotted. These are no amateurs, believe me.'

'Why don't you warn the army?'

'The Canaanites would see them arriving and disperse into the countryside. If we want to find out what they're really up to, we mustn't lose sight of them. I'm no more amused than you are by taking a risk like this – I'd much rather be a guest at a feast and then spend the night with a beautiful girl. Ah, the pretty servants of Kahun and the linen sheets in your beautiful house!'

'You played the servant extremely well,' said Iker, smiling.

'But I wasn't playing. My parents were humble folk, and I'm a man of the people. It doesn't embarrass me to be a servant.'

'How did the pharaoh notice you?'

Sekari smiled broadly. 'One of my many jobs was as a bird-catcher, and I learnt to speak the birds' language. While the palace steward was testing me, with a view to taking me on, a hoopoe got out of the royal aviary. It was so frightened that it would have ended up injuring itself, but I calmed it down by whistling some soothing notes. Senusret saw what happened, and summoned me. The king himself, can you imagine? If you knew how afraid I was! In the face of that huge man, I felt weaker than a new-born baby – and I still do sometimes. I don't doubt for a moment that he's in contact with the gods.'

'Have you often been to Abydos?'

'Abydos, Abydos . . . You're really obsessed with the place.'

'Well, it's the spiritual centre of Egypt, isn't it?'

'Possibly, but we've got other things to think about.'

Iker was thinking of Isis, who lived at that most sacred of all sites, far away and inaccessible. Would he have another chance to speak to her and at last open his heart to her?

'They're moving,' said Sekari.

The two men flattened themselves on the ground, and peered out of the shelter of the tamarisks. The Asians were setting off again.

Ibcha had always made weapons. In Sichem he'd had an illicit forge, but it could produce only enough for small roups, and in any case the Egyptian guards would have ound it before long.

Then the Herald had appeared. Listening to his teaching, bcha had realized that only violence would enable the Canaanite people to drive out the occupiers and become a reat nation, more powerful than Egypt. If killing was ecessary, he would kill. If fighters must be sacrificed in rder to make the enemy feel insecure, he would train them, nd they would die joyfully. At Kahun, Bina and he had lmost succeeded. From now on, many towns would be afraid f being attacked.

With his raiding-party, Ibcha would destroy one of the najor symbols of the pharaoh's power and shatter his soul. enusret was nothing but a king with feet of clay, reliant on is army, and the army was tied down in Canaan, where ightning raids were occurring more and more often. Thanks o the Herald, the rebellion would soon be victorious.

Sure they hadn't been spotted, Ibcha led his men along the rack dictated by Bina. It was a difficult route, which meant hat the journey would take longer, but it avoided all the heckpoints.

During a halt, he told his men what their goal would be. Pharaohs love to build monuments to their glory, and enusret's no exception. At Dahshur he's building a pyramid, where he plans to rest for eternity. We are going to desecrate oth the pyramid and its temple, by damaging them as badly s possible. Then the site will be unusable, the pyramid will e abandoned, and Senusret will know that no corner of his ountry is safe from our raids. The people will lose faith in im and become divided. New provincial leaders will rise up, nd chaos will once again be established.'

42

Djehuty was mayor of the builders' village at Dahshur, and he was proud of the men. With Senankh's efficient help, he toiled unceasingly so that the royal pyramid might produce as much *ka* as possible as soon as possible. The builders had had to live in makeshift accommodation when the work began, but now had comfortable houses.

Despite his failing health, Djehuty shared the craftsmen's daily lives. In his travelling-chair, he could move easily from one part of the site to another and check that the pharaoh's plan was being followed in every detail. The group of structures whose centre was the pyramid followed strict symbolic rules, enabling the stone's magic to shine forth.

Although he felt the cold badly, and suffered from pains in his joints, Djehuty would not hear of rest. By initiating him into the mysteries of the Golden Circle of Abydos and this vital project to him, Senusret had given meaning to his old age. Instead of dozing in some honorary post, every day he summoned up unsuspected resources. He always felt sure he'd never be able to get up the next morning, but somehow he always managed it.

'Anything to report?' he asked the commander of the site guards.

'All quiet, sir,' said the soldier.

Djehuty went to the house of eternity, to the north of the

pyramid, where Tjaty Khnum-Hotep would rest. It was built of bricks clad in limestone, and was decorated with carvings and hieroglyphic inscriptions to ensure the survival of his spirit. The funerary chamber, the room for the funerary jars and the antechamber would soon be finished. By granting his tjaty such a magnificent tomb, the pharaoh was emphasizing the importance of his office.

The curtain-wall, which was punctuated by bastions and redans, was a wall of magic protecting the pyramid, the primordial stone and the channel through which the royal *ka* flowed. By linking himself to the teachings of Djoser and Imhotep, formulated at Saqqara, Senusret was reaffirming the fundamental values of Egyptian civilization. Yes, the pyramid embodied Osiris, reborn and victorious over death. Yes, Ma'at could triumph over *isefet*. Yes, she would free man from the prison of his mediocrity and baseness, so long as he transformed himself into a builder.

The carpenters had just placed the wooden ships in the vaulted shrines. The ship of day, the ship of night, the ship of the Divine Light and the ship of a million manifestations of unity: all would be used for the journey of the royal soul, which never ceased to travel through the universe.

Djehuty walked through the temple, whose pillars were shaped like papyrus- and lotus-stems. Giant statues of the pharaoh bore witness to the king's permanent rebirth in Osiris. Exquisite hieroglyphs gave the names and qualities of the king, who was placed under the protection of the Key of Life, the *ankh*, flanked by two falcons. In the antechamber, gods and goddesses brought the sovereign life and power; in the chamber of offerings, the crowned pharaoh received the subtle strength of the foods. Striking down enemies who emerged from the darkness, recreating the harmony of Ma'at, here Senusret celebrated an eternal festival of regeneration.

The wide roadway linking the southern and northern parts of the site was in itself a work of art. The pyramid's covering of blocks of limestone from the quarry at Tura reflected the rays of the sun, manifesting the power of the Stone of Light, which had emerged at the beginning of time.

The master-builder invited Djehuty to enter the underground section. Hidden at the end of the construction works, its entrance opened on to a corridor leading to an antechamber, which extended into a passageway ending in a rectangular room. To the east was a shrine clad in finely dressed limestone; to the west was the granite house of resurrection, where pride of place went to a red granite sarcophagus, its decoration evoking the palace of the first pharaohs. It would become the ship of the king's radiant spirit when he travelled to the world beyond. Above the funerary chamber was a false ceiling comprising five pairs of limestone beams twelve cubits long, each weighing as much as a sea-going ship.

Djehuty meditated for a long time in this place, outside the world of men. In accordance with tradition, the builders were fashioning a space where the Invisible could reveal itself without fear of outside attacks. From here, the pharaoh set out, truly alive, in and towards the Light.

When he went back outside, it was almost sunset. The craftsmen had left the site, and the mayor was astonished to see only one guard on the threshold of the pyramid temple.

'Where have your colleagues gone?'

'Sir, our commander was informed of a serious incident on the road to Faiyum. He's taken his men and gone to help the wounded.'

'He should have asked my permission.'

'He didn't dare disturb you, sir.'

Djehuty was worried, and warned the master-builder and his workers that the guards were no longer there to protect them. He told them to post lookouts all round the village. Then, his joints on fire from weariness, he went home, drank a little water and lay down on his bed, afraid he'd never be able to get up again.

*

In the far distance, bathed in the gentle glow of the sunset, the half-built pyramid irresistibly drew the eyes of Ibcha and his raiding-party.

'Our ruse has drawn off the guards,' said Ibicha. 'The only people left are the builders, and they'll be tired after the day's work. Like all Egyptians, they treasure the special moment when the sun sinks into the west. They feel deeply peaceful, and won't be able to defend themselves.'

By spreading terror and spilling blood on the Dahshur site, Ibcha would fulfil the assignment Bina had entrusted to him on the Herald's orders: to prevent the pyramid from producing *ka* and to reduce it to a heap of inert stones. Thanks to his revelations, the Asians were beginning to understand that the Egyptians' strength did not lie only in their weapons. To defeat the hated enemy, they must destroy Egypt's magical structures, which emitted a mysterious energy and enabled them to reverse the most perilous situations.

Transforming Dahshur into a heap of ruins would be a stunning victory. The pharaoh would see the work he had destined for eternity smashed to pieces. His certainties would be replaced by doubt and fear.

'Do we spare the women and children?' asked a rebel.

'No, we show no weakness at all, or we'll fail,' replied Ibcha. 'May the Herald's fire destroy these vile places.'

The Asians were on the point of charging towards their target when one of them said, 'Sir, over there, there's a man running.'

'Don't waste a javelin – he's too far away.'

'And another one over there, with a donkey. He's running away.'

'Attack!' ordered Ibcha.

Sekari had never run so fast. He expected to be struck down at any moment, and that made him run even faster.

At last, he reached the entrance to the builders' village. As he dashed inside he bumped into a stone-cutter carrying a hammer.

'Where are the soldiers?' shouted Sekari.

'Gone to help wounded people on the road to Faiyum.'

'Rouse everyone! We're about to be attacked!'

The stone-cutter ran to spread the alarm. Seizing their tools, his colleagues prepared to fight.

'We must defend the pyramid,' ordered Djehuty. 'The women and children must shut themselves inside the houses.'

'May the Golden Circle protect us and give us the strength to fight against *isefet*,' murmured Sekari in his ear.

Their hands joined for a moment.

'Iker has gone to fetch the soldiers,' said Sekari.

'Will they get here in time?'

'A scribe educated in the Hare province is trained never to be late. Take cover.'

'I shall fight like the others,' declared Djehuty. 'What do our deaths matter, if we save the royal works?'

A javelin wounded a craftsman in the thigh. Sekari responded immediately by hurling a well-sharpened copper chisel, which hit an Asian in the throat.

Djehuty brandished his stick. 'To the temple, quickly!'

The craftsmen regrouped inside the temple complex. It had only one entrance, which they barricaded with stone blocks on which spears and arrows would shatter.

'They'll climb the walls,' predicted Sekari, 'and we won't be able to drive them back. Which is the most difficult place to enter?'

'The royal tomb, but I refuse to profane it. We shall defend this sacred place to the last.'

'Careful, here's one of them!'

The hammer thrown by Sekari hit the Asian full on the forehead as he appeared at the top of the wall. He fell backwards, knocking off the man climbing up after him. This failure caused alarm among Ibcha's men, who were already uneasy at invading a temple and provoking the anger of the gods.

But Sekari harboured no illusions. Despite their courage, the craftsmen would soon be overwhelmed.

Suddenly, they heard a loud braying.

'That's the voice of Set!' exclaimed a sculptor. 'He's helping the attackers!'

'On the contrary,' declared Sekari, 'he's giving us the power we need to drive them off.'

Ibcha cut the wounded man's throat, for he had orders not to leave behind anyone who might talk.

'We only needed a little longer,' he said bitterly, as he watched Iker and North Wind bringing the soldiers back to Dahshur.

Ibcha had lost two men, and decided to save the rest of his raiding-party rather than to engage in a fight they might not win. In rage, he fired an arrow at the pyramid and gave the order to retreat.

The Egyptians charged after the Asians, but they were already too far away.

The officer appeared before Djehuty. 'It was a lie. No one needed our help on the road to Faiyum.'

'Letting yourself be deceived by an Asian might just be excusable. But you acted without my authorization and in violation of your orders. I am dismissing you from your post, and the tjaty's court will judge you. Until a new officer is appointed, I am taking command of the troops.'

Djehuty sat down. Iker poured him a cup of wine.

'You have saved the pyramid, Royal Son.'

'Oh no. The credit goes to you and Sekari – and to North Wind's loud voice.'

The peace of the evening enveloped Dahshur once again, as if nothing had happened. But Djehuty's hands were still unsteady.

He said, 'Those barbarians dared to attack a sacred site! We know now that they will stop at nothing and will commit even the worst of crimes. Their leader must surely be the demon who's trying to kill the Tree of Life.'

'That filthy criminal's getting bolder and starting to come out of the darkness,' said Sekari. 'This proves that he feels capable of going on to the attack. Both here and at Kahun he almost succeeded. We must take extra security measures with a view to the next attacks.'

43

'You're sure? You're really sure?' asked Iker.

'I'm afraid so,' confirmed Khnum-Hotep. 'General Sepi is dead.'

Neither Sekari nor Iker could hold back their tears. Sepi had been a wise man and a fine tactician, and had always before managed to escape from the most dangerous situations.

'Nubian looters would never have managed to trap my teacher,' declared Sekari. 'As for the demons of the desert, he dominated them because he knew the words that could immobilize them or send them back to their burning, solitary wastes. Sepi's murderer must be the prince of darkness.'

'Perhaps the same destroyer who's attacking the Tree of Life,' said Iker.

Sekari clenched his fists. 'You're right – of course, that's it. He wanted to prevent the general from finding the healing gold. But this means that the monster is prowling everywhere.'

'We mustn't let our grief distract us,' warned the tjaty.

'Sepi taught me everything I know. If it hadn't been for him, I'd hardly exist.'

'Did you take lessons in hieroglyphs?' asked Iker.

'He took me out into the field with him. I did my writing in the sand; the signs of power I experienced on dangerous tracks, facing savage beasts and brigands of every hue. He forgave me nothing, but he gave me the weapons to defend myself.'

Senankh attempted to comfort Sekari, but they both knew that nothing could ever fill the void left by Sepi.

'You and Iker did well at Dahshur,' said Knum-Hotep. 'The general would have been proud of you. In accordance with Djehuty's demands, the security measures have been considerably strengthened, and the site now has nothing to fear.'

'Dahshur, perhaps, but what about Memphis and the other towns?' demanded Iker. 'The rebels can attack anywhere, at any time.'

No one disagreed.

'We have lost one of the pillars of our country,' said Sekari. 'Let's show ourselves worthy of him and take up his work where death thinks it has been interrupted.'

Sobek's face was openly hostile. 'I am sorry, Royal Son, but you must be searched.'

'As you wish.'

Given who the visitor was, Sobek carried out the search himself. 'You may enter.'

Sobek opened the door of Senusret's office and said, 'Everything is in order, Majesty. Do you wish me to remain in the room?'

'No, you may withdraw.'

The king was seated on the floor in the scribe's position, his back very straight, and had an unrolled papyrus on his knees.

Iker adopted the same posture, facing him. 'Sobek hates me.'

'He believes you have not yet proved your innocence and your faithfulness to the Crown.'

'I shall convince him somehow.'

'That is one of your assignments, my son.'

'My results so far are very poor, Majesty. I found the Acacia of Neith, but it had been burnt to ashes. I found the boatyard where *Swift One* was built, but learnt nothing about the person who ordered her. Lastly, I helped prevent the Asians from seizing Kahun and Dahshur, but failed to arrest the two ringleaders, Bina and Ibcha.'

'What do you think of them?' asked Senusret.

'Ibcha is a killer who knows neither conscience nor remorse. He will carry out his orders to the letter, even if it costs him his life. He led the raid on Dahshur, but he did not launch an attack once our soldiers returned and he could not be sure of winning. That worries me: he was saving his men for a more important attack in the future.'

'He is the principal leader, is he not?'

'At Kahun he obeyed Bina.'

'Does she command all the rebel forces?'

'It is more that she inspires them. She is pitiless, cunning and full of hatred, and she is capable of doing enormous harm. Her leader aims to conquer Egypt, and nothing will make her deviate from that goal.'

'I will consider your words,' said Senusret, 'but the facts do not bear them out. At this moment, there is no leader in Canaan who could lead an offensive against us. If there were one, General Nesmontu would have warned me.'

'This rebellion seems rather like a dried-up riverbed, Majesty. For most of the year it's dry. Then the rains come, and it is transformed into a fierce torrent. Bina and Ibcha are probably hiding in Memphis, where their allies have long been established. It is here, in the capital, that they are planning to strike their decisive blow. And there's one other puzzling thing. The fake desert guard who tried to kill me wasn't an Asian, so who sent him? I fear it may have been a faction of Egyptians who wish you harm. If these two forces come together, our evil enemy will be even more dangerous. He has already proved his efficiency by murdering General Sepi.'

Senusret agreed with Iker. None of the recent incident was the result of chance. They were part of a cleverly plotte campaign which had as its overall aim the death of the Tre of Life.

'Whatever ordeals you may face, do not give in to despair I shall always be at your side, my son, to help you t accomplish a destiny of which you are as yet unaware.'

The young man was astounded. The king had uttered, wor for word, the ending of the last message ever sent to Iker b his old master, the scribe of Madu.

'Majesty, I . . .'

'Rest for a little while. Too much tension hinders clea thinking.'

Trumpet-Nose had been in the guards service for over twent years. An exemplary officer, he hated brutality and carrie out his orders thoroughly but with humanity. He greatl admired Sobek, but sometimes thought him too harsh – afte all, it was as important to be liked by the people of Memphi as it was to be feared. Trumpet-Nose had resolved man domestic disputes in his time, and seldom imprisone revellers who had got a little drunk. He even let himself rela a little now and then, without feeling that he was putting th kingdom in peril.

His latest orders received did not please him. Appointed t guard one of the city's gates, he was to search and questio everyone who wished to enter. At the slightest suspicion, h must interrogate them thoroughly, open a case file and tak them into custody. These hindrances to the freedom o movement would annoy the population enormously an would complicate everyone's daily life. So Trumpet-Nose like his colleagues, was not too zealous. He was content t greet people he knew and traders, and interrogated only a fev dubious-looking individuals.

The pretty brown-haired girl who arrived with a bearde

an with thick arms did not look at all suspicious, but he felt
ke exchanging a few words.

'What's your name, young lady?'

'Cool-Water, Commander.'

'And is this your husband?'

'Yes, sir.'

'I haven't seen you around here before. Where are you
om?'

'The Delta.'

'Why have you come to Memphis?'

'My husband's very sick. We've been told there are
xcellent doctors here, and we're hoping they can cure him.'

'Where will you stay?'

'With my grandfather – he's a sandal-maker.'

Trumpet-Nose ought to have submitted the two travellers
 close questioning but the man seemed so ill that it would
ave been cruel to insist. Besides, the woman, with her fresh
oung face, hardly looked like a bloodthirsty rebel fighter.

Bina and Ibcha passed through the checkpoint without
 rther difficulty and rejoined the other members of the
 iding-party. They, too, had entered Memphis at this entry
oint, separately and at different times of day.

obek was in a rage. Astonished not to have gathered any
 seful information about clandestine Asians, he personally
 spected several checkpoints, doubting that his orders were
eing scrupulously obeyed.

He found three officers who were failing to behave like
 erce guard-dogs. The first to face Sobek's anger was
rumpet-Nose, who tried to excuse himself. 'It is impossible
 distinguish dangerous Asians from the rest of the popula-
on, sir. They're people like you and me, and—'

'I don't think so,' cut in Sobek.

'In any case, even the ones we did interrogate in depth got
 rough. We found no reason at all to throw them in prison.'

'Some of your colleagues have made arrests.'

'Yes, but did they catch real rebels?'

Sobek could not lie: all the suspects had been released. The system he had put in place was not working.

Anxious and frustrated, he reduced surveillance on the gates. On the other hand, he increased the patrols of the area around the city and ordered his men to inform him of every single incident, no matter how small.

Sobek did not try to hide his failure from the king. 'I was presumptuous, Majesty. Memphis is an open city. I thought I could close it to the enemy, but I was wrong. Either the Asians were frightened off by our forces and have gone to ground in the Delta, or else accomplices with secure bases in the capital are sheltering them. Unfortunately, I believe that the latter possibility is the truth, and it has a corollary: the rebels are regrouping in order to attack, and their main target will be yourself. The enemy is hiding in the darkness; I do not know his face; he might strike anywhere and at any time, even inside this palace. So I advise you to limit your movements as much as possible and to strengthen security measures around your person.'

'If I were to prostrate myself like a hunted animal, that would in itself be a victory for the enemy,' objected Senusret. 'I shall continue to carry out my duties in full, with my usual freedom of movement. And you, Sobek, will carry out yours.'

'I am furious, Majesty, for I feel deprived of eyes and ears. Never have I been confronted by such perverse criminals. But I shall do everything I can, you may be certain of that.'

'You are still suspicious of Iker, are you not?'

'Majesty, how can I forget that he tried to kill you? I really want to believe it was a misunderstanding, but all the same, please give me permission to watch him closely. If he is found to be in contact with the Asians, we will have proof of his treachery.'

'I appreciate your outspokenness, Sobek, but I have
ppointed Iker Royal Son. And what he will prove to you is
is loyalty.'

44

In the part of Memphis where their leader lived, the Herald'
disciples remained on alert. Bakers, sandal-vendors an
barbers were so well mingled into the population that nobod
could have dreamt they belonged to a secret network.

Since the arrival of Bina, Ibcha and their men, who wer
immediately sheltered in safe houses, the lookouts had bee
increased and told to watch the surrounding areas both nigh
and day. Not one guard or soldier ventured into the Herald'
domain without being instantly spotted. And the patrols di
not worry the Asians, because innocent-seeming walker
took turns in announcing that they were passing by.

On the first floor of the shop where mats and baskets wer
sold, the Herald continued to preach. His followers listene
but were not permitted to ask questions. As the sol
interpreter of a god determined to conquer the world, h
offered an absolute and definitive truth.

Slaking his thirst with a little salt between two sermons
the Herald hammered home a repetitive message designed t
penetrate the admiring minds of his listeners little by little
They would have no other education or culture, but thi
would be amply sufficient to make them fight until their fina
triumph.

Shab the Twisted drank in his master's words, especiall
when he spoke of the extermination of blasphemers and th

absolute submission of women, who were much too free in Egyptian society. The perfect guard-dog, Shab never forgot to screen the fortunate ones who were authorized to receive the teaching. At the slightest doubt, he would seize the suspect and hand him over to the Herald.

The Herald's soft, cajoling voice died away and his listeners withdrew.

'Summon Crooked-Face,' the Herald told Shab. 'His warriors' many days of training are finally to be put to good use.'

'Are we going to strike at the head?'

'Exactly, my friend.'

'Will there be enough of us?'

The Herald smiled indulgently. 'You need not be anxious. Thanks to our new allies, we shall have the information we need. For our part, we shall spread such terror in the city that the most serious obstacles will be removed. Have some well-dried firewood and rags collected, and distribute them to our faithful. Soon, the fire of Set will come down upon this impious town! Now I shall complete Bina's training.'

The Twisted One frowned. 'Master . . .'

'What is wrong, Shab?'

'Master, I have no intention of disputing your decisions, but this Bina . . .'

'What is the matter with her?'

'She . . . she's a woman.'

The Herald laid his hand gently on the Twisted One's shoulder. 'God teaches us that women are inferior creatures and must remain confined in their houses in order to serve their husbands and their sons. But we are at war, and I use many weapons, including some most surprising ones. Bina is precisely one of those. The Egyptians are so stupid that they cannot conceive of a pretty girl being more dangerous than a well-trained army. I have yet to complete her transformation.'

The Herald entered the darkened room where Bina had

been shut away since her arrival in Memphis. In her veins new blood now flowed, and its quantity must be increased still further for her to become a pitiless killer in the service of the cause. None would be fiercer than this wild beast.

'Wake up, Bina, and look at me.'

Inanimate, curled up, she began to come back to life when she heard her master's voice. Throwing back her head, she stood up slowly, her eyes staring into nothingness, and stood like a statue in the centre of the room.

The Herald pivoted the section of the back wall and took from its hiding-place the acacia-wood box containing the queen of turquoises.

'After exposing this most precious stone to the sun,' he said, 'I shall proceed to your final awakening. Then you will belong to me body and soul, and your obedience will be total.'

The Herald drew back a curtain formed from two mats joined together. A ray of light struck the queen of turquoises, and it emitted a blaze of light which lit up Bina's face.

'Queen of darkness, be the terrifying lioness, greedy for blood and slaughter, travel across the plain and the desert!'

Bina's nails became as sharp as claws, her teeth as powerful as fangs.

The Herald was proud of his work. He closed the curtain again and replaced the stone in the box.

'Don't forget, Bina, you are devoted to your master, and you are to be a lioness only on my orders.'

The pretty brunette seemed to emerge from a profound nightmare.

'Take off your tunic,' he ordered.

He fascinated her as much as he terrified her. Unable to resist him, she stripped naked and let him abuse her.

Despite Sobek's protests, the king took Iker outside Memphis. True, the Protector's best men were guarding them both, but would they succeed in saving Senusret in the event of an attack? Given the ever-present menace, it seemed a bad moment to run such a risk.

A falcon guided them, the king following it in silence until they reached a shady canal. He gazed upon the willows' greenery and walked along the bank. A profound peace reigned.

'Humans, God's flock, were well provided for,' Senusret said. 'He created the sky and the earth for them, the air as the breath of life, since they are in his image, brought forth from his being. He shines in the sun, makes the trees and plants grow and gives them all kinds of foods. The Creator did not devise anything contaminated. No evil featured in the order of his creation. But human beings rebelled, and one cannot remove the poison from the snake, any more than the evil from a bad person. When God laughed, the gods came into being; when he wept, mankind was born. Man, the bearer of injustice and cruelty, is the most formidable of predators. The pharaoh's office maintains and prolongs the divine work on earth, while freeing man from the hand of man. Believing that one can act in favour of humans is always vanity; Pharaoh acts in favour of his father, the master of the gods. No spirituality exists for those who are lazy; there is no spiritual brother for him who does not listen to Ma'at, no day of celebration for the greedy man. Never desire what belongs to others, Iker, never covet anything you cannot achieve for yourself, because envy leads to downfall. The greedy man is a living corpse. This, too, is the king's duty: to fight ceaselessly again the greed of human beings.'

'Did greed not triumph at the end of the age of the great pyramids?'

'Darkness was preferred to light, no one drew teachings from the celestial laws any more, no one respected the earthly laws, evil was called good, the criminal considered a righteous man, immorality a virtue, perversion the norm, the sage a madman, the fanatic a model to be imitated, and the voices of the gods were stifled. Then came the reign of *isefet*, which is injustice, violence, greed, laziness, forgetfulness, putrefaction, chaos and the law of the strongest, enabling murderers and thieves to hold sway. If their triumph endured, the ground would become sterile, the air unbreathable and the water poisoned. As for the sky's fire, it would lay waste our world. Fighting *isefet* constantly is not enough. One must above all affirm Ma'at, by ritualizing the time that passes. Each reign must be the conscious repetition of the process of creation, the "first time", in order to repel the forces of chaos and establish Ma'at. What do you know of her, Iker?'

'When Ma'at is in her place, Majesty, the country stands firm and the heavens are favourable. Daughter of Ra, companion of Thoth, always present in the ship of the sun, she is the pilot who points out the right way.'

'It is thanks to Ma'at that the universe functions,' said Senusret, 'and that the starry, solar and earthly worlds live together in unity. Without Ma'at, our space would be uninhabitable. My will is Ma'at, for only righteousness of the heart is fitting for the pharaoh. My strength is justice. If I distanced myself from it, it would be the end of my reign, for the monuments of a destroyer are doomed to destruction. My prime duty is to raise up Ma'at towards herself, to be the mediator between her and my people, to bring the social order and the cosmic order into harmony. The state that has no celestial dimension and does not make offerings to Ma'at knows not justice, nor reciprocity, nor solidarity. It becomes mired in human conflicts and power struggles. Ma'at orders: act for him who acts. Are you that man, Iker?'

'Such is my desire, Majesty.'

Senusret took Iker to the edge of the desert. In the distance stood Pharaoh Djoser's stepped pyramid.

'Do you know the true name by which outsiders designate a burial-ground?

'It is "the land of Ma'at", is it not?'

'Great, lasting and radiant is the rule of Ma'at. It has never been disturbed since the time of Osiris. It is true that evil, iniquity and their allies are ceaselessly at work in this world and accumulate many misdeeds. But, so long as a few people respect Ma'at, evil will not succeed in crossing the river of life to reach the other bank. And when the end of time comes, Ma'at will remain.'

The king walked over to a small house of eternity dating from the ancient days. There was an inscription on its lintel.

'Read it, Iker.'

'"*Speak Ma'at, do not be passive, take part in creation, but do not go beyond the Rule.*"'

'What is your being made up of, besides your body?'

'My name and my heart.'

'Your name, Iker,* indicates that you are the bearer of something complete and the perfection of a work which is called upon to renew itself unceasingly. May your heart be filled with Ma'at so that your actions may be just. But your *ka* must also be nourished, that vital energy which comes from the other world and towards which you will return if you come through the ordeal of Osiris's court. May your *ba*, your spirit's capacity to move beyond the visible, journey to the sun in search of the light that can guide you in the darkness. And will you be capable of becoming an *akh*, a being of light which death does not touch?'

Iker was speechless. So many doors opening, so many new perceptions . . . The king's revelations made his head spin.

'Look at this stone, my son. It is in the shape of a statue's plinth, isn't it?'

'That is one of the hieroglyphs used to write the name of Ma'at, Majesty.'

'Statues are living beings, born of Ma'at. Climb up on to this plinth.'

*Il-kher-neferet, meaning 'He Who Goes', 'Bearer of Completion'.

The young man obeyed.

'What do you feel?' asked the king.

'A fire springs from this stone, a fire that spreads within me. My sight . . . it's getting sharper!'

'In the war we are fighting against the powers of darkness, the survival of Osiris and his civilization are at stake, so we must arm ourselves with weapons obtained in the invisible world. Today, my son, your initiation into the Mysteries has really begun. Whatever happens from now on, do not leave the way of Ma'at.'

45

A meeting of the King's House had just ended. Sehotep emerged from the council chamber and walked briskly to Medes's office. Medes immediately stopped dictating letters and told his assistants to leave.

'I am at your disposal, Bearer of the Royal Seal. How many decrees has His Majesty formulated?'

'Only one – this time, you will not have much work to do. But the text must be written this very day, and the royal messengers must leave first thing tomorrow morning to spread it throughout the provinces. If necessary, double the number of teams.'

Once again, Medes was one of the first to be informed of a decision by Senusret. But, because it was to be promulgated so urgently, he would have no time to benefit from it.

'The decree is very short,' said Sehotep. 'The pharaoh grants full powers to General Nesmontu and charges him with putting down any attempt at rebellion in Canaan. This will ensure that no inhabitant of the region can doubt our determination.'

'Does he think there may be another uprising?'

'According to Nesmontu's latest report, the Herald is not entirely dead.'

'I don't understand.'

'That sick-minded man was indeed executed, but some of

his followers survived and claim to represent him, with the intention of sowing unrest among the population. That is why Nesmontu must show exceptional firmness.'

'Knowing the general, we need have no fears on that score!'

'Fortunately so, Medes.'

'I would like to employ new messengers and increase the number of transport vessels in order to improve my efficiency. It is important that messages are passed on ever more quickly.'

'I shall speak in your favour to High Treasurer Senankh.'

'Many thanks.'

The information was without interest. So General Nesmontu had come up against grave difficulties in Canaan, had he? Even though people believed he was dead, the Herald was still weakening the occupying power. This decree came across as an admission of weakness. Unable to wipe out the rebels, the king and the general were trying to terrorize the population. If the whole region erupted into violence, what would be left of Senusret's prestige?

As usual, Medes did his work thoroughly and diligently. His employees all knew how uncompromising he was: one mistake meant dismissal. So his department was cited as a shining example, even by the tjaty.

As Medes was beginning the final draft of the decree, using official terminology, an unexpected visitor arrived: Iker, the accursed scribe who should have died so long ago!

Medes got to his feet and bowed. 'This visit honours me, Royal Son.'

'I am to go on an official mission, on His Majesty's orders.'

'We all strive, in all circumstances, to give him satisfaction. May I add that, personally, I am very happy at your appointment? The court cannot suppress its mockery, but its gossips will soon run out of breath. If you have need of me, do not hesitate for a moment.'

'I value your friendship. The king has asked me to carry the new decree to Djehuty, mayor of Dahshur, and to check the security measures there.'

'Many rumours have been circulating about the rebels' attack there. I hope the royal pyramid did not suffer any damage?'

'The attack failed, and the pyramid is intact and will soon be completed.'

'Some say that you behaved like a hero.'

'They are wrong.'

'Do not belittle yourself, Iker. Many braggarts who proclaim their courage run away at the least danger. You, however, confronted dangerous raiders.'

'The merit for the victory goes to Djehuty. Thanks to his cool-headedness, we avoided the worst.' He did not mention Sekari's decisive contribution, because of the need for secrecy: very few knew his friend's true role.

'I shall have the decree ready for you first thing tomorrow morning,' promised Medes. 'May I ask you to congratulate Djehuty on my behalf and wish him better health? The construction of the pyramid at Dahshur will be one of the many high points of the pharaoh's reign.'

Once Iker had left, Medes nursed his anger once again. He knew how to judge his enemies, and this one was particularly dangerous. Of course, Medes would act the perfect courtier and flatter the Royal Son, but that would probably be inadequate. Little by little, he must discredit him in the eyes of courtiers and ministers, making them believe that Iker was a mere schemer, an ambitious provincial with no skills or stature and, worse still, that he was harming the monarch's reputation. By moving forward in small stages, Medes would distil an effective poison.

For now, there was a more urgent matter: re-establishing contact with the Phoenician.

*

The water-carrier was satisfied with his work. In the past few weeks he had succeeded in hiring a number of useful informants, notably his lover, a palace washerwoman, who was observing Medes's comings and goings. And Medes's sumptuous house had been watched for a long time.

On the Herald's orders, the Phoenician was checking that Medes was behaving like a loyal ally. When his visit was announced, the trader was not surprised. Medes must have been alarmed by the latest upheavals, for he insisted on following the usual procedures and being extremely cautious.

He rose to greet Medes, and asked, 'How are you, my very dear friend?'

'What happened at Dahshur?'

'Sit down, and taste a few of these sweetmeats.'

'I want to know, and I want to know now!'

'Don't over-excite yourself.'

'If our collaboration is to be lasting, there must be no shadows between us.'

'Don't worry, the Herald doesn't intend it to be any other way. Dahshur was attacked by a courageous band of rebels but unfortunately unexpected resistance prevented them from damaging the pyramid, which is continuing to produce energy. Given the new protective measures, a new attack would be madness, at least for the time being.'

'Iker was responsible for their failure. That boy is harming our interests – he must be killed.'

The Phoenician gave a slight smile. 'Killed? Or used?'

'Used how?'

'The Herald greatly admires the fire that drives him, and knows how to wield it. This problem will be resolved.'

'When will I see the Herald again?'

'When he decides. He is in a safe place and has the situation well in hand. Shall we congratulate ourselves upon our successes, dear Medes? Our trade in valuable wood is

348

hriving and earning you a fine fortune, isn't it?'

Medes did not disagree. The system was working excellently.

'The time has come to tell you more about my choices,' he Phoenician continued. 'When you know the profound reasons for them, you will be conjoined with us once and for ll in our ferocious struggle against your country.' Although till smooth, the Phoenician's voice had become full of menace.

'I have no intention of giving up,' declared Medes.

'Even when you know that the things we are importing will cause the deaths of many of your countrymen?'

'I have already eliminated certain inconvenient people. Since that is the price to be paid for overturning Senusret and fashioning the country we dream of, I have no hesitation.'

The Phoenician had been expecting more resistance. But Medes seemed to have completely stifled his conscience in order to attain his ends. Now an unconditional adept of *isefet*, an active companion of evil, whose power and necessity he no longer disputed, Medes would not recoil from any crime.

'Let us talk first about the laudanum that your perfume-makers like so much,' said the Phoenician. 'Some flasks contain not only laudanum but also a drug which will remove certain obstacles. Next, let us move on to the moringa oil with which pregnant women anoint themselves. Our customers belong to the best society, and carry within them the country's unborn elite. Why allow that elite to prosper when we have the means to annihilate part of it before it is even born?'

Stunned, Medes no longer regarded the trader as a warm, friendly lover of good living. 'Surely you don't mean . . . ?'

'When the Herald decides, we shall replace the moringa oil with a substance which will cause a large number of miscarriages. Does this excellent plan shock you?'

Medes swallowed with difficulty. His battle was taking an unforeseen turn. This sort of violence had not entered into his plans but, after all, effectiveness was the most important thing. Allying with the Herald really did offer another dimension to the secret war against the pharaoh.

He said, 'I am neither shocked nor hostile.'

'I am glad to hear it, my dear friend. Now you understand why I set up this trade. And that is not all. Egyptian priests, scribes and cooks use different oils, so we shall not restrict our actions to pregnant women.'

Dizzying prospects, but how fascinating! Mortally wounded, pharaonic society would crumble in on itself, watched with horror by the powerless authorities.

'Success will require coordination and subtlety,' said the Phoenician. 'Our networks will be operational in the near future, but let us not forget our most dangerous enemy, the pharaoh. For as long as he reigns, he will find the energy necessary to confront even the worst ordeals.'

'Sobek the Protector has unfortunately been returned to his post,' said Medes. 'I thought I had dealt him a fatal blow, but that accursed man has thick skin!'

'We are well aware of that and of his capacity to do harm. Nevertheless, it now seems possible that we may succeed where we failed before.'

'In killing Senusret? I don't believe it!'

'Traditional methods proved unusable, I grant you, but I have devised some new ones. No matter how many guards there are, we shall get rid of them. I need your help, Medes. I need an accurate plan of the palace, and information on the king's activities and the security system surrounding him.'

'If he survives, will I not be suspected?'

'There will be no risk of that, because we shall leave clues identifying the persons responsible. When I tell you the date and time of the attack, you must arrange to be far

from the palace on that day, and make sure you have many
witnesses. If Senusret dies, our conquest will be swifter than
expected.'

46

Iker could not refuse an invitation to dine with Sehotep. The Royal Seal-Bearer's elegant house was delightful: bunches of flowers in each room, subtle perfumes, elegant furniture, alabaster tableware, paintings of cranes, storks and herons, tiled floors in delicate colours. And the staff, with the exception of a cook whose rotund form proved his love of food, consisted of charming young women, dressed in thin linen gowns and adorned with jewels.

'Participating in the government of Egypt is a rather taxing business,' remarked Sehotep. 'Everyone has his own way of relaxing a little: this is mine. You, Royal Son, seem much more serious. Is it true that you spend your nights reading old treatises on wisdom?'

'They marked the beginning of my education, and they still offer me wonderful nourishment.'

'I know that scribes are advised not to get drunk, but will the former law student nevertheless accept a cup of wine? This fine vintage comes from my vineyard at Imau, and the king himself admires it.'

Iker did not turn up his nose at it. And the meal was a masterpiece, ending with kidneys in a delicious sauce.

'Without wishing to flatter you,' said Sehotep, 'I find it remarkable how you have adapted to this court, which is usually very difficult to decipher. I myself don't yet know all its twists and turns, but you have decided to ignore them all completely. As you know, your appointment has whipped up storms and jealousies. Think how many rich families hoped to see their offspring adopted as Royal Son. And yet His Majesty chose you, an obscure provincial scribe. Everyone expected you to be triumphant and disdainful, but you show such exemplary discretion that it arouses suspicion. Moreover, the king grants you long audiences, alone with him. Can you imagine the assumptions and the anguish? Every courtier and dignitary fears for his post and his privileges. Whom are you going to supplant in his high office?'

'Nobody.'

'That's most unlikely.'

'The pharaoh has offered me a priceless treasure by opening my heart to spiritual realities which I perceived only confusedly and could not put into words. Receiving such teaching is incredible good fortune, and I hope to prove myself worthy of it.'

'Are you aware that storms threaten this tranquillity?'

'The king is preparing me for fierce battles.'

Sehotep appreciated Iker's openness and clear-headedness. Like Sobek, he had had reservations about the Royal Son's character and wanted to know him better. Now he felt reassured, and regretted having doubted Senusret.

'At last, Majesty, at last!' exclaimed Sobek. 'I knew that my men would come up with a result in the end, but it seemed to take a very long time. We suspect an itinerant barber who works in a district near the port. One of my informants is a regular client of his, and they're in the habit of talking freely about this and that. Their last conversation was about the danger that might be posed by Asians from Sichem who had settled illicitly in Memphis. The barber thinks they are good folk, whose grievances are justified. He says our occupation is too harsh, and that Canaan deserves total independence, so that it can better develop.'

'In other words, he supports the rebels.'

'Although he deplores violence, he understands their reasons. He presents himself as a humane man – like certain decadent individuals at your court, whose sole occupation consists of working out which way the wind is blowing.'

The king smiled. 'You are not making very much progress in the field of diplomacy, are you?'

'It's pointless when tracking down criminals, Majesty. A soft, indecisive, snivelling officer puts his colleagues' lives at risk.'

'Did this barber say anything else subversive?'

'My informant did not like to ask too many questions, for he sensed that the loose-tongued fellow regretted going so far. But we at last hold one link of the chain. Breaking it would be stupid. Let us use it to climb higher up the chain of command. I have removed my pawn from the game, so I need a new man, one who will be credible enough for the barber to say more to him.'

'Whom are you thinking of?'

'I am in an awkward position, Majesty. This type of criminal instinctively identifies a guard, even an experienced one. Moreover, our operation must be conducted in the greatest secrecy, which excludes any court dignitary.'

'Then there is only one candidate: Iker. He is still unknown in Memphis.'

'Iker? The Royal Son . . . ?'

'If I do not deceive myself, Sobek, this is the test you wanted to put him to.'

'You have fine hair, my boy, healthy and straight. What would you like? Shaven head, fashionable cut, or waves?'

'A short, simple cut.'

'Sit here on this stool,' advised the barber, 'and sit up straight.'

On a low table lay the equipment belonging to the barber, a friendly, stocky fellow: several razors of different sizes, curling pincers, scissors, and a bowl containing water to which natron had been added.

Iker was the first customer of the morning. The others waited, dozing, playing dice or exchanging a little gossip.

'Your hair's clean, so no need to wash it. Are you new to this district?'

'I'm a scribe and I come from the South. They say that in Memphis a public scribe can earn a good living.'

'With the number of demands sent to the government, you certainly won't go short of work.'

'Doesn't the tjaty try to make the humblest people's daily life easier?'

'That's what he says, but nobody believes in mirages.'

'Well, I think his hands are tied.'

'Why do you say that?' asked the barber.

'Because nobody can oppose the will of a tyrant.'

The razor remained suspended in the air for a few seconds. 'Surely you're not talking about . . .'

'I don't need to say his name: you understand me perfectly. We aren't all bleating sheep and we know perfectly well that only rebellion will give us back our freedom.'

'Lower your voice! Words like that could get you thrown into prison.'

'Others will take my place. And I have already escaped from the guards once, during the Kahun massacre.'

'You were there?'

'I was helping my friends from Asia. We hoped to seize the mayor's house, but we were betrayed. I managed to escape, but many of us were killed. The Egyptians will pay for that.'

'Are people looking for you?'

'Sobek the Protector would dearly like to catch me,' admitted Iker. 'And I'd very much like to see again the young woman who led us. But I expect she was killed.'

'What is her name?'

'If she's still alive, I'd put her in danger by revealing it.

You're an honest man, barber, but like most people you simply endure the tyranny.'

'You're wrong there. I'm fighting, too, in my own way.'

'Do you really want to fight the despot?'

'I didn't wait for you before making a start. Your young Asian girl, she's called Bina.'

Iker looked amazed. 'You mean you know her?'

The barber merely nodded.

'Then she's still alive!'

'Fortunately for us.'

'Where can I meet her?'

'That's asking much too much.'

'Without Bina, I'm lost – sooner or later I'll be arrested. But at her side I could still be useful.'

'Well, I know very little. But I do know someone who may be able to give you some information. He makes face-paints, and has a workshop at the bottom of the street, opposite me. Go there and tell him I sent you.'

The council, presided over by the king, listened to Iker's report.

'It is bound to be a trap,' said Sehotep. 'You should go no further.'

Sobek disagreed. 'The reason why we have failed to detect the Asians' network in Memphis is because it is divided into many separate sections. This barber remains in his role, one of many unimportant pawns. As Iker has taken him into his confidence, the other man allows him to move up the chain.'

'I think Sobek is right,' said nodded Senankh.

'And what if the barber is merely a decoy?' suggested the tjaty.

'Iker neither looks nor behaves like a guard or a soldier,' said Sobek. 'He and the barber took a step towards each other by mentioning Kahun and Bina. So there is no danger in pursuing this infiltration.'

'What is your decision, Iker?' asked the king.
'I shall continue, Majesty.'

The maker of face-paints supplied the city's principal doctors. By combining many varied substances he created beauty products.* But he did not confine himself to these and also created products which were not found in nature. He added medicinal qualities to his creation, making it possible to prevent or treat trachoma, leucoma and conjunctivitis.

As he was mixing some ingredients together, Iker knocked at the door of his workshop.

'This is not a good time to disturb me.'

'The barber sent me.'

'Who are you?'

'An ally of Bina's. I took part in the Kahun rebellion against the tyrant. Since I reached Memphis I've been in hiding, but I'd like to rejoin my friends.'

'Describe the barber to me.'

Iker did so.

'At Kahun, the mayor lives in a modest house,' the craftsman went on, 'but he likes to deck himself out in eccentric, expensive clothes.'

'It's the other way round,' Iker corrected him. 'He lives in a huge house with many servants, and dresses in a traditional manner.'

'Bina is too old to take up the fight again.'

'She is very young and very pretty.'

'What is the password the barber gave you?'

Disaster! The barber had not trusted Iker at all. He must

---

*The ingredients included galenite, lead sulphide, white lead, lead carbonate, pyrolusite, manganese oxide, chrysocolla, hydrated copper silicate and malachite; see the discoveries of G. Tsoucaris, P. Walter, P. Martinetto and J.-L. Lévêque, set out in the *Mensuel de l'X*, no 564, April 2001, pp. 39–45.

instantly find a plausible password, perhaps 'Bina', or 'Kahun' or 'rebellion'. But his chances of success were infinitesimally small, so he played the honesty game.

'He didn't give me a password, only told me that you might help me.'

The man seemed satisfied. 'Leave here, go down the second street on your left and enter the first house on your left. Then wait.'

Iker ought to have told Sobek what was afoot, but he feared he was being watched by the rebels. Moreover, a hunted man such as he claimed to be would lose not a second before going to this address.

The door closed behind him. Plunged into darkness, the entrance hall of the little white house seemed sinister. If he was attacked, Iker would not see the blows coming.

'Climb the stairs,' ordered a rasping voice.

Iker realized how unwise he had been. Sobek did not know where he was, and no guards would come to his aid. And if the young scribe was confronted by one of the Asians he knew, could he be convincing?

But he had never seen the person who greeted him, a short, middle-aged man who hardly seemed fearsome.

'What do you want, my boy?'

'To rejoin Bina and my Asian allies, and carry on our fight against the tyrant with them.'

'They have left Memphis.'

'Where have they gone?'

'To Sichem, to be with the Herald.'

'The Herald? But he has been dead for a long time!'

'No one can kill the Herald. He will spread the divine fire throughout Canaan. We Canaanites will drive the Egyptians from our territory, form an immense army and bring down the pharaoh's throne.'

47

The pharaoh's inner council hung on Iker's every word.

'And that is why Sobek could not dismantle the network of Asians in Memphis,' concluded Senankh. 'They left the city some time ago and took refuge in Canaan, where they have much local support.'

'It is up to General Nesmontu to resolve the problem,' said Sehotep. 'He must extinguish the fires of desire for rebellion by arresting the Herald's imitators, putting them on trial and holding their executions in public. As long as the Herald's reputation encourages other fanatics, there will never be peace in the region.'

'Thanks to Iker,' said Khnum-Hotep, 'we now know that Memphis was merely a staging-post and that the rebels have returned to Canaan. On one hand, that is good news; on the other, it is a serious threat, because if the enemy forces regroup they will become strong again.'

'I am still doubtful,' said Sobek. 'If that were the truth, Nesmontu would have reported more trouble in Sichem.'

'His last report gives some cause for alarm,' Senusret reminded him, 'but he is awaiting concrete evidence before making definite pronouncements.'

'And what if the Royal Son has been duped?' asked Sobek.

'We must not belittle his success,' advised Sehotep.

The Protector looked sullen.

Christian Jacq

'The conclusion is obvious,' said the tjaty. 'The major risk remains Sichem. As a matter of prudence, let us maintain a security cordon round Dahshur and Abydos. On the other hand, I propose re-establishing free circulation of goods and people here.'

The king agreed with him.

Sobek looked at Iker through narrowed eyes, as if he suspected him of having lied.

Several times the Herald's disciples prostrated themselves before their lord. Then, with one voice, they uttered a repetitive prayer to the glory of the god of victories, who would give them supremacy over the whole world.

Shab the Twisted participated with fervour in this celebration, but Crooked-Face was bored to tears. The pantomime seemed pointless to him as regards the only reality worthy of interest: violence. It was through him and his rebel fighters, and nobody else, that the Herald would triumph.

When the prayer ended, Shab the Twisted remained in an ecstatic trance.

Crooked-Face elbowed him in the ribs. 'Come back to earth, friend! You're surely not going to lapse into childish dreams?'

'Why do you remain closed to the Herald's teaching? It would offer you a strength which we all need.'

'Mine is enough for me.'

When the other followers had gone back to their workplaces or observation posts, the Herald assembled the trio charged with preparing the pharaoh's death.

Shab and Crooked-Face were surprised by Bina's transformation. She was no longer a pretty brunette, lively and light-hearted, but a fearsome seductress sure of her own charm. Despite their contempt for women and their feeling of superiority, the two men flinched.

'From now on, Bina belongs to the inner circle,' said the Herald. 'I have directly passed on a part of my power to her so that she may become queen of the night. She will therefore take part in our most important operations.'

Neither Shab nor Crooked-Face dared utter a word of protest. There was such a terrifying gleam in Bina's eye that even they did not wish to provoke her.

'Are your men ready?' the Herald asked Crooked-Face.

'The dried wood has been hidden in the agreed places. At my signal, the plan will be set in motion.'

'I spoke at length with the water-carrier,' said Shab. 'His talkative washerwoman has provided the information we needed, and the Phoenician has given me the phials.'

Gently, the Herald took Bina's hand. 'It is up to you to act.'

'Sir,' said the guard, 'the barber and the maker of face-paints have disappeared.'

'What do you mean, "disappeared"?' demanded Sobek-Khu. 'Weren't they being watched?'

'Of course, but very lightly so that they wouldn't realize it. They managed to give our men the slip.'

'I am surrounded by imbeciles!' roared Sobek.

'Sir, there's something else.'

'What now?'

'The Canaanite the Royal Son spoke to is packing his bags.'

'Well, we're not letting that one escape. I shall deal with him myself.'

Sekari was enjoying one of his favourite occupations: sleeping. He didn't mind whether he got up late, had an afternoon nap or went to bed early. He always fell asleep with a remarkable ease and was not easily roused.

'Wake up,' said Iker, shaking him.

'Wha . . . ? Is it time for the evening meal?'

'The Canaanite has sent me a message. I am to join him to the south of the city. The king wants you to follow me.'

Sekari was on his feet instantly. 'I don't like this, Iker.'

'Perhaps he will provide me with a way to rejoin my alleged allies.'

The guard stepped forward, preventing Bina from entering the palace guards' dining-hall. 'Where are you going with that basket?'

'It's a gift from the tjaty.'

'Open it.'

The soldier found flasks inside.

'Some contain high-quality oil for cooking,' explained Bina, 'the rest contain an ointment which eases pain. I've been told to take them to the cook.'

'How long have you worked at the palace?'

'I've always worked here,' said the young woman alluringly. 'But I've never seen you before.'

'You wouldn't have. I've only just been transferred here.'

'We should get to know each other better, don't you think?'

The guard quivered. Bina smiled.

'Good idea,' he said. 'Are you free tomorrow evening?'

'Tomorrow evening? That's possible,' she murmured, smiling sweetly.

She took a phial, uncorked it, moistened her index finger and ran it gently over the man's neck. He thought he would melt with pleasure.

'See you soon, handsome soldier.'

The cook was no harder to seduce. Bina had all the time she needed to pour oil into the cooking-pots, where food was simmering for the sentries who would go on duty at the first hour of night. They would fall into a heavy sleep from which most of them would never awake. As for the rest of the guards, Crooked-Face's men would take care of them.

'He isn't alone, sir,' said one of Sobek's men. 'There are at least two others on the terrace, and bound to be still more inside. We've stumbled on a whole nest of Canaanites.'

Dusk would make the arrests easier. Sobek sent out a scout.

As he approached the suspect house, a stone from a slingshot hit him on the shoulder.

'They were waiting for us,' said the Protector. 'We shall encircle them. I shall return to the palace and send you reinforcements. As soon as they arrive, attack the house.'

Sobek had an uneasy feeling that this house was only a decoy. If he stayed to direct the operation, he'd be away from the king for a long time, and his instincts told him to rejoin him as fast as possible.

'But the message definitely said this house,' confirmed Iker.

'It looks abandoned,' said Sekari.

'At Kahun, I met Bina in a place like this.'

'In other words, she's probably laid a trap for you. Stay here.'

'Sekari—'

'Don't worry, I'm used to this.'

Iker could not understand how the apparently clumsy Sekari could transform himself into a creature of air whom no obstacle could hinder. He disappeared with incredible agility and was not long in reappearing.

'This dump's empty. The message was just a ruse – they wanted to get us away from the palace. Quickly, we must get back there.'

Ten fires were lit at the same time, near the palace. The dry brushwood burnt fiercely and the flames rose high, causing panic.

One of the fires threatened a government building, and the guards posted outside ran to help the water-carriers trying to save it.

'Here we go,' Crooked-Face told his fifteen fighters, who were armed with short-swords.

Despite his courage, the lone sentry who remained before the main door was soon cut down.

Inside, Bina's poison had proved effective. Most of the guards lay sprawled on the floor of the dining-hall or in the corridors. A few were still on their feet, but half asleep; only a handful had not eaten and were still in a condition to fight. But they could not hold out for long.

Senusret had just lain down on his bed. No matter how many tasks filled his interminable day's work, the monarch never stopped thinking about the Tree of Life. A vital route linking the Earth to the cosmos and the spine of the reborn Osiris, it preserved the fundamental values used as materials by the brotherhood of sages when Egypt was built.

By governing righteously, the king contributed to safeguarding the acacia. Every righteous deed produced food; every ritual celebrated emitted a power capable of driving back the forces of evil.

Suddenly there was the sound of shouts and clashing weapons. The king rose, snatched up a sword and opened the door of his bedchamber.

In the corridor, the last guard fell dead. Only two of Crooked-Face's raiders had been killed.

A heavy silence fell. All eyes converged on the giant figure of the Pharaoh, whose calm demeanour unnerved his attackers.

Even Crooked-Face, who knew no fear, hesitated. Then he recovered and hissed, 'It's him, the pharaoh!'

The Asians lowered their weapons.

'He's only a man!' said Crooked-Face furiously. 'He's alone and there are many of us – he has no chance of beating us. Attack!'

After a long moment, one raider made up his mind.

Although the pharaoh's arm seemed scarcely to move, a bloody furrow cleaved the Asian's chest and he fell heavily on to his back. One of his comrades tried to avenge his companion, but met the same fate. Senusret gazed upon his enemies with a mixture of anger and disdain.

'All together!' roared Crooked-Face.

His men would have obeyed him if two of them had not been felled by Sekari and Iker, who were wielding clubs taken from the guards' corpses.

'Retreat!' shouted an Asian, convinced that massed reinforcements were arriving.

He did not get far, for he ran into an enraged Sobek, whose spear ran him through.

Abandoning his men, Crooked-Face set off down an empty corridor and jumped out of a window. Taking advantage of the general confusion, he disappeared into the night.

48

The pharaoh was safe and sound. Sekari, slightly wounded in one arm, was getting his breath back.

Sobek pointed his spear at Iker, who was leaning against the corridor wall near the pile of Asian bodies. 'I accuse the Royal Son of having organized this attempt to kill the king.'

'You're losing your mind!' protested Sekari.

'Who made us believe the rebels had left Memphis? Iker and the Canaanite. They're accomplices, and that's the truth.'

Iker was very pale. 'On the name of Pharaoh, I swear that I am loyal to the king and ready to give my life to defend him.'

Fearing the Protector might resort to violence, Sekari hastily stepped between the two men. He said, 'Like you, Sobek, we were duped. We were lured away from the palace, fires were lit, the guards drugged. As soon as we suspected something was wrong, we came back as fast as we could. Iker fought bravely; he could have been killed.'

The Protector's wrath abated a little. Sekari's explanation was indeed believable. But Iker had already tried to kill the king once. What if this was a second attempt, better organized than the first?

'Iker's behaviour and his oath should dispel your suspicions,' said Senusret. 'The true culprits lie at your feet.'

'Asians,' said Sobek. 'A few have been killed, but how many more are determined to destroy Egypt?'

*

The Herald calmed his faithful followers. 'The assassination attempt failed,' he acknowledged, 'but none of our valiant fighters has spoken – if they had, the guards would be here already. Those heroes will go to paradise, and we can be proud of their courage and devotion. Because of them, the tyrant will no longer feel safe anywhere, not even in his own palace. It is time to leave this depraved city. Shab, form groups. Each will leave in a different direction so as not to attract the enemy's attention. We shall meet in a safe place, and I will assign new tasks. Our struggle to establish the true faith will constantly intensify.'

Reassured, the followers received their instructions.

The Herald went upstairs and took the acacia-wood box out of its hiding-place. The weapons it contained had not yet expressed their full power.

'My lord,' said Bina, 'I regret not taking part in that fight. Crooked-Face could not keep a cool head. I would have done.'

'You will have other occasions to display your valour. Senusret has proved an exceptional enemy, with extensive powers. His gods have endowed him with extraordinary qualities, and only the superiority of our god will reduce him to nothing. The road will be long, Bina, for the enemy is strong.'

'Victory will be all the more beautiful.'

'Sobek has not found us, but we shall not always have that advantage. Be prudent, queen of the night. Shroud everything you do in darkness.'

Shab was uneasy. Carrying the turquoise's box on his shoulder, he followed the Herald, who ought to have left Memphis with the others instead of going to the Phoenician trader's house. But he must obey his master, even if he took ill-considered risks.

The Twisted One feared they might be intercepted at any

moment by a guards patrol, but the Herald walked along calmly, like any citizen with a clear conscience. And, indeed, nothing happened.

When the Herald entered the reception room, the Phoenician and Medes stood up.

'Senusret is still alive!' exclaimed Medes.

'I know, my friend, I know.'

'We'll all be arrested!'

'Of course not.'

'Sobek will interrogate the wounded, and they'll talk.'

'I don't think so,' said the Herald.

'How can you be certain?'

'Apart from Crooked-Face, the brutes charged with killing the pharaoh ate something which will have ensured that they could not. Even if they had succeeded in killing the king, they would all have been dead less than an hour later.'

Medes stared at him in terror. 'You . . . you've—'

'The chance of success was extremely small, for Senusret is still surrounded by magic. However, we have achieved the result I envisaged: this impious regime knows it is vulnerable. And nothing and no one can help it predict from where or when the blows will fall.'

'Am I to go back to my country straight away?' asked the Phoenician.

'Certainly not, my fine friend. Several of the faithful have already left for the north, but you will stay here, as will the members of the principal network, the shopkeepers, barbers and itinerant traders. You will direct it in my name and keep me informed with exemplary loyalty, will you not?'

'You can rely on me, my lord!' exclaimed the Phoenician, whose suddenly painful scars reminded him of the all-conquering necessity to obey the Herald.

'Your role and Medes's are particularly important. You will inform me about what is happening in Memphis and Senusret's intentions.'

'We shall do our best, but . . . are we to continue our trade with Phoenicia?'

'I see no reason why not, so long as our cause benefits from it.'

'I meant exactly that, my lord.'

'Are you thinking of waiting a while before attacking the pharaoh again?' asked Medes.

'I must deploy my forces in a different way, but there will be no pause. For your part, learn as much as you can about Abydos. For as long as the Acacia of Osiris has a breath of life, there can be no final victory. But we shall soon achieve our first goal: ensuring that no Egyptian sleeps peacefully in his bed.'

As he was about to enter the interrogation room of the main barracks at Sichem, General Nesmontu received a message from Sehotep, relating the dramatic events at Memphis.

This news heated the old soldier's blood and strengthened his desire to flush out the leaders of the Canaanite sedition. Although it was apparently under control, Nesmontu sensed that the fire was smouldering beneath the ashes.

Opposite him, sitting on a stool with his hands tied behind his back, was a young lad with hate-filled eyes.

'Why was he arrested?' the general asked the soldier guarding him.

'He tried to stab a sentry in the back. It took three of us to control him.'

'How old are you?' asked Nesmontu, staring right into the prisoner's eyes.

'Thirteen.'

'Did you tell your parents what you intended to do?'

'My parents are dead. The Egyptian army killed them, so I shall kill the Egyptians. Sichem will rebel, because we have a great leader!'

'What is his name?'

'The Herald.'

'He's dead. He was sentenced and executed.'

'Rubbish! We Canaanites know that isn't true. And you'll soon have proof.'

'Really? When?'

'At this very moment, the Herald is pillaging a caravan to the north of Sichem.'

'You seem well-informed, little crook. But you tell lies as easily as breathing.'

'You'll soon see it isn't a lie.'

'A stay in prison will set your ideas straight.'

'He's only a young boy, sir,' said the guard.

'A young boy ready to kill. Egyptian law applies here, and it stipulates that from the age of ten an individual is fully responsible for his actions.'

As the general was going back to his quarters, his assistant brought him a message: a caravan had been attacked to the north of the town.

'Any deaths?'

'Unfortunately, yes, but there are some survivors.'

'Bring them to me at once.'

As soon as he arrived in Memphis, Nesmontu requested an audience with the pharaoh, who abandoned everything and received him. Given the importance of the general's information, Senusret summoned Khnum-Hotep, Sehotep, Senankh, Sobek, Iker and Sekari.

'The investigation conducted by General Nesmontu has resulted in a worrying conclusion,' declared the king. 'He will set out the circumstances of his discovery. Then we shall have decisions to make.'

'A caravan was attacked recently near Sichem,' said Nesmontu. 'The soldiers escorting it fought bravely, but they were greatly outnumbered. A patrol managed to rescue the only two survivors, a soldier and a merchant.'

'This proves that we must strengthen our military presence a Canaan,' said Senankh.

'I also suggest doubling the escorts,' said Sobek. 'They will dissuade the sand-travellers – willing allies of the 'anaanites – from launching their murderous raids.'

'Those measures will certainly be necessary,' acknowledged Nesmontu, 'but they may not be enough. According to the survivors, the attackers were led by a tall man whom they called the Herald.'

'The Herald is dead,' Sehotep reminded him. 'According to your own report, he was executed.'

'That is what I believed, but clearly I was wrong. The Herald does indeed seem to be alive. From the clues I gathered in interrogations, I have the feeling that he is declaring himself the soul of the Canaanite rebellion. Even children are devoted to him and want to fight in his name.'

'Then if he exists, he must be in Canaan,' said Iker.

His intervention provoked a ferocious look from Sobek. He had not been able to get anything out of the Canaanites appointed to entrap him. All the captives had died of wounds sustained in the attack.

'The Herald must have several armed groups at his disposal,' Nesmontu went on. 'He moves around a lot, and is trying to unite the tribes and create an army capable of facing us.'

'Why have you not arrested him?' asked the tjaty.

'He knows the terrain better than we ever will, and lookouts inform him of our forces' every movement. Nevertheless, I have obtained one useful piece of information: the merchant who survived the attack on the caravan said he once heard the Herald preaching war against Egypt, and recognized him. His real name is Amu, and he leads an ancient nomadic Canaanite tribe renowned for its cruelty and violence.'

'Then all we have to do is locate him.'

'The families of that tribe went into hiding after th
Sichem insurrection. They swore an oath, which the whol
region takes very seriously, that anyone who denounces
supporter of the Herald to the army or the guards will b
killed with the utmost savagery.'

'Then what do you suggest?' asked Senankh.

'I need a very brave man, one who has His Majesty'
complete trust and who is capable of winning the trust c
Amu and those close to him. He must identify the variou
branches of the rebels' network and inform us – with th
greatest prudence, naturally. We shall intervene at the rig
moment and annihilate the enemy with a single blow.
cannot be a soldier – he would easily be detected.'

'Then I am the obvious candidate,' said Sekari.

'Certainly not,' said Iker. 'I am the only one who has th
necessary qualifications. After all, didn't I try to kill the king'

Sobek started. 'Majesty, I advise you once again to bewar
of this scribe.'

'Wherever the Herald is hiding,' Iker went on, 'Bina an
the Asians of Kahun will not be far away – we know the
have left Memphis and are preparing for their next attacks.
have deceived the authorities, but Sobek-Khu knows the tru
and is about to arrest me. The only thing I can do is run awa
rejoin my accomplices, tell them what I have learnt about th
palace and take up the fight against the tyrant again.'

'At last,' exclaimed Sobek, 'you confess!'

Iker turned his gaze upon the Protector. 'Since my wor
cannot convince you of my loyalty, my actions will speak f
me. Either I rejoin my accomplices and you eventually ki
me with unadulterated joy; or else I infiltrate the enemy
ranks and pass on precious information which will enable H
Majesty to root out the evil.'

'A third course seems much more realistic to me,' sai
Sekari. 'You fail, and the Herald puts you to an agonizir
death.'

'I am aware of the danger,' admitted Iker, 'but I have a
ebt to pay and I want to gain the total trust of all those close
▸ His Majesty, Sobek included. His attitude does not shock
ie. I committed a grave offence, and I must wash my heart
lean and fill it with righteousness. That is why I beg Pharaoh
▸ permit me to do this.'

Senusret got to his feet, signifying the end of the council
ieeting.

Silently, everyone except Iker went out.

'Majesty, may I beg a favour before I leave? I would like
▸ see Isis again and speak to her one last time.'

49

Gergu was slumped in a chair, sobbing. 'We must lea
Memphis at once. But where can we hide? Senusret w
pursue us to the very ends of the desert.'

'Stop babbling like an idiot,' snapped Medes, 'and dri
some more strong beer. It will calm you.'

'I'm not thirsty any more.'

'Pull yourself together, man!'

Gergu emptied his cup as though it were to be his last.

'Actually, we have little or nothing to fear,' Medes assur
him. 'According to the rumours, the only one whom Sob
suspects is Iker. The Herald and most of his men are safe, a
the Phoenician's people are still in place.'

Gergu felt a little less anxious. 'Are you sure we won't
arrested?'

'No one can prove we have done anything wrong. All t
trails that might have led back to us have been cut off.'

This time, Gergu emptied the jar. 'Senusret seems inv
nerable. I don't believe anyone will ever succeed in killi
him. We ought to withdraw from this dangerous allian
Medes, and enjoy the fortune we've made.'

'That would be foolish. First, the Herald permits neit
treason nor defection – we'd be signing our own dea
warrants. Second, we shall continue to grow richer, thanks

he Phoenician. Finally, we shall eventually dominate the entire country. Do you really believe in hell, Gergu?'

'The damned burn there in cauldrons, and nothing relieves their suffering.'

'Stupid stories,' declared Medes. 'I believe only in evil, falsehood and greed. Denying them is idiotic, fighting them is ridiculous. The Herald fascinates me, for he uses the forces of evil with supreme skill. It's astonishing that so many men obey him blindly. Do the fools really believe that God has spoken to one man and charged him with imposing an absolute, definitive truth? Stupidity leads the herd, and we must take full advantage of that. It is the most fearsome political weapon. I care nothing for the religion the Herald preaches, but I am convinced it will succeed in conquering the world. By associating ourselves with him, we shall become fabulously rich and powerful.'

Medes's calmness reassured Gergu, and the beer finally relaxed him.

'The King's House lives in fear,' added its secretary. 'Following General Nesmontu's unexpected arrival, I have no decrees to write up. Nothing has emerged of his conversations with the king, but it appears that Iker was summoned. I am going to try and find out more. For your part, discreetly question Nesmontu's entourage. You're bound to find at least one loose-tongued fellow who'll be happy to reveal the reasons for the general's visit.'

The sun was setting over Abydos. Isis slowly climbed the stone staircase to the temple roof, where she would spend the night studying the sky.

Charged by the king with reporting any suspicious activities on the part of the permanent or temporary priests, the young woman had noted, not without relief, that each man was performing his duties meticulously. Another more difficult mission demanded her energy: searching the archives of the House of Life for clues, however small, to a cure for the acacia tree.

It was precisely because one text advised exploring the cosmos that Isis was planning to question the stars, the planets and the decans.

The goddess Isis placed the stars in their proper places, and the seven Hathors influenced destiny. As for the reading of the time, the horoscope, that remained a state secret passed from pharaoh to pharaoh. The initiates, however, knew the message of the thirty-six candles, the decans, also called 'the Living Ones'. They were born and regenerated in the *duat* the stars' matrix, and set the rhythm for the ritual year.

With the aid of a viewer made from a palm-leaf split in the middle and a graduated beam equipped with a plumb-line Isis calculated the positions of the heavenly bodies. She observed Horus-the-bull-of-the-sky, a decisive power leaving no place for human weaknesses; Horus-who-reveals-the-secret; red-Horus, dispenser of strength; the double star of morning and evening, assimilated into the phoenix, bearer of the radiance of the primordial stone; Sebegu at the front of the ship of the sun, opener of all ways.* Together, these planets played a music which one must learn to perceive to understand how the partitioning of the universe, of which they were the eternal interpreters, enchanted the land of Egypt.

None of them showed any alarming signs. On the other hand, Isis wondered why the acacia was not more in harmony with the phases of the moon. At the end of the rising phase of its energy, the fourteenth day, the celestial eye was fished out again, put back together, and shone in the boat as the sun of the night, a light at the heart of the shadows, capable of amplifying shapes hidden in the darkness.

The sun was still fulfilling its function, but the Tree of Life was no longer benefiting from it. According to the writings

*Respectively, the planets Saturn, Jupiter, Mars, Venus and Mercury

nly one power could damage the night sun and prevent it from shining: Set, the murderer of Osiris, Set the transgressor, the violent one, the drunkard, the stormy one, he who separated, cut apart, sowed confusion and disorder.

Isis knew where to find him: at the heart of the front foot of the bull, in the northern sky.*

Pointing her little ivory 'Magic' sceptre towards him, the priestess questioned him. She knew the dangers of doing so – disturbing Set the unpredictable risked unleashing his thunder – but she needed to find out why and how he was harming his brother Osiris by attacking the Tree of Life.

The circumpolars, indestructible stars, remained identical. Servants of Osiris, they maintained the power of Set at the heart of the universe's harmony. On the other hand, the other celestial bodies began to shine with unusual brightness.

Suddenly, Isis had a vision of the hidden reality of this immense expanse she had so often contemplated in admiration, without discerning its true nature. On a lapis-azuli background shone metals and precious stones, fed by the brightness emanating from the sun's ship. The cosmos appeared as a gigantic alchemical laboratory, in which the transmutation of light into life took place unceasingly, projected on to each being, beginning with the Earth. In the bellies of the mountains the metals and minerals from the sky were reborn. Osiris-Moon, the sun at the heart of the darkness, made them grow. A spirit of evil, manipulating the cosmic forces, was trying to interrupt this growth.

Isis was overcome by dizziness. She went slowly back down the staircase, frequently using the wall to support herself. It was too soon to draw teachings from her discovery, but perhaps it would enable her to find new weapons against the enemy.

There was a presence in the half-light of the temple.

That is, in the Great Bear.

'Who is there?'

'I have come to perform my service,' said Bega hoarsely 'The Shaven-headed One asked me to replace you and to continue the observations. Did you note anything unusual in the movement of the stars?'

'No,' replied Isis. She was not lying. It was neither the movement nor the position of the celestial bodies that had opened her consciousness, but their very quality. She could have spoken of this to Bega, who was a renowned mathematician specializing in the ephemerides, but she was still overwhelmed, and preferred to keep silent about her experience.

By the light of the candles, Bega noticed that the priestess looked exhausted. 'How are you feeling, Isis?'

'A little tired.'

'Do you wish me to accompany you to your room?'

'Thank you, but there's no need.'

'I don't wish to give you orders, but you should rest for a while.'

'As for all of us, circumstances forbid it.'

'You won't preserve the acacia's health by ruining your own.'

'If my life could save its life, and that of our country, would not hesitate for a moment to offer it.'

'The permanent priests share that noble thought,' said Bega, 'and are unstinting in their efforts. The result is no such a cause for despair, since the acacia still lives.'

'We are fighting the most formidable of wars and we have not yet lost it.'

As he watched her walk away, Bega was torn by a variety of feelings. How could one not be envious of her beauty and her intelligence? With caution and skill, he must prevent her from rising in the hierarchy and becoming a hindrance – she was already so radiant that many were promising her high office. Fortunately, lacking ambition and solely preoccupied with spiritual research, she had no thoughts of power.

Had she just made a discovery that had deeply moved her? Questioning her would have been unwise, for she would have been surprised by such curiosity. But with persistence perhaps Bega would coax her into trusting him, even transform her into prey for the Herald.

The sun rose in splendour. Isis noticed the exceptional brilliance of the red halo preceding the reappearance of the gold disc, once more victorious over the darkness it had traversed during that night, which the priestess had ended in the library of the House of Life. In consulting Imhotep's alchemical treatise, whose riches she was a long way from exhausting, she had devised an experiment, which she hoped the Shaven-headed One would permit.

When he saw a copper mirror in Isis's hand, he was quick to express his disapproval. 'Have you by chance forgotten our primary duty?' he asked sharply.

'No, have no fear. We are going to water the foot of the acacia with water and milk, but I would like to obtain your permission to carry out a new rite.'

'With that mirror?'

'Hathor was made sacred during the rites of feminine initiation. The one I have at my disposal is the simplest, and its ability to produce radiance is limited. However, I have hopes.'

'Where does this idea come from?'

'From perceiving the metallic nature of the sky.'

'Ah, you have passed through that stage. The king was right.' Grumpily, the Shaven-headed One led the way to the acacia.

After feeding the Tree of Life, Isis angled the mirror so that the morning light lit up a small part of the foliage. Watched attentively by the Shaven-headed One, a few leaves began to grow green again. Then the colour faded, although it did not disappear completely.

'Explain, Isis.'

'The enemy has disrupted the circulation of energy between the sky and the earth. One single power makes metals and plants grow, and the acacia is the king of the plants, participating at once in the world beyond and here on earth. Because of this baleful intervention, it is no longer playing its twofold role of emitting and receiving energy. Only an alchemical treatment can heal it.'

'That is why the gold of the gods is so vital,' said the Shaven-headed One.

'Until we find what we need, we must use other metals that come from the stars. This simple ritual mirror has just proved its effectiveness, however minimal. Others, better made, will help the sap to circulate in its veins.'

'What if we were to arrange dozens of mirrors round the acacia?' asked the Shaven-headed One.

'We would risk burning the little vitality it has and killing it ourselves. Our actions must be cautious and meticulous.'

'Nevertheless, this is a new step in the right direction.'

'My research is not yet finished. The ancient seers have bequeathed major secrets to us. So I shall continue to scrutinize their words.'

50

In the workshop at Abydos the instructions for making face-paints, perfumes and ritual ointments were kept; all were vital for the daily practice of the rites. The Shaven-headed One and the permanent priests knew these texts so well that they no longer paid them any attention. In re-examining them, as well as the columns of hieroglyphs engraved on the walls, Isis set off in quest of an unexpected detail or an allusion to a lost secret which would put her on the trail of the healing metal.

First, she noted down several mentions of the gold of Punt, but could find no details as to the location of this mysterious country, whose reality nobody could confirm; next, she learned of the existence of a 'City of Gold', where a very pure metal with exceptional virtues was mined. There was no indication of where the city might be, either, but the context led her to believe that it was in the Nubian desert.

Exhausted, she rolled up the precious papyri and slid them into leather cases. Then she left the workshop and meditated for a few moments in the silent temple before returning to the outside world.

The sun was setting. In the gentle light of dusk, a huge man stepped forward.

'Majesty!'

'What have you discovered, Isis?'

She told him about her observation of the sky and about the City of Gold.

'I have come to celebrate a ritual designed to drive back the enemies of the Light, in order to protect Osiris more effectively. You will be one of the four priestesses representing the goddesses who assist me.'

In a shrine the Shaven-headed One set up a relic-holder surrounded by four winged, lioness-headed figures. It symbolized the primordial mound that had emerged during creation when the Divine radiance materialized.

Along with three other priestesses of Hathor, Isis made a ball of clay. Each one represented a facet of the eye of Ra, which could dispel the storms raised by Set.

On the relic-holder the pharaoh laid a fifth ball, into which he stuck an ostrich feather, an evocation of Ma'at.

'May the tomb of Osiris be always defended against its attackers,' chanted the king. 'The four lionesses watch at the cardinal points, their eyes never close. May these four directions remain stable and the sky never falter.'

Each carrying her clay ball, the priestesses stood before the monarch. Four times he repeated the words of conjuration: 'Henceforth, the sun has four eyes. The whole of the sky is lit up. Violent gusts, filled with fire, disperse Set and his accomplices.'

He threw the first ball towards the south, the second north, the third west and the fourth east.

'Abydos remains for ever the site that bears the Venerable One, and Set sees himself condemned to bear one who is greater than he, Osiris.'

When the rite was over, Senusret gathered together the permanent priests and priestesses in the temple's pillared hall. 'The protection of the acacia has been strengthened,' he said. 'Wherever the evil being is hiding, the eye of Ra will discern it and thwart his actions. In my absence, one of the initiates will speak the words prolonging the effectiveness of the rite. Isis will watch over the acacia and name the elements of Osiris's ship, "the Lady of Abydos". Because it no longer travels freely, the energy of resurrection is becoming exhausted. Isis will preserve what can be preserved, and we shall continue our fight and search for the healing gold.'

Bega's throat was dry. True, Isis was not yet replacing the Shaven-headed One, but she was acquiring considerable importance and as the representative of the royal will she would inevitably increase her influence. Fortunately, her role was limited to sacred action and touched neither administration nor material possessions. Because of her mystical temperament, the young woman would shut herself away in spirituality and would never notice the traffic in stelae.

As for the final death of Osiris and the destruction of Abydos, she would not see the danger coming until it was much too late.

A soldier worthy of the name did not turn his nose up at good beer, especially if it was a little stronger than usual. Gergu therefore decided to approach one of the elderly soldiers of General Nesmontu's escort, a man near the end of his military service. When he came off duty, the soldier readily agreed to visit the best taverns in Memphis in the company of a man who knew them well.

'I work in the royal vineyards,' lied Gergu. 'After we've moistened our throats with strong beer, I'll get you to sample some fine vintage wines that you'll remember.'

Nobody held his drink better than Gergu. Even dead drunk, he could still understand what people were saying to him. The soldier, on the other hand, lacked practice at the highest level. So, after telling of his exploits, he did not refuse to answer his new friend's questions.

'Why did General Nesmontu come back to Memphis in such haste?' asked Gergu.

'It's a very odd story. A caravan was attacked, and there were civilian and military deaths. And do you know who the leader of the criminals was? The Herald! The man who was executed can't have been him.'

'Is his real identity known now?'

'The general certainly knows it, and he was in a hurry to tell the pharaoh.'

'I expect a vast search of the region is planned.'

'That would surprise me.'

'Why?'

'Because it's already been done ten times, with no result, Nesmontu's a wily fellow. He'll send a spy to infiltrate the Canaanite ranks and find out where the Herald's hiding. Then we shall strike.'

'Good work, Gergu,' acknowledged Medes. 'That talkative fellow has been extremely useful. I shall inform the Phoenician this evening so that he can warn the Herald.'

'My lord, Royal Son Iker is asking to see you,' said a scribe.

Medes immediately left his office. 'How may I be of use to you, Iker?'

'I had accepted your invitation to dinner, but unfortunately I cannot honour it.'

'You aren't ill, I hope?'

'Not at all, but I must leave the court for a while.'

'A mission in the provinces?'

'Forgive me, but I cannot tell you any more.'

'Do you wish to arrange another date?'

'I do not know exactly how long I shall be away.'

'Permit me to wish you a good journey and to say how impatient I am to see you again. As soon as you return, grant me the privilege of being among the first to receive you.'

'That is a promise.'

'Then goodbye, and we shall meet again soon.'

'If the gods will it, Medes.'

There was only one explanation for the Royal Son's hurried departure: Senusret had ordered him, in the greatest secrecy, to infiltrate the ranks of the Canaanite rebels. Iker was not a soldier, and nobody knew him in the region; he would claim to be a supporter of the Herald and would obtain better results than Nesmontu's army.

If Medes was not mistaken, he held the surest means of getting rid of that tenacious little scribe once and for all. The Phoenician would have him followed by his agents, who would hand over to the Herald's disciples. When Iker entered Canaan, thinking he had deceived those around him, he would be a dead man.

Soon he would be in Canaan, a hostile land of danger, loneliness, fear and probably death. Iker had no illusions about his fate but did not fear it. Before that ordeal, which was likely to his last, the palace gardens seemed particularly cool and peaceful. He would have liked to write, for the rest of his life, in the shade of a sycamore tree, to follow the course of the sun to the rhythm of the hieroglyphs set out on a papyrus, to go into the thoughts of the sages and try to word them in a new way in accordance with tradition. But destiny had decided otherwise, and rebellion would be childish.

Suddenly, he thought he was having another hallucination. She was coming towards him, in a dress of palest pink, a lotus-flower in her hair.

'Isis, is it you? Is it really you?'

She smiled at him, radiant as the sun. 'On the orders of His Majesty, I am visiting Memphis to consult certain archives which have not been used for a long time. Before spending long hours in the library of the Temple of Hathor, I wanted to see this place again. Forgive me for interrupting your meditation.'

Once again, words bumped into each other inside Iker's head, and he did not know which ones to choose.

'The pomegranate tree,' she went on. 'Do you remember?
I would like to look at it with you.'

The tree was beautiful. New flowers constantly replaced
the old ones.

They sat down on a wooden bench, at once close to each
other and very far apart.

'I hoped so much that I would see you again, Isis. This will
probably be the last time.'

'Why?'

'I have been authorized by the pharaoh to carry out a
mission which is incumbent upon me: to try to infiltrate the
rebel group led by the Herald.'

'How will you do that?'

'The strategists will tell me.'

'What weapons will you have to protect yourself with?'

'The knife of the guardian spirit that His Majesty gave to
me, an amulet representing the "Power" sceptre and the
experience of fighting I gained during my training.'

Isis seemed aghast. 'But isn't this mission suicidal?'

'As Royal Son, I owe obedience to my father. Still more, I
must serve him without thinking of myself. Today, my place
is in Canaan. If I succeed, Pharaoh will be able to fight the
forces of evil more effectively. If I fail, another man will try.'

'You seem almost indifferent in the face of your destiny.'

'Do not think that I am resigned – quite the contrary. But I
know that my chances of success are very slender, and so I
beg a favour from you, if you will consent to hear me.'

'Please tell me what it is.'

'When I leave for Canaan, I shall have to leave behind my
most faithful companion, North Wind, a donkey I saved twice
from certain death. He has preserved me from bad luck.
Would you take him to Abydos and care for him?'

'Of course, and I shall try to win his friendship. You can be
certain that he will lack for nothing.'

'That will be comforting to know while I am in exile. A

Memphis it's easy to be brave, but how will I react when I am far from Egypt? And even if I discover the Herald's lair, will I be able to warn the king?'

'The magic of Abydos will protect you, Iker. Thanks to you, we shall save the Tree of Life.'

The young man thought of the words of the snake on the Island of the *Ka*: 'I could not prevent the end of this world. Will you save yours?'

Isis stood up.

In a few moments, she would walk away, disappear for ever, and he had still not said anything to her about his feelings. How could he confront death without telling her the nature of the fire burning inside him?'

He, too, got to his feet. 'Isis . . .'

'Yes, Iker?'

'We shall probably never see each other again, and I must confess to you that – that I love you.'

Afraid of her reaction, he lowered his eyes. The silence seemed never-ending.

'The pharaoh has also just entrusted me with an overwhelming mission,' she said, and Iker heard the emotion in her voice. 'Like you, I am afraid I may not be able to carry it out, and I must save almost all my thoughts for it. However, some of them will be with you and will never leave you.'

He dared not hold her back or question her, and he watched her leave, ethereal, almost fragile, so elegant and so beautiful.

All that was left was an empty garden, bathed in light.

POCKET BOOKS

The Tree of Life

Volume One in THE MYSTERIES OF OSIRIS series

In the temple of Abydos, an acacia tree is dying. And its
death threatens all of Egypt. For this is no ordinary tree: it
sprang forth from the tomb of the god Osiris, the first
ruler of Egypt, as proof of his triumph over death. The
great pharaoh Sesostris III immediately joins battle
against the invisible enemy who wishes to lead Egypt to
her doom. But unknown to Sesostris, within his closest
circle hides a traitor, a man who dreams of power and
glory, a man prepared to sell himself to the powers of
darkness in order to achieve his aim.

A young apprentice scribe, Iker, becomes an unwilling
player in the drama. Kidnapped by sailors who refer
darkly to a 'state secret', Iker does not know who is trying
to kill him, nor indeed who is trying to protect him.
Haunted by a vision of a beautiful priestess, Iker senses
that he's being guided or manipulated, and that he has set
out on a path whose end he does not know.

Will the two of them, Iker and Sesostris, the weak young
boy and the great man of power, succeed in preventing
Osiris from dying for the last time, thereby saving Egypt?

ISBN 0 7434 9225 0
PRICE £6.99

**POCKET
BOOKS**

This book and other **Pocket Books** titles are available
from your local bookshop or can be ordered direct
from the publisher.

0743492250	The Tree of Life	Christian Jacq	£6.99
0671018000	Shadow of the Sphinx	Christian Jacq	£6.99
0671017993	Secrets of the Desert	Christian Jacq	£6.99
0671017985	Beneath the Pyramid	Christian Jacq	£6.99
0671010204	Son of the Light	Christian Jacq	£6.99
0671010212	The Temple of a Million Years	Christian Jacq	£6.99
0671010220	The Battle of Kadesh	Christian Jacq	£6.99
0671010239	The Lady of Abu Simbel	Christian Jacq	£6.99

Please send cheque or postal order for the value of the book,
free postage and packing within the UK, to
SIMON & SCHUSTER CASH SALES
PO Box 29, Douglas Isle of Man, IM99 1BQ
Tel: 01624 677237, Fax: 01624 670923
Email: bookshop@enterprise.net
www.bookpost.co.uk

Please allow 14 days for delivery. Prices and availability
subject to change without notice